Literary Criticism and Cultural Theory

Edited by
William E. Cain
Professor of English
Wellesley College

A Routledge Series

Literary Criticism and Cultural Theory

William E. Cain, *General Editor*

Segregated Miscegenation
On the Treatment of Racial Hybridity in the U.S. and Latin American Literary Traditions
Carlos Hiraldo

Death, Men, and Modernism
Trauma and Narrative in British Fiction from Hardy to Woolf
Ariela Freedman

The Self in the Cell
Narrating the Victorian Prisoner
Sean Grass

Regenerating the Novel
Gender and Genre in Woolf, Forster, Sinclair, and Lawrence
James J. Miracky

Satire and the Postcolonial Novel
V. S. Naipaul, Chinua Achebe, Salman Rushdie
John Clement Ball

Through the Negative
The Photographic Image and the Written Word in Nineteenth-Century American Literature
Megan Williams

Love American Style
Divorce and the American Novel, 1881-1976
Kimberly Freeman

Feminist Utopian Novels of the 1970s
Joanna Russ and Dorothy Bryant
Tatiana Teslenko

Dead Letters to the New World
Melville, Emerson, and American Transcendentalism
Michael McLoughlin

The Other Orpheus
A Poetics of Modern Homosexuality
Merrill Cole

The Other Empire
British Romantic Writings about the Ottoman Empire
Filiz Turhan

The "Dangerous" Potential of Reading
Readers and the Negotiation of Power in Nineteenth-Century Narratives
Ana-Isabel Aliaga-Buchenau

Intimate and Authentic Economies
The American Self-Made Man from Douglass to Chaplin
Thomas Nissley

Revised Lives
Walt Whitman and Nineteenth-Century Authorship
William Pannapacker

The Real Negro
The Question of Authenticity in Twentieth-Century African American Literature
Shelly Eversley

Labor Pains
Emerson, Hawthorne, and Alcott on Work and the Woman Question
Carolyn Maibor

For Katharine

Contents

List of Illustrations

List of Cited Collections

American Antiquarian Society, Bolton-Stanwood Family Papers, Worcester, MA

Beinecke Rare Book and Manuscript Library, The Yale Collection of American Literature, Yale University, New Haven, CT

Boston Public Library, Department of Rare Books and Manuscripts (Courtesy of the Trustees), Boston, MA

The Houghton Library, Department of Manuscripts, Harvard University, Cambridge, MA

The Huntington Library, San Marino, CA

The New York Public Library, Berg Collection of English and American Literature and Manuscripts and Archives Division, Aston, Lexon and Tilden Foundations, New York, NY

The Pennsylvania Academy of the Fine Arts, Collection of the Archives, Philadelphia, PA

Schlesinger Library, Radcliffe Institute for Advanced Study, Beecher-Stowe Collection (Folders 150 and 245), Cambridge, MA

Smith College, Authors and Sophia Smith Collections, Fanny Fern and Ethel Parton Papers, Northampton, MA

Harriet Beecher Stowe Center, Acquisitions, Katharine S. Day and Isabella Hooker Collections, Hartford, CT

University of Virginia Library, Elizabeth Stuart Phelps Collection (#6997), Clifton Waller Barrett Library, Special Collections, Charlottesville, VA

Acknowledgments

THIS PROJECT HAS BEEN A LENGTHY ONE, AND I AM GRATEFUL TO THE MANY people who, over the past few years and in different ways, have helped me write it.

First and foremost, I wish to thank members of The Ohio State University's Department of English, especially Susan S. Williams. Susan's knowledge of archival research, nineteenth-century transatlanticisms, and the culture of Victorian professionalism have been indispensable to me as I have developed this manuscript, and I feel fortunate to have had the opportunity to learn from such a thorough and perceptive scholar. I am similarly indebted to Marlene Longenecker and Cathy Shuman (who now works bibliographic magic at MLA), both of whom painstakingly read chapter drafts and provided me with invaluable counsel. Marlene's capacious knowledge of feminist literary history and Victorian literature have done me in very good stead, while Cathy vigilantly reminded me that the world is not made up of dualisms. Although Debra Moddelmog did not directly help with preparing this manuscript, her influence is stamped on every page. There is no one who has taught me more about the political and social ramifications of literature, and every aspect of my professional work has been, and continues to be, influenced by Debra's guidance. And, finally, special thanks goes to Andrea Lunsford (who now resides at Stanford). Andrea asked me questions no one else could, helping me to see my arguments through a rhetorical lens, yet Andrea also has shown me what it means to be a selfless, loving, and gracious human being—and for these lessons I owe her everything.

I am additionally grateful to Steve Fink, Roger Cognard, Anne MacLeod Cognard, Andrew Cognard-Black, Cheryl Gunness, and Jeffrey Hammond for providing me with discerning suggestions. As a result of Steve's impressive apprehension of nineteenth-century American literature, my father's editorial savvy, my mother's creative connections between writer and text, my partner's careful reading skills,

Cheryl's rare ability to see the proverbial forest for the trees, and Jeff's talent for finding subtle inconsistencies, this manuscript is undoubtedly richer and more coherent.

I am thankful for many fellowships and grants that have supported this research. My colleagues at the place I've called home for three years now—St. Mary's College of Maryland—graciously provided me with a Faculty Development Grant to assist me in completing my archival work in London. In addition, the Ohio State University's Graduate School gave me a much-cherished Presidential Fellowship to work full-time on this project as well as a Graduate Student Alumni Research Award to visit archives along the Eastern seaboard. In turn, Ohio State's Department of English granted me two blessed quarter-long fellowships; the Department of Women's Studies awarded me a generous Elizabeth Gee Grant for Research on Women to visit the Huntington in California; and Ohio State's Office of International Studies gave me a Dissertation Research Grant for project pursuits that took me "across the pond" to England. For assisting with permissions costs, matching funds, helping with application materials, and writing letters of support, recognition goes to Larry Vote, Cheryl Glenn, Lisa Kiser, Jim Phelan, and Elaine Showalter.

I owe much to the aid of several proficient archivists. I wish to extend particular appreciation to Jim Bracken, Director of the English, Theater, and Communications Library at The Ohio State University, who took me on more than one whirlwind tour of archival indexes; I could not have begun to write this project without his indefatigable assistance. In addition, I wish to thank the following archivists for their help, both in person and via many letter, email, and telephone exchanges: Margaret Hrabe at the Alderman Library, University of Virginia; Lynn Braunsdorf at the Beinecke Rare Book and Manuscript Library, Yale University; William Faucon at the Boston Public Library, Department of Rare Books and Manuscripts; Rebecca Tuttle at the Henry E. Huntington Library; Jennie Rathbun at the Houghton Library, Harvard University; Melanie Yolles at the New York Public Library, Berg Collection of English and American Literature; Katherine Kominis at the Mugar Memorial Library, Boston University; Jennifer Kuehn and her staff in the Interlibrary Loan Department, The Ohio State University; Judith Edwards at the Routledge & Kegan Paul Archives, University College of London; Mary Maples Dunn at the Arthur E. and Eliza Schlesinger Library on the History of Women in America, Radcliffe College; and Ken Bastura and Audra Zimmermann at the Stowe-Day Library.

I am further beholden to Susan Coultrap-McQuin and Joan Hedrick, whose impeccably cited biographies of Elizabeth Stuart Phelps and Harriet Beecher Stowe became my reference bibles, and I would like to express my gratitude to the late Gordon Haight, who collected and exquisitely edited George Eliot's letters. Without the exhaustive groundwork established by these scholars, my research task would have been arduous indeed.

This project could never have become a reality without the initial support of Kathy Hickok and Judy Jones at Iowa State University. Kathy introduced me to Victorian women novelists—I had never read *Wuthering Heights*, *Jane Eyre*, or *Middlemarch* until she assigned them—and Judy taught me about feminism as a political movement, loaning me books by women I'd never heard of such as Betty Friedan, Gloria Steinem, and Elizabeth Cady Stanton. There are rare instances in one's life when one experiences a true epiphany, and what I learned from Kathy and Judy about women in literature and politics certainly constituted one of these for me.

For a very real-world and essential gift, I thank Chip and Lora Black, who, for three summers now, have been morning caregivers for my daughter Katharine, allowing me the dual necessities of time and quiet. In turn, my St. Mary's colleagues Ruth Feingold, Beth Charlebois, and Kate Chandler have helped in this measure as well, taking-on sections of composition or a literature survey in order to facilitate my having only two preparations in a given semester. This altruism and the laughter and camaraderie these women bring to my life in Maryland sustain me on a daily basis, and for that I am forever grateful.

Indeed I am blessed by the women in my life. When I have gone into seclusion to work on this manuscript—and whenever I have faced personal trials beyond the difficulties of research and writing—Melissa Goldthwaite, Cheryl Gunness, Gianna Marsella, Becky Taylor, Susan Wagner, and Kate Chandler have taken care of me. I will long remember Melissa's aromatic tea and soothing voice, Cheryl's elegant knitting and blessed smiles, Gianna's epicurean table and giant hugs, Becky's down-home advice and contagious laugh, Suze's perfect outfits and wet kisses, and "friend Kate's" back-porch picnics and luxurious care packages. These women got me through, and I thank them all from the bottom of my heart.

To Joanna Murray, my godmother, and the late Donald MacLeod, my godfather, I owe the lessons in self-determination and personal integrity that I draw on each day. I know of no others who have withstood life's trials with the same dignity, honor, or compassion, and I only hope that I can be a tenth of the human beings they are in my own lifetime.

Finally, there are five individuals who deserve my immeasurable gratitude. My sister Elizabeth MacLeod Walls is my life, and the strength of her love is my backbone; I could accomplish nothing without her. My mother Anne MacLeod Cognard is my other self, and I have taken her with me throughout this intellectual journey; in a very real sense, she helped me write every word. My father Roger Cognard is my heart, and I have carried him close in everything; his unflappable belief in me has sustained me when I was sure I would fail. My partner Andrew Cognard-Black is my love and best friend; it is he and he alone who was there each and every day with his endless cups of hot tea and long backrubs, and I thank him with all my heart for his patience, encouragement, and love. And, finally, my daughter

Katharine is my perpetual wonder, my miracle-worker, my everything. It is to her that I dedicate this book.

Narrative in the Professional Age

Introduction

LATE IN HER LITERARY CAREER, THE AMERICAN WRITER ELIZABETH STUART Phelps engaged in a business dispute with the *Century*'s editor Richard Watson Gilder. Phelps denied Gilder's charge that she expected too much for her work, asking, "Have you not welcomed this contributor for thirty years? I know my prices are not small, . . . [b]ut I think I have always accepted what you offered me, in payments without comment—have I not?"[1] Yet Phelps also rejected the notion put forward by Gilder that she must think more of "monied value" than of the moral worth of her fiction. In keeping with her life-long conviction about the affinities between art and morality, Phelps insisted to Gilder that a writer could produce a "successful union of art and ethics."[2]

Although this exchange is brief, Phelps's response to Gilder encapsulates much of her aesthetic theory and simultaneously reveals its inherent reliance on a market economy. At the same time Phelps argues for social morality ("ethics") as a corollary to aesthetics ("art"), she understands that the efficacy of such a communal, aesthetic value ("union") is necessarily commercial ("successful"). Importantly, Phelps depends on the descriptor "successful" to link art, ethics, and the market. By avoiding economic adjectives such as "profitable" or "gainful" and by choosing a word that carries the double meaning of lucrative and popular, Phelps both masks and admits that this "union" requires artistic and moral taste in tandem with an acquisitive sensibility.[3] In essence, she displays the same double consciousness when discussing her own merit as an author. While acknowledging that her fiction certainly has a price, Phelps believes her artistic worth is based on a service model rather than a wage-labor one. Indeed, Phelps invokes her thirty years of service to the *Century* and silent acceptance of payment as the criteria that guarantee her a position above haggling over market cost; in other words, she simultaneously acknowledges her high price as testament to her work's value while insisting on an illusion of disinterested or payless cooperation that distinguishes a high-culture artist from one who produces mere hackwork. As Phelps puts it to Gilder, "You'll pardon me for saying that the case [of how editors treat writers] is a little different with an author of established reputation[.]"[4]

These letters from Phelps to Gilder are saturated with a cultural discourse that came into vogue at the same time Phelps was at the height of her celebrity: the discourse of professionalism. Throughout the latter third of the Victorian period, in all branches of knowledge—from medicine to law to the academy—the new professionals participated in a vocational model that eschewed the language and idea of wage-labor in favor of community service. While professionals on both sides of the Atlantic relied on the prestige a salary conferred on their intellectual ("workless") duties, they created a simultaneous fantasy of paylessness—i.e., expertise performed for social good. At one level, then, my project maps this discourse of professionalism onto the relationships suggested by Phelps's four key terms: successful, union, art, and ethics.

At another level, my project examines Victorian femininity as a metaphor for aesthetic expression within a professional paradigm. Considering Phelps as well as two of her most prominent literary peers—Harriet Beecher Stowe and George Eliot—this study explores how their respective positions as professionals and artists were constantly negotiated by their positions as women. For "successful," "union," "art," and "ethics" not only inhabit the narratives, articles, and personal correspondence by these three writers; these ideas are mediated through Stowe, Eliot, and Phelps's collective theory of feminine aesthetics—an aesthetics that consciously resisted the commodification of literature induced by professional discourse while simultaneously participating in the professionalization of artistic practice, or what Jonathan Freedman has called "aesthetic professionalism."[5]

Thus I choose to locate my project's discussion of Victorian professionalism and feminine aesthetics in the personal and public writings of Stowe, Eliot, and Phelps, and I make this choice for specific reasons—some material, some historical, and some ideological. Materially, these three writers were in direct correspondence with each other from the mid-1860s until Eliot's death in 1880. While Stowe and Phelps knew each other—Stowe was Phelps's childhood neighbor in Andover—I focus, instead, on unpublished correspondence from Stowe to Eliot and from Phelps to Eliot as well as Eliot's individual responses to each of them.[6] In this correspondence, the ways in which Stowe and Phelps address, shape, and employ their shared images of Eliot are strikingly similar, informing not only how both of these writers construed their own status as famous American writers but, too, how they contrived an all-encompassing feminine aesthetic with Eliot as their mutual paragon. Conversely, Eliot's replies to Stowe are quite distinct from her responses to Phelps, primarily as a result of the differences Eliot perceived in how these two Americans presented themselves as fellow writers to their English peer.

Historically, throughout their correspondence all three writers work through contradictions they faced as self-appointed high culture aesthetes in an emerging professional milieu. The rise of British and American professionalism brought with it (and was brought about by) changes in how the transatlantic world produced and practiced communication. With the establishment of such mid-century technologies as the steamship, transcontinental railroad, and the Atlantic telegraph, national and international communications were revolutionized into agents of capitalism that maintained as well as created professional institutions. Thus, the world of art—particularly the literary arts—became increasingly aligned with commercialism and advertising, the fact-based knowledge system of news, and fast-paced entertainment engines like serialized sensationalist fictions and railway novels. As established and celebrated authors on both sides of the Atlantic, all three writers found themselves caught between their traditional, highbrow aesthetic impulses and the realities of how art was increasingly disseminated through circuits of lowbrow or mass culture.

Finally, in terms of their ideological bents, during this same fifteen-year period Stowe, Eliot, and Phelps expressed similar ambiguities as well as certitudes about their theories of aesthetic femininity in the context of professionalized art. In addition to their private letters and published articles, I examine narratives that followed these authors' respective entrées into the sphere of bestsellerdom[7] and that treat the intricate entanglements of an aesthetic ideal at once feminized and reified, professionalized and commodified. For reasons linked to both the advance of professionalism and controversial debates surrounding Woman's Rights, each of these narratives caused critical furor in England and America. For Stowe, I examine *Lady Byron Vindicated* (1870), a treatise that defended Lady Byron's position in her notorious marriage and, to the umbrage of the popular press, charged Lord Byron with having committed incestuous adultery with his half-sister Augusta Leigh. For Eliot, I take up *Daniel Deronda* (1876), a novel that disappointed and disturbed many American readers with the "Jewish half" of the story and that sparked discussion on the "realness" of its heroine, Gwendolen Harleth. And for Phelps, I analyze *The Story of Avis* (1877), a *künstlerroman* about Avis Dobell, an accomplished female painter, and a book Phelps admitted "made so many enemies" due to its perceived radicalism on the question of women's role in marriage and work.[8] Thus, my study moves back and forth between the consideration of a culture of correspondence across the Atlantic—at once literal in terms of letters, fiction, and news as well as figurative in terms of what Malcolm Bradbury has called "fancy . . . , dream and myth"[9]—and an interrogation of the role of readers, reading, and transatlantic literary criticism in a professional age.

Before detailing the above connections more completely, however, it is important for me to pause here and explain why my project treats Stowe and Phelps more thoroughly than Eliot and, indeed, why even the Eliot chapter is read through the lens of nineteenth-century American criticism. The answer is directly related to the material links among these three writers. At the most basic level, Stowe and Phelps's letters are more candid and elaborate in their articulations of aesthetic femininity. In addition, Stowe and Phelps deliberately turn to an idealized image of Eliot as their icon of such an aesthetic, thus making their mutual correspondence with Eliot all the more interesting. While Eliot seems to agree with Stowe's conception of female artistry and, to some extent, offers a complimentary assessment of moral value through highbrow art, she is less forthcoming in her letters, and she does not mediate her sense of herself as an artist through reciprocal depictions of Stowe or Phelps.

Apart from these material realities, however, there is perhaps a broader historical reason for Eliot's reticence on many of these concepts—a reason that emerges when we consider the history of recent transatlantic studies. In such studies, nineteenth-century American writers have been characterized repeatedly as competitive toward their British peers, and the circulation of literary critical commentary across the Atlantic has been called the paper war of the Victorian era.[10] Perhaps the most well-known example of this argument comes from Robert Weisbuch's *Atlantic Double-Cross,* a study that depends on the notion of a Bloomian "anxiety of influence" across the Atlantic, one in which American authors worry whether their art is patently American or a mere pastiche of the English bona fide. "The compulsive need to overcome British literary influence for reasons of pride or even for reasons of sufficient personal and national selfhood," argues Weisbuch, "is real and strong" (xvi).[11]

Certainly, even Weisbuch admits that America functioned as a vision of the future for many nineteenth-century English and European authors and that a number of prominent British writers made lecture tours of the United States as part of their literary popularity (most famously Charles Dickens and Oscar Wilde). But according to what may be termed the "antagonistic thesis" put forward by critics such as Weisbuch, English and European authors maintained a stable, fixed sense of themselves as "good" writers—i.e., writers with the weight and heft of literary history and cultural density behind them—that Americans lacked or felt they lacked. Such a sense of aesthetic inferiority is demonstrated in a comment like this one from an 1883 edition of *Frank Leslie's Illustrated Newspaper*: "[T]here is no such thing as a distinctively American art," claimed the *Newspaper*. "There is no school that can be called the American School. . . . [O]ur art, like our literature and drama, halt before the foreigners" ("American" 178). According to the "antagonistic thesis," then, Nathaniel Hawthorne and Henry James produced numerous English and European novels and sketches in a rather desperate and vexed attempt to appropriate "real" culture, while Charles Dickens and George Eliot did not write analogous American texts (unless one includes the American scenes from *Martin Chuzzlewit*) because, put simply, they didn't feel the need.

Yet the distinction cannot be merely one of quantity, for other popular British novelists such as William Makepeace Thackeray and Anthony Trollope did make brief forays into American fiction, *The Virginians* and *The American Senator* respectively, and Dickens did produce *American Notes,* a travelogue of his first North American tour. Rather, the difference seems to have to do with quality or degree. In broad terms, the "antagonistic thesis" argues that Americans retained a grudging and even embarrassed reverence for all things European whereas the British either ignored or disparaged American cultural value—often satirizing what they believed to be an American preoccupation with money. For instance, upon first landing in New York, Martin Chuzzlewit is told by the Editor of the "New York Rowdy Journal" that the American aristocracy is composed of "intelligence and virtue . . . [a]nd of their necessary consequence in this republic, Dollars" (258). In turn, the narrator tells us that "Martin was very glad to hear this, feeling well assured that if intelligence and virtue led, as a matter of course, to the acquisition of dollars, he would speedily become a great capitalist" (258–259). In essence, then, long after Americans declared their political independence from England, this thesis contends that many maintained a kind of colonial mentality with regard to art, aesthetics, and culture.

But while a certain measure of this dynamic influenced the relationships among Stowe, Eliot, and Phelps, the legitimacy of the "antagonistic thesis" for my particular study is not what one might expect. Although I do not doubt that American authorship was predicated, in part, on a negative impulse to show that one's work was not-English, I am convinced that examining the Victorian literary field in this manner produces but a partial story. Studies like Weisbuch's have focused solely on certain authors—Washington Irving, James Fenimore Cooper, Ralph Waldo Emerson, Mark Twain, Nathaniel Hawthorne, Walt Whitman, and Henry James—and have constructed a one-sided history of anxious influence where American authors resist and abhor their British artistic inheritance. My study, however, complicates this limited model of masculine antagonism by considering literary reciprocities across the Atlantic that are simultaneously connective as well as independent.

As Malcolm Bradbury notes, the 1870s marked a "new American cosmopolitanism, and the transatlantic contacts multiplied, decade by decade" (180). During this time millions of immigrants came to America (approximately ten million between 1860 and 1890), and thousands of Americans made European tours each year. In other words, while cultural bias certainly existed, at the same time more and more Anglo-American fiction writers saw their audience as two-fold, constituted of both American and English readers.[12] By the 1870s transatlantic thought was a way of life. News, art, politics, commercial ventures, technology, and the family were all bound by transatlantic interests, at least through World War II with the clear establishment of the United States as its own superpower coterminous with the advent of second- and third-generation immigrants becoming the bulk of the American population. In turn, it could be argued that all nineteenth-century fictions produced in

America and England were transatlantic fictions, and I don't mean in the limited sense of travelogues or Jamesian expatriate novels. One cannot appreciate, for instance, the widespread social and political dynamics of *Uncle Tom's Cabin* unless one reads about English responses to the novel, including British sympathies with the South and the establishment of a number of antislavery societies in England and Scotland as a direct result of Stowe's two visits across the Atlantic. Reciprocally, in order fully to understand Eliot's influence on the establishment of Anglo-American realism not only as a literary but as a political and cultural movement on behalf of elite cultural groups—spearheaded by John Blackwood in England and William Dean Howells and Henry James in America—one must read what Howells and James have to say about Eliot's fiction. And these are the most obvious examples, for each and every popular novel, whether by Phelps or Dickens, had a dual life on both sides of the ocean, through critical notices and commentaries as well as in the parlors and back bedrooms of many households. In sum, the Anglo-American publishing markets of the nineteenth century were never exclusively limited to an author's home country, and this interconnection became increasingly important with the proliferation of both transatlantic travel as well as the communications and mass distribution technologies that gained prominence after the Civil War.

On the one hand, then, Eliot's reticence on issues close to the hearts of Stowe and Phelps is indeed partly a result of the fact that American writers thought more about England than the English did about America. And I do mean to be precise in this idea of "thinking about" England or the United States through narrative, for it is the relative presence or absence of literary self-consciousness that distinguishes how one nation articulated its ideas about the other. The implications for my study of this aspect of their exchange is that Stowe and Phelps often imagine England as the seat of the arts or Eliot as the "novelist of the century," whereas Eliot speaks but little of America or its writers as "idea." In consequence, Stowe and Phelps self-consciously negotiate their own places as authors as well as their particular visions of feminine aesthetics *vis-à-vis* these images of British poetics and culture in a manner that Eliot does not quite reciprocate. In addition, Stowe and Phelps directly incorporate English or European elements into their narratives—obviously, *Lady Byron Vindicated* is all about British social history, and *The Story of Avis* has Avis Dobell study painting in France for six years—and Phelps produces articles, lectures, and poems about Eliot.

On the other hand, it is important to distinguish between an antagonistic interchange and a relationship of difference. While the imagistic and metaphoric exchange is not equal among Stowe, Eliot, and Phelps, it is interdependent, and the way Stowe, Phelps, and the American public read the interlocking complexities of aestheticism, professionalism, and femininity in *Daniel Deronda* is just as important as how *Lady Byron Vindicated* is received in England by Eliot and British reviewers. Thus, what is striking for me is the simultaneous contrast and complementarity of

Stowe and Phelps's respective relationships to Eliot and, in turn, Eliot's response to each of them. What remains compelling is the mutual reliance Stowe and Phelps seemed to have had on Eliot—Stowe and Phelps requiring Eliot's "lichens," to borrow a metaphor from Hawthorne—as well as, to some extent, the need Eliot seemed to have to believe in Stowe's inherent moral sympathy as an American mother, i.e., as a mother "of the future." As case studies, then, Stowe's and Phelps's correspondence with Eliot in tandem with a discussion of how fictions by all three get circulated and received in England and America provides glimpses into a specific aspect of transatlantic literary history, one that challenges the one-sided view of the "antagonistic thesis" to posit a more complex and varied picture of late nineteenth-century transatlanticisms. For as Stowe points out in her own transatlantic travelogue, *Sunny Memories of Foreign Lands*, "[British] history for two centuries was our history. Its literature, laws, and language are our literature, laws, and language" (II: 18).

VICTORIAN PROFESSIONALISM

Although I will return again and again to different aspects of professionalism throughout this study, it behooves me to paint it in broad strokes here. Roughly speaking, professionalism came into vogue around the same time the United States was undergoing Reconstruction and England was in what historians have called the Age of Improvement. For both nations, this period was marked by furious industrialization and the increase of a specific kind of market production: commodity manufacture and exchange. Such exchange altered representational systems as varied as the novel, painting, and architecture as well as social vocabulary. As cultural historian Thomas Richards has argued of Victorian England, "There were so many new things, . . . that it became impossible to keep them all straight, and a new class of words came into being to describe things in general—words like gadget, dingus, thingamajig, jigger" (2). World fairs abounded, dedicated to displaying these new commodities of industry, science, and national expansion. In London, Prince Albert opened the 1851 Great Exhibition in Hyde Park, where a gigantic greenhouse shaped like a castle, named the Crystal Palace, held one hundred thousand "thingamajigs."[13] In 1876, Philadelphia hosted the Centennial Exhibition, one intended to evince an even wider range of capitalist advances, including artistic productions, than London's Crystal Palace, which had focused solely on manufactured goods.[14] In truth, however, each of these exhibitions had an identical overall purpose: to theatricalize commodities—whether merchandise or *objets d'art*—as symbols of national value by making a show of the nation's industry, affluence, cultivation, and technological eclecticism. In turn, citizens participated in the moral and literal wealth of the nation by procuring these products, demonstrating their taste by what they bought. In this manner, consumerism fashioned a new sphere of highbrow culture, one accessed by the exercise of a discriminating taste—maintained by an appropriate education—and concretized through the purchase and exhibit of highbrow articles.[15]

The advent of transatlantic professionalism was an indispensable part of this intricate network of economic and aesthetic transformations.[16] At its most basic, the material relationships of capitalism were constantly refigured as non-economic social patterns through the symbolic processes of consumption but also through types of work and the inherent power dynamics structured into work categories—including the category of "the professional."[17] In general terms, professional society was organized according to three criteria. First, as mentioned above, professionals adopted an ethic of service as their claim to social authority, a position supposedly workless and classless yet, of course, dependent upon the inevitable existence of a salary—thus exposing the symbiotic alliance between capitalism and professional prestige.

Second, to adequately perform this service, the professional had to make him- or herself an expert, i.e., focus on one field of knowledge, screen all available information pertaining to that field, eliminate all data that had no bearing on solving specific problems, and use the remainder as the basis for confronting all potential issues or concerns. This notion of "expertise" was the perfect embodiment of an ideological oxymoron that, once again, both masked and revealed the professional's reliance on capitalist structures: the oxymoron "universal exceptionalism." Universal exceptionalism purported that expertise was accessible to any and all who wished to be trained as a professional yet simultaneously kept other occupational groups from entry into the professions by establishing structural limitations on who qualified as an appropriate trainee. In so doing, professionals could make clear distinctions between their cultural position and that of laypeople while maintaining a rhetoric of equal access akin to capitalism's rhetoric of equal economic opportunity.

Third, borrowing from ancient guild models, professionals themselves determined the criteria for entering their profession, which usually involved some kind of formal education or certificate coupled with being of the right class, race, age, and gender. And because professionals defined the parameters by which they would be assessed, they could act as "gatekeepers," making sure, as Magali Larson points out, that they achieved monopoly control over the services they provided and, by extension, monopoly control over the economic advantages afforded such a prestigious social position. "Professionalization is thus an attempt to translate one order of scarce resource—special knowledge and skills—into another—social and economic rewards," Larson argues. "To maintain scarcity implies a tendency to monopoly: monopoly of expertise in the market, monopoly of status in a system of stratification" (xvii).

On both sides of the ocean, then, professionals claimed an ethic of disinterested service that supposedly acquitted them of profit motive, fashioned their intellectual acumen as their property, and claimed meritocratic legitimization for helping, and thereby directing, the masses. Historian Burton Bledstein has identified this entire social process as the "culture of professionalism."

Thus, while professionalism in the United States and Great Britain perhaps differed in terms of its relation to class, or at least in terms of the distinct perceptions of class within the two nations,[18] it shared the same basic impulse: the delimitation of clearly defined, service-oriented careers populated by experts and sustained by gatekeeping practice or monopoly control. Throughout the last third of the nineteenth century, these professional precepts infiltrated almost all occupations in England and America, from bricklaying to teaching to practicing law to writing fiction. In a sense, then, the discourse of professionalism cut across economic class; however, paradoxically, that same discourse kept hierarchies of privilege and prestige intact. In other words, professionals, by definition, had to marginalize certain groups in order to function. As Mary Poovey points out in *Uneven Developments*, women often served as the group professionals measured themselves against since women engaged in "natural" production (unaided and unrecognized by authenticating institutions) and were therefore inherently amateurs—untrained, uneducated, and unorganized.

Women intellectuals like Stowe, Eliot, and Phelps, then, had to distance themselves from this image of "natural amateurism" at the same time that they wished to speak on behalf of women as well as raise their own work to professional status—although they simultaneously eschewed certain professional aspects. As such, these three writers chose to revise their own connections to "natural amateurism" into a unique professional schema. Generally speaking, Stowe, Eliot, and Phelps made the mothering implicit in metaphoric femininity—i.e., the symbolic locus of women's moral capital—into the indispensable element of perfect professionalism.[19] As I discuss in the next chapter, Stowe and Phelps used their mutual images of Eliot to fashion such schema, called "strong weakness" and "feminine strength" respectively. Such schema accepted the following: if women were assumed morally superior and carried an innate ability to raise the ethical standards of society, women—especially women who could claim both moral and intellectual capital—should be the ideal candidates for carrying out social service and, in principle, should be the most accomplished of professionals. This theory, however, carried with it at least two problems relative to gender. First, in order for women professionals like Stowe, Eliot, and Phelps to claim the position of expert, they still needed the necessary Other of other women—they needed to distinguish their own authorial expertise as different from the quotidian command of domestic womanhood. Second, by virtue of its reliance on capitalistic exchange, professionalism potentially compromised a woman's virtue. A woman who is not paid and who performs the invisible work necessary for a professional ethos is elided with the position of an upper- or middle-class woman—a respectable, domestic amateur or ornamental lady. On the other hand, a woman who is paid for her labor is defined as a wage-earner, a factory girl, a woman of the working class—the kind of women intellectual professionals seek to guide. But a woman who receives a salary for invisible work—a "professional"—is either an intellectual woman (e.g., an artist, an author) or a prostitute; indeed, both kinds of women work to entertain and sell their entertainments as work.

FEMININE AESTHETICISM

In keeping with William Wordsworth's articulation of the autonomous author as fit subject for poetry (simultaneously a subject in text and a producer of text), the nineteenth century witnessed increasingly individuated definitions of the artist and artistry in both England and America.[20] Such definitions coalesced with the burgeoning of mid-century Aestheticism. A designation Victorians themselves used, "Aestheticism" posed an independent domain for the artist, one that separated the artist and aesthetics from the work and exchange of a capitalist marketplace, or as Kathy Psomiades notes, characterized "the artist as enclosed consciousness and . . . art as a realm separate from the world of politics and economic production" (9). At the same time, and paradoxically, Aestheticism dubbed the artist as the appropriate, incisive critic of bourgeois capitalism.[21]

In turn, with the proliferation of technological media enhancing the production of literature and the visual arts, the aesthetic increasingly acquired a massive, frantic, and ironically tasteless popularity. For the first time in history, art could be accessed through avenues hitherto unknown: before, art was reserved for the cultivated few or the exercise of an innate, self-educated taste; but with the technological inventions of the Atlantic telegraph and photograph that fractured and multiplied aesthetic images and messages in ever decontextualized arenas of consumption, those who could buy aesthetic goods could now accumulate the image of aestheticism rather than necessarily espouse its philosophical content. As mentioned above, art, like other merchandise, now fed on phenomenal representation, and the art object, like the commodity, promised a superior selfhood to those who could apply discriminating connoisseurship. In other words, middle-class individuals demonstrated their aesthetic acumen by purchasing artistic goods on the basis of criteria established by artists functioning as art critics.

Like the professional, then, the aesthete consciously projected himself (for avowed Aesthetes were virtually always men) as a cultural expert and arbitrator whose dedication to social value beyond capitalism set himself apart from the commodity marketplace. As might be imagined, however, also like the professional, the aesthete simultaneously participated in the market and, in many ways, fashioned it through the commercialization of his art and the professionalization of his artistic practice. "For what is the aesthete but the consummate professional," asks Jonathan Freedman, "the possessor of a 'monopoly of knowledge' about the provenance and extent of this mysterious entity, 'the aesthetic'—the man . . . who responds to the demands of a rapidly professionalizing world by forging a career for himself out of the imparting of knowledge about this new 'field' to an awed and appreciative public" (xix)? In keeping with professional custom, this stance guaranteed the aesthete absolute reign over the criteria that would rank his work, in essence granting aesthetes, like professionals, self-authenticating power.

What enabled these contradictions was a metaphor of femininity. As represented in Aesthetic painting—women with white-white skin, rose-colored lips, soulful eyes, and a languid, sensual posture—femininity allowed aesthetes both to participate in yet deny any connection with mass culture. On the one hand, such depictions of femininity put forward an etherealized, aesthetic ideal separate from the praxis of everyday life as well as a feminine form inherently privatized and, thus, inherently removed from social utility or service (Psomiades 3). On the other, this same femininity sold aestheticized art through market vehicles, trading on the paintings' material, sensual allure. In essence, then, by virtue of its contrary nature (private yet public, pure yet erotic, material yet spiritual), aesthetic femininity allowed secluded, individuated artists to remove themselves and their work from the mechanisms of a consumeristic society at the same time that these artists relied on the dissemination of their art through commercial means. Thus, as cultural distinctions were increasingly made in England and America between high art and mass culture, in truth both were contained within a single symbolic system: Victorian femininity.

But while recent studies have analyzed how art objects function like commodities and, in addition, how femininity enables the conflation of art with the commodity,[22] few have considered what it means when the art object is produced by a female artist or what happens when that female artist focuses her gaze on ideas or icons of masculine aestheticism. While other scholars have demonstrated how contradictions inherent in Anglo-American gender ideology and Aesthetics facilitate a conception of art that shuns as well as reifies a market economy, their work limits explorations of gender to representations within art itself (primarily painting) and aestheticism to the academic rubric "Aesthete"—in one sense a catch-all word, but in another sense a very limited category indeed, reserved for self-appointed Aesthetic painters, writers, and critics (all male) now canonized as such in the academy. In other words, even though these projects examine how various aesthetic movements in England and America produce and are produced by popular culture or, in turn, how femininity allows for an expression of aesthetics at once both priceless and commodifiable, these projects fail to consider the import of widely read professional women writers who, while not openly identifying as Aesthetes-capital-A, certainly wielded enormous public influence over what was or was not thought "art" on both sides of the Atlantic.

Unlike the typical Victorian figure of the middle-class female consumer, the professional female artist cannot be elided with either the well-trained, middle-class woman who has been taught what is and what is not art or the uncultured, often working-class woman who cannot distinguish art from the vulgarities of mass culture. The professional female artist is both of these women and neither of them; like traditional Aesthetic femininity, she embodies aspects of high art and mass appeal, art's privacy and its sensational public consumption. In addition, akin to a middle-class woman whose household regulation provides a modicum of aesthetic taste in the domestic realm, this figure carries the role of aesthetic arbitrator in the social sphere, teaching her readers how to understand art. Specifically, Stowe, Eliot, and Phelps attempt to delineate signifying systems within mainstream aesthetics, replacing "weak" and "debased" masculinity with a peculiar version of "strong" yet "pure" femininity—thus undermining the accepted function of sensuous, static femininity in aesthetic representation. Here women aren't relegated to an artistic position that is either masculinized (as the creator of art) or objectified (as the subject of art); they are not passive consumers, passive objects, or mannish artists. Rather, they produce art and art criticism, adopting the authority and agency of masculine professionalism at the same time they retain a core femininity that, they believe, is closer to ideal humanity—to God or the divine.

To perform these discursive feats, Stowe, Eliot, and Phelps distinguish among models of femininity in order to accomplish various objectives: to identify with the common woman reader and "woman" as a social discourse; and to utilize the power endowed by professional systems yet keep themselves separate by being both the exceptional artistic experts guiding the taste of women readers as well as representatives of a new kind of woman—one that adopts masculine strength yet remains theoretically unbound by the commercial taint of professional or market strictures through an immortal, inviolable, maternal, aestheticized femininity. Said another way, while adopting the privilege of the professional, Stowe, Eliot, and Phelps reject the label "professional" in favor of a reified, high-art aesthetic of "strong femininity"—symbolically above and beyond all social institutions or time-bound contexts. This amalgam of professional, aesthetic, and certain feminine concepts allows Stowe, Eliot, and Phelps to legitimize their role as cultural teachers, guiding their audience in how to interpret art, especially art produced by women. In this manner, they hope to revolutionize what they see as the moral bankruptcy of society, elevate readers to highbrow pursuits, and insert a specific aesthetic of "strong femininity" as a universal code of social taste, conduct, and spirituality.

Of course, this adoption of strong femininity as the basis of a new kind of aesthetic professionalism parallels the progression of women's entry into the professions through avenues of social reform (abolition, suffrage, legal debates on women's rights in marriage and the law, the rehabilitation of drunks and prostitutes, etc.) and is thus indebted to the transatlantic movement for Woman's Rights.[23] But while such reform groups used the notion of women's inherent moral capital as grounds for enfranchisement and the legal authorization of their right to own property, Stowe, Eliot, and Phelps translated this notion into their personal correspondence and published narratives, appropriating the argument for women's moral superiority from Woman's Rights rhetoric as part of their aesthetic ideal while keeping their claims at the level of immortal myth rather than immediate social action. For Stowe, Eliot, and Phelps were not in the business of arguing, like Millicent Garrett Fawcett or Elizabeth Cady Stanton, that a woman should have equal rights because she had the same intellectual powers as a man; rather, their sense of "strong femininity" implied that certain exceptional women should have social, political, and spiritual authority because a woman of strong femininity was uniquely and innately entitled to singular valuation. However, their collective belief in each other as exceptional, strong women artists—exceptionally moral and exceptionally talented—stemmed directly from these movements for woman's suffrage, thus allowing Stowe, Eliot, and Phelps to consider one another and one another's work as edifying for the everyday woman reader, a group of women Phelps called the "average minds."

The tensions surrounding these writers' use of strong femininity as their brand of aesthetics were irresolvable. As previously mentioned, an artistic woman engaged in workless pay was inevitably implicated in the cultural image of prostitution. Because Stowe, Eliot, and Phelps inevitably sold their work and themselves as authorial images as part of an iterative, commercialistic, and sensational literary marketplace, they could not escape the innate dangers of trying to adopt professional discourse in the service of a "pure" feminine aesthetic. Stowe's *Lady Byron Vindicated* and Phelps's *The Story of Avis*, for instance, were vociferously condemned by the transatlantic media for their sexual explicitness, knowledge of deviant sexuality, audacity in emasculating men, and seeming sympathies with radical factions of the Woman's Rights movement. In turn, Eliot's *Daniel Deronda* was lauded for the "wrong" reasons, i.e., for its depiction of Gwendolen, not the feminized Daniel, and for its English plot over its Jewish themes. The moral capital Eliot attempted to employ was not palpable in an emasculated, Jewish "container." Yet these authors' mutual fantasy of strong femininity remains compelling, especially given how it exposes the interconnections and incongruities of transatlantic reading practice through discourses of professionalism, aestheticism, and gender.

TECHNOLOGIES OF TRANSATLANTIC READING

After many bungled attempts, the first successful transatlantic telegraph cable was laid on August 5, 1858. The London *Times* proclaimed, "The Atlantic is dried up, and we become in reality as well as in wish one country. . . . The Atlantic Telegraph has half undone the Declaration of 1776, and has gone far to make us once again . . . one people" (Clarke 48–49). According to the *Times*, the introduction of instantaneous cross-Atlantic information brought with it the promise and risk of monoculture, the power to collapse space and time as well as history—partially undoing the American Revolution, the most definitive event in Anglo-American politics. A generation before the telegraph, expanding railroad networks and the ensuing proliferation of popular reading materials had generated an unprecedented flow of news and information about distant events that had worked to undermine the insularity of local populations, including provincial self-definitions.[24] In a similar manner, the technology of the telegraph implied that national self-definitions would collapse as culture was imported and exported along the immediacies of the electric cable. Metaphorically, the media response to the Atlantic telegraph fashioned the wire as an emblem of an imaginary, transatlantic nation—one that would end international hostilities as well as boundaries. At a banquet held for Samuel Morse in 1868, the British ambassador Edward Thornton proposed a toast to the Atlantic telegraph as "the nerve of international life, transmitting knowledge of events, removing causes of misunderstanding, and promoting peace and harmony throughout the world" (Standage 91).

Interestingly, this view of the telegraph as a unifying technology had little if nothing to do with its day-to-day function. The telegraph traded in information that was trivial, repetitive, and sought more for popular appeal than substance. As Henry David Thoreau had foreseen, "[Though we] are eager to tunnel under the Atlantic and bring the old world some weeks nearer to the new; . . . perchance the first news that will leak through into the broad, flapping American ear will be that the Princess Adelaide has the whooping cough" (307). Instead of sequential, coherent narratives connected to an international, national, or local purpose, telegraphic news was a series of competing headlines from people and places both distant and strange. In everyday terms, such technology worked more to fracture and isolate than it did to unify. Thus, like professionals or Aesthetics who sold their social services in the form of information and image, the discourse of the telegraph, on the surface, appeared communitarian but worked as an agent of profit and produced a market discourse, one aligned with patterns of communication we now term "popular" or "mass" or "lowbrow" culture: commercialism and advertising, sensationalist fictions, and, most notably, fact-based knowledge systems.[25]

Indeed, one of the primary reasons the telegraph produced broken narratives was that its grammar traded in fact—disconnected dates, names, figures, and events—and this reliance on facticity was intimately bound up with the rise of professionalism. Since the professional expert craved technological progress while eschewing tradition, intuition, and, above all, spiritual insight, knowledge had to be quantifiable, tangible, provable. "By making words clear, plain, direct, and tangible," notes Bledstein, "Mid-Victorians believed that they were incarnating reality, plumbing its depths, raising its potential, and immortalizing its true nature" (74).

This turn to facticity was indicative of a broad transatlantic shift from a narrative-based to an information-based culture—a shift that, in many ways, was inspired by the complex transformations in communication media that occurred throughout the 1860s, 70s and 80s. This shift reconstituted how Americans and the British defined "reality" and "truth." In terms of politics, for instance, discontinuities between the moral and the empirical, between value and fact, informed debates over Parliamentary representation in England and woman's suffrage in America. Those engaged in discussing the Representation of the People Bill in 1865, for example, found themselves trying to locate a number that would adequately express the worth of political representation. Whether they advocated a one-to-one correlation of constituents to votes or the extent of one's monetary wealth or even one's mental acuity as apt credentials for the franchise, these members of Parliament tried to circumscribe an exact relationship between the fact of one's assigned number and the value of one's participation in the civic arena.[26] A similar tension occurred in America with the widespread disputes over women's participation in government. Agitation for Woman's Rights forced lawmakers to confront a central paradox in republican doctrine: that while religious, political, and educational institutions held up woman's moral superiority—her value—as a national necessity, once a woman took on that "necessary" role of wife and mother, she became nonexistent in terms of the law, i.e., she failed to count.

Of course, echoes of this great shift reverberated through scientific and religious communities as well. With the publication of Charles Darwin's *The Origin of Species* in 1859 and *The Descent of Man* in 1871, Christian orthodoxy on both sides of the Atlantic was destabilized, as sources of proof were increasingly built on fact over faith. Stowe, in the serialized version of *Uncle Tom's Cabin*, included this satiric passage with regard to Tom's faith-based response to the Bible: "I mention this, of course, philosophic friend, as a psychological phenomenon. Very likely it would do no such a thing for you, because you are an enlightened man, and have out-grown the old myths of past centuries."[27] Indeed, for Stowe, Eliot, and Phelps, the turn away from the "old myths of past centuries" as the basis for human understanding and knowledge was more than irritating or perplexing—they believed it was culturally lethal.

Thus, while professionals wanted straightforward and concrete interpretations of reality, this primacy of fact was met with a paradoxical fictionality on the part of writers like Stowe, Eliot, and Phelps—a revision of the fractional, fact-based discourse of telegraphy, law, and science into a fiction of sentimental connection and unity, a fiction not unlike the one created by journalists and statesmen at the inception of the Atlantic telegraph. In one of her letters to Eliot, for instance, Stowe appropriates and domesticates the metaphor of the telegraph, explaining, "I love you—& talk to you sometimes when I am quite alone so earnestly that I should think you must know it even across an ocean—is there no magnetic telegraph for us?"[28] Here, Stowe revises the fragmented and impersonal nature of telegraphic expression into an intimate and relational reading of like minds—in her own way obliterating space and time to fashion a spiritual union between herself and Eliot. Indeed, this phenomenon of refashioning the telegraph as a communitarian metaphor was common among artistic circles. For instance, Henry James remarks in his notice of *Daniel Deronda*, "The 'sense of the universal' [in the novel] is constant, omnipresent. . . . [I]t gives us the feeling that the threads of the narrative, as we gather them into our hands, are not of the usual commercial measurement, but long electric wires capable of transmitting messages from mysterious regions" (131). Importantly, James self-consciously reinterprets the "commercial measurement" of telegraphic cable—or, rather, the print and paper of a book—into a mystical experience, a reader's ability to access "messages from mysterious regions" through reading a certain kind of "universal" (or cross-national) fiction.

This is one reason why Stowe, Eliot, and Phelps were dedicated to sustaining fiction as the vehicle for disseminating moral capital. Fiction, unlike other prose forms, told extended narratives and thereby created an illusion of truth that served as a methodological refutation of growing mass discourses enabled by the telegraph, especially the fact-based discourses of science appropriated by professionals in law, medicine, government, and news media. Indeed, fiction, as Stowe and James demonstrate above, fostered an illusion of worldwide human continuity, not only that A necessarily follows B but that the social progress of humanity is cumulative and inevitable and that hidden universal truths might be gained through reading. Fiction made sense as the genre of choice for Stowe, Eliot, and Phelps in other ways as well. Particularly in America, by mid-century women fiction writers were the most popular authors of their day and thus fiction provided an established avenue of social influence. In addition, fiction constituted crucial patterns of consumption with the proliferation of serialized novels and higher rates of literacy among the middle and working classes. In other words, fiction—like the medium of television in the late twentieth century—affected large groups of people and even national or international policy. One cannot forget that when Abraham Lincoln met Stowe, he supposedly said, "So you're the little woman who started this great war!"; and, in turn, the women of England christened Stowe the universal "impersonation" of antislavery.[29] And fiction was an ideal option for a female artist's talent since Victorian novels had a strong basis in domesticity—parlor scenes over images of the battlefield, legislature, or office. Finally, the largest literary traffic across the Atlantic was in fiction, and so a successful writer could count on gaining effect on both sides of the ocean. Often, fiction written in England sold even better in America and vice-versa, although there were multiple difficulties with international copyright and pirated editions in both the United States and England.[30]

Importantly, however, Stowe, Eliot, and Phelps distinguished between the plethora of sensational fictions on the market and the kind of rare fictions they themselves wrote—narratives they saw as socially responsible, credible, and pursuing a higher understanding of God (for Stowe and Phelps) or humanity (for Eliot). If they were to combat what they deemed the degeneration of culture, these three authors believed they had to seek cultivated readers who would, as Eliot explained to Stowe, gain "power over the social mind" by sharing their aesthetic knowledge with the wider populace; indeed, Eliot felt that the only hope for influencing everyday people through "writing above the common order" was "due to its reception by a few appreciative natures, and is the slow result of radiation from that narrow circle" (Haight, *Letters* V:30).

Thus, all three of these writers worked to establish their narratives as "high art," separate from a group Stowe classed with the likes of Miss Braddon and Mrs. Henry Wood.[31] This move on their part coincided with similar trends in all avenues of art, from painting to music to the theater. Because fiction was simultaneously popular and elite—much like, as Lawrence Levine notes, nineteenth-century opera and Shakespearean drama—novels and narratives were read by large numbers of people, primarily made up of the new middle class in England and America, as well as a much smaller cadre of the economically and socially elite. Primarily a result of the rapid changes in industry, communications, and marketing, the emergence of the middle class accelerated discriminations between intellectual and popular culture. Simultaneously, the word "culture" itself became increasingly conflated with art and aesthetics. "The new meanings," notes Levine, ". . . symbolized the consciousness that conceived of the fine, the worthy, and the beautiful as existing apart from ordinary society" (225).

Stowe, Eliot, and Phelps participated in these cultural discriminations in a number of ways. First, and most obviously, all avoided pulp presses, placing their work in highbrow, belletristic publications. As Nancy Glazener has detailed, magazines in what she terms the "*Atlantic* group" established not only literary realism as a high-art genre but "confer[red] distinction on both the authors who published in them and the purchasers who read them" (7). Indeed, the *Atlantic* and other periodicals like *Harper's* and *Blackwood's* were crucial in consolidating cultural hierarchies as the century progressed. Although distinctions between high and low culture were made throughout the nineteenth century, until the early 1860s, many liked to believe in what might be termed a kind of popular or democratic access to high culture in both America and England. For instance, from 1850 to 1852, the soprano Jenny Lind made a famous tour of the United States that was heralded as a "republican operation." In his *Memoranda of the Life of Jenny Lind*, Nathanial Parker Willis quoted a letter to the editor of the *New York Tribune* in praise of Lind's "democratic" performances, i.e., ones that included operatic arias in both German and Italian: "[T]his great people," exclaimed the letter-writer, "so intent on acquisition, so bewildered at times by the rapidity of their own progress, have not forfeited the capacity of appreciating excellence" (216). After the Civil War, however, *Harper's* began making distinctions among the kinds of music an audience "of the highest cultivation" should prefer. In terms of opera, *Harper's* differentiated between Italian and German librettos. "Italian opera [are] a kind of Mother Goose melodies, good enough for a childish musical taste, but ludicrous for the developed and trained taste of to-day. . . . Because we once read the primer and *Simple Susan* with delight, shall we refuse to own the charm of Shakespeare and of Dante? It is a far cry from *Rigoletto* to the *Götterdämmerung*" ("Editor's Easy Chair" 968).[32]

The magazines that comprised the *Atlantic* group included elite American periodicals as well as certain British journals that American magazines attempted to emulate or best. Stowe, Eliot, and Phelps regularly appeared in a number of these periodicals. For instance, the serialized version of *Daniel Deronda* came out in *Harper's*; "The True Story of Lady Byron's Life" appeared in the *Atlantic*; and Phelps published many short stories and novels in the *Atlantic* and *Harper's* but also in the *Galaxy*, the *North American Review*, and *Scribner's Monthly*—a magazine that eventually became the *Century*.[33] In turn, *Blackwood's* editor published virtually all of Eliot's fiction in England, and the *Cornhill Magazine* serialized Stowe's *Agnes of Sorrento*.

In addition to placing their work in highbrow periodicals, other telling details include what Stowe, Eliot, and Phelps chose to write about and how they went about writing it. Perhaps most obviously, all three authors hoped to strengthen the moral fiber of their readership. Stowe's *Vindicated* tries to teach responsible publishing and reading practice through the exercise of strong femininity; *Daniel Deronda* and *The Story of Avis* both deal with the question of art's role in society as well as who may be an authentic artist; and *Deronda* makes an incisive commentary on racial prejudice in relation to the establishment of aesthetic sensibility and culture. Furthermore, all of these works adopt language and imagery that call attention to their literariness. *Avis* is probably the work most peppered with such examples, incorporating allusions to well-known classical paintings, Greek and Biblical mythology, and Eliot's verse-poem *Armgart*.

In keeping with the orientation of the *Atlantic* group magazines, these writers also responded to an increasing predilection among high-art editors and their audiences for realism. Partly an outgrowth of the social realignment along fact-based lines of inquiry, editors and middle-class readers began to value texts more and more for their everyday representations over idealized portrayals; such presentation was thought to arouse a more refined sympathy than the engrossing tales of murder, deception, and illicit love that sold from the railway stalls. This predilection manifested itself in various critical responses, and Stowe, Eliot, and Phelps were all put in the position of having to defend their work when it embraced what readers deemed "romantic" elements. In terms of *Vindicated*, for example, Stowe was exhorted to prove the merits of her case against Lord Byron by citing "real" events from tangible and authenticated biographical sources rather than Stowe's own self-claimed interview with Lady Byron. For *Deronda*, Americans read Gwendolen as a more realistic character than Mirah, Mordecai, or Daniel, even though the Gwendolen sections of the novel adhered more closely to the conventions of sensational fiction than those dealing with Daniel's forays into Jewish life. And *Avis*'s critics were put off by the mythic sections of the book, especially Phelps's use of the Sphinx as a signifier for perfect womanhood.

Indeed, during the same decade that Stowe, Eliot, and Phelps wrote *Lady Byron Vindicated, Daniel Deronda*, and *The Story of Avis*, the *Atlantic Monthly* published a critique that distinguished between real culture and false culture, suggesting that only certain readers could discern the real from the false. "Some will show no capacity for receiving culture; any wood may be varnished," declared the commentator, "but not every sort receives polish; and so it is with men and women" ("Contributor's Club" 625). Similarly, what Stowe, Eliot, and Phelps hoped to accomplish was a kind of "polishing" of culture; one might say that they wished to "varnish" their readers—particularly women readers—not to a high sheen perhaps as much as to a good gloss, since they themselves were the woods carrying the brightest luster and richest radiance. Much of the discussion throughout the ensuing chapters, then, picks up on these complexities of reading practice across the Atlantic, asking how an aesthetic system marked by difference (strong femininity) tries to function as a producer of universal culture and how writers like Stowe, Eliot, and Phelps claim high-art aesthetic purity when their fictions were, by necessity, participating in professional realms of commercial distribution and consumption.

The larger implications of this use of fictionality are intriguing, if difficult to assess. It is important to remember that these three writers rely on the precepts of a narrative-based feminine aesthetic to rescue culture at the same time that the Anglo-American media proclaimed the ubiquitous moral influence of the telegraph. In 1881, for example, *Scientific American* detailed one of the first instances of worldwide up-to-the-minute reporting on a national tragedy—in this case, President James Garfield's slow death due to a gunshot wound. "[T]he touch of the telegraph key welded human sympathy and made possible its manifestation in a common universal, simultaneous heart throb," explained the reporter. "We have just seen the civilized world gathered as one family around a common sick bed, hope and fear alternately fluctuating in unison the world over as hopeful or alarming bulletins passed with electric pulsations over the continents and under the seas" (Standage 162). *Scientific American* called this phenomenon "a spectacle unparalleled in history . . . and indicative of a day when science shall have so blended, interwoven and unified human thoughts and interests that the feeling of universal kinship shall be, not a spasmodic outburst of occasional emotion, but constant and controlling, the usual, everyday, abiding feeling of all men toward all men" (162–163). What seems significant is not that this version of the telegraph's capacity was finally inaccurate—that the telegraph worked more to muddle than to unify international communication. Rather, what remains striking are the domestic, sentimental metaphors (e.g., "one family" assembled around "a common sick bed," evincing a "universal, simultaneous heart throb") coupled with this notion that the fact-based technologies of science will initiate a "constant" and "controlled" expression of "universal kinship." For

Stowe, Eliot, and Phelps also hoped to amalgamate the necessary technologies of fiction with a kind of universal and self-possessed feminine feeling—not the "spasmodic outburst" usually associated with femininity but the "abiding feeling" afforded by feminine strength "of all men toward all men," or as Eliot wrote to Stowe, the "moral good of men" (*Letters* V: 31).

While a lengthier discussion of the interconnections between telegraphic metaphors and this transatlantic ideology of feminine strength is beyond the bounds of this study, it is important to note what this larger context reveals: that these writers' respective versions of strong femininity mediated an exchange between a continuous and narrativistic sense of transatlantic female artistry and the new professionalization of art that worked to fracture this same narrative. Stowe's and Phelps's letters to Eliot highlight the tensions around this exchange, especially in their attempts to place their ideal of strong femininity beyond the bounds of the consumeristic, information-based discourses of professionalism. In this context, discourse across the Atlantic is reciprocal and generative, and like the mythological image of the Atlantic telegraph put forward by journalists, transcends fixed national borders at the very moment such borders are evoked.

NARRATIVE IN THE PROFESSIONAL AGE

Apart from the material, historical, and ideological interconnections among Stowe, Eliot, and Phelps, there are a number of similarities among *Lady Byron Vindicated*, *Daniel Deronda*, and *The Story of Avis*. To begin with, all three narratives were written after the writers themselves were established authors. By virtue of sales alone, by the time these texts were published throughout the 1870s, each participated in the competing worlds of professionalization, aesthetics, and the transatlantic literary market. In addition, to some extent all three narratives negotiate the roles of the female artist and feminine aesthetics in professional culture, and all three make various aesthetic substitutions, i.e., substituting an ideal of strong femininity for other kinds of artistic production, including, for instance, Gwendolen Harleth's amateur dabblings, Lord Byron's masculine creations, Susan Wannamaker's working-class performances, as well as Philip Ostrander's "deviant" or Coy Bishop's mainstream feminine constructions. Interestingly, all three also play with literary genre. *Lady Byron Vindicated* is both a professional polemic and a pseudo-novel; *Daniel Deronda* is a romance and a novel of social realism; and *The Story of Avis* is a *künstlerroman* as well as a Woman's Rights tract and a mythic tale of female heroism. Importantly, while *Lady Byron Vindicated* is a work explicitly written to Englishmen that takes up an unmistakably transatlantic topic, *Daniel Deronda* and *The Story of Avis* are not transatlantic novels in the Jamesian vein. However, I place all three of these texts in a transatlantic context, examining how they were read on both sides of the Atlantic at the same time that I analyze what Stowe, Eliot, and Phelps had to say about each other's work.

Chapter one looks at how Stowe and Phelps worked through the competing discourses of professionalism, aestheticism, capitalism, and gender by turning to images of England, especially Eliot, as their reservoir of cultural capital. In essence, both of these prominent American writers argued for an aesthetic transformation of society, one that portrayed Eliot's strong femininity as a universal moral code. I argue that Phelps and Stowe's aesthetic philosophies not only appropriated English culture through Eliot as well as Woman's Rights rhetoric but simultaneously struggled with precarious distinctions between high and low art. Indeed, in their attempts to try and filter hack-work from the truly artistic, these writers established elite boundaries of feminine aesthetics. Ultimately, then, their aesthetic ideal actually sustained the marketplace by shaping literary commodities as products seeming to exceed objects priced and sold in the same moment they were consumed through reading what they termed "exquisite" or "moral" fiction. As a result, I contend that Stowe and Phelps's aesthetic schema are necessarily professionalized as the product of an elite cadre of writers and critics.

Chapter two treats the censorious response in England and America to Stowe's two texts accusing Lord Byron of having committed incest, "The True Story of Lady Byron's Life" and its sequel *Lady Byron Vindicated*. By fashioning Lady Byron as a metonym of American social value articulated through strong femininity, Stowe attempted to bring together her burgeoning interest in the Woman Question with the rhetorical ethos of woman, Christian, and citizen she had established writing *Uncle Tom's Cabin*. But because *Vindicated* was published during the insurgence of professionalism as a dominant cultural discourse, Stowe quickly discovered that her established ethos no longer granted her automatic credibility. Instead, after the publication of the "True Story," Stowe was accused of romantic make-believe, at best, and wanton sexuality, at worst. In response to the enormous pressure on Stowe to produce the proof of her claim of incest and, too, because the subject matter compromised Stowe's own artistic position in a "deviant" discussion of incest, Stowe wrote *Vindicated*, a text that adopted both fact-based, professional grammars and the trappings of advertising in the same moment that it clung to a narrative structure that maintained fictional elements—in effect engendering an emergent form of literary realism. What appears with *Vindicated*, then, is a layering of literary styles that highlights the discursive forces at work within and on Stowe's book and points toward the great shift between a narrative-based and an information-based culture that this text simultaneously resists and embodies, produces and fails to produce.

Chapter three examines Eliot's *Daniel Deronda* and the American critical discussion it launched over the "reality" of the character of Gwendolen Harleth. Importantly, the figure of Gwendolen enters American history at the intersection of three events: the reading of realism as a high-art endeavor; the political and social agitation for Jewish autonomy; and the conjunction of advertising as a prevalent social instrument with the rise of the American professional. Interpreting Gwendolen's narrative position through the convergence of these three historical movements, I construe the American preoccupation with Gwendolen's "realness" as a response, first, to her performance of beauty as a representation of "false" artistic professionalism, one that links Gwendolen to advertising and the proliferation of sensationalist fictions and warns readers against the seductions of both. Gwendolen is real to readers because she, like them, is seduced by superficiality—indeed, she is exactly the kind of reader Eliot's novel is meant to educate. In turn, this attraction to Gwendolen's realism must be placed in the context of reading practices codified by such high-art periodicals as *Harper's* and other *Atlantic*-group magazines. High-art journals located the effectiveness of Eliot's realism in her ability to induce both a universal and feminine sympathy, teaching their readers to appreciate realistic qualities that Gwendolen is said to arouse, including an affinity with English culture as well as a sympathy derived from her struggles over aesthetics and social morality. And finally, the parts on Jewish life portrayed as the novel's moral center come at a time when America experienced political agitation for the expansion of Jewish immigration and autonomy. Thus Daniel's adoption of a simultaneously racialized and feminized ethos became a particularly threatening image, and nineteenth-century readers linked Daniel's narrative choices to their own fears over Jewish ascendancy, particularly their fears of the dilution of culture. For these reasons, Daniel must be read as less real than Gwendolen in order to secure a vision of society based on those realistic qualities high-art journals espoused. Because *Daniel Deronda* both creates and explodes dichotomies between professionalism and aestheticism, realism and feminine sympathy, masculinity and femininity, it is an ideal text for exploring the interconnections among these concepts.

Finally, chapter four discusses Phelps's *The Story of Avis*, a novel that plays with the incongruities in the form of the novel itself to amalgamate two distinct social groups through the lens of Woman's Rights: the world of high literary culture and elite professionalism (for Phelps, identified with English authors like Eliot) with corporate systems such as advertising that were increasingly controlling the professional literary marketplace. *The Story of Avis* deliberately represents Phelps's aesthetic of "feminine strength" in a literary form that, at once, tries to cater to an elite group of readers at the same time that it hopes to capture the imagination of the masses—especially those "helpless, outnumbering, unconsulted" women Phelps most wished to influence. Initially the novel invests the heroine, Avis Dobell, with the role of exemplifying this dual nature of feminine strength, but Avis's status is compromised by her position as a painter since such work necessarily engaged erotic perception in the pursuit of high-culture art. In order to try to secure Avis's feminine purity, the tenets of feminine strength are inserted over and over again for all competing aesthetic sensibilities, including those represented through other races, classes, and genders. Yet the sexualization of Avis's aestheticism remains too volatile, and in the end, then, even Avis herself is finally displaced in favor of the novel's ultimate logo of feminine strength—the Sphinx. The figure of the Sphinx is meant to equalize all highbrow/lowbrow ambiguities as the perfect idol of masculinity within femininity or "strength" within "weakness," thus supposedly avoiding the perils of erotic female art. However, the final incongruity of *The Story of Avis* is that while the Sphinx is held up as a mythic symbol beyond the vagaries of the marketplace, the critical reception of *Avis* still condemned the novel for its pernicious sexuality. Phelps herself was taken to task for trying to adopt a highly arcane writing style deliberately reminiscent of Eliot's at the same time that she portrayed a sexually autonomous heroine stronger in her femininity than Philip Ostrander, the novel's emasculated hero. In other words, the kind of novel Phelps hoped to inaugurate—one that would "claim the royal lineage of the Coming Woman" through both high-art aesthetics and mass culture—is a novel the critics were not yet ready to embrace.

Chapter One

"You Are as Thoroughly *Woman* as You Are English"

Strong Femininity and the Making of George Eliot

From the late 1860s to the mid-1870s, Harriet Beecher Stowe and Elizabeth Stuart Phelps made public forays into the controversies surrounding the American woman's movement.[1] As early as 1865, Stowe avowed that the Woman Question was the next great social debate, the cause to which the nation should turn its attention with the Civil War over and Reconstruction underway. "This question of Woman and her Sphere is now, perhaps, the greatest of the age," Stowe suggested in one of her *Chimney-Corner* papers[2]—especially now that America had "put Slavery under foot" ("Chimney" 673).[3] In turn, Phelps couched her rallying call in even more inflated terms, writing a series of women's reform articles for the *Independent* and the *Woman's Journal* from July 1871 to February 1874.[4] "It is no great figure of speech," asserted Phelps, "to say that the 'woman question' is the most tremendous question God has ever asked the world since he asked, 'What think ye of Christ?' on Calvary" ("Higher Claim" 343).

But while Stowe and Phelps claimed this Question "the greatest," "the most tremendous" of the age or even of a millennium, both writers employed this discourse as a vehicle for more immediate aims: to set themselves up as cultural mediators for women readers, simultaneously "just like" their audience yet artists quite apart from them. To achieve this position, Stowe and Phelps adopted remarkably similar rhetorical strategies within the context of Woman's Rights. On the one hand, both formulated analogous models of "strong femininity" that appropriated masculine authority without sacrificing womanly decorum. On the other, both applied this model as the basis of a symbolic system for professional female artistry in a transnational context, constructing images of England—especially of George Eliot and her novels—as evidence of their artistic and professional influence over women readers.

This chapter, then, begins by characterizing this simultaneously aesthetic yet professional model of "strong femininity," a model predicated on the movement for

Woman's Rights. Although Stowe articulates her ideas through a parable of "strong weakness" and Phelps refers to her notions as "feminine strength," these systems represent an intellectual alliance, and so for the purposes of clarity, I cluster their attributes under the aggregate term "strong femininity." In addition, this chapter considers Stowe and Phelps's rhetorical choices through the larger context of the culture of professionalism. I argue that their mutual visions of strong femininity mediated an exchange between a continuous and narrativistic sense of public discourse (based on the novel) and the new professionalization of language in the latter third of the Victorian period. As mentioned in the Introduction, Stowe and Phelps believed that professional language and the systems it served—consumerism, advertising, and the circulation of sensationalist fictions—dangerously fractured and demoralized public discourse through a relentless use of sensationalist, spectacular rhetoric and fact-based knowledge systems. In response, Stowe and Phelps created an alternative professional system, one that privileged aestheticism. Yet unlike the strategies of Walter Pater, Oscar Wilde, or Henry James, theirs embraced an immortal ideal of strong femininity as the aesthetic answer to consumeristic, information-based culture—an ideal mediated by their respective constructions of George Eliot. Thus, this chapter considers how strong femininity is expressed in terms of Eliot as well as other representations of English womanhood and asks two interrelated questions: first, how this expression reflected Stowe and Phelps's own sense of themselves as professional artists, and second, how it put forward a cultural ideal that located social, political, and especially artistic power in the symbol of an exceptional, transnational Everywoman—one embodied in the figure of George Eliot.

STRONG FEMININITY, WOMAN'S RIGHTS, AND PROFESSIONALISM

Even given the striking similarities of Stowe and Phelps's campaigns for strong femininity, their respective projects stemmed from very different circumstances. Take the case of Stowe: until the 1869 publication of her contentious article on Lord Byron's infamy, her participation in the discussion on Woman's Rights remained erratic, indirect, and often private. Following the public outcry induced by the "True Story," however, Stowe found herself set squarely in the midst of contentious discussions on marriage, divorce, and sexuality—debates fueled by John Stuart Mill's newly released *On The Subjection of Women*[5] and the wider circulation of "free love" doctrines advocated by George Sand in Europe and Victoria Woodhull in America. Based on her article's implied indictment of the sexual double-standard and Stowe's long-standing renown, in the early fall of 1869, Susan B. Anthony and Elizabeth Cady Stanton sought Stowe as a contributor and editor to their new suffrage journal, the ***Revolution***. As Anthony put it to a friend, "[M]y ***one*** aim just now—is to be able to announce that [the] ***Revolution*** will commence by next volume . . . ***with a serial from Mrs. Stowe***—Alice ***Cary*** wants I should take one from her—her ***name is good*** but of course ***Mrs. Stowe's*** is the ***Queen Bee*** in that hive."[6] It is little wonder that

Anthony and Stanton coveted the Queen Bee's endorsement; while the "True Story" didn't explicitly denounce gender inequities in marriage or the law, Stowe's article accused Byron of spousal abuse, specifically the misuse of Lady Byron's property as well as her body, at least in a conjugal sense. With the subsequent publication of *Lady Byron Vindicated*, Stowe's critique of marital relations became even more strident, generalizing her local censure of Byron's betrayals to an analog for wrongs perpetrated against women by certain kinds of "devilish" men.[7] "The lesson to woman," Stowe extrapolated, is that "man may sink himself below the brute, may wallow in the filth like the swine, may turn his home into a hell . . . , forsake the marriage-bed for foul rivals; yet all this does *not* dissolve the marriage-vow on her part, nor free his bounden serf from her obligation to honor his memory" (*Vindicated* 119–120).

While the transatlantic press focused on evidence supporting the truth or falsehood of whether Byron had committed incest and questioned the credibility of Lady Byron and Stowe as reliable narrators (topics I take up in chapter two), Anthony and Stanton interpreted the controversy as clamor raised against the audacity of a famous woman libeling the most popular British male of the century.[8] "The true relation of the sexes is the momentous question at this stage of our civilization," Stanton proclaimed in one of the few editorials to praise Stowe's temerity,[9] "and Mrs. Stowe has galvanized the world to its consideration. . . . This is a blow at woman's *natural protectors* that will set many a bond one free, and hasten the day when the worst form of slavery, that of woman to man, . . . shall be no more" (175).[10] Recognizing the media backlash as primarily gender-driven, Stanton commiserated with what she believed to be Stowe's position as a defender of Woman's Rights. She told Stowe's sister Isabella, "Give my [love] to her and my warmest sympathy just now for I know the trial of being denounced by the entire press of the country."[11]

Yet even though Stowe was eager to "galvanize the world" in its consideration of Lady Byron's case and probably wished to have her name linked with grandiose declarations of women's future emancipation,[12] Stowe's basic conception of the Byron controversy differed from Anthony and Stanton's in one crucial way: their respective notions of what constituted strong femininity.[13] For although Stowe advocated female suffrage and equal protection under the law, she held firm to the belief that women deserved the respect of male chivalry and, too, that both men and women should adhere to principles of religious beneficence and sexual purity—principles, for Stowe, embodied and expressed in the character of Lady Byron.[14] Stowe's own reply to the attacks on her "True Story" centered on the godlessness of her American and British censors, their incapacity to appreciate Lady Byron's life of Christ-like suffering over Byron's excessive prurience.[15] Thus, citing the militancy of the *Revolution* and expressing her unwillingness to advocate the elimination of marriage as an institution—i.e., to deem it, as Stanton did, the "worst form of slavery"[16]—the Queen Bee declined Stanton's and Anthony's offer of editorship, a move that rankled Stanton and permanently separated Stowe from activism for suffrage.[17]

In truth, however, Stowe seemed less interested in activist expression on behalf of women; she did not attend rallies or pass out pamphlets or go on the lecture circuit as a spokesperson for Woman's Rights. Unlike the celebrity appearances she made in support of abolition,[18] Stowe's chief involvement in the Woman Question centered on the paper war instigated by the Byron controversy and, even more narrowly, on depicting Lady Byron as a paragon of Stowe's particular version of strong femininity. When an article in the *Revolution* endorsed George Sand's notions of free love as a model for the relation of the sexes, the schism between Stowe and the suffragists widened. Writing to her brother, Stowe scoffed, "Susan Anthony & other honest old maids who know no more evil than an old country ministers horse will suppose of course that [Sand's] Lelia is a womans right tract & bye & bye . . . we shall have the literary editor of the Watchman & Reflector & perhaps Times Herald giving it a lift."[19] For Stowe, strong femininity could never equal the sexual autonomy sanctioned by a writer like Sand, and she resisted the intimation that a sordid novel like *Lelia* might be tendered as a Woman's Rights polemic.

But despite her sarcasm, Stowe was seriously worried about the potential threat to naïve readers of what she termed "sensationalist" novels like *Lelia*. She saw the public endorsement of "licentious" writers as a regression from true culture—the greatest obstacle to the development of a universal (feminine) selfhood through the circulation of moral novels. To explain her version of ideal feminine aesthetics, Stowe tended to make private statements like the following to George Eliot. After reading *The Mill on the Floss*, Stowe interpreted the gender dynamics of the book, explaining, "Tom Tulliver has been heretofore the characteristic Englishman. Tom has made the laws for women & judged women by them but the day is coming when *Maggie* is to judge Tom & show him that there is a higher style of living than ever *he* dreamed of—Maggie whose weakness was stronger than Tom's strength."[20] For Stowe, Maggie Tulliver stood for the kind of woman in most need of influence and direction—for while she is stronger in her weakness than Tom in his strength, Stowe notes that she "didn't know & does not *yet* know how much more than he, she is."[21] In turn, Stowe envisioned women writers like herself and Eliot as the experts who would teach the Maggie Tullivers of the world just how much more they were by training them in what and how to read—namely narratives by herself and Eliot depicting strong women characters such as Dorothea Brooke or Lady Byron.

In a sense, this valorizing of female experience connected Stowe to the kinds of debates Stanton and Anthony were having on the political and social conditions of women. Ultimately, however, Stowe's concept of "strong weakness" was not equivalent to the sexual or even legal independence sanctioned by her contemporaries since Stowe believed a woman's integrity and power issued from her weaknesses, i.e., her charity, sympathy, piety, capacity for forgiveness, and love. These were the human qualities with the potential to "revolutionize" society, remake not just worldly institutions like government or the law but the soul itself.[22] By focusing on

Christian and largely conventional feminine values, Stowe articulated not an immediate political stance but a timeless aesthetic that would transcend national borders and establish a specifically feminine way of influencing social morality through the production and dissemination of novels by certain women writers.

Clearly, Stowe's system for changing social morality was closely tied to the development of professionalism as synonymous with culture. In this manner, Phelps's discourse of "feminine strength" is much in keeping with Stowe's "weakness stronger than strength," although, again, Phelps came to her philosophy through a different political path. Phelps's theory of feminine strength developed over the course of a decade, beginning roughly with the transatlantic success of *Gates* in 1868 and crystallizing with the 1877 publication of *The Story of Avis*. "I believe more solemnly than I know how to say in feminine *strength*," Phelps explained to Henry Longfellow. "Is the lily less sweet because it is the whitest and most self-reliant of flowers . . . ? Always I find the deepest tenderness in the strongest woman; there, too, the largest self-sacrifice, and the most faithful friend. A woman of force without tenderness is not strong but brittle."[23] For Phelps, this basic incongruity of confidence-in-softness evolved to mean a kind of cosmopolitan sensibility merged with nerve and cultivated by fastidious literary training. Like Stowe, Phelps identified a select coterie of women writers who would act as cultural mediators for women readers, and also like Stowe, Phelps saw Eliot and Eliot's work as the lynchpin to her aesthetic vision.

From her early newspaper articles wherein she preached that the "powers of self-management, self-support and self-investment are the inherent needs of the maturing man or woman" to *The Story of Avis*'s focus on an autonomous artist-heroine struggling against domestic traditionalism, Phelps's proclamation of "feminine strength" brought together progressive ideals of self-government with a conventional emphasis on self-justification and displays of legitimacy—the fundamental paradox in any professional system ("Unhappy" 250). Indeed, both Phelps and Stowe shaped their vision of strong femininity into a professional schema, one that challenged (or at least tried to revise) other professional ideologies. For instance, in one of her magazine articles on fiction, Phelps asks,

> What are the elements of permanence? What the sources of power in the tale that one finds it impossible to escape? I think these will be found to be chiefly four: originality, humanity, force, and finish. . . . The literary quality, the ineffable touch which we call style, will sustain these other qualities; but, without them, it will not go on living. . . . ("Stories that Stay" 123)

With statements such as these, Phelps attributed enduring art to the organic élan in an artist, an intrinsic quality "finish" can only support, not create. This distinction was an important one for Phelps as well as Stowe—if art were a mere matter of style, then anyone could be an artist. And Phelps takes this logic one step further, insinuating that true artists have special powers of compulsion, are able to incorporate their work into the very tissue of the reader, even against the reader's conscious will. "My own inclinations," she explains, "seem to have been rather wilful tendrils, reaching whithersoever they chose, and clinging obstinately, whether with or without apparent reason, little concerned with the canons, or with other persons' tastes in the literature of the day" (119). So just as Phelps asserts innate, universal criteria commanding artistic taste, she also dubs her own taste as above and beyond quotidian or group identification, "little concerned with canons." What Phelps means, of course, is that while she is a reader, she is also an expert artist in her own right: powerful, exceptional, chosen.

On the one hand, then, Phelps suggests that the seemingly timeless powers of literary endurance can and should be filtered through an individual reader's subjective and exclusive taste where "[f]ine fiction, like fine friendship, is a personal affair. Your friend is not to be of another's choosing. . . . [H]e must be of your soul's kin" ("Stories that Stay" 118). Stowe makes virtually the same point in a letter to Eliot, asserting that, "A book is *a hand* stretched forth in the dark passage of life to see if there is another hand to meet it—Now in your works if you could read my marked edition of them you would see how often the hand has met the kindred hand. Reviews and book notices are commonly so dreary—so *un* sympathetic."[24] Like Phelps, Stowe sets herself up as having a special appreciative nature; where Phelps recognizes books as "fine friends," Stowe receives Eliot's work via the metaphor of the hand, transforming the cerebral experience of "kindred" text to the tactile experience of literal kin, thus making art palpable but comforting, not carnal. In turn, the receiving hand scripts this moment into another version of materiality—the marginalia that attests to Stowe's understanding of Eliot. The hand of feminine sympathy becomes the instrument of true interpretation, creating a continuous circle, one hand meeting another across the "dark passage of life." Unlike meaningless multiplications of sensational novels or "*un* sympathetic" responses from literary critics, Stowe's interaction is insular and intimate, thereby distinguishing Stowe as an informed and sensitive reader—one quite distinct from the popular social mind and that scourge of sympathy, the book reviewer. In sum, fine literature and, by association, fine authors speak soul-to-soul, author-to-reader, in a manner defying the mere economics of book distribution.

Yet while Phelps assures her readers that taste is a personal affair—albeit one honed by the careful tuning of one's soul—she simultaneously warns aspiring women writers to keep bad prose to themselves. If a publisher doesn't want your work, Phelps explains, you shouldn't be an author: a stance that squarely locates literary taste in market value. "If the magazines will not publish your stories," Phelps quips, "it is a natural inference that you are not exactly a genius, is it not?" ("What Shall They Do?" 519). What becomes clear is not that any literate person can discern fine writing; rather, a special cadre of women writers must map appropriate habits of taste for all "weak-minded women" whose name, Phelps adds, "is legion" (519). This turn in her argument highlights how Phelps and Stowe both imagined themselves in relation to their public. They and their chosen peers made up a narrow circle of responsive natures capable of sensing the fellow artist in the text. In turn, this elite literary circle could potentially raise the aesthetic and moral sensibilities of its audience by the exquisiteness of its art but would forever be battling the widespread desire for spectacular experience—middle-class taste. "But what shall we say of the children of this generation sitting in the marketplace eager only for sensation & with no time to think?" Stowe asks Eliot. "What shall people so solemnly impressed with real living as you do with them?"[25] Thus Stowe equates true artistry with intelligence and "real living," false artistry with phantasmal and thoughtless pleasure located primarily in the instinctual or animal faculties—"thoughtless" sensation. Rhetorically, the real becomes exquisite feminine art, the illusory middle-class economy. This rhetorical slippage was necessary for Stowe and Phelps to create and maintain positions as arbiters of taste, both commiserating with the ordinary woman as well as defining who and what ordinary or natural was, thus placing themselves and their models of strong femininity beyond such classification.[26]

But whereas Stowe's use of the woman's movement as a rhetorical context was limited to her polemics on Lady Byron, Phelps constructed her initial discourse through a series of Woman's Rights articles she wrote over a period of three years. Primarily a result of the unexpected and momentous success of *The Gates Ajar* in 1868, by the time she engaged in reform writing, Phelps felt authorized to speak for whole groups of women:

> [With *Gates*] I wished to say something that would comfort some few . . . of the women whose misery crowded the land. . . . [T]he women,—the helpless, outnumbering, unconsulted women; they whom war trampled down, without a choice or protest; the patient, limited, domestic women, who thought little, but loved much, and, loving, had lost all,—to them I would have spoken. (*Chapters* 97–99)

In these articles that followed *Gates*, Phelps continually characterized her readership in this manner: women "trampled," "patient," "limited," "domestic," of little thought and large love. Assuming her readers were of the middling class, domesticated, pious, and of moderate education, Phelps put together elaborate arguments for allowing such women greater play and power—arguments exposing the hypocrisies of church, family, and state that kept women out of what she designated as "natural" roles in a direct satire of the cult of domesticity. But although Phelps expressed the same kinds of opinions Stowe herself held, Phelps was the one who got intimately and passionately involved in specific debates. In fact, even in Stowe's scattered public commentaries about the Woman Question, she often wrote anonymously, employing the device of a masculine narrator to espouse potentially volatile ideas or asking her brother Henry to publish sensitive essays against the free love movement under his own name in the *Christian Union.*[27] But even these unnamed forays were unusual for Stowe, and she tended to make most of her statements on behalf of women through private correspondence.[28]

We see this difference, for example, in the authors' respective stances on equal employment and self-sufficiency. Even as Stowe explained privately to Eliot that "We are busy now in the next great emancipation[,] that of woman—This session I trust Connecticut will repeal *the whole of the old unjust English marriage property laws as regards woman & set her free* & then I shall be willing to claim Connecticut as my mother," Stowe herself was not directly involved in lobbying for legal change.[29] Rather, Phelps was the one who openly lambasted the laws and customs that kept women from earning and managing money[30] or receiving an equal education with men, arguing against those who supported the so-called female education of women, "*So* female that it has become a commonplace to say that institutions intended for the instruction of women only are second-rate affairs" ("Female Education" 1409). Moreover, Phelps went even further than Stowe had in *Vindicated* to discredit not just brutish husbands but an entire marital system perpetuating women as beholden to men. "Woman is not man's ward," she exhorted. "Man is not woman's guardian. Man is incapable, even if he were called upon to do so, of competently judging for woman in the adjustment of her 'place' in society" ("True Woman" 1).[31]

But even when speaking for the disadvantaged, Phelps maintained her position as the exception, going so far as to discourage "ordinary" women who aspired to authorship, ironically girls and women hoping to emulate her authorial success.[32] Throughout her career, Phelps negotiated a professional position between encouraging women readers to claim autonomy and preempting her own advice to act as their experienced, educated guide.[33] Casting her readers in this all-encompassing manner enabled Phelps to shape a decidedly professional worldview in tandem with her female aesthetic, one in which she herself acted as an exemplar of feminine strength and created similar exemplars such as Avis Dobell in *The Story of Avis* or portrayals of Eliot in various articles, poems, and lectures. For Phelps, as for Stowe, this doctrine became her measure of legitimate womanhood, the test to which any woman—a character in a novel, a reader, a suffragist, a fellow-worker—must live up. Elastic, deceptive, and often contradictory, Phelps's "feminine strength" and Stowe's "strong weakness" were their sublime signifiers, containing their entire principles of aesthetics, religious beliefs, and social theories.

STRONG FEMININITY AND IDEAL ENGLISH WOMANHOOD

A key component of these doctrines of strong femininity was Stowe and Phelps's mutual appropriation of images of England and especially prominent British literary women to serve as their cultivated nonpareil. "Lady Byron has an American name and an American existence," asserted Stowe, "and reverence for pure womanhood is, we think, a national characteristic of the American" ("True Story" 313). In fashioning certain British female prototypes as metonyms of American cultural value—and intimating that Americans were more receptive to perceiving the intrinsic worth of such women (given their audience's fundamental "reverence for pure womanhood")—Phelps and Stowe brought together their private and public discourse on the Woman Question with a republican sense that their highly visible versions of Lady Byron, Elizabeth Barrett Browning, and especially George Eliot would work to disseminate high culture to people of all walks of life, thereby raising the overall aesthetic standards of their American readers. At a certain level, then, Phelps and Stowe's writings on strong femininity worked as national curatives, not merely teaching American readers how to estimate such femininity but educating England how to appreciate its exceptional women—not unlike how Stowe had sought to teach people to "feel right" on the issue of slavery.[34] However, this didacticism was coupled with a strong sense of literary inheritance—which is precisely why Stowe and Phelps felt justified in criticizing England or English authors. In essence, these two writers viewed England through a familial lens, and like mothers or sisters, in one sense they felt that they had the right to moralize to their own brethren. In another sense, however, they felt as though England had a good deal to teach them. Stowe, in particular, held the staunch belief that England was the source of American culture and that the fate of the two nations would be forever intertwined. "Say what we will, an American . . . can never approach the old country without a kind of thrill or pulsation of kindred," she wrote of her own travels to Great Britain. "Its history for two centuries was our history. Its literature, laws, and language are our literature, laws, and language" (*Sunny* I: 18). Indebting almost all aspects of American life from government, history, language, and the arts to English primogeniture, Stowe was easily able to imagine a transatlantic household with a cross-national morality, a morality she could locate in representations of English womanhood that superseded nationality such as the social activism and religious piety of Lady Byron or the writings of George Eliot.

This valuation of England—and especially the positive appraisal of English artistic femininity—is forecast through the many fancied as well as actual journeys Stowe took to Great Britain.[35] Whereas some postbellum writers who sought England as a cultural Mecca found themselves simultaneously resisting the implications of this inheritance, Stowe embraced metaphors of consanguinity. "America is a tall, slightly young shoot, that has grown from the old royal oak of England," claimed Stowe. "[D]ivided from its parent root, it has shot up in new, rich soil, and . . . therefore takes on a new type of growth and foliage, but the sap in it is the same" (*Sunny* I: 18). As Hawthorne did in Italy, Stowe sentimentalized the English landscape as the seat of the creative arts, especially the imaginative faculty. Touring Speke Hall in England long before Hawthorne wrote the *Marble Faun*, Stowe asked, "If our Hawthorne could conjure up . . . the Seven Gables in one of our prosaic country towns, what would he have done if he had lived here? Now he is obliged to get his ghostly images by looking through smoked glass at our square, cold realities; but . . . this [place] is a standing romance" (I: 33, 35–36). For Stowe, creativity stood incarnate in England; bucolic castles and villages straddled the interstice between the fantastic and the real, and inhabitants dwelt at their intersection—or one could say, dwelt in narrative.

Simultaneously, however, Stowe assumed England to be the authentic expression of a fixed and continuous human experience.[36] Against the chaotic backdrop of the transcontinental railroad and transatlantic telegraph, labor-saving devices and assembly lines, talking cures and walking cures and water cures, Stowe found security in her transcendent mythos of English womanhood, the unwavering refinement and artistic excellence she equated with Lady Byron and Eliot. At Speke Hall, Stowe had likened English copses and gardens to "goblin-like" and "bewitched" objects, and she had maintained the old Hall itself boasted an "authentic ghostly squeak" (*Sunny* I: 33, 35). But while an antique landscape fostered these picturesque flights of fancy so crucial to artistic stimulus, such landscape also represented the timeless and permanent connection both Stowe and Phelps would increasingly seek between present and past through the power of narrative.[37] "[S]ince there are two worlds in man, the real and the ideal," Stowe said, narrative must raise and maintain the link connecting history to modernity. "[L]ike this beautiful ivy, with which all the ruins here are overgrown," English stories not only adorn, but "they actually hold together, and prevent the crumbling mass from falling into ruins" (I: 70).

Phelps articulated many of Stowe's emotions about England and English womanhood, although her expressions manifested themselves as an inheritance model wherein Phelps looked to writers like Elizabeth Barrett Browning and Eliot as her personal mentors in feminine strength. When Phelps was sixteen, for instance, she "happened for [her]self" on *Aurora Leigh* (*Chapters* 64). Her adult memory of this event paints an elaborate scene of reading, one where nature interacts with text and reader to produce a glorified ideal of perfect instruction:

> The Andover sunsets blazed behind Wachusett, and between the one window of my little room and the fine head of the mountain nothing intervened. The Andover elms held above lifted eyes arch upon arch of exquisite tracery, through which the far sky looked down like some noble thing that one could spend all one's life in trying to reach, and be happy just because it existed, whether one reached it or not. The paths in my father's great gardens burned white in the summer moonlights, and their shape was the shape of a mighty cross. The June lilies, yellow and sweet, lighted their soft lamps beside the cross—I was sixteen, and I read 'Aurora Leigh.' (*Chapters* 64–65)

Here, Phelps searches for apt imagery and language to capture the experience of burgeoning intellectual womanhood: esoteric rites of initiation against "blazing," "burning" backgrounds—backgrounds as holy (white) as they are intense; a sacred communion between female mentor and pupil in which "nothing intervenes"; and atemporal, even elusive, transcendence accompanying this moment of artistic epiphany. Tellingly, Phelps couches her epiphany as highbrow (the sky a "noble thing"); the sought-after knowledge as permanent and delightful (one is happy "just because it existed, whether one reached it or not"); and the natural as an innately poetic world, one rife with alliteration ("great gardens"), rhyming schemes ("white"/ "moonlights"; "soft"/ "cross"), and personifications (elms' "lifted eyes," the mountain's "fine head"). In a sense, Phelps's lyricism attempts to emulate a prose worthy of Barrett Browning's poetry.

Yet at the end of this reminiscence, Phelps's recondite imagery distills itself into a straightforward assertion: "I was sixteen, and I read 'Aurora Leigh.'" Reading, and more importantly reading a British woman author, becomes a one-to-one correlation with a concrete moment in Phelps's own life, thus connecting her life history to a very specific kind of artistic ardor. As such, this scene of reading introduces young Phelps to a larger community of female artists who excite an "aspiration" in her—as she puts it, "ambition" being "too low a word"—to do "honest, hard work . . . in the World Beautiful, and for it" (*Chapters* 66). Using characters from certain pieces of literature (Aurora Leigh, Dorothea Brooke, Gwendolen Harleth) as well as writers such as Barrett Browning and Eliot themselves as a kind of shorthand familiarity, Phelps conjures commonalties of knowledge delimited in terms of feminine experience. "[W]hat Shakespeare or the Latin Fathers might have done for some other impressionable girl," Phelps reflects, "Mrs. Browning—forever bless her strong and gentle name!—did for me" (*Chapters* 65). In turn, this imagined community supplies affectional and artistic needs Phelps failed to find in the real,[38] and for the rest of her career, Phelps mediates her self-construction through constant allusions to the women writers she held most dear.[39] Importantly, Phelps's inheritance model defines artistic work outside temporal and mundane concerns (not to be equated with ambition but rather "aspiration" or sacred desire) and insists that her own intellectual work, though largely invisible, is "hard" and "honest" and vital to the state of the "World." In essence, Phelps takes on the voice of the professional artist—she is engaged in "necessary" work that produces not moveable goods as much as the tools of potential soul-making: novels.

Conversely, Stowe's relationship to her British peers was less one of homage than one of mutual reliance and support—indeed, even guardianship insofar as Stowe remade these icons in a simultaneous effort to define strong weakness and to bring home these British portrayals for broad American circulation. Turning to Lady Byron and Eliot as markers of permanent culture, at one level it was Stowe's intent to demystify English high art for her American readers. Her travel guide to England and Europe, *Sunny Memories of Foreign Lands*, is an excellent example of how Stowe transformed the inaccessibility of European high culture to a middle-class audience.

Stowe deliberately peppered her guidebook with domestic rituals and allusions, writing the book as a series of travel letters to "Aunt E" and telling stories such as how she picked daisies at Sir Walter Scott's grave. This down-home approach to Great Britain and its culture—what Joan Hedrick calls Stowe's "colloquial, 'folksy' voice"—permeated Stowe's entire attitude about both her travels in Britain as well as her correspondences with Lady Byron and Eliot (269).[40]

As I argue in chapter two, Stowe's rhetorical strategy did not, actually, include adopting folksy language in telling her story of Byron's marital crimes; however, Stowe still crafted a carefully intimate approach in how she fashioned characters of strong English women so that her American readers could identify with as well as deify them.

For instance, the qualities that distinguished Lady Byron's character were purity, exceptionalism, and intelligence—transcendent and timeless qualities Stowe metaphorically constructed as angelic or divine. "Lady Byron was on the whole the purest, noblest & best woman I ever knew[,]" she wrote to a friend, "uniting great strength of mind & excellent sense with great power of feeling."[41] This brief statement collapses the most important attributes of Lady Byron's character: pure and noble—connoting chastity, piety, and majesty; wise and sensitive, with a great power of feeling; and a woman who could function as a symbol for all women as well as an anomaly, an exceptional woman—the purest, noblest, and best. In *Vindicated*, Stowe spends a good deal of time demonstrating how Lady Byron draws from these qualities to act in a manner most fitting an ideal of strong weakness, especially revealing her keen sense of right and wrong and her exercise of an independent intellect. For instance, she tells of Lady Byron's acuity with money. Lord Byron spent "every shilling" he could on himself, but Lady Byron "resolved to spend her whole income" on those in need (*Vindicated* 147). While the decision to spend her entire income on charity flies in the face of social convention, this detail actually highlights the probity of her unorthodox practice, identifying Lady Byron as a model of self-determinism and micro-management.

At one level, then, Lady Byron is a "good manager" and Lord Byron a profligate or "bad manager"; at another, she's a conscientious citizen, helping the poor. Like a professional Lady Byron links a quantifiable number, a monetary amount, both to her own worth and the worth of the people she assists. This pattern reoccurs throughout *Vindicated*: Lady Byron is well versed in other professional discourses and activities, especially charitable ones, and dons a different hat depending on her rhetorical occasion. That said, her stance is never arbitrary. Lady Byron, at least via Stowe's portrayal, interacts with the social through an unwavering expression of strong femininity. At times Stowe depicts Lady Byron as a political activist. While Stowe is careful to let her reader know that Lady Byron contributed sixty-three pounds toward gathering signatures to block slavery in Nebraska and Kansas,[42] she also notes that Lady Byron opposed slavery in all places and in all forms, thus showing that Lady Byron was never swept up by popular trends—since much pro-Southern sentiment saturated British periodicals before and during the Civil War.[43] "It seems that whether Slavery is combined with Aristocracy or Democracy," Lady Byron wrote Stowe, "it infuses a venom into the Principle which was before comparatively harmless."[44] Stowe also reveals her as a cultural critic. "The better class of young gentlemen in England are seized with a mediæval mania," comments Lady Byron in a letter Stowe prints as one of *Vindicated*'s documents. "The chief reason for regretting it is that taste is made to supersede benevolence. The money that would save thousands from perishing or suffering must be applied to raise the Gothic edifice where their last prayer may be uttered. Charity may be dead, while Art has glorified her" (*Vindicated* 225). Here, Lady Byron interprets John Ruskin's emphasis on a return to craft-based production not as the foundation of a great social movement meant to uplift the soul of the individual laborer; rather, she views the project as a material loss, an expenditure without tangible gain for the worker. Again, Lady Byron numerates benevolence. At the very same time, however, Stowe shows Lady Byron as a perpetual proponent of social reform without a price tag. Stowe recounts, "Particularly to be noted in Lady Byron was her peculiar interest in reclaiming fallen women. . . . [I]t is only perfection that can tolerate imperfection; and the very purity of Lady Byron's nature made her most forbearing and most tender towards the weak and the guilty" (*Vindicated* 156–157). What these brief examples illustrate is Lady Byron's tendency to quantify the value of popular movements—the condition of the poor or abolition or the aesthetic movement in England—as well as her expression of an enduring moral quality, an ethic transcending nationhood (in an Aristocracy or a Democracy), aesthetics (when taste is made to supersede benevolence), and social custom (reclaiming fallen women). What emerges from *Vindicated*, then, is a professional ideal that melds "Lady Byron's habits of clear, searching analysis" with her "moral nature" (*Vindicated* 211).

Combined, these features suggest a professional yet cultured feminine character that is innate rather than constructed, an intangible essence acquired via an information-based intellect. And Stowe genders these attributes. Character, with its sincerity and virtue, its emotional worth, is coded as feminine. Method, however, with its intellectual cast, its reliance on the numbers and structures of analysis so prevalent in professional discourse, is correspondingly masculine; this is the stuff of law, medicine, journalism, what makes the professions "professional." Thus Lady Byron achieves her morality, a seemingly transcendent value, through quantifiable methods of meaning-making. Put simply, Stowe's icon of strong femininity attains professionalism by bringing together the best of the feminine and the masculine and "proving" the extent of her character from the "facts" of her benevolence: how many bowls of soup equal a gargoyle or how many antislavery signatures can be secured with 63 pounds. In essence, then, Stowe's depiction both adopts and remakes professional ideology.

STRONG FEMININITY AND PROFESSIONAL AMERICAN ARTISTRY

Such depictions of Lady Byron or Barrett Browning constituted a vital aspect of how Stowe and Phelps self-consciously created public images of strong femininity through their respective constructions of England. But in addition to promotional images of British literary figures, both writers attempted to control their own public image and worked to cultivate outward postures of strong femininity themselves, especially attending to their own professional-yet-womanly characters.[45] Phelps clearly links her right to professional artistry with the arrival of her first royalty check. "From the hour that I received that check for 'two-fifty . . . ,'" she writes in her autobiography, "[I found it] impossible to forget the sense of dignity which marks the hour when one becomes a wage-earner. I felt that I had suddenly acquired value—to myself, to my family, and to the world" (22).[46] As mentioned in the introduction, the precision with which Phelps actually names and then exaggerates the meaning behind this sum epitomizes the professional's need to legitimate her skill or social value—in this case, by employing metaphoric terms attached to material gain. By the 1870s, overstating the social import of one's work by amassing material testaments to that work was crucial for aspiring professionals as established definitions of work and class began to change.

Indeed, Phelps's self-construction follows the professional changes that were happening in the literary marketplace as systems of literary production, distribution, and circulation became more commercial and writing projects became inseparable from the larger field of advertising. Because this conflation invented a consumer desire for authorial star-figures, Phelps had to control carefully both her image and its metonyms—her work and all related appurtenances. American periodicals such as *The Critic* and *The Literary World* were unabashed in how they discussed authors' private behaviors as points for selling fiction. Both regularly published tidbits on where Phelps and other notables spent their summer, what they were wearing when seen in Boston, or with whom they had lunch—much like celebrity gossip in modern-day tabloids.[47] Reducing author appreciation to commercial worth, one 1892 edition of *The Critic* reported that upon asking "a famous syndicate" of London's ***Bookman*** what he considered the "selling value" of various American and British authors, Phelps would outsell Braddon and Hardy, thereby ranking her artistry above theirs.

So at one level while Phelps mused over the widespread secular and sacred response to *Gates* in England and America,[48] at another, she spoke with rapacity of her novel's perpetual commodification. "There was a Gates Ajar tippet, for sale in the country groceries; I have fancied that it was a knit affair of as many colors as the jewels in the eternal portals. . . . There was a Gates Ajar collar—paper, I fear—leading the city counters. Ghastly rumors have reached me of the existence of a Gates Ajar cigar. . . . Music, of course, took her turn at the book, and popular 'pieces' warbled under its titles. . . . Then there was, and still exists, the Gates Ajar funeral piece [made of flowers]" (*Chapters* 113–114). Clearly, Phelps refused to accept any old commodification; rather, she fashioned pedestrian commodities in an image of her own professionalized aesthetic by judging them according to their social function and employing a self-made language of religious spectacle: not just an everyday tippet but a knit affair of many colors likened to the jewels in the eternal portals.

On a broader scale, Phelps established a standard of living that emulated her ascension in belles-lettres. Whereas in young adulthood she had written *Gates* on a "chilly bed" in a "cold room" wrapped in her dead mother's "old fur cape," her financial success allowed Phelps to build her own study (*Chapters* 103).[49] "Of course," she explains, "as is customary in the case of all authors who have written one popular book, requests for work at once rained in. . . . [I]t soon became evident that I must have a quiet place to write in . . . [, and] I was allowed to build over for my own purposes the summer house . . . once used by my mother for her own study, and well remembered by all persons interested in Andover scenery" (115). Not only did this new study serve as a befitting, material testament to Phelps's new-found rank, it furnished her with a space that could be imagined as a sanctuary—as hallowed ground for herself, her mother's memory,[50] those who cherished Andover's literary history, and, finally, the very notion of strong femininity itself.

In her own lifetime, Phelps's private study became a favorite analog for exceptional feminine accomplishment. From depicting the environs around her house as forever green to portraying her self-acquired study as a place of "perfect quiet and retirement,"[51] nineteenth-century biographers constructed lavish descriptions of this room in language connoting both august feminine influence and a refined sense of taste. "Mrs. Phelps," writes one, "[was] trained from her babyhood to feel that 'the study' was to be made *the* room of the house, [and] worked assiduously to furnish such little articles as give to a room that look of grace and culture so few can bestow, so many acknowledge" (Gilman 84). These little articles included a "chromo of the 'Immaculate Conception'"[52] as well as "books, pictures, a few easy chairs, tables, and many of the nothings which ma[k]e a study pleasant," a hammock, and "on the southern broad window sill . . . her [little] terrier" (96, 98).[53]

Such details demonstrate how Phelps's ideal of professional artistry worked hand-in-glove with icons of material success, revealingly couched here as "pleasant nothings." For just as biographers characterized her workspace, they echoed and refined these characterizations as representative of Phelps herself. One biographer, describing Phelps in 1892, writes,

> Her hair . . . is of an exquisite gray. . . . Her eyes, now blue, now gray, are full of sensitiveness. She has no crows' feet and her face is unwrinkled, with the exception of two deep horizontal lines of her forehead, which have been there since childhood. It is a young face, an ideal face, a madonna face, that inspires the reverence of all who see her. Here is the face of a philosopher, a seer and a reformer; it is the face of a true woman who carries on her heart

the sorrows and woes of many—a face of infinite tenderness and of delicate expression.[54]

Phelps's face, like the objects in her study, constitutes a series of pleasant nothings: a nothing in and of itself (it doesn't even have the distinguishing marks of age), her face importantly acts as a *tabula rasa* for a host of *pleasant* nothings, patently feminine expressions simultaneously childlike, ideal, tender and delicate. Indeed, by likening Phelps's visage to her own chromo of the Virgin, Phelps's face takes on the aspect of an immortal expression of perfect Christian womanhood, thereby distinguishing her as a consummate measure of feminine feeling. However, Phelps's face is similarly linked to active intellectual occupation: she has the look of "a philosopher, a seer and a reformer," and she sports thinking lines on her forehead that mark her as an intellectual from childhood. Thus Phelps's appearance is double: simultaneously emotive and cerebral, passive and active, timely (of this earth) and timeless ("infinite," "unwrinkled," "ideal"). In this manner, Phelps's commercial image in tandem with her own self-promotion attempts to construct her character not only beyond the strictures of feminine or masculine qualities but, further, beyond the bounds of time, history, or nation.

And this is the precise rhetorical move both Stowe and Phelps make again and again as part of their respective discourses of strong femininity. By showing Lady Byron's philosophical as well as monetary interest in unpopular "American" social questions or, as I delineate more explicitly in chapter two, by going even further to deify Lady Byron,[55] Stowe performs virtually the same rhetorical logic Phelps does when imagining *Gates* tippets in the fashion of the eternal portals or when her appearance is likened to the madonna. In all these cases, both writers seek character attributes that demonstrate how strong femininity crosses personal, local, national, or worldly interests, making it a representational system more mythic and therefore more symbolically powerful than limited social discussions of Woman's Rights. Taken together—from Stowe's "angel" Lady Byron to Phelps's Sphinx in *The Story of Avis*—these various figurations collapse into a universal sign of a divine feminine life: a model Everywoman.[56]

THE MAKING OF GEORGE ELIOT

Even more sustained than Phelps's interest in the Sphinx or Barrett Browning and even more intimate than Stowe's portrayal of Lady Byron are their respective constructions of George Eliot as their avatar of strong femininity. Beginning with Stowe, by the time she first contacted Eliot in 1869, she had already invented England as culturally dense—a place of gothicisms, fixity, and narrative continuity. What develops through her correspondence with Eliot, however, is the evolution of these basic ideas about England into a systematic and singularly feminine aesthetic, one Stowe creates in direct opposition to commercial and fact-driven modes of value. In resisting the reduction of social morals, Stowe demonstrates through her correspondence an ideal in keeping with the nineteenth-century sense of "aesthetics": artistry enabled by a discourse of creative genius and moral iconoclasm, one set against the utility and mass appeal of the marketplace. Importantly, however, Stowe's discourse is one of continuity, not discontinuity; exceptionalism and isolation are traits shared among an integrated network of gifted women, and emotional ties bind together these socially marginal yet socially powerful artists.

Indeed, in her first letter to Eliot, Stowe clearly felt she addressed a writer whose moral acuity and feminine insight matched her own.[57] "What strikes me most in your writings is the *morale*," Stowe informs Eliot. "You appear to have a peculiar insight into the workings of the moral faculties . . . —so complete is the understanding you seem to have."[58] In keeping with her focus on strong weakness, Stowe goes on to qualify this elevated comprehension as a singularly feminine precocity. "[S]ometimes I read your writings supposing you man but come to the contrary con clusions from internal evidence[.] No my sister, there are things about us that no *man* can know & consequently no man can write—& being a woman your religion must be different from mans."[59] Even at the outset, then, Stowe sees Eliot's exceptionalism as the inevitable result of her intrinsic femininity and, in addition, casts her as part of an interpretive partnership based on woman-identified systems of knowledge. In raising the specter of masculine invention (Eliot as a male writer), Stowe only supersedes it with the exceptional feminine, thereby guaranteeing that even Eliot's choice of a masculine pseudonym doesn't threaten her prominent place in the constellation of Stowe's strong women.[60] Stowe explains,

> The girls & I . . . were all in doubt whether you were man or woman—Hatty [Stowe's daughter] said it was *Totty* opened her eyes—She knew at once only a woman could write so of children. . . . —You are not a mother *in fact* perhaps because so much & peculiarly *mother in heart & nature* that your Father in casting your lot left this *actual* out of your experience.[61]

Functioning as Stowe's symbol, here Eliot represents the widespread belief that women had special sympathetic qualities "in heart and nature" as virtuous, pious, and child-rearing citizens. Yet Stowe's figuration of Eliot appraises aesthetic empathy over "actual" experience and puts the exceptional female artist in the position of delivering the "peculiarities" of strong weakness to those uninitiated Maggie Tullivers. In other words, Stowe privileges the truth of Eliot's artistic motherhood over being "a mother *in fact*," implying that Eliot's ability to write convincing fiction imbues her with superior feminine knowledge more real than the actual experiences lived by the Maggies of the world. And even when Stowe highlights her puzzlement over Eliot's gender, these moments serve to reaffirm that Eliot exemplifies feminine sentience where evidence of this sentience comes directly from Eliot's novels, not catalogues of biographical data or any other kind of fact-based document. Narrative is the best source of the real and exists distinct from fact.

Indeed, according to Stowe, this pulse of reified femininity is more important to the expert woman artist than the accumulation of book learning or even the act of writing novels. As she tells Eliot, "I think it more & believe to be really a woman worth loving than to have read Greek & German & written books."[62] For Stowe, then, it is the distinctive nature of woman that must infuse art over and above a display of brilliant erudition or perfect mimetic prose. In turn, such art furthers the cause of woman not in a specific socio-political way but by existing in a realm outside the buzz and hum of quotidian care. "The day of womans co equal reign . . . is coming," Stowe insists to Eliot, "& *you* dear tho you little think it are helping to bring it in. *Merely by being what you are*!"[63] While this statement seems to define Eliot's fiction as social engagement, Stowe does not depict this work as self-consciously political or dynamic, tied to a distinct locale, cause, or national issue. Rather, Eliot's novels and the popular figure of Eliot herself influence the social simply by "being," by enduring beyond the immediacy of public debate. Put simply, in Stowe's mind Eliot is not an activist; rather, in the manner of an Everywoman, she is a timeless artistic presence.

Importantly, Eliot's status as Everywoman is a direct result of her artistic exceptionalism. Indeed, Eliot's artistry is crucial to Stowe's system of strong weakness, for it is Eliot's work that functions as a vehicle for the exercise and display of well-trained taste. "It is only once in a century," claims Stowe, "that a writer of real genius has the art to tell his story so as to take both the cultivated few and the average many" (*Vindicated* 167–168). That Eliot is in fact Stowe's writer of the century is clear in how she addresses Eliot's work—specifically *Middlemarch*. "You write too well my darling—altogether too well to be pitched into Harper[']s Weekly along with Edmond Yates & Miss Braddon & the sensation mongers of the day," Stowe insists. "Your story [*Middlemarch*] is for the thoughtful—for the artist[,] for the few."[64] As such, Eliot's art captures the "cultivated few" (the thoughtful, the artists) at the same time that her novels are widely circulated by *Harper's*, thereby reaching—and presumably "elevating"—the "average many," participating in a kind of trickle-down theory of cultural capital. Importantly, Stowe envisions her own work in a similar manner, equally above the Mary Elizabeth Braddons yet more than worthwhile for the education of a larger audience in need of strong femininity. Concerned about the possible disinterest in *Oldtown Folks*, for instance, Stowe wrote her publisher's wife Annie Fields that the "book is not sensational & can make no headway with those whose taste is formed by Lady Audley & Mrs. Henry Ward [sic]," warning, "It is not a book to go with a rush."[65] Thus like Eliot's own worry over the lack of popular interest in her fiction—a point I explore in chapter three—Stowe sought ways to entice the average many not only to purchase but fully to comprehend her work.

Notably, Phelps iterates a similar set of sentiments in her first letter to Eliot in 1873. Also speaking of *Middlemarch*, Phelps proclaims, "You have written the novel of the century[.]"[66] This feeling Phelps carries for *Middlemarch* is that it is "pure as a lily, and as strong as the hills"[67]—thus framing her reading through the lens of feminine strength. But whereas Stowe first wrote Eliot at Eliot's own behest,[68] Phelps senses she must justify her unsolicited letter, explaining, "That the honest re-cognition of one's hard work, is never unwelcome, I have learned so well by my own small experiences, that I venture to add to 'the benediction of the air' you breathe, an expression of the feeling which I have about 'Middlemarch.'"[69] Beyond the fact, then, that both Stowe and Phelps discerned an unparalleled quality in *Middlemarch* that marked it as the novel of the century, it is of note, too, that both immediately acknowledge themselves in their initial letters as fellow artists. In her very first sentence, Phelps admits her own "small experience" in that species of fame called "re-cognition," naming herself as one who can bestow an informed appraisal of Eliot's work in lieu of idle or mass identification. In Stowe's case, she explains her delay in contacting Eliot by couching her apology in collegial terms. Upon hearing that Eliot wished to make her acquaintance, Stowe writes that she "Forthwith . . . resolved then and there that I would write to you immediately and tell you some of the *many* many thoughts *you* have caused me—[.]" "But," she continues, "I was at that time heavily taxed writing a story [*Oldtown Folks*] that I am just now with fear & trembling giving to the English world[.] It is so intensely American that I fear it may not out of my country be understood, but I cast it like a waif on the waters[.]"[70] Although Stowe's greeting is more colloquial than Phelps', she too invokes a context of writing and writers, making a reference to her own fame, albeit through a rhetoric of self-deprecation. This prelude allows Stowe an opportunity to accomplish many things at once: in addition to constructing herself as a writer with hardships and worries that must be similar to Eliot's, she makes a play for Eliot's writerly sympathy and acknowledges both her intrinsic difference from Eliot—her story's "intense" American spirit—and similarity since her book travels "like a waif on the waters" of the Atlantic, thus sharing the same audience Eliot herself solicits.

Even so, the intent of these first two missives remains distinct. Stowe's aim is to express her awe of Eliot and the ardent wish that they should become friends. Indeed, Stowe already sees her as a friend by having pored over Eliot's novels. Due to her preoccupation with *Oldtown Folks*, Stowe tells Eliot that instead of writing straightaway, she "took Silas Marner and re read carefully pencil in hand & then the Mill on the Floss. Then . . . Adam Bede & then Romola—I have *studied* all these *more* than read them—& you will therefore see why it is that I *must* begin a note to you 'My dear friend[.]'"[71] Eliot's novels become for Stowe a class of unparalleled letters, and Stowe depicts herself as the most appropriate and adroit interpreter of such communications. "I know you very well without words," she explains. "You have said so much in books that you *need* not to write me letters."[72] Novels, then, are transformed from ink and paper into a kind of mythology that defies the limits of space and time. "[W]hen my soul is walking as it often does alongside of your soul up & down paths of thought and suggestion," Stowe reflects, "it speaks aloud in a sort of soliloquy—This knowledge of a mind purely from its writings when we have never seen the bodily presence is to me the purest expression of what disembodied communion may be[.]"[73] In a manner of speaking, what Stowe later calls Eliot's "impersonal soul"[74]—meaning the bodiless essence within her novels—is transfigured from distanced admiration to a sympathy so like her own self that Stowe actually incorporates Eliot as an extension of herself. Taken in its entirety, then, Stowe's initial letter works to establish a unique relationship, one that defies even the limits of words—for, as Stowe says, she knows Eliot "very well" without them. In essence Eliot becomes Stowe's best self, an icon of perfect companionship regardless of distance or the obvious differences between them, including their nationalities. Indeed, Stowe's entire correspondence with Eliot reveals an intense emotional reliance upon her with very little sense of distinction.[75]

And Eliot's response is similarly intimate, telling Stowe that she "value[s] very highly the warrant to call you friend which your letter has given me" (*Letters* V: 29). Indeed, Stowe's repeated claims on Eliot's special sympathy find a commiserating temper. "The best joy your words give me," Eliot remarks, "is the sense of that sweet, generous feeling in you which dictated them, and I shall always be the richer because you have in this way made me know you better" (V: 29). Eliot, too, privileges the novel as an ideal means of communication, commenting that "Letters are necessarily narrow and fragmentary, and when one writes on wide subjects are liable to create more misunderstanding than illumination" (V: 31). Importantly, however, Eliot trusts Stowe's capacity for "true" interpretation, even of her "narrow" and "fragmentary" letter:

> But I have little anxiety of that kind in writing to you, dear friend and fellow-labourer—for you have had longer experience than I as a writer, and fuller experience as a woman, since you have borne children and known the mother's history from the beginning. I trust your quick and long-taught mind as an interpreter little liable to mistake me. (V: 31)

Here Eliot creates a picture of Stowe via themes Stowe herself would have cherished. First, she connects Stowe's artistic acumen to the compassion of friendship, calling her both a "dear friend" and a "fellow-labourer." In addition, Eliot locates Stowe's distinctive artistic powers in her knowledge and experience as a mother, thus imbuing Stowe with an aesthetic authority arising from natural production. These unique attributes, in turn, classify Stowe as an exceptional and trusted reader, precisely the kind of audience "little liable to mistake" Eliot's intent. And Eliot herself wishes to be a similar kind of reader. When she does receive *Oldtown Folks*, Eliot comments, "I think few of your many readers can have felt more interest than I have felt . . . for my interest in it has a double root: one is my love for our old-fashioned provincial life which had its affinities with a contemporary life even all across the Atlantic . . . ; the other is, my experimental acquaintance with some shades of Calvinistic orthodoxy" (V: 48). Eliot's reading highlights places where her experience and study meet Stowe's, thereby showing Stowe how much her work connects with Eliot's own sympathies "even all across the Atlantic." In sum, then, this initial exchange demonstrates that both Eliot and Stowe perceive each other and each other's work in remarkably similar terms, thus establishing a communication that enables Stowe to identify with as well as anoint Eliot as a paragon of strong femininity.

Phelps's opening dialogue with Eliot is markedly different. Unlike Stowe, Phelps couches her praise in regal and religious terms, naming Eliot a Queen, an Apostle, and George the Great.[76] The need for this exaggerated adulation may have something to do with the specific demands of Phelps's professional standard. While, as we have seen, Phelps promoted herself as a model of feminine strength, she simultaneously sought mentors she felt best illustrated this ideal in order to assure ongoing testaments to her hard-won aptitude. So just as Phelps was the self-appointed expert to "ordinary" or "average" female readers, she fashioned herself as a pupil to certain peers—peers she consciously constructed under the rubric of her own, particular aesthetic. And Eliot held an appeal no other peer could match. At one level, this appeal was certainly a function of Eliot's general association with all things British—both provincial knowledge and poetic legacies as well as civilized, high-aesthetic society. In one of her later letters to Eliot, Phelps admits, "a word from you is not only a great personal pleasure but a permanent intellectual stimulant,"[77] thus conflating Eliot's correspondence with a stable and continuous sense of genius, apropos to a nation whose literature, for many Americans, forever equaled immortal art.

But Phelps's identification with Eliot is too specific, too internalized to be a mere product of national awe or envy. Phelps celebrates Eliot; she does not cower under her momentous reputation or define herself in opposition to Eliot or Eliot's England. Rather, similar to Stowe, Phelps creates a common narrative inexorably linking her work to her British peer's. In fact, Phelps easily assimilates both English and Eliot iconography and nomenclature into her own life and prose—designating, for instance, "Daniel Deronda" as a name and personality appropriate for wholesale femininity ("Deronda is great, white, sad; lovely as the Sphinx"[78]) at the same time it serves as the moniker for "Dan," the little terrier perched at her study's windowsill.[79] Indeed, even christening Eliot "Queen" rings of English nobility as well as a veiled, self-referential compliment: in letters-to-editors and certain American book reviews, Phelps herself was hailed "Queen Elizabeth," perhaps in token of Phelps's own "English" prose—a prose both stylistically ornate and self-consciously bookish (recall, too, that Stowe was similarly designated a "Queen Bee" by Susan B. Anthony).[80] In sum, Eliot represents for Phelps a kind of professional and personal model of feminine exceptionalism endowed by God, limitless in potential and priceless in value, yet able to be sold as an aesthetic commodity. That Phelps's model of strong femininity was perceived as a conspicuously "American" one foreshadows Eliot's reaction to Phelps's earnest solicitations.

For after Phelps calls *Middlemarch* the novel of the century, she reveals a more complex agenda, saying that such an accomplishment is but "one matter." "[Y]ou have almost analyzed a woman—and that is quite another."[81] This second matter, how best to analyze a woman, emerges as the focal point of Phelps's letter. "I say 'almost,'" she explains, "because I believe it remains for you to finish what you have begun, and that Middlemarch itself is the hint and proposition for the study of another problem, with a great solution." Here and throughout the rest of her letter, Phelps provides a condensed version of this other problem "of Woman"—a problem whose solution is not just the prerogative but the duty of certain female artists to address. "The woman's personal identity," Phelps confides to Eliot, "is a vast undiscovered country with which society has yet to acquaint itself, and by which it is yet to be revolutionized." Phelps's missive is no mere fan letter; rather, she outlines her epic project to "revolutionize" society through feminine strength, even more important and immortal than having produced the novel of the century, which is but one matter, temporal and fixed. Ultimately dubbing Eliot the would-be "Apostle of the 'Woman Question,'" it is clear that unlike Stowe, Phelps writes to Eliot not as a friend or an admirer but as a solicitor.

And Phelps's offer is no small matter: she wants Eliot to assume the highest position in her regime. "I cannot tell you how earnestly I feel that it will require a *great novel* to proclaim the royal lineage of the Coming Woman to the average mind, nor what a positive personal longing it has become to me that *you* should write it—if for no other reason to prevent my writing a small one!"[82] This plea combines a number of insinuations. First, it once again sets Phelps and Eliot apart from those "helpless, outnumbering, unconsulted women" whom Phelps had always deemed both pitiful and ordinary, the embodiment of the "average mind." In other words, Phelps intimates a kindred connection between herself and Eliot as elite, educated mentors. Yet because Phelps already criticized *Middlemarch* for failing to articulate feminine strength, this plea also estranges Eliot and Eliot's art from Phelps's "Coming Woman," suggesting that Eliot's work cannot be successful until it adopts Phelps's own, peculiar vision of womanhood. Where Stowe had exclusively spoken of the relatedness between her mind and Eliot's, in essence Phelps highlights their philosophical differences. Finally, even when Phelps adopts a self-effacing stance—pitting Eliot's "great" novels against her own "small" ones—she seems to offer a veiled challenge, intimating that if Eliot won't produce such a novel, Phelps herself will attempt one (which, incidentally, she did with *The Story of Avis*). It is tempting, too, to pay close attention to Phelps's adjective "royal." Without reading too much into this rhetorical choice, it does link the novelistic proclamation of the Coming

Woman to English monarchy and, by extension, suggests that were Phelps to write her own novel of this lineage, she would appropriate Eliot's English culture.

Perhaps comprehending her own arrogance, Phelps closes her introductory letter with a kind of apology. "If I over step the rights, to which, a letter intended only to express my personal interest in you . . . , should limit me," she atones, "why, you will remember that I am an American, and that it is the birthright of Americans to be 'agitators,' and so, pardon me, I am sure?"[83] Thus, where Phelps first dissolves national boundaries by articulating a jurisdiction of universal womanhood, she subsequently reinforces them by highlighting her own difference from Eliot in national terminology. And Phelps exploits this designation as a kind of transatlantic bargaining tool: if Eliot finds her presumptuous, she need only remember that Phelps is an American and hence endemically predisposed to "agitate." But should Eliot reject Phelps, she will do so based on national prejudice, for Phelps is ingenious enough to take for granted English decorum, assuming pardon for her presumptuous letter. In this manner, Phelps technically cannot lose, either gaining Eliot as a progenitor of her proscribed lineage or losing Eliot to Eliot's own inability to move beyond English intolerance for new-fangled ideas, especially American ones.

This letter does, in fact, elicit a response from Eliot, one that runs opposite from Eliot's response to Stowe. Although she begins her reply by using a language with which Phelps would readily identify—"You were quite right in believing that words of sympathy from a fellow-worker would have a peculiar sweetness to me"—Eliot goes on to revise Phelps's request to forge a novel for the Coming Woman as, rather, a comment on the general difficulties of being a writer (*Letters* V: 388). "As to the 'great novel' which remains to be written, I must tell you that I never believe in future books of my own, and always after finishing any work, I have a period of despair that I can ever produce anything else worth giving to the world. The responsibility of the writer becomes heavier and heavier—does it not?—as the world grows older. . . ." (V: 388). So just as Eliot continues to thread her letter with allusions to Phelps as a professional "fellow-worker" (e.g., "does it not?"), she clearly sidesteps Phelps's censure of *Middlemarch* as a book failing to analyze "woman." This strategy—to recognize Phelps as a kind of colleague while eschewing her notions of art, women, and religion—becomes the keynote of Eliot's replies over the course of their sporadic correspondence.

In subsequent letters, for instance, Eliot follows Phelps's own lead, casting her as patently American. In keeping with the stereotypic vision of America on the part of nineteenth-century English writers, Eliot punctuates her letters to Phelps and Stowe with allusions to America as a thoroughly modern nation, one uncontaminated by the entrenched, decadent, or even corrupt cultural history so often associated with England and Europe. "America is the seed-ground and nursery of new ideals," Eliot comments, "[a place] where they can grow in larger, freer air than ours" (*Letters* VI: 317–318). Calling America a nursery of new ideals, a place imbued with freer air, and finally naming it the "land of the Future," Eliot flatters both Phelps and Stowe, intimating that their art must necessarily be large and new. Yet Eliot employs this discourse of Americana in distinct ways, depending upon her audience. With Phelps, this discourse succeeds in heightening the distance between them on geographic and aesthetic grounds, suggesting that, in juxtaposition to Phelps's work, Eliot's own art is ratified by the weight and heft derived from a land of the past.

For instance, Edith Simcox, a friend of Eliot and Lewes, recorded in her unpublished autobiography that on November 17, 1877 Eliot "gave me a book of Miss Phelps to read 'Avis,' which the writer had sent her, seeming to think that her promise to read the book when she could might be supplemented by any charitable judgment I could give more promptly" (*Letters* IX: 202).[84] Only four days previous, Eliot had written to Phelps, "I have read several chapters [of *Avis*], and shall continue to read the work with interest, but as I shall read it slowly, taking it up at odd moments, I cannot defer all sign of my sympathy till I reach the end" (VI: 417). That Eliot felt justified in passing the book to Simcox before finishing it speaks to her marginal interest in Phelps's work, especially when opposed to her eager consumption of Stowe's *Oldtown Folks*. Indeed, Eliot had admitted as much to Phelps, explaining, "In general . . . it is my rule not to read contemporary fiction, and I have had to say so in many cases to country-women of yours. . . . I daresay you will understand that for my own spiritual food I need all other sorts of reading more than I need fiction" (VI: 418). Not only does this reluctance to read Phelps's work seem particularly indifferent given Eliot's warm-hearted appraisal of Stowe's novels, Eliot's indirect refusal to participate in the kinds of exegesis Phelps engaged without hesitation is again couched as a function of nationality. Phelps is lumped in with all the many other cases in which an American country-woman has sent Eliot her fiction, hoping for praise and perhaps, like Phelps, even collaboration. But Eliot does not mince words over her beliefs in such matters, at least in relation to writers like Phelps. "[D]o not expect criticism from me," she implores.

> I hate 'sitting in the seat of judgment,' and I would rather try to impress the public generally with the sense that they may get the best result from a book without necessarily forming an 'opinion' about it, than I would rush into stating opinions of my own. The floods of nonsense printed in the form of critical opinions seem to me a chief curse of our time, a chief obstacle to true culture. (VI: 418)

These statements reveal a good deal about how Eliot felt toward Phelps. First, she implicitly scolds Phelps for presuming to censure *Middlemarch*, calling the critical analysis of fiction the "chief curse of our time." Moreover, she implies that Phelps's own work is both nondescript and uncultured; Eliot generalizes that Phelps's novel is but one more specimen of "contemporary fiction" by American women writers, and, further, she distinguishes literature outside this lot as "spiritual food," meaning by implication that contemporary American women's fiction is culturally destitute. Ultimately, then, Eliot maneuvers the conversation so that Phelps's Americanness is equated with random and depthless art and opinion, whereas Eliot's own Britishness allows her to discern true culture as well as the obstacles that thwart it (perhaps meaning a novel like Phelps's own). But the crowning blow against Phelps and her brash Americanness comes from Simcox's memoirs. After Eliot gives over *Avis*, Simcox recalls Mr. Lewes having observed, "Everyone . . . [has] an American admirer," thereby making a joke of Phelps's adoration (IX: 202). What finally emerges from this correspondence is an uneasiness or unwillingness on Eliot's part to acknowledge Phelps as an aesthetic peer. Unlike the easy accolades offered Stowe as well as Eliot's obvious enjoyment of Stowe's novels—notwithstanding their status as contemporary fiction by an American woman writer—each statement Eliot makes to Phelps on art or artistry adumbrates a careful trace of aesthetic difference, one pitched in national terms.

Eliot's sense of America is much more positive when writing to or about Stowe. Stowe herself invents America for Eliot in juxtaposition to her earlier constructions of England—as a new land that works as an agent of rebirth and renewal. Stowe worried that Eliot's ill-health coupled with Lewes's decline had worked their way into Eliot's fiction, creating a seriousness and lack of spiritual optimism that needed amends. And what better antidote, thought Stowe, than a trip to the United States? "My love," she writes to Eliot,

> what I miss in this story [*Middlemarch*] is just what we would have if you would come to our tumble down, jolly, improper, but joyous country—namely 'jollitude'—(You write & live on so high a plane—it is all self abnegation—we want to get you over here, & into this house where with closed doors we sometimes make the rafters ring with fun—& say any thing and every thing no matter what & won[']t be any properer than we's a mind to be—[)] I am wishing every day you could see our America— . . . so much wealth, ease[,] progress, culture & all sorts of nice things. . . . [I]f you should come you would . . . take a new lease on life.[85]

In a sense, Stowe offers her "improper" nation as well as her irreverent self as Eliot's aesthetic cure, the instruments that will revitalize Eliot's *morale* by taking her out of herself, enacting an almost Paterian aesthetic gesture wherein intense pleasure in the beautiful—in the "tumble down, jolly, improper, but joyous country" of America—circumvents and deconstructs the spiritual bankruptcy of literature without hopefulness or mirth.

Although Stowe was finally unsuccessful in persuading Eliot to venture across the waters, in a letter to Annie Fields about Stowe's offer, Eliot admits that it is "not for want of hope and belief in America as the scene of a great future, . . . that I give up the sight of the great New World" (*Letters* VI: 54). It was both illness and family deaths that prevented Eliot from ever making the literal voyage, but her correspondence with Stowe shows that she, too, participated in this invention of America as a confident, exciting land of "wealth, ease, progress" that worked to temper, as Eliot once put it to Stowe, "English drawing-room talk" (V: 48). Indeed, Eliot felt it was Stowe's Americanness that enriched and enlivened her novels. Responding to Stowe's worry that an English audience might not appreciate *Oldtown Folks*, Eliot insists, "I have good hope that your fears are groundless as to the obstacles your new book may find here from its thoroughly American character. Most readers who are likely to be really influenced by writing above the common order will find that special aspect an added reason for interest and study" (V: 30). Thus national difference is less a tool of separation between Eliot and Stowe than an exchange of productive, complementary images. For her vision of strong weakness, Stowe required Eliot's artistic permanence and import, and in return, Eliot fashioned an idealized notion of Stowe's republican motherhood as well as her life of American progress.

But despite the difference in attitude Eliot displays toward Stowe and Phelps, both American writers attempt to mold Eliot into a particular vision of "Eliot." And since their respective aesthetic paradigms of strong femininity function as professional systems, it is little wonder that just like a professional in science or law or medicine, Stowe and Phelps move to eschew impulses in Eliot's work that do not "fit," especially those that divorce the aesthetic (style, form, finish) from the feminine *morale*. Speaking of *Middlemarch*, for instance, Stowe admits that the book is "for the few—not the many," and "above the lines of ordinary thinking," but the novel fails to excite "any great human tragic vein where all feel in common [as] with Adam Bede." Stowe's difficulty with the novel is its attention to craft over emotion. "[*Middlemarch*] addresses the intellect & the artistic sense more than the heart," Stowe laments. "I have enjoyed reading it because it is *you* tho by no means the highest & best in you. As *art* it is perfect—but perfect art as an *end*—not instrument—has little interest to me."[86] Strikingly, Phelps echoes almost the exact same sentiment in a letter to Eliot a few years later. "I believe if Middlemarch had held the Christian trust of Adam Bede," she asserts, "it would have been *artistically* a greater book than it is, inasmuch as faith is philosophically broader than doubt and art to be perfect, must worship."[87]

Although they articulate their beliefs in different ways, a cardinal aspect to Phelps and Stowe's respective cultural aims is this theme of transcendent connection or the idea that in order for art to be "perfect," it must "worship." In keeping with most all manifestations of British aestheticism and its American counterpart that required an immutable artistic position beyond the immediacy of consumer culture (even while participating in consumerism), Phelps and Stowe insist on an aesthetic ideal embracing ultimate Christian value—or what Stowe calls here "the heart." And even though Phelps's desires and methods are more overt, both she and Stowe remake Eliot and her work not as a discrete artistic phenomenon but as an ultimate criterion of human value—an abstract symbol of strong femininity, exceptional artistry, and moral *geist*. For both women, *Adam Bede*'s Dinah Morris is an ideal figuration, and both oppose what they see in Eliot's later novels as an increasing secularization and attention to stylistic dexterity over what Phelps termed "force" and Stowe "vitality."[88] But while their combined valorization of this aesthetic is a valorization of reified Christian spirituality, it is also, importantly, a beatification of strong femininity. As Stowe says to Eliot, "Now it seems to me that . . . most of the so called scientists who are taking life [on] the basis of physical law tho in themselves pure & good—high in purpose and as poor Dorothea says *meaning* right . . . —yet having no positive triumphant hold on God Christ & the victorious hereafter[,] they have *nothing* by which to help the sorrowful[,] tempted and anguish stricken in such a life as this—nothing."[89] Against this kind of information-based *scientia* that reduces human possibility to fact or a random convergence of biological and other material factors—"nothing"—Phelps and Stowe mount a counternarrative, one that articulates a coherence of human experience distilled to an absolute *esprit de la femme*.

Here I use the concept of counternarrative deliberately. At the same time Stowe and Phelps's aesthetic negates the impersonal language of science and the fragmented delivery of information that passes for social discourse, they also reclaim the symbol and form of sequential, continuous narrative as the only medium for changing culture. "Did you ever think of the rythmical [sic] power of prose," Stowe suggests to Eliot, "how every writer when they get warm fall into a certain swing & rhythm peculiar to themselves the words all having their place and sentences their cadences."[90] Prose, whether a novel or the narrative of a life, offers a designated place for each word, a textual cadence or harmony, a synchronic sense of the present connected to the past. In the work of true artists (vs. false artists—Stowe's Braddons and Byrons), prose could awaken a passionate, dramatic emotion in the receptive reader, could tap the divine, the vital, the pure—a kind of religious ardor. And although not as adamant as Phelps in believing that Eliot need be Christian, Stowe does pester Eliot about the source of her creative power.[91] Locating her own artistic force or vitality in the combination of her strong weakness and Christian piety, Stowe believes her faith could serve as a catalyst for Eliot, bringing Eliot closer to the Christian reverence and power that she had either given up or at least lost sight of in her later fiction, especially in *Middlemarch* and *Daniel Deronda*. "I felt my heart so drawn to you last Sunday in the communion service of the church that it seemed as if my heart bore you and your trials in the infinite Love," she confesses to Eliot, "and I felt sure He would help you."[92] Tellingly, Stowe frames her criticisms through the context of friendship, offering to help "redeem" Eliot—bear her trials—and acting as the synergist bringing Christ (back) into Eliot's life.

This desire to take Eliot's agnosticism into her heart is, perhaps, the key difference in how Stowe responds to Eliot versus Phelps's more purposeful religious entreaties. "Knowing me to be a believing Christian," Phelps explains to Eliot, "you will foresee the points in which I should mourn over your later works."[93] Since religion is inseparable from Phelps's politics of feminine strength, Phelps believes that a novel like *Middlemarch* could actually impede the progress of her Coming Woman. "Give us one more Christian book, I pray you," she exhorts Eliot, "for the sake of Christ, and for the sake of Womanhood."[94] But whereas Eliot humored Stowe's worries over the state of her soul (and the soul of her fiction), Eliot's reception of Phelps's entreaty is markedly cool. "[A] propos of a distinction you seem to make between my earlier and later works, . . . there has been no change in the point of view from which I regard our life since I wrote my first fiction. . . . Any apparent change of spirit must be due to something of which I am unconscious" (*Letters* VI: 318).

Notwithstanding this sober repartee, Phelps became more and more interested in publicly salvaging, or, more appropriately, *saving* Eliot's Christian image for her American audience, especially after Eliot's death in 1880. In an article for the *Independent*, for example, Phelps quotes the above passage from their personal correspondence, grieving, "[W]ith the knowledge obtained from her memoirs [we now know] the alteration in her religious views antedated this period, [and] we may not give to her sensitive reverence the name of Christian belief" ("George Eliot's Short Stories" 2). Yet Phelps goes on to perform linguistic acrobatics in order to Christianize the very work she has just admitted could not be Christian. "What then shall we say of [her later fiction], and of its relation to that beautiful early work? If it was art, not faith, it was art to whose quality faith had ineffably contributed. . . . She was artistically great because she was spiritually great" (2). Here, then, Phelps uses Eliot's own words as a rhetorical loophole, contending that if Eliot was unconscious of any apparent change of spirit, she must have been similarly unconscious of her art's religiosity, its necessary faith.

To wit, in her elegiac poems, Phelps continues to laminate her own religious values over Eliot's life and work. The first, entitled simply "George Eliot," includes this epigraph: "The last book which she read was Thomas à Kempis's 'Imitation of Christ.'" Paralleling Eliot's refusal of Christianity to all "lowly men" who hear or see Christ "and [know] him not," this poem concludes:

> At twilight, as she, groping, sought for rest,
> What solemn footfall echoed down the dark?
> What tenderness that would not let her go?
> And patience that Love only knoweth, paced
> Silent, beside her, to the last, faint step?
> What scarred Hand gently caught her as she
> sank?

> Thou being with her, though she knew Thee
> not. (1)

By conjuring the seeming coincidental evidence of Eliot's last moment of reading, Phelps suggests Eliot's salvation in a manner performing her own imitation of Christ. This poem both names and unnames Christ—imitates him, fictionalizes him (a footfall, a Hand)—while, too, it creates him as a real being, a participant who watches, walks beside, and finally catches the dying Eliot as well as a reader addressed directly as the second-person "Thou" at the end.

Phelps's other panegyric, "George Eliot: Her Jury," completes this same rhetorical feat backwards, summoning fictional characters from Eliot's novels and giving them dominion over Eliot's soul:

> A lily rooted in a sacred soil.
> Arrayed with those who neither spin nor toil;
> Dinah, the preacher, through the purple air,
> Forever in her gentle evening prayer
> Shall plead for Her—what ear too deaf to hear? –
> 'As if she spoke to some one very near. . . .'
>
> A statue fair and firm on marble feet,
> Womanhood's woman, Dorothea, sweet
> As strength, and strong as tenderness, to make
> A 'struggle with the dark' for white light's sake,
> Immortal stands, unanswered speaks. Shall they,
> Of Her great hand the moulded, breathing clay,
> Her fit, select, and proud survivors be?–
> Possess the life eternal, and not She? (927)

Apart from numerous references to feminine strength ("fair/firm," "sweet as strength," "strong as tenderness," the ever-present symbol of the lily), this poem renders Phelps's aesthetic theory in an even subtler manner. Phelps employs Eliot's Dinah and Dorothea as emblems of a sacred definition of womanhood with the promise of infinite survival. Confronted with an immense, unpredictable, and possibly indifferent public made of up those ordinary women and average minds, such strong female characters comfort Phelps. Though chimerical, Dinah and Dorothea act here as necessary mythologies, paradigmatic women both tender and strong who exist forever, pleading redemption for their human, and therefore imperfect, creator. In addition, because these characters are fictional, and therefore simultaneously plastic yet permanent ("possessing the life eternal"), they could hardly offend Phelps's sensibilities or resist her interpretation of them. As such, this poem engineers Phelps's construction of Eliot between the seeming personal proximity of a Dorothea and the frustrating distance of the "breathing clay."

Yet Phelps does not stop there—rather, she makes another rhetorical leap, fictionalizing Eliot herself as an Everywoman who, now dead, can function in the manner of the madonna or Sphinx, a permanent icon. Paradoxically, given her reverence for Christian principle, Phelps revises Eliot's scandalous romance with Lewes as a sanctified component of her pure artistic passion. "In a sense, what must seem to us her personal mistake, *was* the price of her intellectual fame. . . . She had the love capacity of a hundred of what we usually call women—creatures who play at the passions of life. . . . There was no more grimace, or vanity, or self-seeking, in her than in some primeval woman born before Eve, and feeling with the intense simplicity of nature" ("George Eliot" 103). Characterizing Eliot as a primeval woman "before Eve," Phelps suggests that Eliot's relationship with Lewes existed in a sphere before—and therefore beyond—the Fall, thus consecrating her "love capacity" by rendering it outside Christian sin. In this manner, Phelps tutors her American readers (the "us" in this quotation) in how to decipher Eliot; for Phelps, she is not *a* great woman writer but *the* great woman writer, one who cannot be judged by temporal laws of social or spiritual dogma. By fashioning Eliot as this kind of feminine archetype, like Stowe, Phelps mythologizes Eliot, both borrowing from the precepts of traditional myth while revising those very precepts into a unique, even radical, version of feminine authority. In exculpating Eliot's erotic passion, Phelps suggests that there is a realm of feminine power that pre-exists scriptural, and therefore patriarchal, law. And by designating Eliot as the modern-day embodiment of this power, Phelps limns her as a potent, as well as pernicious, figure.

But while Phelps actively worked to remake Eliot in an image that best fit Phelps's own sense of feminine strength, she also used the idea of Eliot to further her own authorial career. In addition to elegiac poems and mythological musings, Phelps wrote articles that, in essence, manufactured a friendship out of an acquaintance. In a tribute to Eliot in *Harper's*, Phelps extracted snatches of their correspondence, insisting that while their letters were "occasional, and by no means confidential," still her excerpts were only those it seemed "right or possible to share with the public" ("Last Words" 568). As such, Phelps fabricated the illusion of confession while retaining a scrupulous, disinterested stance; in fact, this article begins and ends with paragraphs revealing the affected nature of Phelps's appropriations. "Of the great woman whose name stands at the head of this fragment so little has been coherently known, and as yet we are brought so imperfectly into the atmosphere of her personality, that the slightest approach to it becomes a possession which it seems almost an offense to human fellowship to keep to one's self" (568). Here Phelps exonerates her own impulse to gossip over Eliot by characterizing her motives as somehow democratic, a social duty. By the end of the piece, Phelps authorizes herself to rewrite not just her own kinship with Eliot but her readers' as well, arguing, "No healthy heart without perversion of the intellect accepts interrupted relations as final facts. The 'Story with an End' runs on; and she whose abounding personality drew to itself the depths and heights of human fellowship must live despite herself and every prophet of her creed of death, to bless and to resume her bond to us" (571). Phelps nominates herself as the one who will interpret Eliot to the masses, rearrange final facts, and insist that Eliot's "interrupted relations" be consummated, although on Phelps's own terms. This self-appointment as Eliot's agent is clear from the article's title, "Last Words from George Eliot." We are not, as readers, privy to Eliot's actual last words; instead, we are given Phelps's version, and, tellingly, these words occur in a personal letter to Phelps. Thus the final fact of Eliot is decontextualized and reconstructed in a single instance of her writing, an excerpt implying a friendship or sympathy that exceeds the bounds of their actual correspondence.

But perhaps the most vivid example of how Phelps utilized this "revised" Eliot to market both her doctrine of feminine strength as well as her own place in American letters occurred while Eliot was still alive. In the fall of 1876, Phelps delivered a series of lectures entitled "Representative Modern Fiction."[95] For Phelps, these lectures exemplified her professional and artistic acumen: not only was she the first woman in the history of Boston University asked to deliver lectures to the student body, the very site of the University itself worked to promote and serve her professional authority. Elizabeth T. Spring, writing a chapter on Phelps for a contemporary anthology, characterized the lectures in the following manner:

> It was the first thing of the sort ever attempted by a woman in this part of the world, and in the minds of those most interested there was the air of a renaissance in the undertaking. . . .
>
> Her power over the audience is said to have been remarkable. While her voice in conversation is singularly low and sweet, some peculiar penetrative quality made it distinct without the slightest effort for the listener in every part of a large hall. . . . Mr. Whittier, who on another occasion heard the lectures, says, of them: 'They were admirable in manner and matter. I have never heard a woman speak with such magnetic power.'
>
> In treating modern fiction she concentrated her analysis on George Eliot as representative. President Warren of the University says, 'The genius of George Eliot has never been analyzed with superior, if with equal subtility of sympathy and clearness of discrimination.' (569–570)

For a nineteenth-century audience, then, the lectures were less a scholarly study than a political and social statement, touted by the popular press of Massachusetts as a simultaneous argument for Woman's Rights and a spectacle featuring Phelps as a special breed of female orator, one boasting a "peculiar penetrative quality" in tandem with the appropriate modulations of feminine speech, "low and sweet."[96] This peculiarity or rhetoric of exceptionalism permeates John Greenleaf Whittier's comments on the lectures as well. Though claiming to be struck by both "manner and matter," Whittier evidently found Phelps's manner—and gender—more noteworthy, having never heard a *woman* speak with such magnetism. Even the President's commendation focuses on Phelps's feminine sympathy with Eliot as a crucial component of her analysis. Thus, the lectures came to symbolize exactly that balance of power-within-femininity—peculiar, penetrating, sympathetic—that Phelps considered the lynchpin of her artistry.

Upon accepting the invitation to give these lectures, Phelps wrote to Eliot requesting biographical information, but, apparently, Phelps spilled a traveling-flask of brandy on Eliot's reply. Tenacious, she contacted Eliot again, explaining she needed a copy of the lost manuscript. "I make a 'point' in one lecture," she acknowledged, "where, in reading such passages from your letter as <you> felt [me] authorized to use, I want to lift the letter in my hand, that the boys and girls may see it at the audience-distance. The whole motif of one of my pet sentences hangs upon the act" (*Letters* VI: 158). Holding up the letter, of course, was crucial to Phelps as a testament to their intimacy, an authorization for Phelps speak about and on behalf of Eliot to an American audience.

Yet these very passages, ironically, constituted an injunction against those who would use biography for literary analysis. "I certainly feel a strong disgust for any readiness to satisfy that idle curiosity which, caring little for the study of [an] author's work, is pleased with low gossip about his private life and personal appearance," admonished Eliot. "Of every writer worth reading it may be said 'He gave the people of his best; / His worst he kept; his best he gave.' Can we be too severe on the spirit which neglects the 'best,' and eagerly accepts details called biographical, which would be worthless even if they were accurate?" (VI: 163). Given Eliot's scandalous life, it is little wonder that she felt particularly sensitive about the circulation of her own biographical material. But, again, this statement demonstrates Eliot's basic wariness with Phelps, whom she seemed to have regarded as potentially dangerous—much like her sense of literary critics in general. And Phelps certainly is more comfortable with the notion of commercial exchange than either Eliot or Stowe, acknowledged by her participation in the Boston lectures as well as her desire to commodify herself and her artistic paraphernalia (e.g., *Gates* tippets and cigars, her study, her face). Indeed, for the Boston lectures Phelps not only employs biographical information on Eliot;[97] she wields Eliot's handwriting as an artifact miming her selfhood, solidifying the pet sentence not with Eliot's best but with an advertisement, a guarantee that Phelps is an insider on matters George Eliot. Thus, even while Eliot granted Phelps narrow permission to apply biography and assumed Phelps would be above satisfying "idle curiosity," Phelps proved to be more interested in selling her personal connection with Eliot, brandishing and quoting from the corroborating letter. Comparatively, then, Phelps demonstrates an ease in a culture requiring authorial spectacle whereas Eliot expresses mortification at tabloid mentalities, needing to mask her image to the point of telling Phelps exactly what parts of the letter she may read from.[98]

A mere speculation, it is nonetheless compelling to presume that Eliot's prejudiced attitude toward Phelps had something to do with Phelps's reputation in England. In contrast, even though her Anglo-American relationship soured after the "True Story," when Stowe visited England for the first time, notwithstanding public statements in favor of anti-abolition in the States, she was treated as royalty. As Hedrick so vividly describes, when Stowe first stepped off the *Canada* in Liverpool, "Amassed as far as the eye could see was a crowd of English men, women, and children who were straining for their first glimpse of the author of *Uncle Tom's Cabin*. . . . Such receptions swelled in size and enthusiasm as Stowe made her triumphant tour of Great Britain, where sales of *Uncle Tom's Cabin* were more than triple the already phenomenal figures of the United States, reaching a million and a half in the first year" (233). Inversely, Phelps's *The Gates Ajar* met with English books and pamphlets that, for the most part, censured the novel's unorthodox views of heaven and, in turn, Phelps's American audacity. In her pamphlet *"The Gates Ajar" Criticised and Corrected*, one anonymous Englishwoman asserted, "Truly, the book needs an 'apology,' and the best apology that can be found for the sentiments it introduces to English minds is, that the work is thoroughly *American*" (iii).[99] While Stowe was viewed for many years as an American hero, Phelps was consistently seen as a "painted woman," a kind of confidence man hustling people with her depictions of a secular and domesticated Heaven. Another British pamphleteer wrote that such "degrading views of eternity [as found in *Gates*] are worthy rather of a Red Indian's expectation, than of a Christian's" (Dean 46). This writer continued,

> The poor heathen, when he is dying, slays his favourite dog, who, with his best bow and arrows, is buried with him, fondly dreaming of the heavenly hunting-grounds where he hopes to join his ancestors! More rational far than the puerilities of this lady, who, having sagely observed that 'the principal joy of a child's life consists in eating,' naturally resolved never to tell her little girl that heaven *was a dinnerless eternity*!'" (46)

In a sense, then, long before Phelps first contacted Eliot, Phelps and her work had been placed in a compromised position: to Britons, her views were like the heathen's, not the Christian's, and her narrative practice imitated the "barbaric" rituals of Native Americans, not the civilized tradition of British literature.

Being tagged "thoroughly American" certainly granted Phelps a kind of panache and the right to invoke her nationality in service of a desire to know and be known by George Eliot. Perhaps, however, this rhetorical move served to paint her as a fraud, at least to Eliot. With Phelps's high-minded insistence that Eliot Christianize her novels, it may be that Eliot—who was certainly attuned to the popular feeling surrounding certain authors (though she denied having any interest in her own reputation)—found this appeal not only brazen but hypocritical.

Regardless of Eliot's differential treatment, however, Stowe and Phelps's respective models of strong weakness and feminine strength created remarkably similar social discourses—ones that worked to establish universal modes of feminine meaning-making. In her very first letter to Eliot, Stowe comments, "You are by nature so *thoroughly English* . . . —besides you are as thoroughly *woman* as you are English."[100] While Stowe begins by making an innate national distinction, she articulates common ground from which to construct empathy: like Stowe herself, Eliot is thoroughly *woman*, not American or English. And, indeed, throughout the years of their correspondence, both Phelps and Stowe repeatedly viewed their work as a complement and extension of the woman-centered, moral visions they sought in Eliot's novels. Taken together, Stowe and Phelps recognize themselves and Eliot as "fellow-workers" (to use Eliot's term): artistic specialists in a peculiar and potentially communal feminine sympathy. It was Stowe and Phelps's mission to comprehend this sympathy via the best, most exquisite novels (Eliot's) and then deliver it, in narrative form, as an ideal to other appreciative natures, in turn initiating a moral transformation among the *fæx populi*. Thus, this complex articulation of strong femininity through a professional lens seems to negate an information-based professional culture, posing, instead, an alternative mode of social morality.

What finally sustained Stowe and Phelps, then, were their images of familiarity and shared exceptionalism across the ocean, whether those images were accurate or fantastic. Stowe had once said that the "highest class of mind in all countries loses nationality, and becomes universal," and, indeed, Stowe and Phelps's invention of Eliot *vis-à-vis* their own self-creations details a mythic story of a consummate, universal Everywoman, one that borrows both from English refinement and American innovation (*Sunny* I: 69). Symbolically, this Everywoman exemplified an admixture of the rich history and definiteness of England as well as the spirited growth of American newness. In its ideal representation, their icon of strong femininity collapsed national distinctions and provincial sensibilities, slowly working toward what Eliot had once specified to Stowe as the "moral good of [all] men" (*Letters* V: 31).

Chapter Two

"The Wild and Distracted Call for Proof"

Harriet Beecher Stowe's Lady Byron Vindicated *and the New Professionalism*

In a cartoon from the October 1869 *Merryman's Monthly*, Harriet Beecher Stowe wields a huge quill and conjures Lord Byron in the shape of a satyr. Byron rises on a dark cloud from a great black inkwell; a snake at Stowe's feet reads "scandal"; a horned toad sits on copies of *Uncle Tom's Cabin* and *Dred*; and a human skull as well as a jarred fetus rest on a shelf in the background. The caption reads, "Mrs. H— B— S—'s Great Incantation. Who have we here?— The great poet Byron or the D—l?"[1]

The surface critique is obvious: the cartoonist equates Stowe's writing with witchcraft. More subtly, however, the parody targets three specific attributes that had comprised Stowe's authorial ethos ever since the publication of *Uncle Tom's Cabin*: her tripartite position as woman, Christian, and American activist for abolition.[2] The Christian critique is the most apparent. An emissary of the D—l (his propinquity made manifest in the serpent that names her writing practice scandal), Stowe's art transforms Byron from a great poet into a Satanic incarnation. In other words, Stowe's own writing is not great; it can only defile and debase the great. In turn, the elements of witchcraft, especially the pickled fetus, insinuate that Stowe's womanhood has gone awry. Rather than nurture and protect the republic's children, her writing or sorcery kills them, polluting the domestic idyll. And, indeed, the entire portrait is not just magic but black magic: the stuff of Stowe's art, her ink, drips thick and black; and the representative productions of this art, *Uncle Tom's Cabin* and *Dred*, are Stowe's two slavery novels. By inference, the sketch racializes all of Stowe's writing, suggesting that her treatment of Byron is inflected by a quintessentially American quality—threatening, sinister blackness.

This British cartoon is but one response to Stowe's article "The True Story of Lady Byron's Life."[3] Published simultaneously in the September 1869 issues of the *Atlantic* in America and *MacMillan's* in England, this piece initiated a transatlantic media blitz so virulent and wild that Oliver Wendell Holmes called it the "Byron

Figure 2.1. Cartoon, *Merryman's Monthly* (October 1869).

whirlwind" (Morse II: 183).[4] The "scandalous" center of the article accused Lord Byron of committing incest both before and during his marriage; and while such an accusation could, in and of itself, explain the caustic nature of the media's response, the reasons motivating Stowe's almost universal condemnation are less transparent. Certainly Stowe had received negative press as a consequence of *Uncle Tom's Cabin*,[5] but the rhetorical position of woman, Christian, and citizen that had made this novel a transatlantic bestseller and launched Stowe into cosmopolitan celebrity in 1851 no longer guaranteed her standing as a credible author by 1869. Rather, as is evident in the *Merryman*'s cartoon, the press attacked Stowe for those very same qualities and repeatedly called on her to produce "proof" of Byron's crime. In the early 1850s, proof had been a matter of effecting a convincing narrative to arouse Christian sympathy. Now, as Joan Hedrick points out, "writing about real people and facts that could be disputed, Stowe could make no use of her most powerful tools, her ability to create realistic dialogue and a texture of presumed fact" (366).

But the difference wasn't one of mere subject matter, for Stowe had successfully treated controversial real-life stories in works like *A Key to Uncle Tom's Cabin*.[6] The reason Stowe's audience now failed to appreciate the value of her article was that her readership no longer assumed Stowe's credibility; rather, her audience was increasingly shaped by the new discourse of professionalism—a discourse that reversed literary qualities Stowe held most dear by divorcing knowledge from meaningful contexts, removing "bookish" or narrative attributes from public rhetoric, and relying on fact as the measure of supreme value. With the advent of such a professional milieu, Stowe found herself in the unforeseen position of having to prove her accusation of incest with discrete and tangible facts, especially as the nucleus of her argument was a cipher, an unsubstantiated conversation she had secured from Lady Byron meant to be taken on faith by the reading public. According to one journalist from the London *Standard*, Stowe wasn't credible precisely because of her reputation as "an American authoress . . . known to the public by a clever but uncandid romance" ("Stowe-Byron" 56). This critic refused to quote from the "True Story" because doing so would "allow the authoress . . . to employ over again in these pages the well-known dexterity of the romance writer when fiction has to be made to look like fact" (56). In other words, this commentator accused Stowe of engaging in a kind of artistic witchcraft, relying on the rhetorical conventions of a romance where a story stands in for what is true. But the climate in which Stowe offered her article required not truth but fact, i.e., a separation of truth from story, and as such, Stowe's piece failed miserably on both sides of the Atlantic.

Thus, the new discourse of professionalism led Stowe to appraise and approach facticity in a new way. In less than six months, she re-wrote her "True Story" into a book-length study entitled *Lady Byron Vindicated*, one that emphasized facticity and reframed Stowe's rhetorical position from woman-Christian-citizen to that of a professional witnessor. These two versions of the same story provide a rich case study for exploring the development of crucial aspects of professional culture: a certain strain of literary realism that relied on fact-as-value as well as the workings of commercial advertising in professional exchange. In part, then, Stowe's double account of Lord and Lady Byron's life exposes the mutual and often conflicting histories of gender, nation, artistry and professional culture in the 1870s and reveals how Stowe tried to manage her own changing position at their intersection.

LADY BYRON VINDICATED AND THE "PROOF" OF PROFESSIONAL DISCOURSE

In essence, Stowe's original essay and its sequel adapted the same story as their centerpiece: on a trip to England in 1856, Lady Byron granted Stowe a *tête-à-tête*, one in which Stowe learned the secret reason behind her marital estrangement, that Lord Byron had fathered a child with his half-sister Augusta Leigh and maintained an incestuous relationship even after his marriage—all the while blaming Lady Byron's frigidity as the source of his dissipation. Thirteen years following this confidence, Stowe happened upon a memoir by Byron's last mistress, the Countess Guiccioli, a reminiscence perpetuating this oft-repeated portrayal of Lady Byron as a "narrow-minded, cold-hearted precisian" who stifled Byron's art and drove him to seek solace in other women ("True Story" 295).[7] Stowe then alleged to have come across an article in England's celebrated *Blackwood's* praising this memoir and offering it as an authentic representation of Byron's wedded woes.[8] Angered at what she felt to be a one-sided attack on Lady Byron's character and frustrated that no English writer came to her defense, Stowe argued that since "Lady Byron has an American name and an American existence, and reverence for pure womanhood is, we think, a national characteristic of the American," she deserved a conclusive "refutation of the slanders" from an American author ("True Story" 313).

At one level, then, Stowe's text attempted a national corrective, not merely one woman speaking in defense of another's honor but America tutoring England on how to treat its pure women. However, at another level Stowe's article troubled the very rhetorical positions she had always claimed as her authenticators; in addition to cartoonists, literary critics denounced her impropriety as a woman, Christian, and American. Indeed, her detractors repeatedly invoked Stowe's gender and self-claimed piety, accusing her of behaving in an unwomanly and ungodly manner by spreading sexual scandal and breaking feminine confidence. The editor of London's *Illustrated Times* jibed, "[Stowe's] rash and utterly unjustifyable conduct only illustrates once more the melancholy truth that man's inhumanity to man is as nothing compared with woman's uncharitableness to woman" ("The Lounger" 231). And another critic for *Public Opinion* cried, "[Stowe] is false to the instincts of her own sex; it is theirs to draw the curtain over the faults of the living, and to cherish sympathy for those whom genius endows with her noblest gifts" ("The Byron Scandal" 381). Still other editorialists seized on Stowe's nationality, likening her to an environmental pollutant—"the Tweed and Mississippi freely mingling with our classic Thames"—and classifying her disclosure as "pre-eminently un-English" ("Stowe-Byron" 106, 115).[9]

Part of the reason Stowe's rhetorical delivery failed in 1869 where it had succeeded in 1851 had to do with the new media of Anglo-American communication developed during and just after the riotous success of *Uncle Tom's Cabin*—media that were, in fact, magnified by the unprecedented sales of her novel. With the development of the Atlantic telegraph, news became a series of disconnected ideas from remote and unfamiliar places—a nonsensical string of competing headlines. Although the transatlantic novel business flourished in the last decades of the nineteenth century,[10] what's important is not that news replaced novels (it didn't) but that the structure and delivery of news no longer resembled a novel. Instead, writing news became its own distinct profession, replete with special knowledge and instruction, ceremonies and prizes, habits of thought, and, of course, jargon and syntax. Above all, news traded in tangible fact. Straightforward, plain language performed the real, and whereas *Uncle Tom*'s readers had not maintained rigid distinctions between fiction and nonfiction, Stowe's 1869 audience expected words packaged as fact to render certitude.

But rather than offering outside, independent, objective, or technical evidence to support her article, the "True Story" read like fiction. Stowe confused dates, misquoting how many years Lord and Lady Byron had been married. She used Byron's poems as if they were unalloyed autobiography, referring to passages from *Don Juan* to demonstrate his mistreatment of Lady Byron in the guise of Donna Inez and from *Cain* and *Manfred* to show how he "justified himself in incest" ("True Story" 304). In keeping with the style of historical romances, she referred to herself as "the writer," never providing her name or signing the article.[11] In fact, her overall writing style was characteristic of the techniques upon which she had founded her career as a novelist, techniques Jane Tompkins has distinguished as "heuristic and didactic rather than mimetic" (xvii). Stowe's syntax was the opposite of economy, a maze of sinuous constructions, stacks of adjectives and embedded clauses. Her piece spoke in euphemisms and analogies and relied on sentimental allusions, including the requisite tears: "Lord Byron's 'Fare thee well . . . ,' was set to music and sung with tears by young school-girls, even in this distant America" (296). Importantly, the article also followed the allegorical pattern of *Uncle Tom's Cabin*, embodying the redemptive love of Christ in a "Little Eva" exemplar—"Lying so near the confines of the spiritual world, [Lady Byron] seemed already to see into it"—and making a prophetic analogy between Byron and a fallen angel whose evil doings had influenced gullible readers (310–311).

Even the plot structure of Stowe's article resembled that of a moral tale, establishing first the story as consumed by an innocent multitude—one in which Lady Byron was characterized as hard-hearted; moving next through a retelling of the same story, supplemented with all the damnable actions on the part of Byron—the "secret adulterous intrigue with a blood relation" and the fact that he asked Lady Byron to allow a "continental latitude" in their marriage, "in which complaisant couples mutually agreed to form the cloak for each other's infidelities" (306); and, finally, remaking Lady Byron not just as a wronged woman but, again, as a suffering and compassionate Christ-figure—a move calculated to re-educate all Christians who had ever condemned her. In short, Stowe misassessed her rhetorical situation and made stylistic and organizational choices worthy of the sentimental novelist, not the journalist.

Readers were quick to condemn her essay's prosiness and especially Stowe's lack of verifiable evidence. In a series of private letters to Stowe's sister Isabella, Isabella's husband, John Hooker, vividly captured the tenor of the postwar reading public and its aversion to Stowe's lack of "proof."[12] The four letters I cite here react to a development that occurred in the last stages of preparing *Lady Byron Vindicated* for press. One result of "True Story" was the publication of a spate of ad hoc biographies, digests, and treatises related to the case. Medora Leigh, the supposed child of Lord Byron and his half-sister Augusta Leigh, published her memoirs in an attempt to acquit Byron. This autobiography included letters between Leigh and

Lady Byron, and John Hooker, as well as other readers, felt that the simple existence of such a correspondence proved that Medora could not have been illegitimate. While Calvin, Stowe's husband, contended that Leigh's book actually corroborated Stowe's case, Hooker thought this evidence the crowning blow against her lack of professional documentation in the "True Story."[13] "As it now stands," Hooker wrote Isabella on November 18, two months following the publication of Stowe's article, "with Lady Byrons letters to Mrs. Leigh, [Stowe's book] must be *solid argument — downright facts*—Mere fine writing will do no good—will really be worse than nothing. Those letters, if genuine (& nobody seems to claim they are not, though they look like fabrications) would seem to be decisive & beyond the power of any other facts to overcome—I hope she will not give the public any thing that shall seem a mere appeal to feeling—but that she will make it (what alone is of any use) a logical, unanswerable ***argument.***"[14] As a Connecticut state legislator, Hooker had found nothing in the "True Story" to satisfy his definition of proof: no downright facts, no logic, no solid argument. He had witnessed the transatlantic press cast aspersions on Stowe for her ineptitude and naiveté, and with no similar public cry against Medora's autobiography, he assumed that the letters were genuine or, at least, that they would be regarded as genuine. Hooker viewed words not as an expression of human feeling or communal value but as a final, permanent reference to a specific writer's avowals, and, by extension, as an enduring testament that could be used to damage a writer's reputation.

Two days later, Hooker further clarified his initial assertions, claiming not only that Stowe should avoid fine writing and a mere appeal to feeling, but, in addition, as narrator she should not "assume the position of a guarantor of the truth of Lady Byron's statement[s] to her—that is wholly Lady Byron's matter—not hers—She will make a great mistake if she admits herself bound to sustain the charge. She can present her facts ***as a contribution to a discussion that the public is taking a deep interest in***, and not as an argument of one who has identified herself with the cause."[15] Here Hooker's professional bias toward common sense is even more overt; if every word is interpreted as potentially damning in an age of fact as proof, Stowe must detach herself as much as possible from the word, abjure responsibility that could result in a judgment against Stowe as one who had endangered civilization with her "dirty book"—the promulgation of fiction as truth. In Hooker's opinion, Stowe risked her entire career should she try to pass off an impassioned vindication as a studied, considered, impartial argument. "[T]here must be *iron facts*—nothing else," insisted Hooker, almost two weeks later. "It will be a great mistake if Mrs. Stowe touches the matter any further & does not put the case beyond question on her side. . . . If it is sentiment, and a defense of Lady Byron's sanity & purity, & an array of probabilities merely, it had better never come out. A ton of mere probabilities wont weigh a feather now."[16] Hooker's tirades culminated in a foreboding prophesy, one that turned out not to be without merit. If Stowe could not meet proof with proof, she would ruin her reputation; further, even if she accumulated hard evidence such as facts, figures, and events, above all she should not claim that her version of her story was the truth. As a narrative strategy, Hooker surmised, believing that one knows the truth is tantamount to rhetorical suicide. "[T]he proofs against her charge are insuperable—& I feel as if I *know* that she will only infame her reputation by reasserting it. . . . If she goes on & repeats the charge & does not prove it beyond a question, she will receive no mercy at the hands of the public & will expose herself terribly to damages in a court of law . . . —and it should no where assert the truth of the charge but merely give the evidence that tends to prove it." Hooker concluded, "Mrs. Stowe is walking in a most perilous path."[17]

Hooker's private letters mirror the public criticism Stowe received in both America and England and the incredulity, even chastisement, she met with from family and friends. For instance, *The Independent*, a newspaper that had printed many of Stowe's articles over the years, carried a prototypic indictment from its editor, Theodore Tilton: "Startling in accusation, barren in proof, inaccurate in dates, infelicitous in style, and altogether ill-advised in publication, her strange article will travel round the whole literary world and everywhere evoke against its author the spontaneous disapprobation of her life-long friends" ("Byron Revelations" 1).[18] In turn, Stowe's brother Henry, primarily writing to gloat over the media blitz—"Sometimes it is one, sometimes another of [those] Beechers, that keep people in hot water[.] Now, it is *your* kettle that has boiled over"—finally asked his sister, "Had not Lady Byron *documents* which establish the facts beyond all controversy?"[19]

This critical response left Stowe in a vexed position. "The course of the papers surprises and grieves me. They are not as good as I thought them," she wrote her publisher, James Osgood. "The wild and distracted calling on me for proof, utterly ignoring the only kind of proof that I have to give, shows that the public is yet not in a proper state to weigh anything."[20] In response, Stowe decided to write a book-length study of the case, *Lady Byron Vindicated*, and she took steps to remake her argument into a professional instrument: an archive of dates, documents, cross-referenced data, and named sources.

As Stowe sought to meet the rhetorical demands of a public calling for proof, she appropriated words from the emerging professions, especially journalism, law, and psychiatry.[21] "As it is too late to have the securities of a legal trial," Stowe explained, "certainly the rules of historical evidence should be strictly observed. All important documents should be presented in an entire state, with a plain and open account of their history" (*Vindicated* 322). Indeed, Stowe attempted to cast herself in the role of the impartial, investigative journalist, the one who would provide the "plain and open account" of all "documents." By inference, Stowe also assumed the role of the lawyer, the one who would put Byron on a literary trial, and, in addition, she simulated the voice of the psychiatrist, the one who would establish Byron's moral illness and its infection of the entire British nation. The consequence of miming such professional postures, however, was the tension Stowe created against her own novelistic prose and impassioned, sentimental appeals—in other words, a tension against her own established artistry.

The form and tone of much of *Vindicated,* so distinct from the "True Story," were designed to teach her public the "proper state" in which to read and "weigh" both her text and her own position as a professional female artist. Stowe not only autographed the book but referred to herself as "I" and "me" instead of "the writer." Punctilious in naming names and quoting sources, Stowe dedicated an entire chapter to her argument's core, the notorious interview, providing the who, what, where, when, and how hitherto absent. She numbered, footnoted, and dated; she moved through her polemic in a rough chronological fashion, inserting an entire chapter abstracting the most salient events. She justified the error she had made in her original article over the marriage dates by precisely citing her source, impugning someone else's faulty research. For the most part, she turned away from Byron's poems as biographical material to analyze his personal correspondence.[22] Overall, the substance of her approach changed from what she herself characterized as the "most general terms" of her original article to "just where I would stand were I giving evidence under oath before a legal tribunal" (*Vindicated* 261, 258).

Within the evocation of this classic professional context, a courtroom, Stowe appropriated the language of expert witnesses as well as the voice of a defense lawyer. For the chapters in *Vindicated* requiring data to demonstrate the "criminal" aspects of her case, Stowe quoted pertinent documents at length, often in their entirety, and adopted the organizational structure of a legal brief. Here is one example of many:

> IV. Aug. 9, 1817.—Gives to M. G. Lewis a paper for circulation among friends in England, stating that what he most wants is public investigation, which has always been denied him; and daring Lady Byron and her counsel to come out publicly. Found in M. G. Lewis's portfolio after his death; never heard of before, except among the 'initiated.' (79)

By placing the date first, Stowe makes it appear as one in a series—a reassurance that the following information is linked to a specific day in a specific year. Sentence fragments form the body of the paragraph as if Stowe, the investigator, merely jotted down the most striking facts. All of Stowe's information comes from a designated document with a particular addressee, one she names, and Stowe provides her reader with what she believes is the "plain and open account" she had said was imperative, the knowledge of who had the documents, where they were found, and how preserved. Finally, in reference to Byron's actions, she chooses two words connoting culpability, "daring" and "initiated": Byron dares Lady Byron like an overgrown child picking a fight—he doesn't request, demand, or expect her to make a public accusation—and clearly Stowe wants her reader to believe that Byron is a member of some mysterious band called the initiated. Indeed, the quotation marks around "initiated" imply that the word is Byron's own, further implicating him in some covert activity.

To make Stowe's expropriation of legalistic discourse all the more evident, consider the following paragraph from the original "True Story":

> Madame de Staël commenced the first effort at evangelization immediately after [Byron] left England, and found her catechumen in a most edifying state of humility. He was metaphorically on his knees in penitence, and confessed himself a miserable sinner in the loveliest manner possible. Such sweetness and humility took all hearts. His conversations with Madame de Staël were printed and circulated all over the world, making it to appear that only the inflexibility of Lady Byron stood in the way of his entire conversion. (297)

Not only is Stowe's syntax here literary, consisting entirely of independent clauses rather than fragmentary pieces of information, but Stowe applies a string of value-laden descriptors to highlight Byron's artifice ("edifying," "miserable," "loveliest"); affects metaphor ("[his] sweetness and humility took all hearts"); and elevates her diction ("evangelization," "catechumen," "penitence"). There are no dates or documents. Distilled to its informational content, this excerpt has very little in the way of hard fact: Stowe's reader knows Madame de Staël got involved in some way to persuade the public that Lady Byron was at fault for the separation, although de Staël's manner of involvement is not specified, and the reader learns that Byron engaged in confession, but the transcript of this confession is absent.

On the other hand, in *Vindicated* Stowe moves fluidly from one professional accent to another. Taking on the voice of the psychiatrist, for instance, Stowe devotes an entire chapter to what she calls her "Physiological Argument"—a chapter intended to convince the reader that Byron was an alcoholic hysteric. When needing the opinion of an expert witness, especially a medical man, Stowe quotes long passages from work by scholars in the field, in particular Dr. Forbes Winslow and his article on "Obscure Diseases of the Brain and Nerves." But Stowe also goes one step further to ventriloquize medical discourse herself:

> Modern physiological developments would lead any person versed in the study of the reciprocal influence of physical and moral laws to anticipate the most serious danger to such an organization as Lord Byron's, from a precocious development of the passions. Alcoholic and narcotic stimulants, in the case of such a person, would be regarded as little less than suicidal, and an early course of combined drinking and licentiousness as tending directly to establish those unsound conditions which lead toward moral insanity. (*Vindicated* 374)

Now Stowe's diction insinuates scientific jargon and suggests an educated perspective with such high-brow turns of phrase as "reciprocal influence," "precocious development," and "unsound conditions." By forgoing the use of "I" in favor of a third-person, passive voice, Stowe suggests a universal, objective point-of-view; further, Stowe's writing hints that she herself is one of those people versed in this esoteric study without actually having to claim that she is or is not. This example mimes classic textbook prose, adopting the inflection of a distanced, intelligent narrator whose opinion is axiom.

PROFESSIONAL DISCOURSE AND LITERARY REALISM

Taken together, these multiple concessions to a public calling for "Proof!" serve to throw into relief points in *Vindicated* where Stowe returns to the voice of the novelist, revealing something about the narrative that necessitates a fictional stance. Stowe adopted just such an approach for her most sensational chapter "Lady Byron's Story as Told Me"—the one relating the all-important moment of Lady Byron's confession. I say all-important for it was this piece of evidence—or, rather, the lack thereof—that produced the most incredulity and backlash in the transatlantic press. For instance, one thread of criticism accused Lady Byron of having jealous hallucinations. In a letter to the editor of the *Pall Mall Gazette*, a contributor claimed that "women, especially when jealous, are not very scrupulous in their assertions, and, moreover, after a certain time actually believe in the truth of their assumptions. They will in fact, to use a common expression, stick at nothing" (3).

Thus Stowe had to reclaim a position of authority, especially regarding her charge of incest. For this most important and contestable chapter—a chapter containing no material documents to bolster its claims, no outside witnesses to attest to its merit—Stowe chooses to construct scene, setting, dialogue, and character. In short, she chooses to write fiction.[23] Even this chapter's title is telling, "Lady Byron's Story as Told Me." All preceding chapters from Part I of *Vindicated* offer no sense of a first-person "I" or "me" in the text: "The Attack on Lady Byron"; "Résumé of the Conspiracy"; "Results after Lord Byron's Death"; and "The Attack on Lady Byron's Grave." In turn, all subsequent ones lose this "I": "Chronological Summary of Events," "The Character of the Two Witnesses compared," "The Direct Argument to prove the Crime," "Physiological Argument," and "How could she love Him?" (Indeed, the chapter just prior to the infamous one of disclosure is the only other to affect a first-person narrator, entitled "Lady Byron as I knew Her"—a point to which I will return.) As such, these titles suggest that Stowe's summaries, arguments, and résumés devolve organically from a nether realm of truth—they are not authored, like fiction; they represent an absolute veracity, a compendium of publicly owned evidence. Moreover, these chapters add thick layers of documental evidence on either side of her book's core, its narrative climax, sandwiching the cipher at the center of Stowe's text to create an illusion of inner substance as well as a further mystification of the terrible secret.

Stowe's difficulty with this pernicious chapter rests primarily with her milieu's dependence on print as its legal medium—clear, precise words that functioned as the binding vehicles for all professional institutions and their exchanges. To a nineteenth-century public, the printed word connoted prestige, authenticity, objectivity, and history (or as many others have noted, the masculine Public) while the spoken implied hearsay, personal opinion, and the immediate (the feminine Private). The printed word persisted, the spoken evaporated. Stowe's audience could scrutinize a letter, an affidavit, even a poem; they could debate its meaning, interpret the flow of its argument or inference. By wrapping her volatile chapter in so much professional text, *Vindicated* responded to this typographic prejudice in like form, admitting that writing more closely approximates the truth. However, by feeding this prejudice, Stowe's book also reveals its dependence on intimate, private exchange and oral testimony, thus subverting its own logic. As such, Stowe had to remake oral practice into a valid form of witnessing and, further, herself into a professional witnessor.

For this reason, Stowe includes a chapter on "Lady Byron as I Knew Her." Stowe explains, "Lady Byron's communications were made to me in language clear, precise, terrible; and many of her phrases and sentences I could repeat to this day, word for word" (*Vindicated* 202). Here the confessional idiom apes the requirements of professional language; Burton Bledstein's stipulation that the nineteenth-century professional's words be "clear, plain, direct, and tangible" are precisely what emerge from Lady Byron's mouth—"clear, precise, terrible." In turn, like written discourse that can be quoted "word for word," in lieu of manuscript Stowe represents her own memory as lexic. It's not that she cannot remember Lady Byron's testimony; rather, if she had immediately reproduced her language, as the critics suggested, word for word, "the public horror and incredulity would have been doubled" (202). Thus Stowe takes on the role of cultural arbitrator, the expert who circumscribes locutions that, from a professional viewpoint, convey brutal, irrevocable truths. This move further serves to maintain Stowe's feminine decorum, for womanly modesty as much as professional restraint are at work.

Once Stowe rationalizes her initial reluctance to produce brash statements, all the while insisting that the most significant statement can be produced verbatim or "scripted," her next step is to credentialize her source:

> I am now about to complete the account of my conversation with Lady Byron; but as the credibility of a history depends greatly on the character of its narrator, and as especial pains have been taken to destroy the belief in this story by representing it to be the wanderings of a broken-down mind . . . , I shall preface the narrative with some account of Lady Byron. (204)

While Stowe obviously means to amend Lady Byron's integrity, she also alludes to those critics who accused Stowe of having misheard or misunderstood what Lady Byron said. So Stowe's brief history of her subject's repute is an analog of her own damaged reputation, and the qualities Stowe chooses to highlight—purity, exceptionalism, and intelligence—stand as testimony to Stowe's own role as a professional witnessor.

First, Lady Byron's virtue is located in the body—clothes, comportment, and physical attributes. Stowe describes Lady Byron as a study in whiteness, with "silvery-white" hair, "pearly" white hands, and "transparent," "pure" white skin (206). Of course, Stowe links virtue to the body (and to whiteness) because it is the body, its female sexuality and knowledge of a "dark" desire like incest, that threatens Lady Byron's purity of motive. Moreover, because Stowe is speaking of Anglican womanhood, the metaphors are monarchical, both royal and divine: "Her spirit seemed as seated on a throne" (206). Since part of Stowe's claim is that Lady Byron lived with her husband after he revealed his incestuous affair so as to redeem his soul, Stowe must be doubly careful to etherealize and Anglicanize (whiten) her subject. Reciprocally, since part of the criticism leveled at Stowe was her own black or racialized bias as the author of *Uncle Tom's Cabin*, this bleaching effect allowed her to reclaim her own white power and to whitewash her own articulation of incest, the "secret crime" of slavery.

Relatedly, exceptionalism is revealed via Lady Byron's intelligence. Not only is her deportment singular, but also at their first meeting, Stowe remembers how Lady Byron engaged the topic of abolition. Her remarks, recalls Stowe, "caught my ear . . . by their peculiar incisive quality, their originality, and the evidence they gave that she was as well informed on all our matters as the best American statesman could be" (207). Like Stowe's own, Lady Byron's intelligence is measured in how well informed she is about American politics and how well she reproduces text from memory. Stowe finds in Lady Byron a kindred intellect, an exceptional, encyclopedic genius able to remember "the whole" of documents with "perfect clearness" (207). Lady Byron's mind, like Stowe's, is rich in professional assets. To these ends, the balance of Stowe's chapter details Lady Byron's thoughts on religion, literature, worker's reform and British imperialism as noted in her personal correspondence to Stowe and others. Overall, the chapter's aim is to recast Lady Byron and, by inference, Stowe herself as professional minds.

Having proven their mutual qualifications as accurate and conscientious witnessors, Stowe now turns to relay the "most painful interview which has been the cause of all this controversy" (232). Set at almost precisely the midpoint of her work, this locus influences everything that follows it and, of course, informs and revises everything that has come before. One way for Stowe to concretize this moment is to revert to a novelistic format wherein she delivers the climactic conversation in dialogue and gains a sense of the dramatic as well as the feeling that the interview is happening before the reader's eyes. Yet, with the blatant insertion of a specific "me" in the text, a self-referential narrator simultaneously the teller and sole witness to this event, Stowe risks compromising her carefully calculated positions as journalist, lawyer, or medical expert. Although other chapters certainly include Stowe making statements in the first person,[24] this chapter requires that she take the dual part of critic and subject.

At one level, this scene's writing style returns to the kinds of descriptions, details, and images abundant in the "True Story," albeit in muted form. As mentioned, in the "True Story" Lady Byron was characterized as a class of Little Eva and "the writer" was compelled by her capacity to suffer and forgive. In *Vindicated*, Lady Byron is less an artless, puerile embodiment of Christ and more a rational Christian, one who approaches religion from a position of maturity and consideration. Yet *Vindicated* still represents her as a type, a stock representation of pure womanhood, as is evident in the following excerpt:

> She answered quickly, and with great decision, that . . . she felt sure [Byron] had finally repented; and added with great earnestness, 'I do not believe that any child of the heavenly Father is ever left to eternal sin.'
>
> I said that such a hope was most delightful . . . , but that I had always regarded the indulgence of it as a dangerous one. . . .
>
> She looked at me so sadly, so firmly, and said,—
>
> 'Danger, Mrs. Stowe! What danger can come from indulging that hope, like the danger that comes from not having it . . . ? The danger of losing all faith in God, . . . all hope for others, all strength to try and save them.' (247)

Here, I could discuss other aspects of sentimental convention and Christian tautology Stowe employs at the crux of *Vindicated*, even though these narrative techniques are not as exaggerated as in the "True Story." I could certainly argue, a la Tompkins, that Stowe drew on her audience's rich literacy as novel readers, their recognition of certain archetypal characters and scenes and the sympathy she expected to realize from their use. Stowe had written to Oliver Wendell Holmes that "[t]he interview had almost the solemnity of a death-bed confession"—clearly a familiar theater (C. Stowe 453).[25]

However, until this juncture I have tacitly separated novelistic from emerging professional discourse, juxtaposing the traits of Stowe's fictional prose against those she appropriated from journalism, law, and psychiatry. But the stories of these Victorian professionals are surprisingly close in their purpose and even their structure to the stories of novelists. Victorian professionals studying human behavior provided particular interpretations of a set of human events and evidenced their interpretations with examples—character case studies, perhaps, or generalizations about a certain group of people. Unlike the work of an empirical scientist whose subject of study has no interiority of its own (a leaf, a planet, a liver), interpretations made by journalists, lawyers, psychiatrists and, yes, novelists could not be tested for their falseness but would be accepted or rejected on the basis of linguistic prowess, the detail and depth of explanations, the appropriateness of examples, and the credibility of their narrative positions. And all such professionals have didactic and even moral intents: the Victorian psychiatrist wants to curb sexual deviance; the lawyer wishes to argue that women should be allowed limited rights of property in marriage; the journalist hopes to convince his readers that they can improve the city's sanitation by walking to church instead of taking a carriage. Milieu, métier, and personal bias restrict all such writings.

Stowe's book arrives at a historical moment in which human interest professionals started to remake their work in the guise of science. Certain professionals ventriloquized the language of science by writing journalistic exposition instead of narrative; structuring their prose in rational, logical, argumentative fashion; and focusing on groups of people instead of individual psyches or turning to individual psyches to illustrate group tendencies. *Vindicated* mirrors these expectations: the bulk of Stowe's writing is journalistic; her organizational structure is hyperbolically logical; and the book contains multiple perspectives and refrains from delineating a single, complex psyche—indeed, its final purpose is to indict learned men of the press on both sides of the Atlantic.

In this new professional culture, the technical supplanted the moral; or, rather, the technical *was* the moral. By the early 1870s, it was not enough to argue that Byron was a libertine or that having sex outside marriage was immoral, and it was futile to offer the Bible or a novel as proof. Like a doctor, Stowe had to pathologize Byron, demonstrate that standard psychological theories exposed his mental instability. Like a lawyer, she had to produce credible witnesses attesting to Lady Byron's character and collocate dates, names, and events to corroborate Byron's guilt. At the same time, however, novelists and these human interest professionals were responsible for providing images of and for their culture, even though the new stories abjured individual authorship and held up, instead, data and method as the things that "speak." The new information-based atmosphere pieced together its stories from bits of data issuing from everywhere and nowhere at once. It was the scientific method that authored a particular version of history, identity, or truth, not the minister, the philosopher, or the novelist—or, at least, not the kind of novelist Stowe had been for two decades. In terms of Stowe's troublesome chapter, then, what emerged was a species of realism, one held in suspension with Stowe's romantic and domestic literary tradition. This obligatory moment of true confession, sans documentary evidence, induced Stowe's text to cross sentimental writing with professional technique and realigned narrative discourse into mimetic representation. In other words, Stowe put fiction in service of fact, which is one way to define literary realism.

As such, the chapter "Lady Byron's Story as Told Me" opens with a paragraph of exposition providing backstory, key characters, and setting. "My sister and myself were going from London to Eversley," begins Stowe. "On our way, we stopped, by Lady Byron's invitation, to lunch with her at her summer residence on Ham Common, near Richmond . . . as she said she had a subject of importance on which she wished to converse with me alone" (232). So might a George Eliot or an Edith Wharton novel start, with the evocation of a class-bound *donnée* and the slightest hint of social intrigue. From here, Stowe telescopes her focus to Lady Byron until setting the stage for the *tête-à-tête*: "After lunch, I retired with Lady Byron; and my sister remained with her friends" (233). Once alone, Stowe constructs and arranges her two characters, the credible witness—calm, dignified, quiet, lucid—and the professional witnessor, the one who will turn the oral into the textual, going so far as to admit the possibility of error in order to accent the words Stowe will insist are exact. "In recalling the conversation at this distance of time, I cannot remember all the language used," she confesses. Yet "[s]ome particular words and forms of expression I do remember, and those I give" (234–235). Now Stowe is ready to furnish the terrible accusation, "word for word":

> There was something awful to me in the intensity of repressed emotion which she showed as she proceeded. The great fact upon which all turned was stated in words that were unmistakable: 'Mrs. Stowe, he was guilty of incest with his sister!' She here became so deathly pale, that I feared she would faint. (235)

Thus Stowe brings together sentimental and professional grammars. The narrator experiences an "awful" emotion, or "awe-ful"—an allusion to the awe-inspiring, intense empathy of an ecstatic witness—while her subject of study enacts a "deathly pale" aspect, reminiscent of Christ's death as well as of the paleness and propensity to faint that connote feminine virtue. Juxtaposed against these Christian soteriologic transformations, however, is the "great fact" stated in words "unmistakable" of incest.

Here, then, is the true center of Stowe's book: "Mrs. Stowe, he was guilty of incest with his sister!" To witness this moment with accuracy, Stowe is required to speak plain, exacting, harsh language. To make up for the deficiency of documents to prove her claims, Stowe is equally required to textualize the moment in the way that will best render the accuracy of how this event occurred via verisimilitude in setting, dialogue, and the portrayal of convincing character. To guard against the kinds of criticisms she had already received—that her word was just a woman's word and/or just an American's word and/or the word of a blasphemer—Stowe is required, finally, to articulate the charge of incest but professionalize its articulation, delivering it through an informative lens.

Paradoxically, however, just as Stowe evokes realism, her very technique indicates the fictionality of her story. By reasoning that she could not "remember all the language used" yet would provide "[s]ome particular words and forms of expression" she recalled, Stowe puts into question, for her reader, what parts of the chapter are literatim, what parts "the substance of what was said." Stowe attempts to render the oral as a kind of transcript or permanent document, yet her medium presents her message as fiction. Form cannot be divorced from function, and as such, Stowe's techniques disclose rather than conceal the fictional nature of her prose. In fact, a section of dialogue such as the following not only indicates but constitutes the form of fiction:

> I inquired in one of the pauses of the conversation whether Mrs. Leigh was a peculiarly beautiful or attractive woman.
>
> 'No, my dear: she was plain.'
>
> 'Was she, then, distinguished for genius or talent of any kind?'
>
> 'Oh, no! Poor woman! she was weak, relatively, to [Byron], and wholly under his control.'
>
> 'And what became of her?' I said.
>
> 'She afterwards repented, and became a truly good woman.' (245)

Stowe's devices for textualizing this moment actually alert her reader to invention in her writing: she uses the dialogue tag "I said"; quotation marks to bracket speech; a line of indirect dialogue; and she molds everyday speech, which, when transcribed, is riddled with breaks, pauses, and incoherencies, into a seamless, polished exchange. Moreover, the reader must suspect Stowe's assertion that these are the exact, "particular words and forms of expression" used by Lady Byron and Stowe thirteen years earlier. Could Stowe possibly recollect whether Lady Byron had said, "No, my dear," or "My dear, no"? How about the order of "Oh, no!" and "Poor woman!"; might not Lady Byron have exclaimed, "Poor woman! Oh, no!"? And if the reader disputes these superficial phrases, Stowe cannot insist on the exactitude of the whole.

That Stowe *does* insist on just that points toward a use of fiction as fact or, reciprocally, fact as fiction—i.e., literary realism. "Of course," Stowe says, after having recited the whole of the interview, "I did not listen to this story as one who was investigating its worth. I received it as truth. And the purpose for which it was communicated was not to enable me to prove it to the world, but to ask my opinion whether *she* [Lady Byron] should show it to the world before leaving it" (251). Because Stowe must portray herself as a friend of Lady Byron's at the moment of confession, Stowe cannot be the investigator she claims. A friend receives a painful disclosure as truth, not as a statement that must be reviewed, contested, substantiated. A credible witnessor must observe an event from an ingenuous position; above all else, Stowe must convince her audience that she had nothing to gain from telling this story. But Stowe makes her role as professional witnessor liable by claiming full responsibility for the truth of her story—exactly what her brother-in-law Hooker had warned against.

Of course, the very terms of Stowe's claim refuse truth from a professional standpoint. By insisting on the precision of her text, Stowe denies her own fictional technique. In the very same moment, however, she calls into question the gender ideologies assumed by her detractors. As Stowe wrote to her publisher Osgood, "Nobody has ever called for *proof* from any of the numberless writers who reported their conversations with Lord Byron."[26] The inverse is true for the problem of silence: since Lady Byron failed to assert her side of the story in her own lifetime, her reticence worked as "proof" of her culpability, even though silence, in and of itself, suggests no conclusions. Lady Byron's silence was consequently scripted by Byron's poems and letters into slander (her silence meant she had something to hide), and because Byron was male, his assertion was accepted without proof. "Of course," notes Stowe, "there is no stronger power than a virtuous life; but, for a virtuous life to bear testimony to the world, its details must be *told*, so that the world may know them" (160). Telling, bearing witness to Lady Byron's story, is the precise act that in itself is true. Again, in a society that demands information in order to ascertain the real, there is no choice but to speak, to write, to aggregate information in a palpable form. Stowe claims that the instant she takes up the pen, her fiction becomes fact. "When a noble name is accused, any person who possesses truth which might clear it, and withholds that truth, is guilty of a sin against human nature and the inalienable claims of justice. I claim that I have not only a right, but an obligation, to bring in my solemn testimony upon this subject" (196). Thus the vindication Stowe achieves in her book is three-fold: a vindication of Lady Byron, a vindication of Stowe herself, and a vindication of literary realism, i.e., the crucial role of the novelist in all projects of culture-making, even in a fact-based climate.

In a sense, then, Stowe invites her persecutors and doubting readers to become parties to the libel. If they require more proof than Stowe has to give, by inference, they cannot accept Byron's version of his marriage and divorce. In turn, if they believe Lord Byron in spite of his own lack of proof, they must simultaneously accept Stowe's version. "All this is not proof," Stowe says, referring to the iteration of Lord Byron's allegations. "It is mere assertion, and assertion made to produce prejudice. It is like raising a whirlwind of sand to blind the eyes that are looking for landmarks" (319). What Stowe doesn't say, however, is "all this is not real." What she's describing is how one writes realistic fiction, and, of course, this is the exact method Stowe employs.

PROFESSIONAL DISCOURSE AND COMMERCIAL ADVERTISING

There is a final layer to these series of paradoxes so rife in Stowe's book. The repetition of an assertion to such an extent that the concept becomes truth is not only a technique of the literary realist but, too, a key component of advertising, although advertising repeats assertions in combination with images until the idea or statement is synonymous with its image. Advertising as a corporate industry in America didn't emerge until after the Postal Act of 1879, an act that provided cheap mailing privileges to periodicals; but even a decade earlier, Stowe's *Vindicated* provided a powerful venue for Stowe to link her text with potent, conspicuous images.

In *Vindicated*, the key components were the documents—so much weight in facts, figures, and dates. Before the 482 pages of *Vindicated* went to press (463 pages longer than her original article), Stowe stipulated to Osgood that he "choose a good, clear, plain type for the ***documents*** so that nobody may skip them as fine print, and then have a larger type for my own words. The documents are the very marrow of the thing, and every care must be taken to make them flash clearly on the eye at a glance."[27] Stowe manipulated the same documents she used to inculpate Byron to serve her own claims to truth. The typeface itself was to perform the effect of her words—"good, clear, plain" type would equal Stowe's good, clear, plain purpose. Ultimately the substance of the Byron documents mattered little; they provided visual support for the "larger type" of Stowe's own text, flashing "clearly on the eye at a glance."

Even early on, writing *Uncle Tom's Cabin*, Stowe had valued image as medium, its power to evoke the kind of emotion in a reader argumentative prose often failed to achieve. She claimed to appreciate the inherent objectivity in pictures, their unambiguous reflection of the world. "My vocation is simply that of a painter," she had told Gamaliel Bailey, editor of the *National Era*—the periodical that ran *Uncle Tom's Cabin* between 1851 and 1852. "[M]y object will be to hold up in the most lifelike and graphic manner possible Slavery. . . . There is no arguing with *pictures*, and everybody is impressed by them, whether they mean to be or not."[28] Of course, while a realistic painting or a photograph works precisely in this manner—devoid of syntax, and, thus, devoid of both the capacity to argue with the world and the world's capacity to mount arguments against it—Stowe always traded in series of propositions, ones that could be taken apart, disputed, even demonstrated as false. Regardless, Stowe tried to market *Vindicated*'s documents as advertisement, not language but image—advertisement fashioned to rouse an inevitable, incontestable agreement from her readers. Indeed, it was crucial for Stowe to retender these documents as surface, not substance: ironically, since they were the "marrow," the vital life-blood of her case, she had to disinfect them so as not to further promulgate Byron's contaminants, the language that was his lie. Otherwise Stowe might breed infection in the sentence, since, after all, she sought to engage in exactly the enterprise she most reviled in Byron: writing slander.

But the logics of advertising worked against Stowe as well. While Stowe had comprehended the import of speaking out on such a topic and against such a favorite as Byron—especially as a woman and an American—she couldn't have foreseen the universal wrath she would incur for having uttered what Stowe later came to call "that one word"—incest. "The world may finally forgive the man of genius anything," Stowe jeered, "but for a woman there is no mercy and no redemption" (*Vindicated* 74). And, indeed, Stowe was condemned for using propaganda similar to Byron's own and for spreading an even more virulent social disease. "The ruthless hand of the sensational authoress of 'Uncle Tom's Cabin' has invaded our shores," cried one columnist for *Vanity Fair*, "and torn the veil from the figure which might just as well have remained veiled" ("Byron Scandal" 146). Thus Stowe metamorphosized from defender to invader, advocate to assailant, cure to infection. "Mrs. Stowe has been guilty of . . . extremely bad taste," pronounced another writer in *The Saturday Review*. "[S]he has let loose a flood of immoral talk and immoral speculation on loathsome subjects which has deeply defiled, and will long defile, European and American society" ("Byron Case" 343). Like her own treatment of Byron in the "True Story," Stowe was accused of seeking fame, seeking money, or according to one satirist in *The Period*, merely living up to her own artistic evolution.[29] "If we were to dissect her encephalon, we should in all probability find imprinted upon the inmost recesses of her brain the words she has herself placed in the mouth of one of her most popular characters: *'I 'spects I'se awful wicked'*; for only by natural and innate weakness can we account for the mischievous character of her writings" ("Polychromatic" 2).

Like the depiction of Stowe as a black-magic witch in the *Merryman's Monthly*, many a satirist made race the central dynamic of his or her slander, a throwback to the media contention surrounding *Uncle Tom's Cabin* but also a typical Victorian elision, collapsing sexual with racial degeneracy and, in so doing, threatening Stowe's most powerful claim to social power—her whiteness. If Stowe's brain was inscribed with Topsy's famous phrase, Stowe, herself, harbored an essential blackness—a constitutional weakness but also, by association, a lurking animalism. The black woman in Stowe denoted her wickedness, her sexual knowledge, but especially her knowledge of incest, for, as the logic goes, who would know more about incest than a black slave woman? In a *Will-O'-the-Wisp* cartoon, for instance, Uncle Tom crouches behind a horrified-looking Stowe and asks a weeping Little Eva, "How could she paint one of her own brethren so *black*?"[30] From *The Comic Monthly*, another cartoon shows Topsy telling Byron, "I'se so glad you'se come. Is'e got company now. Is'e wicked—but Missis saz you goes ahed o' me," while still another pictures Uncle Tom, playing a great harp and pleading, "Go 'way from me, Massa Byron—my Missus saz you're too wicked to 'sociate wid spectable cullud sperrets."[31] In these various caricatures, Stowe herself is often in the act of self-blackening or striating black streaks across a gleaming statue of Byron or performing black magic. Alternately, she is a prim-and-proper Alice-in-Wonderland type, besmirched with the very mud she slings; a witch, brewing a cauldron of calumny; or a hag, scuttling up Byron's noble visage, trailing muck from her hands and feet.[32]

Figure 2.2. Cartoon, *Will O' the Wisp* (25 September 1869).

As these examples demonstrate, the backlash against Stowe became an enterprise of advertising. The sacred connotations she had hoped to instill with strong femininity—Lady Byron as a noble martyr and herself as her fearless defender—were quickly drained of their import through a process of massive and swift trivialization. By distorting Stowe's image in the popular press, showing her here as a witch, there as a peevish old woman, her image was exhausted—sensational gossip from a ridiculous woman, another juicy bit for today's press. Even those periodicals that claimed moral indignation against Stowe's "one word" served to proliferate the sensationalism surrounding the tale, for the technologies of mass distribution that had just started up when Stowe wrote *Uncle Tom's Cabin* were in full forward motion by 1869.[33] In 1852, transatlantic readers saw her portrait in the frontispiece to her novel or, perhaps, in a shop-window, a pirated copy from an engraver's original. If her face sold anything, it sold her book or, by abstraction, the American abolition movement: serious items and ideas. But the convergence of mass transit, mass media, and mass information deprived Stowe's face of its gravity, using it, instead, to sell trivia and sensation: "entertainment." Thus the meaning of Stowe's critique wasn't in the content of her analysis but was transferred to the act of consumption itself, to whatever the consumer wanted her face or text to mean. Since Stowe had tried to portray Lord Byron as a liar and a cheat, the press retaliated in kind. England and

Figure 2.3. Cartoons, *The Comic Monthly* (October 1869).

Figure 2.4. Cartoon, ***Fun*** (18 September 1869).

America, especially English and American media men, disliked Stowe's commodity, and, so, they realigned the terms of the market by revising the look, and thereby the meaning, of what she had tried to produce. And once Stowe and her text no longer stood for righteous action or decorous womanhood, once the symbol was detached from its rational signification—which pretty much defines the process of advertising—it failed to carry any cultural relevance. In other words, Stowe no longer stood for the idea of a professional female artist figure—at least, not the idea she had helped to create and continued to revere. "Sold" as the paragon of American abolitionism and pure womanhood with *Uncle Tom's Cabin*, with *Lady Byron Vindicated* Stowe was now "sold" as an American sensationalist and, of course, as an American whore: an impious, indecorous woman out to make a quick buck.

George Eliot, writing to her long-time friend Sara Hennell, commented, "As to the Byron subject . . . , [t]he discussion of the subject in newspapers, periodicals and pamphlets, is simply odious to me, and I think it a pestilence likely to leave very ugly marks. One trembles to think how easily that moral wealth may be lost which it has been the work of ages to produce, in the refinement and differencing of the affectionate relations" (*Letters* V: 56). With the desecration of linear, traditional narratives as the basis of meaning-making and the advent, instead, of a fragmented story without a moral center—one valorizing the rapture of advertising—Eliot was correct to worry that the "moral wealth" she had spent her life's work trying to promote was undergoing rapid-fire annihilation. But while Eliot understood that the press had made Stowe's story as well as Stowe herself into a "pestilence," she also comprehended the writer's own motive, writing to Stowe, "[W]ith regard to yourself, dear friend, I have felt sure that in acting on a [unique] basis of impressions, you were impelled by pure, generous feeling" (V: 71).

And, in fact, Stowe's critique of Byron from within his own providence reveals a tenacious "feeling," one that is "pure" if not necessarily "generous." For Stowe clearly believes in an aesthetic transcendence that rises above and stands beyond all other social discourse—reified, perfect, and, one might say, pure. To criticize Byron for using his poetry as propaganda is to posit that true literature is not commodifiable or is somehow beyond the designation of mere advertisement. Stowe censures Byron for possessing an inadequate aesthetic, a bankrupt notion of what literature is and should be. By showing Byron's art as insufficient—deficient in moral ideality, miming the workings of information culture—Stowe pays allegiance to a perfect, continuous realm of art through the very mechanism of her critique. At the same time, Stowe intimates that she is the true artist, one through whom the divine makes itself known to the world. If sanctioned by a higher ethic, art based on strong femininity makes even the most transgressive sexuality beautiful. For Stowe, false aesthetics are grounded in the moment, in history; they are specific, political, immediate—anti-narrativistic. On the other hand, real art and its icons constitute an ahistorical trope; they are universal, apolitical, timeless—narrativistic. Ultimately, then, Stowe's attempt at the new professional discourse serves as a critique of itself.

Chapter Three

"A More *Living* Interest"

George Eliot's Daniel Deronda *and the Politics of American Reception*

FROM FEBRUARY TO SEPTEMBER OF 1876, *BLACKWOOD'S MAGAZINE* IN ENGLAND and *Harper's New Monthly Magazine* in America carried simultaneous installments of George Eliot's last novel, *Daniel Deronda*. By the time of *Deronda*'s publication, Eliot was one of England's most celebrated fiction writers and was equally esteemed in America, as evidenced by the widespread sale and discussion of her work, especially *Adam Bede*.[1] But with the advent of *Deronda*, her new novel quickly became her most anticipated, debated, and lucrative.[2] Each installment was closely observed by the media. Periodicals on both sides of the ocean (e.g., *The Athenaeum*, *The Atlantic Monthly*, *The Spectator*) followed each monthly episode with a commentary or a review, in recognition that their readers were taking part in what one reviewer, Edwin Whipple, called "an important literary event" (31); and *The Edinburgh Review* captured the tenor of the "universal extension of interest" in *Deronda* by detailing "the anxiety of critics who have not even waited for its completion, but have discussed it piecemeal as an object of national interest" (450).[3] Put simply, *Daniel Deronda* was the transatlantic talk of the town.

In fact, *Daniel Deronda* was the talk of many towns, securing international attention; the novel was translated into German, French, and Hebrew and sold in Australia and Holland as well as in America and England. Yet this widespread interest was strikingly split into what Stowe termed the novel's "two heads—English life & Jewish life."[4] On one hand the first Hebrew translation of *Deronda* excised the Gentile portions of the novel and focused on Mordecai's pronouncements at the Red Lion Club. Among nineteenth-century Jewish readers, this edition initiated a heated debate in England and Germany on *Deronda*'s implicit sanction of Jewish nationalism and the proto-Zionist movement.[5] On the other hand, most Christians were bored, frustrated, embarrassed, or even angered by the novel's depiction of Jewish life, and many nineteenth-century American readers believed that the Jewish subjects should be cut out entirely and the novel retitled *Gwendolen Harleth*.[6] "I confess," Stowe admitted to Eliot, "that my hearts blood vibrates more toward Gwendolin [sic] than Mirah & that I feel a more *living* interest in her feelings, struggles & sorrows. . . ."[7]

This particular fascination with Gwendolen in American periodicals and letters represents a compelling strand of nineteenth-century commentary. At one level, the parts of the narrative dealing with English life had a time-honored appeal for American readers. The scenes of hound-chasing and archery, courtship and amateur tableaux had been staples of imported drawing-room novels since Jane Austen. In addition, Gwendolen's story relied heavily on the kinds of plot twists and characters derived from popular British novels that—at the same time *Deronda* came out in its serial installments—writers like Stowe deemed sensational: unlike Mordecai's lengthy polemics, the sections on English life told of seduction and betrayal, entrapment and murder. At another level, the world of Gwendolen's England resonated with the American desire to appropriate Great Britain and its history as a world of culture—one that offered images of continuity and tradition in juxtaposition to American fragmentation, newness, and primitivism. For even in novels by Wilkie Collins and Mary Elizabeth Braddon, ultimately the "correct" ancestral lineage is reinstated through the consummation of a long-thwarted marriage, while the allocation of the appropriate rank and property is bestowed on "worthy" characters.

Thus, the English story of Grandcourt's tyranny and the unrequited love between Daniel and Gwendolen could potentially have secured a comfortable race narrative at a time when Americans were celebrating their Centennial yet becoming increasingly split over questions of ethnic immigration and race relations.[8] In either version of the novel, Grandcourt would have had to die, but in the "comfortable" one, through some twist of fate, Daniel would have been restored as Sir Hugo's rightful heir and Gwendolen's lost father would have emerged—if only through the discovery of a will—to bequeath on her the rank and fortune befitting her beauty, comportment, and accomplishments. Then the novel would have established a genial picture of a kind of democratic gentry, one in which worldly clergy like Mr. Gascoigne are on visiting terms with the Sir Hugos of society and beautiful stepdaughters of military Captains marry philanthropic heirs apparent. Even more importantly, the novel would have ended with legitimate procreation, banishing Mrs. Glasher and her illicit children as well as the suspicion of Daniel's illegitimacy and "taint" as a member of the Jewish race.

Indeed, as the sections on Jewish life emerged with Book III, American critics and readers focused on Gwendolen with increasing preoccupation, and while anti-Semitic expressions were not necessarily overt in reviews of *Deronda*, this obsession with Gwendolen revealed Americans' prejudice.[9] Interestingly, however, Gwendolen's American appeal took a decided track: readers debated her decisions and actions as if she were real—a friend, family member, or neighbor—and called attention to that very quality of realness in their reading. Given the critical turn in the 1870s from romanticism to realism in influential periodicals like *The Atlantic*, *Harper's*, and *The Nation*, it is not particularly surprising that American readers were interested in the verisimilitude of Eliot's work; however, this emphasis on Gwendolen as a kind of next-door neighbor is discontinuous with the anti-realistic, sensational logic Gwendolen's own character embodies and enacts.[10] In other words, because the Gwendolen sections of *Daniel Deronda* are indebted to the genre of the sensation novel—a genre that relied on and in many ways engendered spectacular systems of literary production, including advertising and consumer culture—it is all the more curious that Gwendolen would be deemed "real."

In fact, Gwendolen seems to be the antithesis of the famous statement on realism or "characters of the commonplace" in chapter seventeen of *Adam Bede*—a novel many of Eliot's American readers thought her best.[11] "[D]o not impose on us any aesthetic rules which shall banish from the region of Art those old women scraping carrots with their work-worn hands," admonishes the narrator of *Adam Bede*. "It is so needful we should remember their existence, else we may happen to leave them quite out of our religion and philosophy, and frame lofty theories which only fit a world of extremes. Therefore . . . let us always have men ready to give the loving pains of life to the faithful representing of commonplace things. . . . There are few prophets in the world; few sublimely beautiful women; few heroes . . . half so frequent as your common laborer, who gets his own bread, and eats it vulgarly but creditably with his own pocket-knife" (159). With Mordecai as its prophet and Gwendolen as its sublimely beautiful woman, it is almost as if *Daniel Deronda* represents a self-conscious, hyperbolic satire of this very passage, reveling in lofty theories, extremity, and stereotypically hyperbolic characters.[12] Of course Daniel is the novel's hero, but he does not adhere to heroic conventions—a point to which I will return.

Nevertheless, Gwendolen's American readers seemed to find her as prosaic as a carrot-scraping old woman. "[I]nfinitely the most interesting character to me is Gwendolin," confided Stowe to Eliot, "—Of the artistic *vitality* of the character I need no other proof than that I have been called at various tea tables to defend her as earnestly as if she had been an actual neighbor giving parties round the corner[.]"[13] A. V. Dicey, reviewing *Deronda* for *The Nation*, reiterated Stowe's sentiment, asking a series of rhetorical questions to demonstrate the strength of *Deronda*'s widespread appeal, notwithstanding the expletives of a group Dicey termed "carping critics":

> Is it not a fact that Gwendolen's character has been analyzed in every drawing-room with the care with which most persons weigh the characters only of their intimate associates? Was not her marriage as interesting to many persons as the wedding of a private friend? Have there not been hundreds of readers who have invented for themselves the catastrophe to which her marriage was to lead up? Is it not almost as certain that George Eliot must

> have been pestered by requests to break off the engagement between Gwendolen and Grandcourt as it is that Richardson was harassed by correspondents who prayed hard for the life of Clarissa? ("I" 230)[14]

In both Dicey and Stowe's responses, it is the intimacy with which Gwendolen has been internalized by her readership that proves the artistic *vitality* of Eliot's characterization. Seemingly, Dicey and Stowe are applauding Eliot for the perfect realism of her novel, its ability to make Gwendolen into a woman whose actions are defended at tea tables. "It is not given to anything but genius," concludes Dicey, "to make the world thrill with interest over the fate of imaginary beings" ("I" 230). Thus Eliot's genius, or art, is dependent upon her ability to make the word flesh, render imagination as reality. And Gwendolen becomes a focus of keen interest in America because she is taken to be as real as her readers—she, like them, analyzes intimate associates (especially Grandcourt and Daniel), plans a wedding, doubts her engagement, and wishes for the death of her brutish husband. Apparently, according to Dicey, these are universal schemes and desires rather than aspects of a singular life—even the invention of a catastrophe to end one's marriage is the fantasy "hundreds of readers . . . have invented for themselves." In other words, Stowe and Dicey portray Gwendolen's fictional subjectivity as a factual depiction of real-life experience, and Dicey's rhetorical questions begin with this very claim, asking, in essence, "Is it not a fact" that Gwendolen is "fact."

But this applause for Eliot's verisimilitude simultaneously points out her position as Gwendolen's creator; the query "Is it not a fact" inherently contains the second possibility that, indeed, it is *not.* If, for instance, Eliot is "pestered by requests to break off the engagement," it is clear that Gwendolen herself cannot do so and that nothing Americans discuss in their drawing-rooms or over tea will make one whit of difference to the final outcome. Unlike a flesh-and-blood intimate a reader might defend or analyze or influence, the reader has no potential sway over Gwendolen. And, importantly, what such readers find fascinating about Gwendolen is not the expected fascination one has for a character in a realist, "commonplace" novel; rather, their fascination stems from the sensational aspects of her story—her beauty, her gambling, her marriage, and her murderous intents. If anyone is the real character in *Deronda* it is Daniel—a character epitomized by a rich interior life as well as a focus on the interior lives of others. But as Dicey points out, "George Eliot's readers were interested in the fate of Gwendolen, and not one in a hundred cared whether Daniel did or did not turn out to be a Jew and become inspired with Mordecai's enthusiasm" ("I" 231).

Why this American fascination with Gwendolen? Why this insistence that Gwendolen is somehow, ironically, more real than Daniel and his search for a Jewish identity? Answering these questions requires an investigation of three historical movements occurring at the same time that Eliot published *Daniel Deronda.* First, Gwendolen enters the American literary theater when advertising and modes of mass literary production intersect with the ascent of the professional as an arbiter of culture, including, of course, artistic culture. By juxtaposing Gwendolen's performance of beauty as a representative of "false" artistic professionalism against Klesmer's music as a representative of a "true" aesthetic economy, the novel links Gwendolen to advertising and the proliferation of sensationalist fictions, in a sense warning readers against the seductions of both. At one level, then, Gwendolen is real to readers because she, like them, is seduced by superficiality—in fact, she herself is the kind of reader Eliot's novel is meant to educate.

At another level, this attraction to Gwendolen as real must be placed in the context of reading practices that codified realism as a high-art endeavor in such periodicals as *Harper's New Monthly Magazine*, the same magazine that serialized *Daniel Deronda*. Unlike their assessment of novels by Howells or James, however, critics located Eliot's realism in her ability to induce both a universal and decidedly feminine sympathy. In essence, *Harper's* and other high-art journals taught their readers to appreciate precisely the realistic qualities that Gwendolen arouses: an affinity with English culture as well as a sympathy derived from her struggles over aesthetics and social morality.

Finally, everything in *Deronda* that doesn't deal directly with Gwendolen—namely the scenes with Mordecai, Mirah, and Daniel—are portrayed as the novel's moral center at a time when America was experiencing political and social agitation for the expansion of Jewish immigration and autonomy. As a result of this social context, Daniel's adoption of a simultaneously racialized and feminized ethos became a particularly threatening image for a nineteenth-century American audience. Indeed, for some American critics, Daniel's weakness becomes conflated with the figure of the Alcharisi as the racialized artist-mother, a character who carries an intimidating knowledge of race and sex as part of her marked, performative body and stands as the novel's corporeal symbol of an othered history and cultural heritage. Thus American readers linked Daniel's narrative progression to their own fears over Jewish ascendancy, particularly their fears of race-mixing, including the "dilution" of culture. For these reasons, Daniel must be read as less real in order to secure a vision of society based on those realistic qualities high-art journals espoused.

GWENDOLEN AT THE MIRROR

To explore these questions of American reception, we must begin by tracing the spoor of Gwendolen's allure. This task is not an easy one since the novel itself opens with a series of questions that troubles the location of Gwendolen's attraction:

> Was she beautiful or not beautiful? and what was the secret of form or expression which gave the dynamic quality to her glance? Was the good or the evil genius dominant in those beams? Probably the evil; else why was the effect that of unrest rather than of undisturbed charm? Why was the

> wish to look again felt as a coercion and not as a longing in which the whole being consents? (7)

This opening paragraph is both a reverie on the part of Eliot's narrator and also a set of questions in Daniel's own mind—which is important, since Daniel will eventually uncover for himself a fixed identity in his Jewishness and is a man whom Gwendolen will increasingly rely on as a secure source of moral interiority.[15] In confronting a series of binary oppositions as the introduction to Gwendolen's character (beautiful/not beautiful, form/expression, good/evil, coercion/longing), the reader grapples with an identity that stems neither from origin (something innate) nor from attributes (something learned); neither from performance (action) nor from composition (knowledge). At least for the first paragraph, the typical operations of "character" in a novel are suspended: Gwendolen is not shown in action or at rest, in relation to other characters or in solitude. Indeed, the very quality that will soon crystallize as the lynchpin of her character—her beauty—is the first thing that is questioned.

Gwendolen's nature is first a cipher, a vacuous space. But these questions do lean toward one opinion over another—"Probably the evil." The idea that the wish to look again at Gwendolen is a form of coercion comments not only on Daniel's and other characters' interest but the reader's as well: a novel spins "evil," coercing its audience to look again and again, even when the subject creates the effect of unrest or unease. In this manner, the introduction to Gwendolen piques curiosity and resistance: readers are invited to feel uneasy over the intimation that this fiction will compel and overpower them at the same time that they wish to look again and again. As such, the novel structures the reader's engagement parallel to Gwendolen's own instrument of meaning-making, where looking and being looked at constitute her only reality.

When Gwendolen faces the second loss of the novel—the first being the double loss of money and luck at the roulette table—she turns to the mirror to gain compensation.[16] Gwendolen must wrestle with having lost more than a family fortune; she has lost everything that has ever meant anything to her—especially a "destiny [that] must be one of luxurious ease, where any trouble that occurred would be well clad and provided for" (16). In this moment of supreme loss, Gwendolen's first impulse is to gaze at her own reflection in the looking glass:

> [H]appening to be seated sideways before the long strip of mirror . . . she turned to look at herself, leaning her elbow on the back of the chair in an attitude that might have been chosen for her portrait. . . . She had a naïve delight in her fortunate self . . . [a]nd even in this beginning of troubles, . . . she sat gazing at her image in the growing light, her face gathered a complacency gradual as the cheerfulness of the morning. Her beautiful lips curled into a more and more decided smile, till at last she took off her hat,

> leaned forward and kissed the cold glass which had looked so warm. How could she believe in sorrow? (18)

For Gwendolen, the "gain" here is a recuperation of power; although she may not have money or luxury, she has something that, for her, seems just as good—the tender of her beauty. But like a coin or a bill that merely symbolizes the power of purchase, Gwendolen's beauty merely reflects and represents power—it, too, promises a certain value of exchange without actually procuring anything, here offering only a cold surface in lieu of warm reassurance. Indeed, given the workings of the glass, looking and being looked at are the only mode of exchange, and as a result Gwendolen flattens out her own identity into this single attribute: the value of her prime commodity, beauty. Hence Gwendolen's *naïveté* about any aspect of herself that cannot be discerned through the look: the glass cannot represent her inner turmoil—since her gaze cannot penetrate beneath her image—and so, at least for Gwendolen, the inner turmoil ceases to exist; as Eliot's narrator ironically notes, "How could she believe in sorrow?" Rather, Gwendolen repackages her troubles as an outer, superficial reflection of complacency and cheerfulness through the adoption of a "decided smile." At the very beginning of the novel, then, Gwendolen erases the struggling interiority that would normally define a realistic character in favor of a superficial model, reforming the complexity of her private struggle as the simplicity of public cheer.

For though seemingly acted out alone, there is a kind of public in this scene, the appreciative audience that Gwendolen requires in order for her beauty to have worth. First there is the evocation of the portrait-artist, appraising Gwendolen's attitude. Clearly, the theoretical portrait-artist's gaze is one of admiration, for the Gwendolen in the mirror takes precisely that posture that might be chosen for her portrait. Then there is the otherness of Gwendolen herself, her own essentialized double. This audience member, too, is a flattering one—ever beautiful, ever happy, ever reflecting back to Gwendolen an approbatory glance. And, of course, there is Eliot's omniscient narrator relating Gwendolen's thoughts and actions as well as exposing them, through irony, for their shallowness. However, even the cynical narrator notes that Gwendolen's egotism is a product of sustained visual pleasure, suggesting that the additional public in this scene—Gwendolen's readers—should at least partially indulge Gwendolen's triviality as an expected outcome of so many years of gratification: "[A]ny but the harshest saintliness will have some indulgence for . . . a girl who had every day seen a pleasant reflection of [herself] in her friends' flattery as well as in the looking-glass" (18). In other words, Gwendolen is always on display, both the product and producer of image, and, importantly, Gwendolen's display is aimed to please. Thus, rather than the specters of seriousness and sorrow that one expects when a character loses her fortune and future, Gwendolen produces a simulation of happiness, for indeed "How could she believe in sorrow?" when sorrow is nowhere present in the self-replicating and self-mimicking world of Gwendolen's stunning self-image.

In this manner, Gwendolen's moment at the mirror replicates the operations of nineteenth-century advertising—an industry that was just beginning to be widely institutionalized, especially in America, by the time of *Deronda*'s publication.[17] Like Gwendolen's vision of herself at the mirror, Victorian advertising created the simulation of emotion and depth through the proliferation of certain images, linking particular feelings and desires to fixed pictures and basing its success in the economy of the gaze. Interiority was simplified, exteriorized, and sold through the consumption of a certain product. Reciprocally, consuming the representation replaced the need to feel authentic emotion, or in the case of Gwendolen, by consuming her own mirror image, she eradicates her complex feelings in favor of the purchase of a grin.

In fact, Gwendolen is so enthralled by the advertisement of herself that she mistakes the copy for the real thing, kissing "the cold glass which had looked so warm." In a sense, then, Gwendolen behaves like her American readers—those who wish to believe in Gwendolen's flesh-and-blood reality, or in Dicey's words, who "thrill with interest" over the destiny of an imaginary being. The imaginary being in the glass thrills Gwendolen; in turn, the imaginary being in the text thrills her readers. In other words, American readers were at some level willing to accept Gwendolen's initial advertisement of herself, substituting the complexities of character for the acquisition of pleasure or, rather, the weight and heft of highbrow artistry for the thrill of sensationalism.

But while the scene at the mirror ostensibly casts Gwendolen in the position of adoration of her beautiful image, the novel works to expose the falsity of this dynamic, taking on both Gwendolen's self-representation as well as the culture (both within and outside the narrative) that desires and demands it. In particular, the narrative links Gwendolen's coercive beauty to advertising, consumerism, and sensationalist fictions as well as to the rise of capitalist-driven professionalism in order to critique these same systems. Specifically, the novel constructs Gwendolen as a kind of "professional beauty"—wherein she professionalizes certain aspects of her knowledge, skills, and expertise—but simultaneously judges her as well as the kind of sensational fiction Gwendolen represents against a superseding aesthetic economy, one typified by ethical art. In so doing, the novel differentiates among different kinds of professionalism, linking Gwendolen's to "false" professionalism, i.e., the kind that merely adopts the trappings without caring about the professional's duty to social good. This aesthetic economy parallels the one Eliot herself espoused in resistance to corporate professionalism and the sensational literary marketplace, and the novel's critique of the advertising-consumer relation poses a simultaneous critique of those readers who would, like Gwendolen, be taken in by image over substance.

GWENDOLEN AS A PROFESSIONAL BEAUTY

It may seem forced to name Gwendolen a "professional beauty" since Victorian beauty—unlike law, medicine, or academe—seems not to demand the requisites of the professional, namely those outlined in the Introduction, including the acquisition of extensive and elite tutelage, having competence in an esoteric body of knowledge, and utilizing one's professional authority for the public good. Unlike Phelps's Avis Dobell, Gwendolen does not procure European training to achieve artistic cachet; and unlike Stowe, Gwendolen does not resist a particular social evil in order to use art to teach readers how to "read right." Instead, Gwendolen's artistry is avaricious and self-indulgent.

However, Gwendolen's occupation of "being a beauty" is construed throughout *Deronda* as a self-conscious, practiced, and codified undertaking. Where intellectual acumen and its exercise become the property and trading-value of the professional, Gwendolen's beauty is attained through years of self-regulation and performed at a higher level than anyone else's. Like the professional's privilege, Gwendolen guarantees that her special kind of beauty is scarce, thus limiting others' access to her position. Professionals are distinct because they control their own work and set their own price; they resist outside evaluation and yet must have the approbation of the elite classes that sponsor them. And Gwendolen's practice conforms to these qualifications: she believes herself to be the master of her own beauty, deciding how and when and where it will be exercised as well as what price it will catch. She creates the standards of her own evaluation—making sure that she meets or exceeds them—and certainly garners the endorsement of the gentry, especially Sir Hugo's, the novel's prototypic patrician. Indeed, just like a professional, Gwendolen's chief assets are invisible and her payment unquantifiable: her privilege isn't based on the material accumulations of wealth, property, patronage, or capitalist entrepreneurship. Certainly money adorns her credentials in the way that medical tools, books, a clean suit, and a comfortable office service a doctor. But the image of her worth stems from capital as elusive as intellect—sheer splendor. And Gwendolen translates her scarce resource into another ware—social reward. Thus, in many ways, Gwendolen's beauty functions as a professional system.

A few examples illustrate Gwendolen's particular mode of professionalism. In the first part of the novel Gwendolen demonstrates that she is a well-practiced and matchless beauty, both highly proficient and exceptional. As with Gwendolen's mirror double, the role of any beauty is to be ever appealing to an on-looker, ever on the alert for the most favorable dress, hairstyle, jewelry, posture, and backdrop. In the manner of a painting or statue, the beauty must stick and fix herself in an ideal attitude, courting an audience's gaze. But in order to be a consummate, professional beauty, one must be an expert—the only person in the room with the discernment and skill to execute beauty in its most appropriate form according to the occasion. All of Gwendolen's thoughts, actions, decisions, and movements are calculated to achieve such a winning effect.

For instance, she measures rooms and hallways by their potential efficacy as backdrop, and with the discernment of an *artiste,* molds herself to fit each scene. When Gwendolen first comes to Offendene, she is convinced of its worth as a place to live only after she is satisfied that it will serve as an appropriate setting. As the family inspects the rooms, Gwendolen comes across an organ and tells her mother that she will be painted as Saint Cecilia—the patron saint of music:

> [Gwendolen] . . . seated herself before the organ in an admirable pose, looking upward; while [the housekeeper] took out the one comb which fastened the coil of hair, and then shook out the mass till it fell in a smooth light-brown stream far below its owner's slim waist.
>
> Mrs Davilow smiled and said, 'A charming picture, my dear!' not indifferent to the display of her pet, even in the presence of a housekeeper. Gwendolen rose and laughed with delight. All this seemed quite to the purpose on entering a new house which was so excellent a background.
>
> 'What a queer, quaint, picturesque room!' she [said]. (26–27)

Gwendolen experiences a similar thrill the first time she visits an aristocratic estate, Quetcham Hall:

> No youthful figure there was comparable to Gwendolen's as she passed through the long suite of rooms adorned with light and flowers, and, visible at the first as a slim figure floating along in white drapery, approached through one wide doorway after another into fuller illumination and definiteness. She had never had that sort of promenade before, and she felt exultingly that it befitted her: any one looking at her for the first time might have supposed that long galleries and lackeys had always been a matter of course in her life. (43)

In both of these scenes, Gwendolen remakes a living space into a background and alters her own stance according to the parameters of the milieu. The "queer, quaint, picturesque" room in Offendene is an ideal setting for paintings from the Pre-Raphaelite school—works often set in cloistered, dark rooms with medieval, mythic, or religious women as their centerpiece.[18] As Gwendolen intuits, such women are simultaneously sensual and sanctified; Gwendolen turns her eyes heavenward as befitting a saint yet also takes down her hair in a classic gesture of female sexuality.[19] At Quetcham, however, Gwendolen is quite another figure. Unlike the corsets and crinolines typical of late 1860s dress—clothes that took up a good deal of room, spread awkwardly, and often required that a fully dressed lady carry between ten and thirty pounds on her back—Gwendolen's "white drapery" imitates the lines of classical art, a kind of dress first used extensively in Greco-Roman sculpture to "reveal the body to advantage, emphasize its movements, and caress its contours" (Hollander 3). Here, again, Gwendolen amalgamates propriety with erotics. Mid-century English paintings—especially, again, Pre-Raphaelite work—interchanged and intermingled classic drapery with "hair [that] . . . seemed more like a version of drapery than like a physical attribute" (Hollander 73). Perfectly aware of her genteel setting, however, Gwendolen knows better than to let down her hair; instead, she substitutes a suggestive, yet "aesthetic," drapery to convey her vibrant sexuality, a material simultaneously "floating" and "white" (ethereal) yet delicate enough to reveal her "slim figure." Even her slow promenade mimics the romantic realism of Pre-Raphaelite painting. With each step, Gwendolen becomes more "illuminated" and "definite," stippled in luminous color and with a clarity of definition the Pre-Raphaelites were known for.

True to the incongruities inherent in aesthetic femininity discussed in the Introduction, Gwendolen both commodifies herself (as a kind of living art) at the same time that she repudiates commodification—in this manner applying aesthetic femininity in much the same way as a professional artist. At Offendene, Gwendolen slips out of the typical artistic trap, refusing to be "killed into art" through the traditional dynamic: male artist (eye)/female art (body). By keeping the pose under her own representational control and displaying herself in front of a coterie of women who are incapable of oppressing her with an acquisitive eye (which is perhaps why Mrs. Davilow is easy about the presence of the housekeeper at this little family ritual), Gwendolen plays both artist and sitter, on-looker and looked-at-object.

At Quetcham, Gwendolen performs yet another slippage between aesthetic subject and object, reality and representation. As Alison Lurie points out in her study of clothing as a cultural sign system, the more decorated and useless the Victorian lady, the higher her commodity value; by wearing crinolines and especially corsets—a garment that atrophied back muscles, deformed internal organs, and kept women from breathing regularly or deeply—a Victorian woman "announce[d] to everyone that she [was] willing to be handicapped in life in relation to men . . . [and men] reward[ed] her for this by finding both her and her clothes attractive" (221). Pacing the promenade, Gwendolen denies this particular version of exchange by robing herself in what would have been unconventional attire for the period. This decision, while still engaging in the well-worn sexual traffic between woman-as-object, male-as-on-looker, does provide Gwendolen a modicum of power: not only does she exult in her own magnificence, she embodies a position of rank that, in truth, she does not hold. Gwendolen's enactment of the perfect beauty for the occasion creates an illusion so complete that "one looking at her for the first time" would believe she was a woman of title and fortune. Gwendolen herself takes on the sweeping opulence of the manor house; she *is* her environment. As such, she performs beauty better than anyone else—she is the supreme expert.

Yet the implicit danger of not just creating but actually representing Victorian female beauty is just this conflation of subject with object, a lesson Gwendolen first learns portraying the statue of Hermione in a domestic *tableaux.*[20] In truth,

Gwendolen is a poor actress; her interest in playing Hermione is not in the role itself but to show off a favorite Greek dress (more classic drapery) and display her instep. In some ways, however, this makes Queen Hermione an apposite part. In Shakespeare's play, upon seeing his wife's likeness, King Leontes says, "The fixture of her eye has motion in't, / As we are mocked with art" (V.iii). Like Gwendolen's everyday aesthetic enactments that mock viewers with their obvious and desirable corporeality, Hermione's statue tends toward the animate. Hermione is supposed to be a badly acted sculpture, revealing to the King who she really is by making the statue too lifelike to be art. As such, it seems apt that Gwendolen has no intention of playing the statue-like Hermione but, rather, wishes merely to flaunt her own statuesque self. But where Hermione's transformation from art to life symbolizes rebirth—the renewal of familial ties after a long period of death or "winter"—Gwendolen's performance reverses the course, prefiguring Gwendolen's death-in-life. Precisely when the queen is supposed to come to life, Gwendolen is rendered an even truer piece of sculpture as a hidden panel swings open to reveal the painting of a woman fleeing from a dead face: "[Gwendolen] looked like a statue into which a soul of Fear had entered: her pallid lips were parted; her eyes, usually narrowed under their long lashes, were dilated and fixed" (61). Where Hermione's eyes expose their materiality through too much motion, in the same moment Gwendolen's eyes, "dilated and fixed," transform her body into a dead thing.

This scene establishes a clear reversal for Gwendolen, one in which she loses professional control. The moment is accurately interpreted by Herr Klesmer, the novel's representation of an authentic professional artist. Klesmer applauds Gwendolen's show of fear as a "magnificent bit of *plastik*" (61).[21] Ironically, to the cultivated and appraising male spectator, Gwendolen executes her best performance when she ceases to perform—she is the most convincing when she ceases to act, move, and court the gaze. It is only when she resembles *plastique*, the plastic arts, that Klesmer finds her compelling. Gwendolen is most attractive when she no longer takes on the professional role of artistic creation but is reduced to mere article—the accepted place and position of beautiful women in aesthetic art. The artifice of her pallid and immovable body becomes, for Klesmer, an honest expression of passion because the only safe place for a woman to figure passion—anger, lust, or ambition—is as a lifeless sculpture. Of course, it is telling that this particular show of passion is fear. This emotion serves to disempower Gwendolen even further since before, in front of the glass, she had subordinated any such conflict of feelings to her irresistible self-presentation.

It is tempting here to recall a mythic echo, the story of Pygmalion and Galatea.[22] In Ovid's version, Pygmalion—a woman-hater and an artist—vows never to marry. However, he creates a statue so beautiful and lifelike that he falls in love with it, thus damning himself to playing at love with a cold representation. Venus takes pity on Pygmalion's suffering and rewards his many offerings to her by turning the statue into a living woman. Bringing together female beauty and art through a potent allegory of masculine creation, what the Pygmalion story teaches is that artistic men have the power to instill life in beautiful women and, further, that a beautiful woman is a symbol of a male artist's mental life, his soul. In turn, women cannot bring themselves, as art objects, to life. Even Hermione is not allowed to come back from the metaphoric dead until her husband recognizes her "reality," chastising himself for his own unfounded hatred of women.

Even Gwendolen's name, at some level, augurs her ultimate association with false over true artistry. As Eliot herself notes in a journal, "Gwen" in Welsh has the double sense of the color white and the designation of "woman"—together meaning a whitened or marbleized woman, i.e., a static or dead representation.[23] For the outward visage that had originally promised so much power for Gwendolen turns against her. Where at first she believed she could mold her shape in expert fashion to flatter herself and her circumstance, now this same ability reveals itself as Gwendolen's entrapment. Particularly with the arrival of Lydia Glasher's diamonds after Gwendolen marries Grandcourt, Gwendolen's reliance on surfaces exposes itself as a cheap imitation of art—as an advertisement of beauty.[24] "[T]he casket fell on the floor and the diamonds rolled out. [Gwendolen] took no notice, but fell back in her chair again helpless. She could not see the reflections of herself then: they were like so many women petrified white. . . ." (359). The choice of description is important here, "petrified" meaning both frightened and fossilized in the manner that diamonds are ossified coal.[25] Although the multiple mirrors magnify numerous Gwendolens, like the set of diamonds, these images are finally just one: the same white, cold, hard substance again and again. Significantly, Gwendolen cannot *see* herself in the glass, hence her helplessness. Without the visible reassurance of her beauty's power to overcome any obstacle—which is her only access to identity—she views herself as having no identity, not as an expert professional but as just another petrified woman or, rather, just another married woman.[26]

COMMERCIAL ECONOMY VERSUS AESTHETIC ECONOMY

Thus Gwendolen's future hardens into a firm, fossilized image, and she is unable, now, to transform herself with that chameleon-like rapidity she once enjoyed. "Day after day," we learn,

> the same pattern of thinking was repeated. There came nothing to change the situation—no new elements in the sketch—only a recurrence which engraved it. The May weeks went into June, and still Mrs Grandcourt was outwardly in the same place, presenting herself as she was expected to do in the accustomed scenes, with the accustomed grace, beauty, and costume; from church at one end of the week, through all the scale of desirable receptions, to opera at the other. (604)

Just like her initial self-advertisement at the glass, this representation does not allow for conflicting elements that cannot be incorporated into a one-dimensional performance of "grace, beauty, and costume."

But even though such self-display once provided Gwendolen a sense of agency and self-control, actually her commodification has always worked in the same fashion. Gwendolen's repeated image makes an endless circuit through set patterns of social distribution, whether they be the earlier ones of *tableaux*-parties-riding or the pattern she enacts with Grandcourt of church-receptions-opera. In the precise manner of her initial exchange with the glass, Gwendolen still circulates through "accustomed scenes" or backdrops as an object—or in the parlance of advertising, as image. The single difference is that after the arrival of the diamonds, this exchange signifies a calamity instead of an advantage. Indeed, in a worldview where everything is equal to surface, it is little wonder that Gwendolen's exterior circumstances are interchangeable with her interior desires. At the crucial moment of Grandcourt's death, Gwendolen believes she witnesses the enactment of her secret longings outside herself wherein one's internal emotions are realized as an extrinsic and visual truth. "I only know," she says, explaining Grandcourt's drowning to Daniel, "that I saw my wish outside me" (696). This, of course, is the precise function of advertising, to project secret desires as visible presentations.

As such, Gwendolen exposes how false artistic professionalism—artistic professionalism dependent on representational systems such as advertising—relies on the capitalist marketplace yet tries to obscure that reliance through the contradictions inherent in Victorian female beauty. Indeed, Gwendolen's specific delusion is her belief that by professionalizing her beauty, she will sidestep the predicaments of aesthetic femininity. While on the one hand she fully appreciates the snares of courtship—musing that "[t]o be very much sued or hopelessly sighed for as a bride was indeed an indispensable and agreeable guarantee of womanly power; but to become a wife and wear all the domestic fetters of that condition, was on the whole a vexatious necessity" (39)—on the other she utterly fails to see how her claim to professional beauty must and will fail:

> [T]his delicate-limbed sylph of twenty meant to lead. For such passions dwell in feminine breasts also. In Gwendolen's, however, they dwelt among strictly feminine furniture, and had no disturbing reference to the advancement of learning or the balance of the constitution; her knowledge being such as with no sort of standing-room or length of lever could have been expected to move the world. She meant to do what was pleasant to herself in a striking manner; or rather, whatever she could do so as to strike others with admiration and get in that reflected way a more ardent sense of living, seemed pleasant to her fancy. (39)

Because Gwendolen's exceptionalism declines even the pretense of wider public service—the "advancement of learning" or the "balance of the constitution"—and because her performance of special knowledge is too narrow and self-serving to be "expected to move the world," the novel refuses her the option of claiming to benefit the public good in an attempt to remove herself from the contaminations of the market.

Indeed, precisely because Gwendolen's item of professional exchange is her beauty, she is caught within the meshes of nineteenth-century aesthetic femininity outlined in the Introduction. As widely documented and discussed, Victorian femininity required two functions of difference: first, that femininity be separate from the political and economic domains of society, and second, that femininity be both a readable exterior appearance coupled with an illegible interior knowledge—usually construed as sexual knowledge.[27] As such, femininity was an ideal vehicle for nineteenth-century aesthetic sensibility, allowing aesthetics a separation from the wiles of the public marketplace and a simultaneous participation in that marketplace.[28] Gwendolen's case reveals and undermines this system of signification, casting her artistic forays into the public sphere as necessarily sexualized and commodified as well as aestheticized. Thus Gwendolen's professionalism exposes its dangerous prostitution, and in the effort to reveal this perniciousness (the hidden, unknown, and threatening depth behind her surface—manifested particularly in her knowledge of the Glasher affair), the novel effectively demonstrates that Gwendolen and the models of false professionalism she represents are finally commercial economies, even as they mime aesthetic ones.

In essence, Gwendolen's circulation through the novel itself imitates the economies of established literary and marketing modes, especially those of advertisements and sensationalist fictions. According to the narrator, the on-going and iterative recurrence of Gwendolen's "sketch" or image "engraves" it, like the technology of printing plates, producing more and more precise copies of the fashionable Gwendolen for consumption (604). As such, Gwendolen's distribution replicates the wide dissemination of mid-century ads and popular railway fictions. As explicated in the last chapter, ads are predicated on linking a static image to an idea or emotion—thus making them synonymous through widespread duplication—in an effort to compel a consumer to buy this emotion or idea through the product on display. Yet, in effect, ads are always the same, always an appeal for money. In like manner, as Eliot gibes in her early essay "Silly Novels by Lady Novelists," popular novels all feature a heroine who is usually an heiress; "[h]er eyes and her wit are both dazzling; her nose and her morals are alike free from any tendency to irregularity; she has a superb *contralto* and a superb intellect; she is perfectly well-dressed and perfectly religious; she dances like a sylph, and reads the Bible in the original tongues" (140).[29] These works, Eliot quips, are "remarkably unanimous in their choice of diction" and construct similarly discordant scenes of a "quite modern drawing-room society— . . . yet we have characters, and incidents, and traits of manner introduced, which are mere shreds from the most heterogeneous romances" (147, 153). In short, though the content of individual popular literatures may appear distinct, in fact such novels merely recirculate the same basic characters, settings, plots, and hyperbolic style—meaning that the railway novels, like ads, are just monetary markers, bits of theatricalized exchange.

Eliot herself deplored popular sensational novels and the kind of commercial economy epitomized by advertising.[30] "I sicken," she tells her editor Blackwood, ". . . with despondency under the sense that the most carefully written books lie, both outside and inside people's minds, deep undermost in a heap of trash. I suppose the reason my 6/ editions are never on the railway stalls is [that] . . . [t]hey are not so attractive to the majority as 'The Trail of the Serpent'; still a minority might sometimes buy them if they were there" (*Letters* IV: 309–310).[31] In comparison to the "heap of trash" perpetuated by a commercial economy, Eliot frames a kind of aesthetic economy—one that attempts to disseminate the best that has been thought and said in literature, and, indeed, one she terms "cultured" after Matthew Arnold.[32] This aesthetic or cultured economy distributes carefully written books, vital or original works that influence the moral life of those who read them. In a letter to Stowe, Eliot elaborates her vision of this economy:

> I have good hope that your fears are groundless as to the obstacles your new book may find here from its thoroughly American character. Most readers who are likely to be really influenced by writing above the common order will find that special aspect an added reason for interest and study, and I dare say you have long seen . . . that if a book which has any sort of exquisiteness happens also to be a popular widely circulated book, its power over the social mind, for any good, is after all due to its reception by a few appreciative natures, and is the slow result of radiation from that narrow circle. I mean, that you can affect a few souls, and that each of these in turn may affect a few more, but that no exquisite book tells properly and directly on a multitude however largely it may be spread by type and paper. Witness the things the multitude will say about it if one is so unhappy as to be obliged to hear their sayings. . . . Both travelling abroad and staying at home among our English sights and reports, one must continually feel how slowly the centuries work toward the moral good of men. (*Letters* V: 30–31)

A number of Eliot's points here deserve attention. First, characteristics that constitute "exquisite" writing defy local or even national distinctions. While Stowe worried that English readers might dislike the intense American flavor of *Oldtown Folks*, Eliot contends that true readers should like it even more for that very reason, since exceptional art functions as an originary and timeless piece and shouldn't be appraised according to mundane or parochial valuations. Second, though Eliot admits her reliance on literature's market economy, at the same time she separates her novels (and Stowe's) from the trash that employs the same avenues of distribution. Obviously Eliot doesn't deplore, per se, the idea of railway stalls and cheap novels; rather, she is disgusted by what the popular mind chooses to read, buying a Mary Elizabeth Braddon over a George Eliot, and what certain women writers are willing to print. "Society is a very culpable entity, and has to answer for the manufacture of many unwholesome commodities, from bad pickles to bad poetry," Eliot asserts. "But society, like 'matter,' and Her Majesty's Government, and other lofty abstractions, has its share of excessive blame as well as excessive praise. Where there is one woman who writes from necessity, we believe there are three women who write from vanity . . ." ("Silly" 162). Thus, like Stowe, Eliot sees writers, publishers, and readers as similarly culpable: writers should know better than to produce trashy fiction (unless they "write from necessity"); publishers should abstain from selling novels like advertisements; and readers should avoid works like *The Tail of the Serpent* in favor of a book "above the common order" such as *Oldtown Folks*. Finally, even though Eliot keeps a rigid distinction between the few sympathetic souls who understand great art and the uncultured multitude who speak ill or ignorantly about such work, she firmly believes that good writing has the potential to influence the moral good over a period of many centuries. In this manner, Eliot affirms both Stowe's and Phelps's conviction that authors are under an ethical obligation to write edifying fiction as well as instruct their readers in how best to interpret their work and incorporate its teachings into their everyday experience.[33]

In effect, then, Eliot denounces the sphere of the false professional, the one epitomized by Gwendolen. By setting exquisite art or high culture in a reified place beyond commonplace art or popular culture, Eliot articulates an aesthetic economy that is simultaneously dependent on the market for its influence yet breaks with the iterative, unproductive, and damaging results of advertising and sensational fictions. Through *Daniel Deronda*, Eliot exposes false professionalism's pernicious influence, and by choosing Gwendolen as her representative false professional, Eliot rejects any artist's removal from public utility or service.

THE TRUE PROFESSIONAL AND GWENDOLEN AS THE IDEAL READER

But since Eliot herself is dependent on the realities of commerce, what keeps her superseding aesthetic standard from being yet another version of false professional artistry, masking its participation in market exchange under the guise of social reform? As with Stowe, Eliot's aesthetic is indeed a consummate form of artistic professionalism, but Eliot's attempts at distancing herself from this sphere are worth exploration, especially since they inform how critics in America interpreted both Eliot as an author and *Daniel Deronda* as a novel.

In Catherine Gallagher's penetrating analysis of the various economies at play in *Deronda*, she contends that while Eliot touted the supreme value of original work, she "never equate[d] productivity with natural generation" (47). In making this claim, however, Gallagher conflates Eliot's notion of "original work" with Eliot's separation of "culture" from "nature." And, indeed, the *Theophrastus* essay on moral currency emphasizes an idea from Sainte-Beauve that culture is not innate—that it is not equivalent to nature. Yet Eliot did believe, at least at some level, that the ingenuity of fine literature springs from an intuitive organicism, specifically a creative genius originating from "natural generation." On more than one occasion, Eliot esteems Stowe's artistic sympathies on the basis of her experience as a child-bearing woman. Noting that she has no anxiety over Stowe's intrinsic ability to comprehend both her novels and her letters, Eliot explains, "for you have had longer experience than I as a writer, and fuller experience as a woman, since you have borne children and known the mother's history from the beginning. I trust your quick and long-taught mind as an interpreter little liable to mistake me" (*Letters* V: 31). Clearly, then, Eliot accepted the idea that generative novels—as well as the ability to appreciate such work—stem from a keen connection to natural production. The split between culture and nature has to do, instead, with Eliot's sense of how original novels are circulated. As noted above, Eliot was adamant that the popular reading public couldn't be trusted to discern trash from carefully written books. Rather, in order to teach culture, she felt writers and publishers were bound to instruct people on how and what to read—thus the process of acculturation was not native but acquired.

This distinction is crucial since Eliot's belief in the natural origins of great genius provides the basis of her professional argument, permitting her to take advantage of commercial exchange yet occupy an aesthetic space apart from Mary Elizabeth Braddon and Gwendolen Harleth. This philosophical separation of true professional artists from sensation writers and advertisers is epitomized in a scene where a financially destitute Gwendolen consults Herr Klesmer about whether her talents would allow her to pursue a singing or acting career. While waiting for Klesmer to arrive for their *tête-à-tête*, Gwendolen catches her image in a mirror and walks toward herself:

> Dressed in black, . . . and with the warm whiteness of her skin set off between her light-brown coronet of hair and her square-cut bodice, she might have tempted an artist to try again the Roman trick of a statue in black, white, and tawny marble. Seeing her image slowly advancing, she thought, 'I am beautiful'—not exultingly, but with grave decision. Being beautiful was after all the condition on which she most needed external testimony. If any one objected to the turn of her nose or the form of her neck and chin, she had not the sense that she could presently show her power of attainment in these branches of feminine perfection. (251)

In keeping with occasions mentioned earlier, here Gwendolen takes confidence in her body as a specimen of rare art, affirming once more the all-important role of an audience in the construction of both her beauty and self-assurance. The need for outside affirmation is so compelling that Gwendolen becomes her own admirer in lieu of others, proffering the necessary "testimony" to her "power of attainment" with the "grave decision" of a discriminating judge. Again, the novel highlights Gwendolen's affinity with cultures of advertising—if consumers disfavor the promotional packaging of the product ("the turn of her nose or the form of her neck and chin"), the product immediately loses value. Not only is Gwendolen's success dependent on the interest of others, her worth is forever removed from her own control, solely consisting of "external testimony."

Of course Herr Klesmer also participates in a consumeristic trade, peddling his artistic faculties; he, too, is reliant on the interest of an audience. Yet the novel is careful to distinguish Klesmer's wares from Gwendolen's, and the distinction has everything to do with their respective source. The life of the true artist, Klesmer explains to Gwendolen, "'is out of the reach of any but choice organisations—natures framed to love perfection and to labour for it; ready, like all true lovers, to endure, to wait, to say, I am not yet worthy, but she—Art, my mistress—is worthy, and I will live to merit her'" (253). By definition, then, Klesmer's own expertise incorporates contradictory principles: it embodies a universalistic sanction insofar as it projects a standard set of rules that any artist may follow as long as he or she is willing to labour, endure, and wait for commendation, while it simultaneously claims an innate source, thus distancing true artists from groups of mere workers. As Klesmer explains to Gwendolen, in theater she could certainly trade on beauty alone, "donning the life [of the artist] as a livery" (253). "'[O]n the stage,' Klesmer notes, 'beauty is taken when there is nothing more commanding to be had'"—for acting, unlike music or painting, may be imitated without prior instruction (260). Yet Klesmer clearly finds such positions ignominious, especially in the case of beautiful women. "'The woman who takes up this career is not an artist,' Klesmer asserts, 'she is usually one who thinks of entering on a luxurious life by a short and easy road—perhaps by marriage—that is her most brilliant chance, and the rarest'" (260).

Consequently Klesmer constructs a triple partition between his own acumen and Gwendolen's incompetence or amateurism. The apparati that surround art exercise the first measure of gatekeeping; only a certain few have access to fine artistic training or the motive to practice, and Klesmer makes it clear that Gwendolen is both ill-trained and not likely to dedicate herself to study and effort after twenty years of middle-class ease and inactivity. In addition, even with training, Klesmer argues that a true artist must be predisposed, ***a priori***, to the sympathies of art and the aesthetic lifestyle—only "choice organisations" are "framed" for the arts. Though a woman, and therefore potentially able to claim a connate connection to natural generation, Gwendolen denies this avenue to artistic insight. Before her marriage,

Gwendolen is anything but domestic-minded; after, she is "reduced to dread lest she should become a mother" (672–673). Reproduction, for Gwendolen, represents one of two terrible options: imprisonment, as in the case of her own mother's child-bearing (all those superfluous sisters by way of a brutal husband), or prostitution, as in the instance of Lydia Glasher. The threatening entrapment of propagation is so alarming that Gwendolen loathes it when men make love to her; she desires attention without a physical pledge. Indeed, in addition to the arrival of the diamonds, a concomitant reason for the hysteria on her wedding night is this physical debt Gwendolen now owes Grandcourt; by "owning" or becoming the diamonds, she simultaneously occupies the position of debtor or Grandcourt's mistress. In this manner, Gwendolen alienates herself from a primary sense of feminine creativity, a natural connection to artistic sensibility. Finally, Gwendolen makes a dubious figure as a potential artist in her own right. Presented as a choice piece of Roman marble, even before her marriage to Grandcourt, Gwendolen herself is a metonym for "mistress Art"—at once coveted, exalted and yet despoiled. On the one hand, her beauty grants her entrée to the world of art where feminine splendor is prized as the highest result of passionate masculine creation, yet on the other, her claim to the position of artist is deleterious. A woman who sells herself with nothing more commanding than her looks is by definition a courtesan—one who, like an advertisement, has nothing of worth save the lure of spectacle.

Once Klesmer makes it plain that she can never be a true artist, Gwendolen feels that "[a]ll memories, all objects, the pieces of music displayed, the open piano—the very reflection of herself in the glass—seemed no better than the packed-up shows of a departing fair. For the first time since her consciousness began, she was having a vision of herself on the common level, and had lost the innate sense that there were reasons why she should not be slighted, elbowed, jostled—treated like a passenger with a third-class ticket, in spite of private objections on her own part" (262). Klesmer's visit reveals how Gwendolen's art is necessarily adulterated, both hackneyed and short-lived. Until this moment, her beauty was the cement that held together miscellaneous aspects of Gwendolen's professional aesthetic—her memories, the objects she arranged, the music she sang to display herself, and of course her repeated reflections in mirrors as well as in other people's eyes. These created a mirage of permanence and renown—now "packed-up shows," deceptive and temporary. Because Gwendolen's art is amateur, a bit of bad theater, her "innate sense" of superiority is a false sense of aesthetic origins; hers is not, after all, a "choice organisation." Rather, Gwendolen's constitution is "common," thus giving her no argument against ordinary treatment—treatment that includes jarring verbs of sense, awakening her to the position of being a female body over a feminine image, "elbowed" and "jostled" without her consent. Precisely because Gwendolen's beauty inspires sexual desire in men, her aesthetic power is inevitably external and embodied, an indecent allure. Klesmer's artistry, however, is internal and immaterial; it carries immortal and paramount qualities, thus linking the origins of true art not only to natural generation but to universal perspicacity.

In this manner, the novel argues that true artists are true professionals, quite separate from those amateurs or false professionals like Gwendolen. False professionals shape self-defined and self-privileging careers through a careful process of exercising specialized—not comprehensive—knowledge. Necessarily narrow in training, false professionals are limited to the functionality of delivering a single sphere of understanding. And while even false professionals may assert an ethic of service as their *raison d'être*, they do not claim a natural or innate connection to universal wisdom or insight. Rather, their expertise is a patently learned one, codified through credentialized institutions or systems, tied to temporal modes and means, often couched as the most up to date or stylish. When Klesmer excoriates Gwendolen's singing, it is because he surveys her music as narrow and serviceable, "a form of melody which expresses a puerile state of culture—a dandling, canting, see-saw kind of stuff—the passion and thought of people without any breadth of horizon . . . , no cries of a deep, mysterious passion—no conflict—no sense of the universal" (49). As Klesmer concludes, "It makes men small as they listen to it" (49). In turn, Klesmer marks off his own professional position as *recherché*, his own music as the antipode of Gwendolen's folk songs, ballads, and hymns: mysteriously passionate and complex, with a wide view of the cultural horizon simultaneously past, present, and future. By inference, Klesmer's music links men to immense, immortal emotions and experiences: his music makes souls.

By contrasting Gwendolen as the representative of a false commercial economy against Klesmer as the representative of a true aesthetic one, in a sense, the novel warns its readers against the seductions of surfaces—of advertising and sensationalist fiction—by following the trajectory of Gwendolen's shallowness, self-love, and eventual entrapment. Thus it is of even more interest that throughout *Deronda*'s serialization, American readers found Gwendolen to be a living, breathing incarnation of a close intimate. Although the claim that characters were "true to life" was certainly a cliché in nineteenth-century reading on both sides of the ocean, it is not the mere fact that American readers found realistic elements in the novel that inspires speculation and intrigue. Rather, it is the fact that the logics of the novel itself suggest that the reader's focus should be on Gwendolen's superficiality and, further, that readers should actually repudiate this superficiality as banal, thereby rejecting art or artistic representation based on systems of advertising and sensationalism.

However, since Gwendolen has been her own "reader" since the very first moment she beheld herself in the glass, Gwendolen is also the representative of the kind of reader who, having been seduced by superficiality and sensation, has the possibility of being redeemed, of finding a soul. Unlike Klesmer who intuits what has substance, Gwendolen confuses surface with substance or pleasure with art. Yet throughout the novel Gwendolen carries with her an innate something that wants to know the difference between false and true culture, and it is this something that spurs her repeatedly to consult Daniel for advice on how to acquire what Daniel himself calls "real knowledge" (451).

At the beginning of the novel, the narrator explains that "[s]olitude in any wide scene impressed [Gwendolen] with an undefined feeling of immeasurable existence aloof from her, in the midst of which she was helplessly incapable of asserting herself" (63–64). In a manner precisely opposite to Daniel and his sympathetic investment in people and ideas beyond his own ken, Gwendolen finds it impossible to have interest or sympathy in a world beyond her own small cares. But at the very end of the narrative, when Daniel tells her that he is a Jew, that he is leaving and will be gone for many years, and that he is marrying Mirah, this same fear of the unknown becomes Gwendolen's catalyst for change:

> The world seemed getting larger round poor Gwendolen, and she more solitary and helpless in the midst. . . . There comes a terrible moment to many souls when the great movements of the world, the larger destinies of mankind, which have lain aloof in newspapers and other neglected reading, enter like an earthquake into their lives. . . . That was the sort of crisis which was . . . beginning in Gwendolen's small life: she was for the first time feeling the pressure of a vast mysterious movement, . . . and getting a sense that her horizon was but a dipping onward of an existence with which her own was revolving (803–804).

After this epiphany, the novel leaves Gwendolen in a state of becoming. The last time the narrative shows her, she hasn't yet figured out how to exist in a world of substance. Although she abandons the mirror, explaining that she hasn't looked at herself, this separation from her only sense of identity leaves Gwendolen in an hysterical fit—swallowed, in a sense, by that new horizon around her. "Through the day and half the night she fell continually into fits of shrieking," the narrator explains, although she also "cried in the midst of them to her mother, . . . 'I mean to live'" (807).

In a sense, Gwendolen's reading habits are being transformed. Though painful, she is learning how to divorce herself from advertising and sensation in order to appreciate the destinies of mankind found in newspapers as well as other neglected reading such as, almost surely, highbrow novels. By pledging to Daniel that she will try to live a purposeful existence, Gwendolen forces herself to participate in the flesh-and-blood life beyond surfaces, divorcing herself from systems that mimic sympathy in favor of the experience of authentic sympathy—or what Daniel has stood for all along. Put simply, Gwendolen must engage in the real.

In this manner, Gwendolen exemplifies *Daniel Deronda*'s perfect reader. Though a product of the kind of sensational, "rubbishy literature" that at one point in the novel Rex Gascoigne laments "people choke their minds with" (707),

Gwendolen is finally able to begin to emulate what Eliot termed to Stowe an "exquisite" book—a book that "affects souls." Thus the very critique that places Gwendolen in the position of false art or false professionalism becomes the instrument of her authenticity. It is her struggle to embrace the realness of life that, in turn, makes her real to her American readers. As Stowe explains to Eliot, "A frivolous or hard, or worldly selfish woman would have worn the diamonds with a self satisfied grin & taken the good the Gods provided without too many reflections on how or at whose expense she came by them."[34] For Stowe, Gwendolen is worthy of sympathy because she has a moral conscience, because she shows herself to be, ironically, beyond frivolity, hardness, or selfishness.

REALISM, SYMPATHY, AND HIGH-ART PERIODICALS

Placing Gwendolen's narrative metamorphosis into a larger context, one begins to see links between the how Americans interpreted the realness of Gwendolen and how high-art periodicals like *Harper's*, *Scribner's*, or *The North American Review* taught their audience to read realism. Eliot herself was defined in such periodicals as a writer who could see humanity through a universal lens; indeed, much like the novel's realization of Klesmer's art or Daniel's wide sympathy, in review after review of *Deronda*, Eliot was cast as a kind of mystic and immortal soul-maker. Edwin Whipple, analyzing the book for the *North American Review*, commented that "[t]his general largeness of mind, this tranquil grasp of the outlying problems of human life and human destiny, distinguishes [Eliot] from all the other novelists of the age; for she not only looks at things and into things, but she looks through things to the laws of life they illustrate and by which they are governed" (32). Henry James in *The Nation* concurred, noting that "[t]he 'sense of the universal' is constant, omnipresent" (131). And *Scribner's Monthly* agreed: "To write with sympathetic zest of Jewish life, as [Eliot] does here, requires, not alone careful and exhaustive study, but a broadly human spirit, a penetration and a dramatic sympathy simply wonderful" (133).

If these brief critical comments can be taken as representative, they allow an authorial ethos to emerge: for Americans, Eliot was distinguished as unique, omnipotent, sagacious, and sympathetic.[35] Eliot did not merely engage in "careful and exhaustive study" of her subject in the mode of a false professional; she also moved beyond, carrying a "broadly human spirit," a "dramatic sympathy" that was somehow outside book learning, part of her sum and substance, enabling her to see through things to the workings of the universe—"the laws of life" and how they are "governed." And while *Deronda* circulated as a novel and therefore was part of the commercial market, its effect was not market-bound. Rather, Eliot's art, like natural generation, recast commerce because that which was being produced was priceless, profound, and paradoxically both universal and one-of-a-kind. As James noted, her work transmits oracular *communiqué* from "mysterious regions," transforming the material of print and paper into a mystical, global medium (131).

In addition, like Stowe and Phelps who turned to Eliot as an ideal of strong femininity, American critics looked to Eliot's work as an ideal of feminine sympathy. As is obvious from the excerpts above, by the 1870s reference to Eliot's sympathetic genius was commonplace in American periodicals. W. H. Browne, writing for the *Southern Magazine*, struck a keynote in his survey of Eliot's work. "[T]he author goes with us every step of the way, admiring, pitying, judging, excusing, as sympathizing and as amused as we are ourselves with her little living world. No writer that we know of has carried this sympathy so far as George Eliot" (380). Importantly, however, Eliot's broad-minded sympathy was correlated with the elemental compassion of Victorian femininity. In contrast to her American male contemporaries—including James and Howells who "study crude life on the surface"—George Willis Cooke found "heart-nearness" in Eliot's novels, and credited her for "lov[ing] her characters" and "pour[ing] out her motherliness upon them" (120). Though Cooke identifies Eliot as a thorough realist, he portrays her as "a realist with a wide and attractive sympathy . . . , too great a genius to believe that the novelist can describe life as the geologist describes the strata of the earth" (120–121). Whipple's review of *Deronda* makes a similar comparison, calling Eliot's scrutiny of Gwendolen "as relentless as that of a naturalist who has a jelly-fish under his microscope, and as tenderly considerate as that of a mother who holds her new-born babe in her arms" (42).[36]

This dual capacity for universal yet also a decidedly feminine sympathy became the basic criterion through which Americans were taught to value Gwendolen Harleth. As mentioned in the Introduction, the American reading public of the 1870s had become accustomed to a certain kind of elite literature from the pages of magazines like *Harper's*, *Scribner's*, or *The North American Review*.[37] Not only did this literature tend to eschew sensationalism and embrace a style at once straightforward and sympathetic, but it also took for its subject matter activities and attractions of the new leisure class—from the European tour to yachting to the lives of famous personages to rules of etiquette. Running alongside the serialization of *Daniel Deronda*, for instance, *Harper's* included articles on "Talks, Walks, and Drives in and around Lea Castle, Near Kidderminster, England," "Vassar College," and "The Art of Dining," various views of Windsor Castle, a biographical piece on "Mary, Queen of England," a reminiscence on the "Poetry of Steeples," an essay on gothic architecture, and a botany piece about the valve of the utricularia. This seeming hodgepodge actually creates a rather coherent set of interests ranging from cultural history, landscape, and architecture to scientific investigation. The subjects are simultaneously factual in nature—consisting of real places, people, or things—yet inflected by a diction of sympathy (the botany piece, for example, debates whether the utricularia's valve is particularly "sensitive"). In other words, *Harper's* courted a style concomitantly fact-based and emotive, real precisely because it was sympathetic.

As is clear from these brief conjunctions, much emphasis was placed on English topics. *Harper's* readers could accurately appropriate English culture at the same time they learned to feel strongly about "foreign" people and places. The richness, sophistication, and cultural density of England could be appreciated as entirely other at the same time that it offered Americans the opportunity to inhabit English life. And Gwendolen satisfied this desire for cross-Atlantic appropriation in addition to a desire to exercise universal-yet-feminine sympathy in the name of high realism. Because Gwendolen was a woman (and therefore like Eliot innately connected to moral capital) as well as an individual struggling through an aesthetic or worthy problem, these qualities allowed *Harper's* readers to identify with her debility. "The reader looks upon [Daniel] more as a force than as a person," explains R. R. Bowker in the *International Review*. "On the other hand, the reader's attention is concentrated upon Gwendolen, this throbbing, bleeding heart, torn by the thwarting circumstances we all know to our pain, herself the product of circumstance and the battle-field of opposing character—because this is human and near to us" (70).

Thus the exercise of universal, feminine sympathy becomes the mark of the most real of novels. Through the pages of high-art periodicals, readers were taught to demonstrate their aesthetic appreciation by connecting with the human or universal aspects of a character's struggle through a demonstration or understanding of feminine morality. Interestingly, Gwendolen's struggle was so wholly annexed as real by the American reading public that she finally came to symbolize a kind of democratic fellow feeling. Called "fresh," "frank," "natural," "consistent," "known," "felt," and "free," Gwendolen's representation became interchangeable with core values of American character.[38] Even Eliot's style in the Gwendolen sections of the novel was equated with American sincerity and strength. A reviewer for *Scribner's Monthly* likens Eliot's delivery of Gwendolen to "that of the broad, steady current of the Ohio" (135), and a critic for the *Galaxy* comments that "after a long stay in the Mordecai-Mirah atmosphere, [and] we at length emerge upon the words, 'And Gwendolen?' author and reader seem to share a sigh of relief. . . . [E]verything marches more freely" (699). The story of an innately sincere personality brought low by the perils of an inimical society was a familiar one to American readers, especially to a writer like Stowe who found Gwendolen "far from being an exceptionally selfish unworldly woman" but rather one who "stands in the midst of a heartlessly selfish & utterly worldly state of society a creature of higher impulses sensitive to the very first suggestion of moral right."[39] In Gwendolen, then, *Harper's* American readers discovered a woman whose habits, desires, and woes signaled apposite identification—Gwendolen, unlike Daniel or Mirah or Mordecai, carried the kind of highbrow conflicts over art and appropriate representation that *Harper's* upper-class readers (or those who associated themselves with the upper class) were taught they should condone, pity, or admire.

JEWISH IMMIGRATION AND *GWENDOLEN*

But the American focus on Gwendolen as more real cannot be fully understood without considering the reception of what Stowe called the novel's other "head." Eliot explains in a letter to Stowe:

> I expected from first to last in writing it, that [the Jewish element] would create . . . resistance and even repulsion. . . . But precisely because I felt that the usual attitude of Christians toward Jews is—I hardly know whether to say more impious or more stupid when viewed in the light of their professed principles, I therefore felt urged to treat Jews with such sympathy and understanding as my nature and knowledge could attain to. . . . There is nothing I should care more to do, if it were possible, than to rouse the imagination of men and women to a vision of human claims in those races of their fellow-men who most differ from them in customs and beliefs. (*Letters* VI: 301)

Where Eliot deliberately held Jewish people up for "sympathy and understanding," however, her postbellum readers found these parts of the novel the least convincing. In an article for the *International Review*, Francis Maguire states simply that as "Gwendolen's personality grows fuller and richer[,] Deronda['s] still remains in outline" (31). And in Henry James's notable essay "Daniel Deronda: A Conversation," two of his three conversants—Constantius and Pulcheria—echo Maguire's assessment, claiming that the Jewish characters are lifeless because they "produce no illusion." Pulcheria complains, "They are described and analyzed to death, but we don't see them or hear them or touch them. Deronda clutches his coat-collar, Mirah crosses her feet, and Mordecai talks like the Bible; but that doesn't make real figures of them," and Constantius accedes, "Deronda, Mordecai, and Mirah are hardly more than shadows" (421, 422).

Perhaps the reason American readers couldn't "rouse [their] imagination" to offer sympathy for races who "differ[ed] most from them in customs and beliefs" had something to do with a simultaneous historical movement: *Deronda* was published during the same period that marked a swell in the tides of Jewish immigration. Although it is estimated that before the 1870s, Jewish immigrants numbered only 300,000 in an American population of over fifty million, between the late 1870s and 1914, two million Jews came to the United States, many of them fleeing political persecution in Eastern and Southern Europe.[40] High-art literary journals reacted with hostility to this influx of what one writer for the *North American Review* called a "semi-barbarous" population, "willing and used to living in filthy crowded conditions" (Powderly 165). And, in fact, as increasing numbers of Jewish immigrants were lured by a proliferation of jobs in the postbellum industrial North, more and more sought shelter in slums. As historian Lee Friedman notes, "Their dwellings were the back-yard unsanitary tenements, in decaying decrepit dwellings which, in a long-forgotten past had seen better days. Sweatshops . . . were almost unregulated . . . [and e]ndless hours, starvation wages and unspeakable living conditions were the lot of these miserable refugees" (177).

This perception that a "barbarous" and "filthy" Jewish population might infect the purity of American civilization exposes deep class anxieties on the part of American elites. Particularly as Jewish labor leaders began agitating for better working conditions and increasing numbers of Jewish immigrants moved from factory jobs into much more lucrative and prestigious professional occupations, certain Americans believed that Jewish immigrants posed civic, economic, and social threats to upper-class authority. Indeed, even by the late 1870s, Jewish Americans could claim their own culture: many big-city newspapers and journals were dedicated to Jewish interest pieces and even published their articles in Yiddish; one famous female reformer, dubbed the "Polish Jewess," had been agitating around the country for universal female suffrage since the 1850s; and a man by the name of W. D. Robinson had published a book encouraging Jewish immigrants to found a community in the United States by purchasing a large tract of land in the Western territories.[41]

So even more threatening than the flock of poor Jews to inner-city ghettos was the concern among highbrow critics that such immigrants would inter-marry with Christians, thereby polluting the genetic pool. With reference to Catholic and Jewish immigrants, the *Atlantic* called such refugees "peasants" and labeled their ancestral stock "as inferior as [that of] American negroes" ("European Peasants" 233). "Our original population have never been slaves," continued the *Atlantic*. "Compare the origin and nurture of these free men with those of the ordinary laborer of Europe and we see at once the gravity of the danger which the mass of European immigrants brings to us. The American commonwealth could never have been founded if the first European colonist had been of peasant stock" (233). Thus this specific threat—the threat of literal and cultural miscegenation—points toward a specifically feminine, racialized, and natural threat to white superiority, embodied in *Daniel Deronda* as the figure of the Alcharisi.[42]

In a sense, the Alcharisi is the origin of all Jewish characters in the novel; she is the race mother who engenders the entire Jewish plot. The Alcharisi carries Daniel's roots as part of her racially and sexually marked body—thus providing access to his material heritage and also his intellectual one, bearing the chest of his father's records, the documents that witness his racial past. Thus the Alcharisi enables the Daniel-Mirah-Mordecai plot to unfold in the same manner that Gwendolen enables the Grandcourt-Glasher plot: both women act as vehicles for establishing unorthodox, even deviant, inheritance plots wherein the Jewish head culminates in Daniel's adoption of Judaism and the English head ends with Grandcourt and Glasher's illegitimate son falling heir to Sir Hugo's fortune. Indeed, in the scenes where the Alcharisi tells Daniel of his heritage, she is deliberately depicted as a kind of doppelganger to Gwendolen. Like Gwendolen, the Alcharisi wanted money, success, and power without having to marry. Also like Gwendolen, the Alcharisi had no inherent desire for children. "Every woman is supposed to have the same set of motives, or else to be a monster," she explains. "I am not a monster, but I have not felt exactly what other women feel—or say they feel, for fear of being thought unlike others" (628). And in the same manner that Gwendolen cannot engage emotion apart from surface representation, the Alcharisi acts her feelings. "[E]xperience immediately passed into drama, and she acted her own emotions" (629).

Importantly, however, unlike Gwendolen's amateurism, the Alcharisi is portrayed as a true professional artist of the caliber of Klesmer. Upon showing Daniel a picture of herself as a young woman, she interrogates him, "Had I not a rightful claim to be something more than a mere daughter and mother? The voice and the genius matched the [beauty of my] face. Whatever else was wrong," she insists, "acknowledge that I had a right to be an artist. . . . My nature gave me a charter" (664). In other words, like Klesmer's claim to true professional art via natural selection, the Alcharisi insists that her inherent talent demanded that she live for her art. Thus the naturalness of the Alcharisi's superb artistry becomes equated not only with Klesmer but with the double meaning of natural production critics used to distinguish Eliot's own genius: intrinsic ability coupled with a peculiarly feminine gift.

But the Alcharisi is missing a crucial facet of Eliot's aesthetic economy. "I am not a loving woman," she admits to Daniel before they part for the last time. "It is a talent to love—I lacked it. Others have loved me—and I have acted their love" (666). This confession circles the narrative back to the portrayal of Gwendolen in front of her mirror at the novel's onset. Like Gwendolen's initial solipsism, the Alcharisi cannot feel for anything or anyone beyond the self; but unlike Gwendolen, she is not in a position to learn emotion. Rather, the novel's potent articulation of a strong female artist is sacrificed in lieu of investing her son with this universal, feminine sympathy.

And, indeed, American critics came to conflate their uneasiness over the Alcharisi with what they interpreted as Daniel's inappropriate femininity. Importantly, Daniel's feminization is a function of his race. The "naturalness" of Daniel's Judaism (inscribed by nature as part of his body) is credited with having endowed him with his broad-based, sympathetic morality. And so even though he carries the talent to love that the Alcharisi lacks, he, too, becomes a threat to the highbrow realist aesthetic represented for American readers and high-art literary magazines by Eliot's universal, feminine compassion, Klesmer's aesthetic economy, and the process of Gwendolen's metamorphosis. In charged language, A. V. Dicey finds Daniel "incurably weak" and "a slave to circumstances" ("II" 246). Tellingly, Dicey summarizes, "He has, it is true, a charm. His mother calls him a 'beautiful creature,' and throughout the whole description of the interview between son and mother you feel it difficult to think she is not addressing a daughter" ("II" 246). In turn, R. R. Bowker classifies Daniel as a species of strong femininity, "strong with man's strength, tender with the tenderness of woman," yet says it is Daniel's "literary misfortune that he is placed in conditions which in many minds attribute to him effeminacy" (71). For just as the Alcharisi's bid for true artistry is undermined by her mannish qualities (her inability to love), Daniel's bid for occupying the moral center of the novel is undermined by his weakness, beauty, charm, and tenderness. In either case, their gender is deemed somehow inappropriate—or to use the Alcharisi's term, monstrous. And what is more monstrous to class-anxious American readers than the specter of watered-down heredity, in these cases represented as mannish womanhood and feminine manhood? Thus Daniel's essential Judaism works to emasculate him as a character—at least in the eyes of certain American readers—and keeps him from performing the role of a traditional romantic hero.

In order to contain and even excise this threat of racial taint, Daniel and the entire Jewish entourage are read, in the words of James, as "hardly more than shadows," thus alienating them from the perniciousness of their racial embodiment. In turn, of course, this critical assessment makes *Deronda* into a gap-ridden narrative, splitting the Jewish from the English story line and giving what Stowe called her "heart's blood"—the "pure" blood of commiserating, white, highbrow readers—to Gwendolen over Daniel, the representation of secure Anglo femininity. In this manner, Gwendolen's realness works as a security over what is deemed Daniel's Jewish impotence.

The desire to excise the racial threat posed by Daniel and the Alcharisi was strong enough that an anonymous American author wrote a sequel to *Daniel Deronda* in 1878. Named *Gwendolen* and subtitled "Reclaimed," the novel's first three pages have Daniel admit to the "gradual obliteration of his Jewish orthodox views—consequent upon his observing Jewish life *in reality*" (emphasis added 27). When substantiated beyond an abstract, spiritual quest for nationalism, in keeping with the realistic rhetoric of high-art journals, Daniel finds the Jewish people "degenerate," "debased," and with both a "depravity of nature" and a "parvity of honor" (64). Witnessing Jewish people up close, Daniel comes to the conclusion that "as a nation they would only unite gross traits, and that even as individuals they were totally unqualified and undesirable rulers over themselves, much less over others" (64). In other words, when Jewish people are no longer part of the philosophical, idealistic, and romantic plot of Eliot's original novel—when they become embodied or "real"—Daniel finds them loathsome and uncivilized. He gives up his quest for a Jewish nation-state not because he rethinks his theology; rather, he is disturbed by the corporeal perseverance of Jewish people, and he does not wish to see "gross traits" perpetuated.

Early on in *Gwendolen*, Mirah dies a sudden death, and when Daniel buries her, he also happens to find the grave of the Alcharisi—an unmarked grave consigned to anonymity since she died outside the faith. This sacrilege is so powerful to Daniel that he kneels before his mother's blank tombstone, making a vow that "from hence forward her persecutors were his enemies" (74). The next day, the narrator tells us, the "bodies of his wife and mother were placed in Christian sod, and a fitting monument erected over them" (74). Thus *Gwendolen* enacts a number of "reclamations," erasing the triple threat of race, gender, and class as well as the specter of mannish or deviant female artistry/productivity. Of course, *Gwendolen* concludes with the final, and most important, "reclamation" of Gwendolen by Daniel, and the two are married in a Christian ceremony. (Gwendolen, too, is purged of all former infectious behavior—Lydia Glasher becomes the repentant Widow Glasher, and the narrator repeatedly affirms Gwendolen's chastity, piety, and purity of heart.)

As such, this sequel serves as a resolution of all prior disjunctions, eliminating the two heads of *Deronda*'s narrative, redeeming the sexual-racial body of both the Alcharisi and Daniel, eradicating the complicated position of female artistry/productivity, and rewarding Gwendolen as the repository of real American value—specifically the values of *Harper's* primary readership. Further, this sequel brought *Daniel Deronda* firmly into the theater of mass production: *Gwendolen* itself is an unabashed sensation novel, replete with European monasteries, secret messages, Parisian rendezvous, and a mysterious Oriental mogul who orchestrates and finances the Daniel-Gwendolen reunion and, in the end, turns out to be the long-lost childhood love of Gwendolen's mother, Mrs. Davilow. But apart from its affinity with novels Eliot disparaged most, the American cultural desire for and consumption of a sequel like *Gwendolen* exposes the popular culture appeal of Eliot's work in the United States. Paradoxically, while American critics championed *Deronda*'s aesthetic excellence and Gwendolen Harleth's realistic sublimity in attempts to cast Eliot and her work as art beyond time, milieu, and the market, the appearance of *Gwendolen*—like Eliot's own treatment of Gwendolen Harleth—reveals *Deronda*'s reliance on the very systems the book discredits, namely advertising, consumer culture, and the false professionalization of nineteenth-century authorship.

Chapter Four

"Proclaiming the Royal Lineage to the Average Mind"

High-Art Aesthetics, the Novel, and Competing Femininities in Elizabeth Stuart Phelps's The Story of Avis

Appearing a year after *Daniel Deronda*, the publication and reception of Elizabeth Stuart Phelps's *The Story of Avis* serves as a culminating case study of the historical, political, economic, and aesthetic trends encountered by Stowe, Eliot, and Phelps throughout the 1870s. Where Eliot had repudiated false professional strictures, Phelps amalgamated the market role of the professional within her own aesthetic vision. Where Stowe had tried to claim an aesthetic and specifically feminine sensibility akin to, but decidedly removed from, Woman's Rights, Phelps saw her art as intimately bound up with the suffrage and worker's rights movements, going one step further than Stowe's representation of Lady Byron to articulate, in *Avis*, both a blatant artist-heroine as well as a mythological country of womanhood—a country symbolized by the metaphorical concept of an all-encompassing Sphinx. And where both Stowe and Eliot had resisted commercial trends (even when employing them), Phelps had less difficulty commodifying her artistry and selling it to the group of readers she most hoped to influence: those "helpless, outnumbering, unconsulted" women.

Like *Lady Byron Vindicated* and *Daniel Deronda*, *The Story of Avis* appeared after Phelps had secured a prominent position as a well-known writer. A little less than a decade before *Avis*, Phelps published *The Gates Ajar*, a novel she claims to have written to ameliorate suffering from women who had lost husbands, sons, and fiancés in the Civil War. Because *Gates* depicted heaven as a domestic idyll—replete with hearths and puppies and ginger snap cookies—many in America and England found the book's message blasphemous. Yet American sales neared 100,000 before the end of the century, and British sales exceeded even that.[1] Prior to this success, Phelps had been an obscure writer from Andover, Massachusetts.[2] Afterward, however, she became an important part of the New England literary community—as well as a member of the elite circle of *Harper's* contributors—thus participating as a full-fledged professional in the transatlantic literary marketplace.

But while *Gates* and her other novels served self-conscious social functions, for Phelps *The Story of Avis* came to represent a specifically artistic endeavor. A year after publishing *Avis*, she wrote to Henry Wadsworth Longfellow that it was the only book that from "a literary point of view, I am at all willing to own."[3] Unlike the novels Phelps explicitly wrote to palliate suffering or encourage reform, her investment in *Avis* rested on its merit as an aesthetic work.[4] "'The Gates Ajar' was by far the most popular of all my books, and I have myself little doubt that it has done the most good," she explained in a letter to one of her fans. "[But] I regard [*The Story of Avis*], as altogether my best, in the literary sense of the word. My heart goes with its purpose, too, most unreservedly."[5] Perhaps this need to assign unique and personal praise to *Avis* was partly the result, as Christine Stansell suggests, of the novel's autobiographical features. "The same age as Elizabeth Stuart Phelps," Stansell notes, "Avis [Dobell] is also single and from a small seminary town, beautiful, vibrant, and a brilliant artist. . . . [S]he is . . . obviously Miss Phelps' ideal self" (247). Yet Stansell's tidy one-to-one correlation does not suggest why, with regard to *Avis*, aesthetics should take precedence over other aspects of Phelps's "ideal self."[6]

I believe Phelps emphasized *Avis* as a testament to her aesthetic competence because she wished to position herself in relation to high-culture connoisseurship, while still employing the form of the popular novel—a kind of middle-class, consumeristic medium. Indeed, by exploiting incongruities inherent in the form of the novel itself (simultaneously a high-art as well as a commercial genre), Phelps attempted to write a book that would bring together, through the lens of Woman's Rights, the world of high-literary culture and the emerging discourse of professionalism with advertising and other commercial systems that were increasingly organizing the corporate marketplace. To these ends, *The Story of Avis* is Phelps's literary articulation of her ideal aesthetic—as I explained in chapter one, one she called "feminine strength." Itself paradoxically elite and plebeian, enduring and disposable, this ideal of feminine strength allowed Phelps to write both a learned, arcane sort of novel (a type of high art she equated with Eliot) while still believing that *The Story of Avis* could capture universal appeal.

But in order to allow *The Story of Avis* to function as both a high-culture and commercial genre, the novel had to enact a series of rhetorical displacements, substituting the narrative's own peculiar brand of feminine strength for all competing aesthetic models that might upset or threaten the position adopted not only by the heroine Avis Dobell but by Phelps herself as the progenitor and prophet of the "Coming Woman." Initially the novel invests Avis with the role of representing feminine strength, effecting the illusion that an exceptionally talented, middle-class, white woman artist like Avis is a permanent icon; that her artistic productions are immortal; and that she will, in homage to other great women of history, usher in the advent of this Coming Woman. To secure what is in effect Avis's professional exceptionalism, the novel substitutes Avis's feminine strength as the reigning moral aesthetic for all other artistic or ethical possibilities, including those represented through other races, classes, and brands of femininity. Indeed, by incorporating images that evoked the public debates on gender, race, and class (suffrage and workers' reform), the novel appropriates current political discourse in service of the high-culture ideal of feminine strength while maintaining a rhetorical sympathy with these broader-based social movements and, by inference, with the "ordinary" or "average" woman. But Avis's status as a professional female artist is inherently compromised by her work as a painter; because the autonomous ideal of a highbrow nineteenth-century painter necessarily engaged his (or her) sensual perceptions in order to produce good work, Avis's aestheticism is inherently sexualized. Thus the novel's attempt to have Avis act simultaneously as a figurative Everywoman as well as an exceptional artist fails.

In the end, then, even the remarkable Avis is finally displaced in favor of the novel's ultimate logo, if you will, for the professional institution of feminine strength—the Sphinx. The novel's figure of the Sphinx attempts to equalize and unify all highbrow/lowbrow ambiguities as the perfect idol of masculinity within femininity, genius within silence, history within modernity, and commercialism within art—thereby avoiding the erotic perils of a woman painter. But the final incongruity of *The Story of Avis* is that while the Sphinx is held up as a permanent emblem of high culture at the same time that the narrative packages, sells, and circulates this immortal exemplar through market systems of mass manufacture and advertising, the critical reception of *Avis* in England and America once again found such feminine strength socially volatile, condemning Phelps for self-consciously adopting a highly arcane writing style—one deliberately reminiscent of George Eliot's—at the same time that reviewers censured the novel's affinities with Woman's Rights, in particular its portrayal of a sexually autonomous heroine stronger in her femininity than the novel's emasculated and sexually deviant hero, Philip Ostrander. In other words, the kind of novel Phelps hoped to inaugurate—one, as she told Eliot, that would "claim the royal lineage of the Coming Woman"—is a novel the critics were not yet ready to accept.

HIGH-ART AESTHETICS, THE NOVEL, AND ENGLISH WOMEN WRITERS

To begin to tease out the disparities between high-art aesthetics and mass culture appeals throughout *The Story of Avis*, it is important to keep in mind that unlike her other fictional works, Phelps wrote *Avis* to emulate and pay direct homage to British women writers—specifically Elizabeth Barrett Browning and George Eliot. Throughout the 1870s to the mid-1880s, Phelps was quite successful in achieving a widespread association with Eliot in the American literary press. Before Eliot's death, for instance, American critics characterized Phelps as an "apt pupil" of Eliot, Eliot being described as a writer "whom Miss Phelps very nobly worships"—though in matters of style and technique, Phelps was almost always characterized as being at a decided disadvantage to her British peer (Preston 486). That Phelps was repeatedly coupled with, yet simultaneously marked as an artist inferior to, Eliot must partly arise—apart from issues of literary taste—from Phelps's own rhetorical stance. Time and again, Phelps denied commercial or sycophantic motives for her homage by constructing a position as Eliot's American emissary, a mere conduit for the greater author's voice. "[I was t]he miserable victim selected for this sacrifice," she informed Eliot, speaking of the lecture series at Boston University she gave on Eliot's works,

> determined to conquer or die under your great banner. . . . [But] I write to tell you how great the interest seems to have been in my *subject*. Hundreds were turned away from the little College Classroom, for whom there was no admittance; and outside the University, the interest felt in the matter by the Boston people . . . was very kind. This I attribute to my subject, since I have never lectured in public, and have little fitness to attract an audience.[7]

Here Phelps performs two discursive feats. On the one hand, she fashions herself not just as an amateur lecturer (with "little fitness to attract an audience") but as a "victim," selected by some unknown group or person for the "sacrifice" of giving these talks. As such, Phelps suggests an unwillingness to carry out the lectures and is only able to bolster her seeming lack of self-confidence through the depiction of Eliot as the real speaker—the subject that garnered such "great interest." On the other hand, Phelps still details her own fame by cataloging the various kinds of attention she received at Boston University and in the city itself: the lecture hall was packed, "[h]undreds were turned away," and the Boston press was "kind" in showing its "interest," though Phelps is careful not to specify what, precisely, interested the greater Boston public—Phelps herself or her subject matter. Indeed, nowhere in the letter does Phelps actually stipulate that anyone told her how much he or she was taken by Phelps's theme; rather, Phelps attributes the community's admiration to Eliot, allowing herself the privilege to promulgate both Eliot-as-artist as well as Phelps-as-public-figure. Here and elsewhere, then, Phelps enjoys her own role as a popular figure patronized by Eliot as her aesthetic mentor. Rhetorically speaking, this dual performance circumscribes Phelps as the civic mouthpiece for a literary celebrity (the representative of popular culture) and Eliot as the great artist (the sign of eminent creation), thereby allowing Phelps to participate in theaters of American production at the same time that she claims an aesthetic acumen and superiority equated with British belles-lettres.

Indeed, so intertwined was Phelps's American image with Eliot's that by the time she wrote *The Story of Avis*, critics claimed to discern the imprint of "the greater novelist" on virtually every page—"so that it may be fair to wonder," one mused, "whether this novel would have been written if 'Middlemarch' had not appeared"

(*Nation* 202). In his commentary on *Avis*, Bayard Taylor called Phelps's reliance on Eliot the most marked feature of the entire work. "[T]he strongest characteristic of the story," he asserted, "is its unconscious betrayal of intellectual influences which have been working upon the mind of the author. . . . [A reader] will find George Eliot, in the author's constant comment upon and explanation of the words and actions of her characters" (367). Of course, the appeal in miming Eliot's fictional style stemmed from Phelps's desire to appropriate culture; *The Story of Avis* deliberately rewrote the transcendent experience Phelps claims to have had reading *Aurora Leigh* as well as a good deal of the plot from Eliot's *Armgart*, a verse drama on the spiritual and moral development of a female opera singer.[8] *Avis*'s reliance on prior *künstlerromane* by Barrett Browning and Eliot signals a dual desire: Phelps's need to assert and exploit an intimate relationship to prominent British women writers as well as to produce a high-culture piece of art. Indeed, it is perhaps no coincidence that Phelps chose to revise an epic poem and a verse drama, thereby linking *The Story of Avis* to two of the most highbrow forms of English literature.

But while Phelps self-consciously appropriated style and content from *Armgart* and *Aurora Leigh* to replicate intellectual art, she also broke with this same tradition, writing her *künstlerroman* through the most popular literary form of the mid- and late nineteenth century—the novel. This choice points to Phelps's conviction that the novel was the best medium for disseminating her ideal of feminine strength to the populace, and in terms of the literary marketplace, Phelps was quite right. As discussed in the Introduction, while the fact-based practices of telegraphic news informed its readers of real-world events, even a quick perusal of such pieces shows that while engrossing, they were often harsh, limiting, or mean and served to fracture, rather than unify, a cross-Atlantic discourse. Poetry, of course, was the literature of the elite and a financial risk to publish in book-length form; while an epic such as *Aurora Leigh* might be compelling enough to captivate a well-educated Andover girl of sixteen, most middle-class families were exposed to verse in magazines, restricted to lyrics and occasional poems. It is true short stories were favorites of Phelps, and late in her career she contended it had long been her conviction that "more art, so to speak, is required for the making of a good short story than for the making of a long one" ("Stories that Stay" 118). But in terms of *Avis*, the novel had two advantages over short fiction: it allowed Phelps to develop her main character over space and time, thus deepening her argument for feminine strength, and it potentially linked people across states as well as the Atlantic in ways a story or a poem could not. As Ronald Zboray has shown in regard to American literary history, the explosion at mid-century in novel-making and its wide dissemination by rail provoked a crisis in the cohesiveness of provincial communities yet, too, proffered a solution "in the form of illusory, print-oriented connectedness that could pose as community" (79). If Phelps's high-art conception of feminine strength was to reach the widest readership possible, Phelps understood how it must be packaged and sold. The novel would allow her readers a kind of multiple citizenship—in their own communities, their own nations, the transatlantic community, and, of most importance to *The Story of Avis*, the country of womanhood, a country accessible only through an international circulation of popular print.

PROFESSIONAL PERILS FOR THE FEMALE PAINTER

In order to narrate this transatlantic country of womanhood, then, Phelps looked to a fictive paragon, a character who could integrate Phelps's aesthetic ambition with her market savvy. As such, Phelps embodies this ideal in the character of Avis Dobell, a professional painter, proto-feminist, and woman of unusual beauty. The novel's primary tension turns on Avis's precarious position between the aesthetic's notorious and almost requisite display of artistic passion and the newly dispassionate workings of professional artistry that were developing at the same time Phelps wrote and completed *Avis*.

Notwithstanding the proliferation of professional venues for American artists between 1850 and 1880—including art academies, international art exhibitions, and the establishment of professional organizations for artisans—prior to the Civil War, American women did not have sustained access to such schools and organizations.[9] If women pursued visual arts like painting, they were instructed within the family or by securing private tutors under an apprenticeship model of vocational training. Should a woman obtain the opportunity to attend a formal academy through some special dispensation (such as being the daughter of a well-known artist), still she was not permitted to attend classes alongside men, paint or draw from the life, or hear anatomy lectures—activities assumed to compromise decorum. Even public galleries were deemed offensive to young ladies: in 1856, the Board members for the Pennsylvania Academy of Fine Art resolved that "a close fitting, but inconspicuous fig-leaf be attached to the Apollo Belvidere, Laocoon, Fighting Gladiator, and other [statues] as are similarly in need of it" in their galleries (Huber 12).

This tension, of course, resulted from the slippery convergence of three designations—"professional," "middle-class woman," and "artist." Though a middle-class woman did not perform professional work per se, as mentioned in the Introduction, like the professional her work was largely invisible, not easily translated into discrete products. Also, while a middle-class woman could not admit the kind of aesthetic and sensual passions integral to the work of a nineteenth-century artist, she was imbued with higher sensibilities, often described as her organ of sympathy. And with the new social insistence on credentialized skill as a marker of middle-class status, women who aspired to artistry sought the kinds of training afforded men. Female artists went so far as to form their own life classes, private salons for painting *être au poil*—a practice that in the eyes of many risked their propriety. One outraged citizen wrote to James Claghorn, President of the Pennsylvania Academy:

> Does it pay, for a young lady of a refined, godly household to be urged as the only way of obtaining knowledge of true art, to enter a class where every feeling of maidenly delicacy is violated, where she becomes so hardened to indelicate sights and words, so familiar with the persons of degraded women and the sight of nude males, that no possible art can restore her lost treasure of chaste and delicate thoughts! There is no use in saying that she must look upon the study as she would that of a wooden figure . . . ! Living, moving flesh and blood, is not, and cannot, be studied thus. The stifling heat of the room adds to the excitement, and what might be a cool unimpassioned study in a room at 35°, at 85° or even higher is dreadful.[10]

Here the threat of studying art is more than a passing taint—like a woman who loses her virginity, once the female artist's "delicacy is violated," the damage is permanent with no means to restore the "lost treasure" of her sexual ignorance. Though it is tempting to read this critic's tirade as the revelation of personal eccentric fantasies (the writer does, after all, seem to relish the details of "[l]iving, moving flesh and blood" as well as the "stifling heat" and affected "excitement"), American art institutions took such commentary to heart, and while some few formally admitted women on a regular basis as early as the 1850s, the National Academy of Design did not introduce a Life School for women until 1871, while the Pennsylvania Academy waited until 1877—the same year Phelps published *Avis*—before allowing its female pupils to draw from the male nude (Rubinstein 40).[11] This public controversy parallels *The Story of Avis*'s primary anxiety: the question of how to professionalize a "lady artist" without risking her virtue.[12] Not surprisingly, the novel's attempted remedy is feminine strength.

THE TAINT OF "FRENCH" AESTHETIC INFLUENCE

The novel begins its instruction on professional female artistry by introducing Avis as a set-apart expert—like Lady Byron and Gwendolen Harleth, an exceptional woman. Throughout the beginning of the book, we are privy to scenes supporting Avis's exceptionalism. She grows up in Harmouth, an Eastern university town where it is "quite the proper thing" for girls to be "somewhat seriously intelligent" (16). Her mother, who dies while Avis is still a child, was an actress before marriage, a "freak for the stage" quip the Harmouth ladies (21).

But according to Avis's father Professor Dobell, her mother was a true artist, "not like most women, given to magnifying every little aesthetic taste into an unappreciated genius. She had, beyond doubt, the histrionic gift. Under proper conditions she might have become famous" (25). In a sense, then, Avis is endemically predisposed toward genius and fame, and these predilections do seem to manifest themselves as part of her basic constitution. For instance, she despises ordinary housework, and her reactions to cleaning, cooking, and sewing are immediate and visceral: "I hate to make my bed; and I hate, hate, to sew chemises; and I hate, hate, hate, to go cooking round the kitchen," Avis insists, adding, "It makes a crawling down my back to sew" (27).

In addition to her "natural" predilection for intellectual work, Avis also undergoes special training that excites and develops her intrinsic genius. While still a child, instead of making pudding, Avis steals away to read *Aurora Leigh* in the seclusion of an apple bough. In a style associated with Phelps's own initiation to Elizabeth Barrett Browning's poem, Avis "plunge[s] into that idyl of the June, that girls' gospel" (31). And like Phelps herself, Avis is a prime receptor for such induction: "As few poems are ever read, as only an imaginative girl can read those few, Avis in the apple-bough read on and on" (31). Once Avis perceives Barrett Browning, she feels armed in reading, and declares to her father a vocational ambition quite distinct from that of typical Harmouth women: "I have decided this morning that I want to be an artist. I want to be educated as an artist, and paint pictures all my life" (33). From here, Avis is begrudgingly allowed to train in art, taking to her task with "stern, ungirlish doggedness" (37). She is mentored for six years in Europe, and under this hard-won tutelage, Avis "plunge[s] into a life which extremely few women in America found it either possible or desirable to lead" (35–36). Upon her return, we are informed by Avis's best friend Coy Bishop that she has "got into the newspapers" for selling a painting in London (8). "It was seldom that a Harmouth woman got into the papers," confides Coy. "It was only men—at Harmouth: indeed, the University existed," Coy supposes, "for the glorification of men" (8). Clearly, then, Avis's exceptionalism is predicated on a series of ungirlish or masculine traits—traits both innate and a result of environment. Avis demonstrates native intelligence as well as native ambition; she has the taste of an aesthete; she resists parental authority; she applies herself to her vocation with diligence; and by the time she becomes a professional artist, Avis is a self-made individual successfully competing in a marketplace for profit, selling good pictures in London, making it into the papers—a public persona.

Yet even at the outset, the novel works hard to secure the "weakness" within this "strength": Avis's femininity. Importantly, this femininity is chaste and class-bound, clearly set apart from improper or plebeian forms of womanhood. At a reading Avis attends in the novel's opening chapter, for instance, her decorous clothing and aspect are juxtaposed against an artistic reaction she has to a carmine curtain—a reaction both elaborate and sensuous. While the color carmine is said to impress Avis so much as to feel that she would beat herself against it—"even if she had beaten her soul out with it"—her clothes are the quintessence of modesty, with a "very full white undersleeve, . . . [that] completely concealed the outline of the arm," and a profile, silhouetted against this luscious curtain, said to retain "the harmony of a strong antique," implying her looks are old-fashioned and of the proper rank (7).

This ploy of depicting a conventionally feminine yet self-reliant woman—obviously a model of feminine strength—might have proved convincing to Phelps's readership had Avis not been an artist. Five years after Phelps published *Avis* she wrote *Doctor Zay*, a novel attempting to balance similar gender tensions around the issue of a professional female doctor—yet, in the end, a book that could take for granted Doctor Zay's stoicism: her professional demeanor whose clinical severity affirmed her feminine virtue. But Avis is an artist. Carmine is not a mere color; rather, it excites a "positive wave of pleasure" in Avis from "sight and contact" (7). As a child, Avis is "electrically prescient" to nature; indeed, when spring comes the year she meets Philip Ostrander, her narrative foil, Avis "throb[s] to it as if perplexing magnetisms played upon the lenient May air" (53). Studying art in Paris, she finds the ambiance of a Catholic church "tropical," and upon glimpsing Philip in this holy place, a "great tidal wave of color surge[s] across her face" due to the "eye of that amber god across the Madeleine" (39). Consequently, a crucial element of Avis's exceptionalism is her sensual passion; the narrator often tells us that Avis sees the world through the eyes of an artist, and as such, feels with a subtler sensibility.[13]

Thus, in Avis's attempt to claim the position of both professional and artist—positions necessarily opposed to typical women's work (i.e., visible, productive, domestic, iterative)—she blurs the boundaries not simply between these terms but confounds her role as a middle-class woman. As such, Avis must display her credentials and her purity in order to ensure her femininity and her strength, but this necessity is jeopardized on a number of levels. For one, she is the offspring of an actress, and while her father's social status in Harmouth guarantees Avis a unique environment for artistic development and expression, the trace of her mother's questionable predilections troubles Avis's social position at the level of primogeniture. In addition, Avis is anything but a typical Victorian woman; dedicated to her painting, she has no intention of marrying. Instead, she treats her work as wedlock. "My ideals of art," Avis tells Philip Ostrander, "are those with which marriage is perfectly incompatible. Success—for a woman—means absolute surrender, in whatever direction. Whether she paints a picture, or loves a man, there is no division of labor possible in her economy" (69).[14] With this assertion, Avis reveals that her work is both sexualized and domesticated, equated with the "absolute surrender" of erotic passion yet also with "labor" and "economy"—which, in this case, make Avis's art interchangeable with a woman's role in marriage ("loving a man").

But Avis's professional training is the practice that incriminates her the most. During the 1870s many middle-class Americans made European tours. These tours were, in part, attempts to dramatize one's social supremacy, especially in terms of fashion, theater, etiquette, and the arts. Experiencing Europe marked a middle-class family as "select." Yet at the very same time that the Continental Tour distinguished the American middle class as consumers and appropriators of European culture, certain aspects of that culture were deemed potentially deleterious, especially to young women. France, in particular, emerged as one of the focal points of American anxiety, especially after the 1867 Paris Exhibition, when the notions of the painter's garret and groups of free-love bohemians became a romantic staple for aspiring American artists. Thus Avis Dobell, as a young and innocent American girl, compromises her textual standing for receiving French tutelage.[15]

Clearly, Avis travels to Europe to learn painting because Europe, on a broader scale than England alone, represented cultural depth and continuity. And just as Phelps herself turned to an idea of Eliot as her artistic predecessor, Avis must learn her art at the "source"—in this case, the source of great nineteenth-century painters like Courbet or Verlaine: Paris. Indeed, shipping Avis off to study in Paris was commensurate with the practices of real-life Victorian women artists in the 1860s and 70s—and they, too, encountered gender prejudice. For instance, May Alcott, sister of Louisa and an aspiring artist in her own right, recalls "the brave efforts made by a band of American ladies some years ago" against exclusionary art scenes in France:

> [ladies] who supported one another with such dignity and modesty, in a steadfast purpose under this ordeal [of not being allowed in life classes], [that] even Parisians, to whom such a type of womanly character was unknown and almost incomprehensible, were forced into respect and admiration of the simple earnestness and purity which proved a sufficient protection from even their evil tongues. (48–49)

In an attempt to safeguard the reputations of American women studying in France, Alcott sets up an essentialist distinction between "the indiscreet, husband-hunting, title-seeking butterfly" (Alcott's version of the typical American girl abroad) and serious, modest artists who are a type of woman "unknown" to the French (48). In this manner, Alcott sterilizes what is, in truth, a rather incriminating movement—groups of women establishing their own life classes in Paris. Ironically, Alcott casts the butterfly as the imprudent and improper figure, utilizing her charms to procure a husband and a title, while it is the earnest and pure women artists who gather together to sketch naked forms in private salons. Indeed, Alcott is so defensive that she attributes an overall cleansing influence to these artists, women who not only dignify artistic practice but rehabilitate the moral meanness of Parisians in general, introducing them to a class of woman apparently incomprehensible to degenerate French imaginations.

Avis, then, imperils her standing as a virtuous and innocent heroine by becoming the mentee of Thomas Courture, a painter best known in America for his 1847 work entitled the "Romans of the Decadence" (or more commonly "Orgy")—a sensuous portrayal of semi-naked, bacchanal Romans.[16] And it is without question that in order for Avis to become what the fictive Courture believes she has the potential to be—a great artist—she has to study the naked body in both life classes and anatomy lectures.[17] While it is never affirmed that Avis has had such training, her attention to physical beauty and her sensitivity to the sexual gaze (e.g., feeling Philip's eyes "concentrated upon her—upon her lifted face, her arrested motion, her *responsive attitude*—like a burning-glass") serve to implicate Avis in a knowledge that, given her upbringing, could only come from exposure to representations of sex and sexuality (emphasis added 38–39).

Indeed, the very first piece of Avis's work the novel mentions is a charcoal sketch of Una; we are told Avis's lion follows her Una "in a shadow almost as heavy as that which hides the Jupiter in Correggio's Io,—dark, vague, and inscrutable as fate" (9). This allusion to Antonio Allegri da Correggio's "Jupiter and Io" (1531) further reveals Avis's understanding of sexuality by exposing an attraction to mythic subjects in which women are ravished. In Correggio's rendering of the myth, Io, rapturous under Jupiter's nimbuic embrace, epitomizes a sexually enthralled woman. Like Una, Io "succumbs" to a transmogrified God; in Correggio's painting, Io's capitulation is portrayed as willing compliance—her lips open to his kiss, her left arm embracing his form, her head tilted back, eyelids half closed. And although Philip discerns Una's readiness for flight in Avis's painting—"[e]very nerve and muscle" tense—the narrator tells us that it is "impossible to look upon this woman, and not say, 'She sees the man she loves.' Her eyes leaped to him; her lips leaned to him; her whole being gravitated to him" (9). These details are direct appropriations of Correggio's accommodating Io.

But perhaps the most culpable moment comes when Courture tells Avis that she, in effect, has graduated. "Mademoiselle," he declares, "I will give you two years to make a reputation" (37). Avis has an orgasmic response to this assessment:

> Avis, standing with her slender thumb piercing her palette, and her brushes gathered with it, thrust out her empty hand with a gesture which the great artist admired more thoroughly than he understood. Her magnificent, rare pallor swept over her face, and the quality of her features heightened. . . . She reminded him at that moment of Soddoma's [sic] Roxana, in the Alexander's marriage at Rome. (37)

Without reading too much into this description, it is hard not to dwell on the narrator's choice of diction, especially verbs of sense. Avis's thumb "pierces" her palette; she "thrusts out" her hand; and a dazzling pallor "sweeps" over her face. This moment, then, is encoded with the language and imagery of sexuality. Importantly, the moment is also likened by Courture to a highly erogenous painting by Giovanni Sodoma, entitled the "Marriage of Alexander and Roxane" (c1512). In Sodoma's painting—one of three commissioned frescos on the walls of Chigi's bedroom in the Farnesina in Rome—Roxane waits, disrobed, poised in a seductive attitude on the edge of her bed while a cherub draws her lover towards her. Raphaelesque in subject and manner, the "Marriage" has been characterized by art historians as a work that evokes a "pleasurable atmosphere of sensuousness" using "warm-shadowed" colors and naked cherubs in an overtly erotic scene, "intending a more luxurious appeal [than] the intellectually-planned sonorities of Raphael" (Freedberg 140–141). For

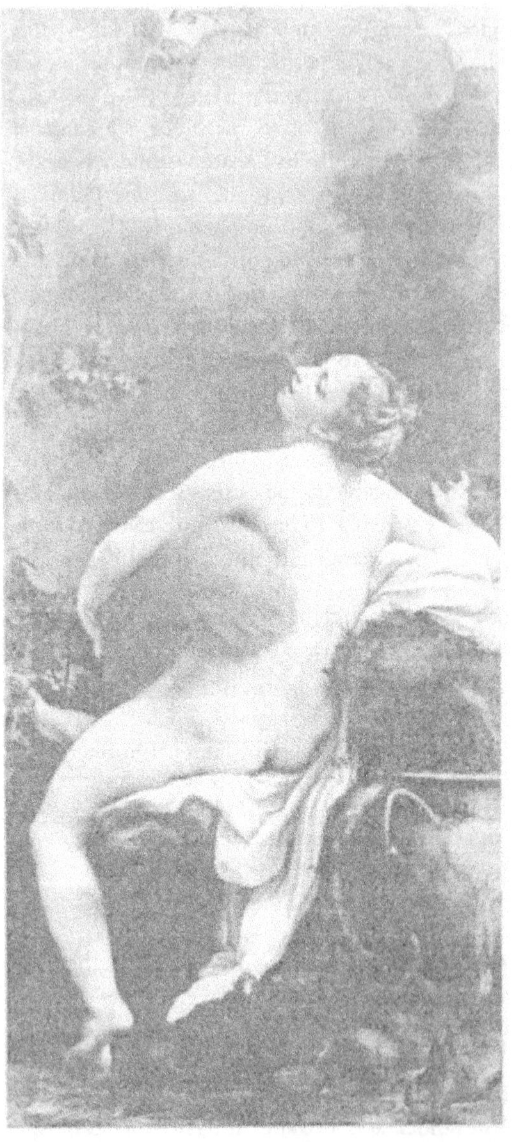

Figure 4.1. Antonio Allegri da Correggio (1489/94–1534), "Jupiter and Io" (1531), canvas, 163.5 × 74 cm, Kunsthistorisches Museum, Vienna, GG274.

Avis, then, achieving an expert's recognition results in a loss of innocence akin to sexual initiation. In turn, this makes Avis's exceptionalism deeply erotic as well as deeply European, thus removing her further and further away from the mainstream audience Phelps claimed she wanted Avis to influence.

Figure 4.2. Giovanni Sodoma (1477–1549), "The Marriage of Alexander and Roxane" (c1512), fresco, Farnesina Villa, Rome.

FEMININE STRENGTH AND NARRATIVE DISPLACEMENT

Taken together, then, Avis's innate qualities and subsequent foreign experiences accrue to eroticize as well as exoticize her position in the novel, putting into question her modesty, innocence, middle-class status, and the appropriateness of her designation as an American female artist. As *The Story of Avis* unfolds, then, the novel must employ increasingly extravagant tactics to assuage Avis's "Frenchness" and eroticism in favor of her feminine strength, especially as Avis evolves from a specific, exceptional personality into a mythic, Everywoman figure—a figure with whom all readers are supposed to identify. This necessity results in a series of rhetorical displacements, beginning first with substituting Avis's feminine strength in place of Philip's masculinity; then inserting Avis's whiteness and middle-class status in the place of other racially "degenerate," class-bound, or conventional female characters; and, finally, supplanting the transnational and epic symbol of the Sphinx in place of Avis's own compromised position as a "French" artist.

In terms of Philip Ostrander, the first thing the narrator notices is his voice—"Musical was the word assuredly" (6). Although described as modest and simple in accent, for Avis its timbre "suffuses" her body with "a penetrative sense of pleasure, of unexplained organic joy" (6). Combining this voice with Philip's interpretative sagacity (he provides the perfect exegesis to Avis's sketch of Una) it is clear that, at the outset, we are meant to find Philip both aesthetically sensitive and sexually exciting—Avis's double. Phelps herself appreciated men such as Philip, whom she defined as literary, serious, intuitive, in delicate health, and, of premiere importance, able to perceive and revere genius in women. Phelps applauded Longfellow for these reasons, especially his admiration of *Avis.* "I have, in fact," she asserted, "never met any other man who showed, from the author's point of view, such a marvelous intuition in the comprehension of an unusual woman; or of what the author of 'Avis' tried to do, in relating her history. 'The Story of Avis' was a woman's book, hoping for small hospitality at the hands of men" (*Chapters* 157). *The Story of Avis* fashions Philip in a manner echoing this sense of Longfellow: Philip is alive to Avis's unusual talents and intellect; his profession is academics; his health is indeed susceptible. But whereas the logics of Phelps's later novel with a similar theme, *Doctor Zay*, follow the hero's progression from a rather insensitive and conservative bourgeois position on women doctors to one that esteems Zay as a professional in her own right (i.e., a novel tracing the progression of a man from solipsist to viable life partner), *The Story of Avis* works in the opposite manner, establishing Philip as the seeming ideal only to expose him as immoral and insensible to Avis's excellence.[18]

The novel's portraiture scene first renders this vivid contrast between Avis and Philip. Avis is the professional, thrilled with the opportunity to put her skills to work ("I am so glad to be at work!" she says—"so gravely, greatly glad!") and clinically observant of her customer (54). "This young woman regarded the contour of a man's face precisely as a physician regards a hectic flush or a bilious eye-ball" (54). And yet, as an artist, Avis must exhibit a sensitivity to beauty and emotion, not just execution. In other words, Avis constructs her aestheticism in terms known to the Romantic and Transcendental poets—harnessing her sexual energy into artistic inspiration. Avis, "like the child of the desert, with her ear at the lips of the sphinx," convinces herself that the "whole world had leaped into bloom to yield her the secrets of beauty" (54). As such, Avis exposes an endemic masculinity, representing her material as, respectively, an inscrutable sphinx or a blooming girl, both offering up their secrets to the watchful, penetrating eye ("I") of the artist. Avis even speaks to Philip as a sexualized object, she the worldly aesthete: "I rarely meet," she tells him, "with beauty in men. I have known several beautiful women" (54).[19]

But even the theater itself—a garden in early spring, a gorgeous man, a beautiful woman—cries out for a romantic interlude, an intercourse exceeding this commercial exchange. And Philip answers, apropos to the moment. In turn, Philip's sexual response returns the artist to art object. When Avis's dress falls with a "faint electric touch against his hand," Philip surprises Avis into a look he perceives as "wide, grave, imperious" (54–55). "Was it the sensitiveness of a young man's wounded vanity," asks the narrator, "that led him to fancy that her lips parted with something of the dumb and delicate scorn that the lips of that Ludovisi Juno, alone of all sculpture that he had ever seen, commanded?" (55). Like Klesmer's assessment of

Gwendolen in the *tableaux*, Philip's image of Avis as Greek sculpture—a dumb one, imperious—serves to fix her in the classic position of aestheticized femininity: silent, inscrutable, deathless yet dead. And the narrator informs us that Avis, though a meticulous professional, indeed enjoys and even courts the masculine gaze—echoing, again, Gwendolen Harleth's inclinations.[20] "She was alive to the nerves of her soul. She was still an unwon woman. She felt even glad sometimes, that there were men in the world who loved her. . . . Men usually married. And it was pleasant to remember that she was not unlovely or unlovable" (55). This admission further feminizes Avis in a traditional heterosexual matrix, putting into question her professional disinterest.

Even the very act of painting a portrait qualifies Avis's bid for disinterested professional status. Not only had Courture enjoined her not to paint too many portraits (for portraits are profit-makers, cheap sell-outs, American versions of art),[21] but the exchange between the portrait artist and her sitter is a flesh-and-blood one, suggestive of life classes and anatomy lectures, those taboo subjects of study.[22] *A priori*, any scene of portraiture is sexualized through this dynamic of scopophilia, an erotics of the gaze, and this particular moment affords the added titillation of a woman as the controlling spectator with a man as the passive and beautiful recipient.[23] The fact that this painting is indeed spectacular is apparent when Coy tells Avis, "I may say that the greater part of Harmouth is familiar with the history and progress of this portrait" (59). Thus, despite the novel's insistence on Avis's exceptionalism and her objective, methodical procedures (even, in the end, her virginal horror at Philip's infidelities), the narrative's logic falters; the supposedly protected status of Avis's expertise is undermined as a function of femininity-gone-public.

This logic grows increasingly complicated and compromised as Philip's wooing develops. In order to preserve Avis's authenticity as a female artist during and especially after courtship, Philip must, by force of circumstance, be sacrificed in terms of his proscribed gender role. Where we were first led to believe in Philip's aesthetic delicacy, we find a hollow performer, a man whose erotic interest quells as soon as his prize is won. Where we thought the experience of war and physical suffering would strengthen his spiritual character (Philip goes off to fight in the Civil War and returns a wounded soldier), we discover, rather, a threatened manhood. Philip turns out irritable, indecorous, incapable of sustained intellectual inquiry, and irresolute, first blaming Avis for soggy cracked wheat and cold coffee; then pursuing a flirtation with Avis's acquaintance Barbara Allen; then losing his position at the college because he can't focus; and, finally, disclaiming his love for Avis and abandoning his two children for a year.

Even his sexual preference is obliquely questioned: Philip's nickname in Harmouth is the Antinous of the college Faculty (60). Antinous was the Emperor Hadrian's teenage lover in the 130s A.D.; after his mysterious death, Antinous became, partly due to Hadrian, a divinized mortal. His popularity stemmed from his unsurpassed beauty; over 2,000 sculptures of Antinous are known either to exist or as discursive artifacts. By the time Phelps wrote *The Story of Avis*, Antinous was a scandalous figure in both England and America. In 1878, one year after Avis's publication, John Addington Symonds applied to the British Museum for assistance with an essay he was writing on Antinous's legacy in art, especially coins and medallions. The only reply Symonds got was that it was "very courageous to ask even artistic questions about him" (Lambert 9).

Thus, with each successive trial Avis must face in her marriage and with each roadblock placed between Avis and her pursuit of art, the reader's sympathies are finessed, meant to be embittered at Philip's selfishness and then led to accept his feminization as inevitable, a sign of his malignity—or, rather, his unprofessional status. "Evil in the Mid-Victorian theodicy stemmed from the inability to realize one's potential," argues Burton Bledstein, "the inability to commit oneself to place and time, to subjugate carnal desires and their distractions, to approach life professionally" (113). When Philip literally dies in Avis's arms—falling from his horse, languishing until Avis comes to rescue him—the novel consummates its own logic. Avis can now remember Philip in the ideal, disinfect his noxious threat to her self-definition, and still manage to claim the position of the professional—the very role Philip himself was meant to occupy, a role both staunchly autonomous and always in a state of progressive becoming.

But without a price? One consequence of this move is Philip's unbelievable ineptitude to Phelps's contemporary audience. Admittedly, the novel tries to subsume Philip's unhealthy femininity into Avis's feminine strength—or to use the novel's own language, "a certain manhood" in Avis, "latent in every woman . . . [,] an instinct of strength or an impulse of protection which lent its shoulders spontaneously to the increasing individuality of her burden" (178). Through the regulating discourse of *The Story of Avis*, Avis's subject position must be elided into an all-determining gender position, privileged over any other identity which might trouble her professional status. At one level this means emasculating Philip, removing all symbolic social markers of white, Victorian, professional male authority, such as achieving prominence in a vocation, supporting a family, having a strong constitution, avoiding sexual indiscretion, and engendering a son (indeed, his son Van is so weakened by a childhood illness that he dies while Philip is abroad). But like the critical response to Daniel Deronda's feminine attributes, nineteenth-century critics were dismayed at Philip's portrayal, and their comments reveal a dual fear of feminized men as well as mannish women. *The Literary World* found Philip "unnatural, because self-contradictory" (98), while *Harper's New Monthly Magazine* saw him as "exceptionally and unnaturally weak" (310). Other periodicals denigrated the novel for its affinities with Woman's Rights politics. *The New York Times*, for instance, thought *The Story of Avis* presented "a partisan defense of woman's rights; the best men are but sad specimens of humanity compared to the intricate and thrilling souls of women" (2). This same reviewer exonerated Philip in the classic reasoning of double-standardism: "[T]he rude, impartial reader, if he be a worldling, will feel very sorry for Ostrander, notwithstanding the little weaknesses of which he is guilty" (2). Some readers actually felt Philip deserved the chance for rebuttal. The *Chicago Tribune* held that "Ostrander's defense should be undertaken. . . . The errors and shortcomings of Ostrander—which were of no very heinous character—are magnified to the utmost" (9). And Gail Hamilton, writing a four-part review of *Avis* for the *New York Daily Tribune*, scoffed at the story's violation of the laws of novelistic romance. "But having made Philip noble in order that Avis should be able to love and marry him," reasoned Hamilton, "it becomes necessary to make him ignoble in order that Avis should have her Story. Instantly Miss Phelps turns about and strikes him down into a commonplace, or rather below a commonplace, vulgar domestic villain" (2). Indeed, Hamilton's assessment summarized most opinion on the subject of Philip: "A man who could so appreciate and admire and satisfy a woman like Avis is rare. A man who could be capable of such slow, cold, unwinking ferocity toward a wife is also very rare. That these two should be the same man is impossible" (2).

Yet the novel goes even further than substituting Philip's masculinity with Avis's feminine strength: in addition, the narrative displaces class and racial subjectivities other than bourgeois whiteness—elided into a single other—with Avis's normalizing gender position, one inherently white, cultured, and, paradoxically, exceptional. Avis's "unique" gender—a gender contradictorily expounded as the norm—is advanced as the inevitable result of her race and class.[24] In terms of race, Avis's "magnificent, rare pallor" (as sexualized by Courture) appears again and again throughout the book, especially at moments when Avis displays the inappropriate masculine emotions of anger or lust. When Professor Dobell dismisses Avis's appeal to become a professional artist with "Poh, poh!" and "Nonsense!," Avis's anger literally whitens her body: "At that moment she became, for one of the very few times in her life, absolutely pale" (33). In turn, when Courture is aroused by Avis's pallor—and she by his compliment—he equates its rareness with a work of art.[25] Similarly, at the climax of the novel when Philip flirts with Barbara and is accidentally discovered by Avis, she is again paralleled to art—this time to white marble, a reproduction of the Milan Venus:

> His wife in the doorway . . . stood colossal. She was paler, perhaps, than need be, in that red drapery. She gathered it, for it had fallen almost to her knee, in one hand. The other was thrust into the empty air. She had never reminded [Philip] of her great Venus as she did at that moment. In the blind action of her arm and figure was something of the same shrinking as of a creature from whom a shield had been torn away. . . . By degrees her pallor deepened dreadfully. Her features seemed to grow thin and sheer like a marble medallion of a spirit. (185)

This hyperbolic bleaching occurs only in moments when the reader is meant to sympathize with Avis's strength—when Avis claims a masculine prerogative to inappropriately strong emotion and, consequently, action. Following these respective "decolorizations," Avis defies her father, claims her right to be a great artist, and leaves her husband. Yet the narrative's iterative portrayal of Avis as timeless art supposedly allows her the ability to claim masculine, middle-class whiteness without hazarding her femininity.[26] And because Philip is renounced and written out of the book—the embodiment of normative masculine whiteness—Avis claims this title in place of Philip, seizing its power for herself and, by association, bequeathing it to her daughter Waitstill, the novel's substitute for patriarchal legacy.[27]

But masculinity and whiteness are not the only appropriations the novel makes for Avis. In terms of class, Avis's feminine strength is set in comparison to "degenerate" or incomplete women as represented through the character of Susan Wanamaker. Susan is delimited as degenerate by her questionable class rank, which is a function of her racial background. And unlike other novels where Phelps's heroine does not have the added threat of artistic passion with which to contend, Avis must also be set-apart from—and preferred over—not just bestial men or working-class women but women who occupy various standards of white, middle-class femininity: Philip's mother Waitstill Ostrander, Avis's Aunt Chloe, the coquette Barbara Allen, and even Avis's best friend Coy Bishop.[28]

Reminiscent of other deformed, indigent, working-class women in Phelps's prose fiction—*The Silent Partner*'s Catty Garth; "The Tenth of January"'s Asenath Martyn; or Sary Jane and her sister in "The Lady of Shallot"—the character of Susan Wanamaker is a deliberate narrativistic insertion.[29] In this case, as a symbol of the laboring woman, Susan works to secure Avis's class and trouble Philip's by laminating Avis's artistic eroticism and sexual knowledge over Philip's degenerate past. The narrative tries to assert, with incidents involving Susan and later Barbara, that Avis is a lady because the idea of an affair would never cross her mind. Further, Susan as the would-be wife of Philip, Avis's doppelganger, is kept in a necessary position of abjection, the victim of domestic abuse, scarred and uncouth. Susan is a book peddler, a designation blatantly demonstrating her non-professional status as a hawker rather than a creator or mass distributor of books, and she bears a literal scar upon her forehead to complement the figurative injury upon her heart—that Philip seduced and left her after they were supposed to be married. Indeed, it is tempting to read symbolic import into Susan's scar. Where Avis's source of power stems from her connection to Pallas Athena—the white-browed goddess of wisdom who sprung whole from Zeus's forehead—Susan is oppressed by the book trade and marked as one who is not an intellectual nor privy to the luxuries of high culture such as leisure reading.

True to the gender reversal already established by the narrative, Philip is exploited as an object of sexual exchange between Susan and Avis. The difference lies in how the two women deal with Philip's sexual indiscretions rather than the question of whether one will win him. Both in manner and look, Susan's entire approach is coarse:

> 'I saw you at the funeral,' proceeded [Susan] abruptly, disregarding Avis's words. . . . 'And once I went to the chapel-church to see you. I don't blame him. Why, I shall see that face of yours till I die! And I'm a woman. *He* was a man. Oh, you think I've come to taunt and torment you! Women do such things. . . . I'm not jealous: I'm only desperate. I'd like to see the man that was worth, down at the core of him—worth a woman's getting jealous for. . . . When I knew him, he was such a handsome boy! Oh you've got him—and I've got a brute! That's the difference between us. It's a monstrous difference! It's a monstrous difference!'
>
> She unfolded her thin hands from the old shawl in which she had held them wrapped while she stood talking. . . .
>
> There is a force peculiar to itself in the mere anatomical appeal of an emaciated hand. It is difficult to believe in the grand despair of a person with plump fingers. . . .
>
> '[Philip] got tired of me. I thought he would get tired of every other woman.' (163)

Although Avis is nonplused at first—"at a dead loss how to conduct a scene like this"—she grows "paler and paler" under Susan's indiscreet talk, indicative, of course, not of weakness but of a gathering control (161). When she finally speaks, the narrator characterizes her demeanor as aloof and cultured, as if her initial bewilderment is conquered by good breeding: "'We will not discuss my husband any more this morning, if you please,' said Mrs. Ostrander, collecting herself, not with severity, but with a touch of stateliness" (163). By adopting a "stately" comportment and the language of bourgeois protocol ("if you please"), Avis maintains an advantage over Susan, even in the wake of realizing she has made the mistake of marrying her own brand of brute. Importantly, the narrator refers to Avis as "Mrs. Ostrander" in this moment, a rare appellation, one that distinguishes her own marital fidelity as well as her proper class status. And all of these aspects of Avis's behavior are coded as essentially feminine, from her politeness to the insertion of her married name to her stately "collection" as opposed to the barbarism of "severity."

Susan, on the other hand, has lost her bid for femininity precisely because she failed to marry the man who aroused her erotic desire. As such, Susan's own passions are masculinized as well as racialized in order to cleanse Avis's artistic, feminine ones. Not only is Susan married to an alcoholic abuser (and in Phelps's fiction, alcoholic men are invariably of the laboring class or a "brown" race), Susan's manners are lacking, her talk crude, and her body emaciated—all plebeian or masculine markers, ones that are presented as innate to any woman bearing such a scar, "coal-cold eyes," "meagre dress" and an emotionless, "monotonous" voice with which she talks of unsavory topics (161). Even the narrator's attempt to construct this scene as an intimate one between women is finally undermined. Although we are told, "It is not often that we are reminded of the quickly-flashing capacity for passionate attraction and generous devotion which renders the relation of woman to woman one of the most subtle in the world," the next sentence reveals that "[t]his little wretched, excited creature turned her face from Avis with a sense of having divinely outwitted her" (164). Thus Susan is duly stripped of her subjecthood, a "little wretched, excited creature," while Avis retains her name and dignified individuality. Despite the narrator's insistence to the contrary, there is no egalitarian woman-to-woman relation here.

In the end, proving Avis's superiority *vis-à-vis* Susan is easy. Like pitting Avis's demeanor and comportment against Philip's degenerate inclinations, both substitutions are finally a rather conventional insertion of highbrow for lowbrow culture. But to privilege Avis's feminine strength in relation to women of her own race and class proves more tricky. With Philip's mother Waitstill, Avis's assertiveness and self-will are juxtaposed against the mother's typically feminine self-effacement. Because the mother has never reprimanded Philip for his disregard or indifference of her, Waitstill is a victim of her own timid reticence, left "sick and alone" and without any outside help. The only time Avis meets her is when the old woman is about to die, and during this brief interview, Avis gleans that it was Philip who kept his mother from coming to their wedding and that Philip refused to bring Avis a prized pair of wedding-slippers her mother-in-law had specifically saved for her. But the mother doesn't actually tell Avis these things; she merely says, "He was a good boy—he was always a good son to me. I never lacked for any thing" (146). Instead, Avis learns of Philip's neglect through a kind of heightened feminine sentience, an almost telepathic exchange between them:

> [S]omething seemed to stir from eye to eye between them, and to crawl cold about the heart of the wife. . . .
>
> Had Philip . . . *neglected* his mother,—his old mother, sick and alone? It was not a question for the wife to ask: it was not one for a mother to answer. Like spirits, the two women met each other's eyes, and neither spoke. (145–146)

This moment marks the first time in the novel that Avis fully realizes that her husband is a selfish, petty man, and whereas the mother had always kept quiet about Philip's character flaws, Avis increasingly rejects and repudiates them from this point forward. Through this flash of insight, Avis takes up the mother's unspoken sorrow, turning the expected silent suffering of conventional womanhood into a forceful and vocal rejection of men's wrongs. This initial substitution of active feminine rebellion in lieu of traditional feminine acquiescence is symbolized in two important ways: first, Avis takes the cherished wedding-slippers home with her, ironically noting that "Perhaps Philip could not be expected to know what a sacredness it would have added to her marriage-day to have worn [them]. Perhaps no man could" (147). Second, Avis names her daughter after Philip's mother, deliberately teaching her daughter to live a life quite opposite of the one in which Waitstill Ostrander remained quite "still," "waiting" for her son.

But such a literal substitution—the second Waitstill for the first—is less common throughout the novel than ones requiring more intricate substitutions and relying more heavily on ambiguous cultural distinctions. As previously mentioned, Avis rejects housework on the grounds that it produces a crawling down her back. "[M]amma never cooked about the kitchen," she insists, "I think that is a servant's work" (27). Housework does not befit Avis's natural temperament—the crawling is a physical response, presented as innate—and she is too finely organized to engage in servant's work, the mindless labor of the working class. In order to justify Avis's pretensions as well as equate her stance with Woman's Rights rhetoric (i.e., equating housework to slavery), the novel constructs domesticity as the province of comic, foolish, or simple women. Avis's Aunt Chloe is the one who cooks, sews, and makes beds in the Dobell house—the spinster aunt. Often the comic butt of the novel, she is said to have "high ideals in cupcake" (26). In fact, even though Aunt Chloe's social status is equal to Avis's, she is depicted as ridiculous, with not much more on her mind than "pickles and hot biscuit" and the proper digestion of her brother's stomach. Here the novel plays on a stock comic character in nineteenth-century American fiction, the fastidious New England old maid.[30] And even though Avis and the narrator mock Aunt Chloe in order to place Avis's domestic scorn in a cultural space above Aunt Chloe's mundane preoccupations, it could be argued, too, that the ridicule itself accentuates Chloe's oppression, thus bolstering, in another way, Avis's position as a kind of mouthpiece for Woman's Rights.

For example, there is a tender scene in which Avis asks Aunt Chloe if she ever wished for a career. "My dear Avis," Chloe begins in a subdued voice, "I suppose all of us have times of thinking strange thoughts, and wishing impossible things. I *have* thought sometimes—if I could begin life over, and choose for my own selfish pleasure, that I would like to give myself to the culture and study of plants. I should be—a florist, perhaps, my dear; or a botanist" (114). As such, Avis's repudiation of the physical, repetitive work of servants might be said to elevate Chloe's professional consciousness; after their heart-to-heart, Chloe knits a pair of "stone-china colored stockings" with "Turkey-red toes," an insignia of Chloe's own, quiet rebellion (115).[31]

But perhaps the most difficult comparison occurs between Avis and two other young women of equal age: Barbara and Coy. Both are generally "useless" as a middle-class woman is expected to be: Barbara is known for her curls and accomplishments at the piano, Coy for her piety and conventional views. Like Avis, their work is largely invisible: where Avis's is primarily brain-work, their use-value remains hidden beneath pretty observances and turns of head. Indeed, because both Barbara and Coy could be considered of equal or higher worth to a woman such as Avis, it is of paramount importance that Avis's "culture" be distinguished from and elevated above theirs without resorting to the kinds of displacements used to disempower Philip, Susan, or Aunt Chloe. As a result, the novel portrays Barbara as a flirt and, moreover, an unwitting one. Not only does she serve as the instrument of Philip's ultimate degradation, but when she, herself, finally understands the possible magnitude of her imprudence (allowing a married man such as Philip to hold her hand and compliment her curls), she is quickly placed out of the narrative frame, relegated to the position of mere feminine conceit—a place that denies the kind of "culture" Avis embodies. "[Barbara] had made up her mind that it would be best for her to marry before long. . . . Barbara had never been in the least in love with Philip Ostrander. But, strictly speaking, it could not be said that she had ever quite forgiven him for not having fallen in love with herself before he married Avis. . . . Barbara thought she should marry a minister" (196). Barbara's brand of femininity finally fails to threaten Avis's bid for professional female artistry because she is so obviously Avis's mental and moral inferior, a woman who cannot comprehend the aesthetic and spiritual value of representation—merely the representation itself.

Coy, however, is more complicated. At one level, Coy appreciates Avis, fully understanding the value of an exceptional woman. In fact, in the opening line of the novel, Coy asks the book's central question, a question echoing *Daniel Deronda*'s initial question about Gwendolen Harleth: "What *was* it about her?" (3). Of course, this is the question that the inquisitive and receptive reader is supposed to ask, ponder, and answer over the course of reading the novel.

In addition, like Courture and Philip, Coy sees classical and antique features in Avis, ones that transcend temporality, likening Avis to the immortality of art. At one point Coy asks Avis, "Did anybody ever tell you [your arms] were like the arms of Mme. Recamier, in David's picture?" (18). In the latter half of the nineteenth-century, Jacques Louis David was best known for his imitations of antique subjects and attitudes in combination with realistic depictions: "his ideal [was] the synthesis between style rigorously applied and nature truthfully recorded"—an ideal Avis herself seems to desire (Leymarie 22). David's portrait of Mme. Récamier (1800) strikes a viewer by contrasting the thin lines of static furniture with the reposed figure of Mme. Récamier—curved, animate, and lithe, bare-headed, bare-footed, and, importantly, bare-armed. Thus Coy guides the reader to liken Avis to refined sensuality with perhaps an added intimation to regard Avis as a figure of self-sacrifice in service of a larger project. Although Récamier's portrait itself does not invite such an interpretation, much of David's fame in the 1870s rested on an historic painting, "The Oath of the Horatii" (1784). This painting galvanized Parisian emotions over the French Revolution and was said by Victorian art critics to have launched the art of painting into the modern era. Classically figured, "Horatii" celebrates "the

Figure 4.3. Jacques Louis David (1748–1825), "Madame Récamier" (1800), oil on canvas, 174 × 244 cm, Musée du Louvre, Paris, INV 3708.

Roman virtue of self-sacrifice in the cause of one's country" (Leymarie 18). Because Avis is similarly martyred for the cause of the "country of Womanhood," it is tempting to interpret Coy's analogy within this larger framework.

But even beyond Coy's ability to appreciate the aesthetic of Avis's comportment, like Avis herself, Coy's imaginative power is creative, organic. For instance, she introduces her personal theory of human temperament, that people resemble metals, by imagining Avis as a magnet, "without alloy, loadstone. . . . Avis had that one particular coloring about her (Coy decided to call it coloring), which is, in a woman, powerful above all beauty, wit, or genius,—that subtile something which we name *charm*" (5). Yet Coy is also ironically aware of the hypocrisy of representation, its inability, for her, ever to transmit the substance of experience—which, for Coy, means an authentic emotive response to nature. "I think it must be very uncomfortable to be an artist," she tells John Rose, her future husband. "You're always looking at Nature with a professional squint: you can't put yourself on any sort of terms with her, I should say, more than a photographer can with a complexion, or a dentist with front-teeth" (12). So even while Coy exhibits perceptions and emotions akin to Avis's, she eschews the profession of artistry, its adulteration of one's natural, or "feminine," encounters with nature.

With the demonstration of these refined and intelligent qualities, Coy poses the most unmanageable juxtaposition to Avis's consummate position; she cannot be handled like Philip or Susan or Aunt Chloe or Barbara, cast as a class or racial or gendered stereotype to be superseded by Avis's supreme culture. The novel's solution? To depict Coy as too conventional, in the end, to transcend her prescribed gender role in keeping with Avis's nobler feminine claim, yet sensitive enough to Avis's greatness to regard her, as she does in the final scene, with "puzzled, affectionate eyes" (249). In other words, Coy epitomizes the sort of woman for whom *The Story of Avis* is written: like Gwendolen Harleth, she is our ideal reader, which is why she both begins and ends the narrative. Rather than displacing her subjecthood, then, in favor of Avis', the novel places Coy on a continuum toward genuine Womanhood, one with Avis's daughter Waitstill as its potential exemplar.

In the end, however, the novel seems to argue that Avis Dobell herself is finally too volatile to represent feminine strength, at least in such a manner as to influence a wide readership. Perhaps this is a function of the kinds of criticism the novel seems to have anticipated and, indeed, received. To nineteenth-century reviewers, all of these various displacements coupled with Avis's overt rejections of traditional feminine roles in marriage and childrearing were perceived as dangerous to middle-class values, and contemporary reviewers blamed Phelps for writing an immoral and pernicious book. On one level, critics were concerned that *The Story of Avis* would influence young women against domestic aspirations. "[Miss Phelps'] influence is dangerous when she urges young girls, who are too often restless and eager for excitement, to leave off giving tasteful touches to the old homestead and go out into the world," warned a writer for the *Galaxy.* "The idea that a woman must be a failure in a home if she has a decided talent for art or literature is a gross libel" (857). This anxiety was specifically targeted at Avis's exceptionalism; writers like Harriet Preston in the *Atlantic* argued that young girls should be more interested in marriage than art, for "marriage is the great central fact of human relations, whereby they exist and must continue. It is not quite so involuntary as birth or so inevitable as death, but ranks so near them that we may fairly apply to it the serene and triumphant saying of Marcus Aurelius: 'That which is universal *cannot* be a calamity'" (488). "In short," concludes the critic for the *Chicago Tribune*, "the Story of Avis is a grossly-partial plea in favor of a gifted, incompetent woman, who weakly, rashly undertook—like too many of her sex—the onerous, yet sanctified, duties of a wife; and then threw upon fate and her husband the blame for hardships for which her own criminal ignorance and selfishness chiefly should be held to an account" (9). What intrigues about these comments is that they apply to Avis the very critique the novel applies to Philip, calling Avis "weak," "selfish," and "ignorant." Of course, the comments also reveal an utter rejection of a novel that tries to make a high-culture, masculine endeavor such as art substitute for a middle-brow feminine norm of marriage—in a sense, rejecting the very idea that popular, conventional novels (often written by middle-class women) may be made to imitate highbrow aesthetic forms.

On another level, however, reviewers deemed the book's influence as exotic—indeed, as a kind of foreign threat to a female readership. The *Philadelphia Inquirer* claimed that in *Avis*, "the author represents unhealthy and abnormal moods of mind and emotions as being natural and typical. . . . There is that about its moral atmosphere suggestive of an air sick and heavy with strange and cloying scents" (273). These critiques compound to suggest that *The Story of Avis* is not just immoral but alien; the *Philadelphia Inquirer* likens *Avis* to illness ("unhealthy," "sick"), disorders ("abnormal"), and deviant sexuality (a "moral atmosphere . . . heavy with strange and cloying scents"). According to the critics, then, *The Story of Avis* was simultaneously dangerous to young women as well as different from them—not at all universal and decidedly exotic. Said another way, the sensuality inherent in Avis Dobell's position coupled with the novel's unconventional amalgam of highbrow and mainstream aesthetics must be kept separate and contained from impressionable female readers—the very readers Phelps had hoped to engage.

Thus, tainted by her training in France, Avis is too sexually aware for a proper middle-class woman, and armed with her Woman's Rights views on work and marriage, she is too stridently mannish to be an icon of universal feminine strength. Yet the novel clearly wishes Avis to take the position of icon, and so the narrative makes another, more extravagant substitution—one that removes the representation of Avis from any specific nationality, gender identity, or immediate political movement by making her the worldly emissary of the Sphinx, a symbol meant to designate immortal, perfect womanhood. To these ends, the final few pages of *Avis* define the novel's epitome of such womanhood not just in professional or artistic terms but mythic ones:

> We have been told that it takes three generations to make a gentleman: we may believe that it will take as much, or more, to make a WOMAN. A being of radiant physique; the heiress of ancestral health on the maternal side; a creature forever more of nerve than of muscle, and therefore trained to the energy of the muscle and the repose of the nerve; physically educated by mothers of her own fibre and by physicians of her own sex,—such a woman alone is fitted to acquire the drilled brain, the calmed imagination, and sustained aim, which constitute intellectual command. . . . (246)

The final transformation for Avis, then, is to become a Sphinx—like Stowe and Phelps's depiction of Eliot, a symbolic Everywoman, the exceptional yet also, paradoxically, the archetypal precursor to this new generation of "WOMAN." As such, the novel can still appropriate contemporary discourse on enfranchisement and equal representation without actually locating its critique of female oppression in an apparent and fixed social context that limits the potential of Avis's art.[32] In fact, each of Avis's previous displacements are rehearsals for this mythic one, wherein Avis—the quintessence of WOMAN—prepares the arrival of a utopic class and race of women who "still await" their apotheosis, embodied, of course, as her daughter "Waitstill."

In order to accomplish this mythic metamorphosis, ironically Avis must relinquish the very aspect of herself that has been causing the trouble all along: her art. Until her visit to Florida at the end of the novel, Avis's artistry has been carefully equated with a divine gift, the misuse of which would be a heresy against God; in this manner, the narrative strives to decorporealize and purify Avis's artistic passions: "God gave her the power to make a picture before he gave her the power to love a man" (69). In order for this logic to play itself out, Avis can only "give in" to her (erotic, bodily) love for Philip when the novel has made it clear that not to do so would constitute a lie against her own soul and God's love, a sacrilege. By transferring her sacred organ of artistic feeling to the love of a man, the narrative attempts to redeem both her own questionable, foreign passions and Philip's weaknesses. Once Philip dwindles and dies, Avis can then restore herself and Philip to sacrosanct status by sterilizing and consecrating their married love to the point that it, too, becomes equated with God. Just after Philip's death in Florida, Avis returns home, "tearless and excited":

> She felt strong and strained. As yet she was filled less with a sense of loss than love. . . . Only [Philip's] ideal visited her heart. She was not without a strange, exultant sense that now she never could see a weakness or a flaw in him again. . . . Their relation seemed to her to run on quite uninterrupted. He leaned over her shoulder to read their undivided life. He had but turned a leaf before her in the story without an end. (242)

Here Avis's love is transformed into one that is ideal, holy, infinite—"without end." What is lost in this transaction, however, is Avis's creative fervor; once her sexuality is self-conscious, undeniably located in the body and not her painting, her artistic vision must wither; indeed, her own great painting of the Sphinx is the last masterpiece she ever creates.

But even this divine love Avis creates for her husband is not traditional—rather, like the rest of the novel, it too is actually blasphemous. For in keeping with all other aspects of subjecthood that trouble Avis's feminine exceptionalism, even this divine love must ultimately come to equal WOMAN rather than God. The novel achieves such transpositions via a series of allegorical substitutions, wherein Christian, Greco-Roman, and English myth are retold as stories about the benevolence and wisdom of omnipotent womanhood with Avis as the mythic heroine. For instance, at one juncture Avis is likened to the Greek Ariadne, a mortal who provides Theseus with the ball of string to get him out of the labyrinth and who is later abandoned by him on the island of Naxos. At another point she is equated with Eve, blamed by Adam for the fall of humanity, and at still another moment she becomes Brünhilde, forsaken by her lover Siegfried in old Norse mythology. In the traditional versions of these myths, each of these women is abandoned or used as scapegoats by their male hero-partners. Like Avis's revision of Waitstill Ostrander's life of "waiting, still," Avis's story transposes the mythic figures' combined helplessness into a narrative in which she—as Ariadne, Eve, and Brünhilde—leaves Philip. But Avis doesn't just abandon the story's pseudo-hero; rather, in the mode of an artist, after his death she remakes his image into a vision of manhood in the service of WOMAN, thus placing herself closer in kind to yet another divinity whom she is said to resemble, Isis—the Egyptian fertility goddess who brought her brother-husband Osiris back to life.[33]

Of all of these mythic transpositions, however, the most pervasive and striking is the revision of the myth of the Sphinx as a myth of universal WOMAN—at first glance an odd revision to choose, given that the Sphinx is a violent, rapacious monster rather than a goddess of fertility or virginity or a protectress of women.[34] Yet the Sphinx serves the narrative as a plastic signifier, able to contain any and all elements and render them WOMAN, whether they be traditional feminine markers, masculine designations, or renegade elements such as all that is not-white, not-genteel, not-American, or not-English. Indeed, the Sphinx subrogates all aspects of perfect WOMAN that have been articulated throughout the novel: the figure of Avis herself, the philosophy of feminine strength she articulates, and the sanctity of Avis's art.[35] As such, the Sphinx is actually an apt symbol for Avis because she encompasses the same contradictions and dangers inherent in the novel's formulation of feminine strength: she is a literal man-eater, a woman-creature with a recognizable torso and monstrous lower half, implying sexual threat. Yet she also represents knowledge and the precise balance between feminine sensibility and masculine power.[36]

In Avis's early dream-vision, which induces her to paint a celebrated picture of the Sphinx, this creature comes to mean, quite clearly, the impenetrability of all womanhood—regardless of race or social position, religion or level of education:

> They swept before [Avis] in file, in procession, in groups. They blushed at altars; they knelt in convents; they leered in the streets; they sang to their babes; the stooped and stitched in black attics; they trembled beneath summer moons; they starved in cellars; they fell by the blow of a man's hand; they sold their souls for bread; they dashed their lives out in swift streams; they wrung their hands in prayer. . . . [B]ut surely at last, and with piercing vividness, . . . [s]he saw a low, unclouded Eastern sky; fire to the horizon's rim; sand and sun; the infinite desert. . . . In the foreground the sphinx, the great sphinx, restored. The mutilated face patiently took on the forms and the hues of life; the wide eyes met her own; the dumb lips parted; the solemn brow unbent. The riddle of ages whispered to her. The mystery of womanhood stood before her, and said, "Speak for me" (*Avis* 82–83).

Figure 4.4. Elihu Vedder (1836–1923), "The Questioner of the Sphinx" (1863), oil on canvas, 92.07 × 107.31 cm, Museum of Fine Arts, Boston, 06.2430.

This repeated image of Avis listening intently to the whispers of the Sphinx undoubtedly comes from a famous painting by American artist Elihu Vedder, Phelps's contemporary. Vedder's painting, "The Questioner of the Sphinx" (1863), shows an Egyptian man, hand covering his own mouth, crouched before the great ruins of the Sphinx with his head pressed to the Sphinx's lips. In a similar manner, Avis is both listener-pupil to the Sphinx as well as the appointed the interpreter of the Sphinx's universal womanhood—like Vedder, Avis becomes the Sphinx's "author." In a sense, then, the narrative circles back on itself, first creating Avis as the icon of Phelps's feminine ideal, then mediating Avis through the mythic vision of the Sphinx, and finally granting Avis, through the Sphinx, the power Phelps herself claims as a literary artist—to "speak for" universal womanhood.

MYTH AND THE COMMODIFICATION OF HIGH-ART AESTHETICS

Nina Auerbach offers an incisive argument against these mythic substitutions in *Avis*. Though she admits feminist issues dominate the novel, she contends that "the archetype of the removed woman artist permits author and reader to abjure attaching to them a local habitation and a name" (482). As Avis is circumscribed as the eternal feminine, placed above market value, the "artist [is] so rarefied a being that she is never threateningly representative," insists Auerbach, and "by equating art with nunlike devotion," *The Story of Avis* "effectively remove[s] it from the sphere of society" (481). In other words, the narrative works in an historical vacuum, rendering Woman's Rights a political consciousness without language, form, or nation.

Auerbach sees this sort of narrative logic as fanciful, at best, and dangerous, at worst. But rather than attack *Avis* as a weak feminist or even antifeminist novel—so defined in terms of its real-world exegesis of political enfranchisement—I am inclined to ask why Phelps dehistoricizes Avis's experience. Why would Phelps be committed to portraying feminine strength outside of a specific socio-economic or political movement? Simply to make her critique "safe" by placing it beyond the bounds of her own milieu? It seems to me that when one reads *Avis* against the prodigious feminist and personal writings by Phelps, one sees precisely the reason why she chooses this vehicle for Woman's Rights. Phelps's activism, like her Christianity, deliberately exists out of time, out of nation, in an utopian and mythic setting because Phelps sought to replace Calvinist Christianity with proto-feminist Christianity. As such, she had to write narrative that mimed myth.

Ironically, this Christian proto-feminism actually allows *The Story of Avis* to be commodifiable in the literary marketplace at the same time that it tries to articulate that uncommodifiable commodity, "WOMAN." *Avis* serves to isolate and safeguard what was one of the most essential social rituals of Victorian society: eliminating the importance of natural feminine productivity to secure the pleasures of mass, mechanistic productivity and consumption.[37] (The Sphinx, at the close of the novel, is photographed to pay Philip's debts—sold into the equivalent of *Gates* cigars and collars.) But whereas the *Gates* series depicted a heaven in which impermanence was made into "permanent" commodities—i.e., spiritualism made manifest in never-ending supplies of gingersnaps—*Avis* undertakes a more difficult substitution with regard to consumption. Here, consumption is not just the pleasure of instantaneous and perpetual ownership as with *Gates*; rather, in *Avis*, consumption requires pleasure in the very effort it takes to acquire ownership. As Burton Bledstein and Magali Larson note, those who strive for professional status must engage in processes of delayed gratification, and so such a highbrow form of consumption is another mark of the novel's attempt to professionalize *Avis*'s narrative— to cast it as a high-art genre.[38] Yet this emphasis on an aesthetic, rather than economic, view of Avis's art finally backfires: Avis's art, and thus her bid for professional stature, dies when she, herself, is "owned" by Philip's love; when the narrative itself, however, "owns" Avis—

romanticizing her into a mythic Sphinx figure meant to attract a universal audience through processes of mass circulation—conversely Phelps's novel "dies" at the hands of critics.

Like Stowe and Eliot, Phelps participated in the literary marketplace at a precise cultural moment, one when advertising converged with capitalism and professionalism to synthesize a highly stratified cultural matrix of book production and circulation across the Atlantic. When Phelps first entered the literary marketplace in the late 1860s, it was the commodity that made and sold cultural value via trained systems of strategic advertising—advertising that included, and in some ways depended upon, the commodification of literature.[39] Indeed, with the advent of mid-Victorian bestsellers, a transnational marketplace, and successful systems of advertising, literature was increasingly conflated with its own promotion and publicity: with puffs, reviews, and popular talk. Literature "sold" identity, and widely read writers like Phelps were touted by publishing houses as spokespeople who represented the yearnings, morals, and values of their audience *en masse*.

While the novel's ambitious project—to articulate a country of womanhood out of time and therefore out of history yet one with fictive bonds strong enough to hold women on both sides of the ocean united in a common cause—is indicative of the paradoxical nature of a widely disseminated high-art novel, the irony is that Phelps's novel didn't sell particularly well. Phelps failed to engage a broad audience, either through her articulation of the Coming Woman or through her figuration of the mythic Sphinx. In the novel's attempt to garner a devoted following through the revision of medieval, biblical and classical myth as well as the placement of the Woman's Rights debate into a mythic sphere, Phelps actually lost her readership as well as her mythological country of womanhood and its citizens. Phelps was perplexed and dismayed by the onslaught of bad reviews of *Avis*, deciding, finally, that like those who resisted her political commitments to temperance and, later, antivivisection, *Avis*'s detractors simply didn't have the sensibility with which to appreciate this new brand of highbrow/lowbrow novel; they were all, ultimately, a bunch of bumbling, crude Ostranders. "If there be one lesson above another which experience in moral reforms teaches a fair-minded person," writes Phelps many years after publishing *Avis*, "I think it is patience with the averseness of those who do not join in our own particular methods of improving the world. Lack of sympathy with these is quite as likely to signify want of head as want of heart; or simply to indicate a deficient imagination, or one strung below its key" (*Chapters* 227).

In the abstract, Phelps's belief in a middle-class medium put to high-art ends—ends not elite but universal, available to all—reveals a democratic, rather than meritocratic, commitment to aesthetic access. She implored Eliot to write "a *great novel* to proclaim the royal lineage of the Coming Woman to the average mind," precisely what *The Story of Avis* attempts to do, combining, in a sense, the patrician ethos denoted by diction such as "proclaim," "royal," and "lineage" with a desire to reach and elevate through this ethos the "average mind."[40] But a redefinition of the novel along these lines proved critically fatal, and her critics were simply not ready to accept her vision. In a sense, Phelps herself became a kind of Waitstill—at the close of her own life, still awaiting the public recognition for *The Story of Avis* she fervently believed the novel deserved.

Afterword

To raise the question of the relation of Stowe, Eliot, and Phelps to such concepts as "professionalism," "femininity," "aestheticism," "transatlanticism," and "reading" is to embark on a problematic journey. First, the very notions of these concepts are hard to understand or explicate fully. Each encompasses a broad cultural arena; for instance, we know from a myriad of feminist historians that the idea of Victorian femininity permeated everything from the parlor to politics, slavery to imperialism, theater to portraiture, midwifery to mercantilism. Further, each concept has behind it an excess of historians and literary critics who debate its meaning. Nineteenth-century femininity alone has been understood to mean both an essential, inborn trait and a societal construct; it has been touted as a sort of personal or group power and, of course, as an instrument of political oppression; it has been relegated to middle-class, white, heterosexual status and been called integral to the formation of working-class, homosexual, and/or racial identities; and it has been located in contradictory places—madonnas and whores, privileged whites and black slaves, prepubescent bodies and full, maternal figures. In addition, even if historians and literary critics establish certain parameters for defining each of these abstractions, their application to specific authors and their texts still proves a difficult task. Not only is one constrained by the limits of cultural criticism—the impossibility of reconstructing precise discursive or ideological formations no matter how detailed or involved one's research, not to mention the hindrance of occupying a late-twentieth-century worldview—one is also curtailed by just how far any claim can be made that, say, writers like Stowe or Eliot took such-and-such a stance in relation to professionalism or aestheticism or the process of reading each other's novels. The cultural critic is forever caught between the desire to attribute certain literary threads to this or that social movement and the snares of presuming any sort of authorial intention.

However, I want to suggest that it is the confounded nature of this study that actually offers the greatest potential for critical insight. The work of Stowe, Eliot, and Phelps might be examined most provocatively not as discrete bodies of "American" or "British" literature, or as representations of a domestic or realistic literary terrain, or even as illustrations of proto-feminist thought. Rather, the writings of Stowe, Eliot, and Phelps initiate, at least for me, questions about the complex and often contentious position of writers in relation to what we have come to call culture. When this project began, I intended to study a rather traditional theme (traditional, at least, in terms of feminist literary history): the depiction of a female artist figure in novels and letters by Victorian women writers in both England and America. As my research progressed, however, it became clear that such images were in conversation with historical and social trends beyond the prose. Most notably, I stumbled on recurring links between female artists both within and outside of texts simultaneously creating and being created by the precepts of professionalism. In turn, I began to see disjunctions between different kinds of professionalism and how these were incorporated into literature and literary practice. It became clear, for instance, that professionalism demanded contrary allegiances to the realms of highbrow aesthetics and lowbrow marketeering or, as I mentioned at the beginning of this study, the illusion of "payless" work and the status afforded by salaries. And these disparities begot more, especially as I began to examine simultaneous cultural trends dealing with gender, reading, art, the market, or transatlantic communication technologies.

Thus I came to realize that images of artistic femininity cannot remain in local contexts if one is to explore the connections among literature, history, and cultural power that move beyond literary or aesthetic particulars to consider how texts articulate and are articulated by the social. What I've discovered is that while each of these concepts informs my reading of Stowe, Eliot, and Phelps, at the same time insights offered by, say, the narrative of professionalism often countermand those culled from a study of aestheticism. In other words, putting these three authors in dialogue with "professionalism," "femininity," "aestheticism," "transatlanticism," and "reading" brings about a greater sense of paradox than it does resolution. Yet I am convinced that this approach, while messy and incomplete, accomplishes at least two things of value: it more closely imitates the workings of nineteenth-century culture itself—multiple, contrary, and palimpsestic; and it enlarges itself as it progresses—prompting me, in retrospect, to ask what has been left out of this study and what I need to consider next.

Notes

INTRODUCTION

[1] Elizabeth Stuart Phelps [ESP], letter to Richard Watson Gilder, 13 November 1908, Richard Watson Gilder Papers, Manuscripts and Archives Division, NY Public Lib., NY. By 1908, Phelps went by her married name Elizabeth Stuart Phelps Ward, but for the purposes of clarity, this study retains her unmarried name throughout.

[2] ESP, letter to Richard Watson Gilder, 10 November 1908, Richard Watson Gilder Papers, Manuscripts and Archives Division, NY Public Lib., NY.

[3] For a discussion of economic language and its relation to the rise of professionalism in the United States, see chapter two on "Space and Words" in Burton Bledstein's pioneering study *The Culture of Professionalism.*

[4] ESP, letter to Richard Watson Gilder, 10 November 1908, Richard Watson Gilder Papers, Manuscripts and Archives Division, NY Public Lib., NY.

[5] See Jonathan Freedman's *Professions of Taste.*

[6] For a summary of Phelps's relationship with Stowe, see Phelps's autobiography, *Chapters from a Life*, pages 131–140. Not only was Phelps a visitor to the Stowe household in Andover, she was once a guest at Stowe's summer home in Mandarin (or as Phelps erroneously names it, "Magnolia"), Florida.

[7] Stowe, of course, became a best-selling author with the serial publication of *Uncle Tom's Cabin* in 1851–1852. *Uncle Tom's Cabin* is purported to have made Stowe $10,000 from the first three months' sales alone, what a reviewer for the *London Times* called "the largest sum of money ever received by an author, either American or European, from the sale of a single work in so short a period of time" (Hedrick 223). In the first week, the novel sold 10,000 copies, and in the first year that number climbed to 300,000. The novel sold even more copies abroad than in America; by the end of 1852, various legitimate and pirated editions made for one-and-a-half million sales in England, and the book was translated into more than forty languages, including Dutch, Swedish, French, German, Italian, Danish, Flemish, Polish, and Magyar (Mott 118). Indeed, the sales and distribution patterns of *Uncle Tom's Cabin* are often

credited with creating the very category of modern-day "best-seller." In turn, Eliot's most popular work was *Adam Bede*, published in three volumes in 1859. In England, *Adam Bede* went into second and third editions (unusual for three-volume novels), selling more than 10,000 copies in the first year, and in America, *Adam Bede* outsold every other Eliot novel, at least until the end of the nineteenth century. Indeed, J. Henry Harper noted in *The House of Harper* that "[s]ome critics have assumed that the stories by George Eliot would appeal rather to the thoughtful few than to the great world of novel readers, but our experience with the sale of her works shows this supposition to be ill-founded" (388). The novel was translated into German, Dutch, Hungarian, French, and Russian. As Eliot's modern biographer Gordon Haight notes, "No book had made such an impression since *Uncle Tom's Cabin* swept the world" (*George Eliot* 279). Finally, Phelps launched her literary fame with *The Gates Ajar* in 1868, a novel that sold even better in England than it did in America and that reached a total of 81,000 copies in the United States by 1897. Like *Uncle Tom's Cabin* and *Adam Bede*, *The Gates Ajar* spawned numerous pirated editions and was translated into Dutch, Italian, German, and French. Reviewing *Gates* for *Blackwood's Magazine*, Margaret Oliphant noted that the "wonderful success of the 'Gates Ajar' is of itself one of the most touching facts of literature . . . [, and this] little book sold, we believe, as many as a hundred thousand copies" ("American Books" 436). Indeed, over twenty years after its publication, *The Literary World* told a sentimental tale of how James T. Fields of Fields, Osgood and Company decided to take a chance on *Gates*, much to his benefit: "The success of the work was phenomenal . . . , and Miss Phelps's name was on the lips of everybody. She had struck a new vein in fiction, and imitators of her style and manner sprang up on all sides. Less than two years after *The Gates Ajar* had seen the light, a friend dropped into Osgood's cozy library one night, and seeing him with a book in his hands, asked him the name of it. '*The Gates Ajar*,' he replied, 'and a mighty good book it is, too. We are printing our fortieth thousand.'" See *The Literary World*, 20 (27 April 1889): 148.

[8] ESP, letter to Henry W. Longfellow, 27 February 1879 (bMS Am 1340.2 [5815]), Houghton Lib., Harvard U., Cambridge, MA.

[9] This quotation comes from Bradbury's outstanding study on material and metaphoric traffic across the Atlantic, from the conquistadors to modern-day treks of the Concorde. "It's a well-known fact that the wide Atlantic Ocean, which, according to your viewpoint, either links or separates the continents of Europe and America," comments Bradbury, "has generated a roaring trade not just in gold and silver, slaves and sugar, cotton and crack, Scotch and Bourbon, the Rolling Stones and Madonna, but a stranger and more elusive commodity: images" (1). See *Dangerous Pilgrimages*.

[10] Although there is a century-long tradition of literary criticism devoted to transatlantic study, see, most recently, Malcolm Bradbury's *Dangerous Pilgrimages*, Peter Conrad's *Imagining America*, Marcus Cunliffe's *In Search of America*, Hugh Honour's *The New Golden Land*, Christopher Mulvey's *Anglo-American Landscapes*, and Robert Weisbuch's *Atlantic Double-Cross*. Bradbury's study is the most even-handed in its depiction of literary influences both ways, although he, too, falls prey to limiting his discussion to male writers.

[11] Weisbuch defines this anxiety as two-fold, encompassing a possible lack of outer and inner resources in American writers, including both resonating material from which to write (such as a sense of national history or culture) and a finely attuned sensibility that is the hallmark of good writing. In Weisbuch's formulation, it is necessary for him to perpetuate the very constructs of nationality his study claims to break down, in particular "British cultural stability" and "American instability." Accordingly, the British can claim originary status—and thereby authorship—whereas the Americans flail about, unable to locate their aesthetic origins either in the nation's landscape or in an author's soul that has not been Anglicized. Not only does Weisbuch invoke and maintain artificial stabilities and instabilities, then, he writes a literary history that requires antagonism, where "enmity is the keynote" (xviii).

[12] For instance, after finishing *Oldtown Folks*, Stowe wrote to Eliot about her trepidations that the book was about to be published in England. She fretted that her novel was so "intensely American" that she feared "it may not out of my country be understood"—yet in good faith, she "cast it like a waif on the waters[.]" In turn, Eliot was conscious of both the disapproving and positive press *Daniel Deronda* received in America, and because Phelps had read the contentious British pamphlets published on *The Gates Ajar*, she worried how *The Story of Avis* might be perceived in London. Harriet Beecher Stowe [HBS], letter to Mary Ann Evans [George Eliot], 15 April 1869, Berg Collection, NY Public Lib., NY.

[13] Thomas Richards's study details the symbolic value of the Crystal Palace as a "monument to consumption" and links its representational import to mid-century depictions of the commodity in Dickens's novels, industrial paintings, Morris-style bric-a-brac, and Victorian architecture. See *The Commodity Culture of Victorian England.*

[14] In addition, two Paris Exhibitions were held in 1867 and again in 1889 to commemorate the French Revolution, and the World's Columbian Exhibition was held in Chicago in 1893, the latter honoring the four-hundredth anniversary of Columbus's voyage to the New World. See Alan Trachtenberg's *The Incorporation of America* for more on the Columbian Exhibition and its display of American technological acumen coupled with aesthetic refinement through the erection of the "White City": four-hundred temporary buildings covered in white plaster of paris designed to emulate Renaissance palaces and cathedrals as well as neoclassic temples and domes.

[15] In addition to Freedman's monograph on the interstices between aestheticism and commodity culture, see Lawrence Levine's *Highbrow/Lowbrow.*

[16] Thorough historical studies on professionalism in nineteenth-century America include Burton Bledstein's classic work *The Culture of Professionalism*, Stuart Blumin's *The Emergence of the Middle Class*, and Gerald Geison's *Professions and Professional Ideologies in America*. For an in-depth monograph devoted to professionalism in England, see Harold Perkin's *The Rise of Professional Society*, and for a sociological study treating nineteenth-century professions in both America and the United Kingdom, see Magali Larson's *The Rise of Professionalism.* Specific to authorship, see William Charvat's pioneering work *The Profession of Authorship in America*, and specific to women writers' negotiation of the professionalization of Victorian

letters, see Monica Cohen's *Professional Domesticity in the Victorian Novel* and Sharon Marcus's "The Profession of the Author: Abstraction, Advertising, and *Jane Eyre.*"

[17] For example, in American popular discourse, often the commodity itself was transformed into the signifier for the entire history of its own production, collapsing its raw material, factory work, fancywork, distribution, and sales into a single representation: the final object. As Stuart Blumin demonstrates, between 1885 and 1890, *Harper's Monthly* ran a series of articles that summarized respective trades and industries, yet the titles and pictures accompanying the features merely recorded the finished product: "A Pair of Shoes," "A Suit of Clothes," "A Glass of Beer" (262).

[18] Put simply, until the latter part of the century, American professionalism seems to have been more "democratic," infusing professional rhetoric and the institutional organization of careers in occupations from factory work to medicine. In England, however, professionals tended to distance themselves from the mercantile classes through the embrace of behavior patterns associated with the gentry. Yet even this distinction gets muddied. On the one hand, as Blumin spends a good deal of time arguing, while Americans liked to believe that they were a classless society, the "all-encompassing American bourgeoisie, . . . may well have been a class after all—the power of its values serving to reinforce rather than to destroy social class boundaries" (3). Lydia Maria Child wrote to a friend in 1877, "No observing person can help being aware of an increasing tendency toward a strong *demarcation of classes* in this country. The genteel classes do not inter-marry with the middle classes; the middle classes do not intermarry with the laboring class; nothing is *said* about it, but there is a systematic avoidance of it. Moreover, they don't mix socially; they are as much strangers to each other, as if they live in different countries." On the other hand, professionals in Great Britain certainly participated in middle-class activities and had an investment in notions of salary-for-service that "true" gentry hardly ever entertained. Lydia Maria Child, letter to Sarah Blake Shaw, 31 July 1877 (bMS Am 1417 [155]), Houghton Lib., Harvard U., Cambridge, MA.

[19] As Monica Cohen reminds us, devoting one's cultivated knowledge of a specific intellectual task (e.g., novel-writing, law, medicine, ministry, teaching, etc.) to the service of others makes the professions an elected vocation. In theory, professionals come to their vocation with the desire to change and/or help society, thus distinguishing their "work" from wage-labor as well as aligning it with middle-class domesticity, i.e., "work" that aids the family, the community, and the nation. Cohen calls this alignment "domestic professionalism" and argues that the female professional, regardless of vocation, carries the "home" into her "work." In other words, a female novelist is judged as an artistic mother, a female doctor as a surgical mother, a female teacher as a didactic mother—all such professionals are always metaphoric mothers.

[20] Throughout this study, I use the terms "artist" and "artistry" rather than "author" and "authorship." I make this choice for deliberate reasons. First, although "author" and "artist" are words concerned with myths of origin, containing within their etymologies an emphasis on beginnings, their relative emphases are distinct. "Author" is derived from *auctor*—a founder, a begetter—and is the root of "authority" or *auctoritas,* which may be translated as

"power." "Author," because it requires a single focal point, locates it in an individual "genius," thus perpetuating an axial narrative of the individual author. In turn, this axial narrative underpins the entire construction of Western aesthetic history and criticism, a narrative with the central belief that authors beget: they produce, cause, invent. They also possess what they create; Edward Said delineates a "constellation of linked meanings" from the word "authority" to *auctor, autos, suis ipsius, propsius,* "property" (83). Capitalized, Author is synonymous with God. Beginning roughly with Michel Foucault's article "What Is an Author?" in 1969 and, a decade later, Sandra Gilbert and Susan Gubar's literary history *The Madwoman in the Attic,* the question of how one goes about defining authorship has spurred criticisms that suggest not only that the position of author is a highly invested cultural site—a nexus of power dynamics that maintain a notion of authorship that is, of course, as privileged as any God might be—but also that the use of the idea of an author in literary criticism inevitably carries with it this trace of myth: that powerful image of an exclusive creator producing singular works.

"Artist," on the other hand, comes from *artis,* meaning "to join together," and has evolved from the archaic noun form *artigino,* a craftsman or scholar. Thus, where "author" focuses on the fixed point from which unique art comes, "artist" centers on the skill and acumen needed to bring together various ideas and substances. At one level, then, I choose to focus on artistry rather than authorship in order to circumvent this trace because the artists who inform my project remain clearly uncomfortable with monolithic definitions of authorship. Indeed, to a large extent, Stowe, Eliot, and Phelps emphasize how they "join together" previous literary or political or religious work, even as they claim originality. Their artistry is carefully and insistently shaped as layers upon layers of text, discourse, idea, and spirit brought together in unique ways but ways not entirely of their own making: Eliot takes on a male pseudonym; Stowe and Phelps claim that God dictated *Uncle Tom's Cabin* and *The Gates Ajar.* Put simply, their collective uneasiness with a God-like idea of autonomous authorship is the foundation of their uneasiness with professionalism as an aesthetic movement.

At another level, I choose "artist" because of another meaning: "a skillful plan," *artificium,* an artificer. At the same moment artists presume the ability to create, their "authority" is mimetic, an illusion, an imperfect copy of the authentic or real. Thus the French derivation of "artist"—*artiste,* "a skilled public performer." "Author" does not connote this meaning; rather, it perpetuates the illusion of originary power. But "artist" contains an acknowledgment of performance even as it strives toward representing the actuality of human experience. This central paradox is inherent to the aesthetic philosophies of the women writers who make up this study—writers who create characters like Gwendolen or Lord Byron who perform art yet fail to achieve an authentic expression of art as well as characters like the Alcharisi or Avis who produce bona fide art only to be interpreted by others as artificers because of their gender.

21 "'Aestheticism,'" writes Freedman, "is one of those terms in literary criticism that are impossible fully to define. . . . Of whom, for example, do we speak when we refer to the 'aesthetic movement'? Is Ruskin the central force behind aestheticism in England? Is Rossetti its

truest practitioner? Or is Swinburne, or Pater, or Wilde? And what of its provenance? Is aestheticism merely a French import . . . ? Or does it signal the incorporation of the doctrines of German idealist philosophy into British criticism . . . ? Or does aestheticism represent the last flourish of British Romanticism? After all, the link between Wordsworth and Keats (via Browning and Tennyson) and the Pre-Raphaelites or poets of the 'decadence' is an obvious one" (3–4). Yet while Freedman demonstrates the elasticity and oftentimes incoherence of the terms "aesthetic" and "aestheticism," he simultaneously insists on a relatively strictured view: while complex and even contradictory, Freedman's definition is still limited to the ideas of traditional male writers and critics, all self-selected avatars of "Aestheticism." For analyses of how various female artists and writers participated in (or were excluded from) the Aesthetic movement in England, see the wide-ranging anthology edited by Talia Schaffer and Kathy Psomiades, *Women and British Aestheticism*.

[22] See Freedman's *Professions of Taste*; Regenia Gagnier's "A Critique of Practical Aesthetics" and *Idylls of the Marketplace*; Lori Merish's *Sentimental Materialism*; Kathy Psomiades's *Beauty's Body*; and Jennifer Wicke's *Advertising Fictions.*

[23] Monica Cohen explains, "The assertion of woman's rights as merited by a female's inalienable connection to others (whether experienced as a blessing or a curse, biologically determined or culturally mandated) precedes and in some ways foreshadows the professional's conception of his or her service as a sign of entitlement" (7).

[24] For a history of these technological developments in America and their relation to reading practices, see *A Fictive People* by Ronald Zboray.

[25] Since my study is not primarily concerned with distinctions among these terms, I cannot devote a lengthy discussion to how they are similar or different. However, let me say here that I follow Lawrence Levine's suggestion that such terms, themselves, were used interchangeably in the second half of the nineteenth-century, "cluster[ing] around a congeries of values, a set of categories that defined and distinguished culture vertically, that created hierarchies which were to remain meaningful for much of [the twentieth] century" (224). At basic, then, I cluster together such terms as "high," "higher," "highbrow," "elite," "cultivated," "cultured," "pure," "beautiful," and "aesthetic" into one group and "low," "lesser," "lowbrow," "vulgar," "uncultured," "mass," and "popular" into another. In so doing, I mirror the application of these adjectives throughout latter-half nineteenth-century texts in England and America.

[26] I base my summary on Catherine Gallager's *The Industrial Reformation of English Fiction*, especially chapter nine, "The Politics of Culture and the Debate over Representation in the 1860s."

[27] The serialized version of *Uncle Tom's Cabin* ran in the *National Era* in weekly installments from June 1851 through April 1852.

[28] HBS, letter to Mary Ann Evans [George Eliot], May 2, [1869], Berg Collection, NY Public Lib., NY.

[29] See Mrs. Eliza Wigham, letter to Mary A. Estlin, 22 March 1853 (Ms. A.9.2.27.18), Department of Rare Books and Manuscripts, Boston Public Lib., Boston.

[30] When *The Critic* solicited Phelps's opinion on international copyright, she said, "It seems to me there can be but two opinions on such a matter, and that they cannot be unlike those of the burglar and of the burglar*ee*" ("An Appeal" 65).

[31] See HBS, letter to Mary Ann Evans [George Eliot], 23 September 1872, Berg Collection, NY Public Lib., NY; and HBS, letter to Annie Fields, 9 May [1869] (FI 3985), Fields Papers, Huntington Lib., San Marino.

[32] Levine's *Highbrow/Lowbrow* provides a brilliant discussion of this hierarchical consolidation in America, and he devotes an entire section to opera as a kind of cultural case study.

[33] Although Phelps is long-forgotten in the twentieth century, in her day she was classed with the most prominent realist writers coming out of the *Atlantic*-group set. "The *Atlantic* had a great opportunity when it was founded," writes a journalist for *The Literary World.* "What American periodical has had choicer blood in its veins? Emerson, Longfellow, Whittier, Holmes, Lowell, Aldrich, Howells, Phelps, Thaxter, Preston, Cranch, James, 'H. H.'—these are among the brightest names on the page of later American literature, and these are distinctively the *Atlantic*'s writers" ("Five American" 392).

"YOU ARE AS THOROUGHLY *WOMAN* AS YOU ARE ENGLISH"

[1] For an informative discussion of Stowe's vexed relationship to the American woman's movement, see Joan Hedrick's exhaustive biography of Stowe, especially her twenty-sixth chapter "Woman's Rights and Woman's Wrongs: 1869–1872." In turn, for various overviews of this period in Phelps's career, see "Women's Wrongs, 1868–1871" in Carol Farley Kessler's *Elizabeth Stuart Phelps*; "'The Most Tremendous Question': Phelps's View of Women as Revealed in Her Magazine Articles," the third chapter in Lori Duin Kelley's *The Life and Works of Elizabeth Stuart Phelps*; and what I consider to be the best survey in terms of its thoroughness and accuracy, "The Female Reconstruction of Society," the fifth chapter to Susan Coultrap-McQuin's doctoral dissertation on Phelps.

[2] Republished in *Household Papers and Stories, 1865–1867.*

[3] Four years later, Stowe articulated an even more adamant investment in the Woman's Rights movement to her former pupil and friend Fanny Fern. "The more I think of it," she wrote, "the more absurd this whole government of men over women looks." HBS, letter to Sara Willis Parton [Fanny Fern], 25 July [1869], Parton Papers, Sophia Smith Collection, Smith College, Northampton.

[4] The *Independent* was a weekly first popularized for its participation in abolition, and the *Woman's Journal* was specifically created to promulgate arguments for female suffrage. All but one of Phelps's reform articles were first published in the *Independent* and then reprinted in the *Woman's Journal*; "A Few Words to the Girls" was written exclusively for the latter.

[5] "[N]ow I lay my commands on you —," Stowe informed Fanny Fern. "You and Mr Parton *both* must without delay get and read John Stuart Mills book just published by the Appletons—It has wholly converted me—I was only right *in spots* before now I am all clear." HBS, letter to Sara Willis Parton [Fanny Fern], 25 July [1869], Parton Papers, Sophia Smith Collection, Smith College, Northampton.

[6] Susan B. Anthony, letter to Paulina Wright Davis, n.d. [August or September 1869], Isabella Hooker Collection, Harriet Beecher Stowe Center, Hartford.

[7] Abstracting the specifics of the Byrons' marriage in her "True Story," Stowe maintained, "The most dreadful men to live with are those who thus alternate between angel and devil. The buds of hope and love called out by a day or two of sunshine are frozen again and again till the tree is killed" (304).

[8] Lord Byron was a man who, according to one Stowe detractor in England, was "one of our grandest poets; every line he has written has added a stone to the temple of Britannia's fame" (1). See "Let the Dead Rest."

[9] Three other woman's rights advocates came to Stowe's aid, although their praise is more tempered than Stanton's: Julia Ward Howe in the *Woman's Journal*, Charlotte Wilbour in the *Revolution*, and Lydia Maria Child in the *Independent*. Another proponent was George William Curtis, the editor of *Harper's New Monthly Magazine*, who, although convinced by Stowe's argument, arrived at a rather different conclusion than her female allies as to why the media aspersed her. "The indignation with which Mrs. Stowe's disclosure has been generally received in this country may be regarded as a pleasant tribute to human nature—as evidence of the universal unwillingness to believe any man guilty of so hideous an offense" (189). Like Stowe, however, Curtis agreed that the "facts" of Byron's account were "chiefly the assertions and insinuations of Lord Byron and his friends" (189). Stowe kept a scrapbook of all the essays and commentaries supporting her side of the cause; this scrapbook is held at the Schlesinger Lib., Radcliffe Institute for Advanced Study, Cambridge.

[10] Stanton simultaneously published this editorial, "The Moral of the Byron Case," in the 9 September 1869 issues of *Revolution* and the *Independent*. I quote from the reprint in Elizabeth Ammons's anthology, *Critical Essays on HBS*.

[11] Elizabeth Cady Stanton, letter to Isabella Beecher Hooker, 1 September 1869, Isabella Hooker Collection, Harriet Beecher Stowe Center, Hartford. This letter announces Stanton's intention to print an essay on Stowe and Byron in the *Revolution*: "Next week I shall have an editorial on Mrs Stowe & Byron," she writes, asking Hooker, "Is there anything you would like to have me say." Hooker did, in fact, take an active role in helping Stowe manage negative publicity, and she assisted her in researching and organizing *Vindicated*, going so far as to correspond with Osgood on how to procure the necessary documents for Stowe's appendix. See Isabella Beecher Hooker, letters to Fields, Osgood & Co., 29 November [1869], n.d. [29 November 1869], and 2 December [1869] (HM 24372–74), Fields Papers, Huntington Lib., San Marino.

[12] Twenty-five years earlier, the women of England had dubbed Stowe the "impersonation" of antislavery efforts; it is easy to imagine that Stowe might have hoped to be the same for the Woman Question. "Mrs. Stowe seems the general pivot of effort at present & I do not regret it at all, although to honour her is small anti slavery—yet to get the public enthusiastic on the A. S. question of which she for the present appears the impersonation is a great matter." Mrs. Eliza Wigham, letter to Mary A. Estlin, 22 March 1853 (Ms. A.9.2.27.18), Department of Rare Books and Manuscripts, Boston Public Lib., Boston.

[13] For a review of how Stowe incensed Stanton by placing an editorial in the *Woman's Journal* warning suffragists against the free love movement, see Hedrick, pages 373–375.

[14] To her brother Henry, Stowe insisted, "The New Testament is the only ground on which we can fight both sides—[t]he free lovers who claim licence for women instead of liberty & the Major Pendennises who claim licence for men & slavery for women." *Pendennis* is a novel by William Makepeace Thackeray. HBS, letter to Henry Ward Beecher, n.d. [summer 1870], Beecher Family Papers, Sterling Memorial Lib., Yale U., New Haven.

[15] To her colleague William Patton, Stowe wrote, "Such a scoffing at Christs spirit in a professed Christian country I have not seen since I saw half the professed Christians of America on their knees before the fugitive slave law." HBS, letter to William Patton, 10 September 1869, Authors Collection, Smith College, Northampton.

[16] In fact, Stowe made distinctions between the compulsory, corporeal slavery of Africans and other forms of metaphoric servitude such as the "bounden serfdom" of marriage. For instance, in 1852 Stowe entered into a correspondence with Arthur Helps, a British essayist who argued, in *Fraser's Magazine*, against Stowe's conflation of the experience of the English labourer with that of the American slave. Specifically, in *Uncle Tom's Cabin*, Augustine St. Clare notes to Miss Ophelia, "Look at the high and the low, all the world over, and it's the same story,—the lower class used up, body, soul and spirit, for the good of the upper. It is so in England; it is so everywhere; and yet all Christendom stands aghast, with virtuous indignation, because we do the thing in a little different shape from what they do it" (319). To Charles Norton, Helps labeled this comment an "exaggeration," the same claim he put forward in *Fraser's*: "But if there be no exaggeration . . . as regards the condition of slaves in America, there is, I am sorry to say, an exaggeration in the statements which are made in the course of [*Uncle Tom's Cabin*], and are not contradicted, respecting the condition of the English labourer." Stowe replied to Helps via his publisher, "I perceive, on reading the article in Frasers magazine . . . that I am addressing a man of benevolence & feeling & one who will excuse the liberty I take of replying to some of the sentiments that have interested me." Stowe further explained, "I am perplexed how to reconcile the impressions received from your article as to the condition of the English poor, with those I have received from much current English literature. I will name for example Charlotte Elizabeth [Tonna Brown]'s 'Helen Fleetwood' & the 'Little pin hinders'—many of Dickens's writing & latterly 'Alton Locke['] & [']Yeast.'" While Helps dismissed her sources as suspect (as fiction, not fact), he focused most of his response on explaining his theory of slavery, namely, that if a man has free will and the hope of education, he can never be an intellectual slave like blacks in the American South. "Many slaves & numberless Seals & Walruses are happier, I have no doubt, than either you or I can pretend to be," he wrote Stowe, "and probably, on the other hand, there are many slaves who are, physically considered, a great deal worse off than we are. But I contend that neither their happiness nor their misery bears the full fruit of instruction which all human sensation was intended to produce. The shadow of misery is wisdom, or at least self knowledge. The suffering of slaves are blank, shadowless, comparatively speaking unproductive. In short, free will, as men can give it scope in their intercourse with one another, is necessary to

work out the best part of continuous Education, & thus to give the full meaning to the life of man, which, otherwise, would be a very poor & limited affair." Although Stowe never retracted the opinion expressed by St. Clare, two years later in *Sunny Memories*, she commented, "One cannot read the history of the working classes in England . . . without feeling sensibly the difference between oppressions under a free government and slavery. So long as the working class of England produces orators and writers . . . ; so long as it has in it that spirit of independence and resistance of wrong . . . ; and so as long as the law allows them to meet and debate, to form associations and committees, to send up remonstrances and petitions to government,—one can see that their case is essentially different from that of plantations slaves" (1: 68). Overall, this correspondence reveals two important things: first, that Stowe discerned subtle commonalties and differences among varied kinds of oppressions and second, that both textual literacy and the opportunity to professionalize distinguished the purely economic from physical, inherent indenture. Perhaps this insight spurred Stowe to endorse women's enfranchisement after the Civil War. See Arthur Helps, letter to Charles Eliot Norton, 9 July 1852 (bMS Am 1088 [3373]), Norton Papers, Houghton Lib., Harvard U., Cambridge; HBS, letter to Arthur Helps, 22 August 1852, Acquisitions, Harriet Beecher Stowe Center, Hartford; and Arthur Helps, letter to HBS, 9 October 1852 (Autograph File), Norton Family Papers, Houghton Lib., Harvard U., Cambridge. For a persuasive article on how supporters of the Woman's Right movement appropriated the concept of slavery from abolitionist polemics, see "Bodily Bonds: The Intersecting Rhetorics of Feminism and Abolition" by Karen Sánchez-Eppler.

[17] "[N]either of Lyman Beecher's daughters could see themselves on the masthead of a journal called the *Revolution*," explains Hedrick. "They inquired of Stanton and Anthony whether the name might be changed to something a trifle less shocking to public taste" (361). Stanton rejoined that "a journal called the *Rosebud* might answer for those who come with kid gloves and perfumes to lay immortal wreaths on the monuments which in sweat and tears others have hewn and built." See Elizabeth Cady Stanton, letter to Susan B. Anthony, 28 December 1869, *In Her Own Right: The Life of Elizabeth Cady Stanton*, Elisabeth Griffith (NY: Oxford University Press, 1984), 131.

[18] I should note, however, that even these appearances were constrained. Stowe's husband Calvin or brother Charles usually spoke for her while she sat on the sidelines. On her first trip to England when large public meetings were held in her honor, Hedrick points out that "Stowe sat in side galleries and respected the convention that forbade women from speaking in public" (238). Hedrick links this behavior to Stowe's desire always to act in accordance with the precepts of true womanhood, performing "privately and properly" while "nevertheless speaking publicly" through the widespread sale and distribution of her novel, *Uncle Tom's Cabin.*

[19] HBS, letter to Henry Ward Beecher, n.d. [July? 1870], Beecher Family Papers, Sterling Memorial Lib., Yale U., New Haven. Eugene Benson's "George Sand and the Marriage Question" appeared in the *Revolution* the summer of 1870. Primarily as a result of this debate over marriage and sexuality, in 1869 the Woman's Rights movement itself split into two

camps. Stanton had warned Anthony of this eventuality as early as 1853: "I feel this whole question of woman's rights turns on the point of the marriage relation, and sooner or later it will be the question for discussion" (DuBois 56). Stanton's new National Woman's Suffrage Association (NWSA) continued to stress reform on a number of fronts, including divorce and "free love," while the American Woman's Suffrage Association (AWSA) focused on securing the vote. (Incidentally, the President of the AWSA was Stowe's brother, Henry Ward Beecher.) The AWSA underwrote the *Woman's Journal.* I should note that, in histories of the American suffrage movement, AWSA is often described as "conservative" and NWSA "radical," but these terms should be considered with caution for they cannot be applied ahistorically. For instance, Elizabeth Stuart Phelps was a regular contributor to AWSA's *Woman's Journal*, and her articles might very well be deemed "radical," or at least "liberal," in the context of Victorian America. Campaigning for suffrage, Phelps asked in one article, "Is your husband afraid his buttons will not be sewed on . . . ? Who will make the dessert when you are at the polls? How can you run for office and keep the parlor dusted? Did not Paul say that a man was the head of a woman? Too many negroes voted, and it is safer for fifteen millions of women to embroider little petticoats. . . . A disfranchised race, class, sex, is a child in guardianship of and under subjection to the race, the class, the sex which administrates government for and upon it. The baby in your arms, madam, becomes one day your virtual sovereign" ("The Gist" 226). For a broad overview of the American woman's movement, see Mari Jo and Paul Buhle's anthology, *The Concise History of Woman Suffrage*, and for a brilliant historical study of the genesis of the Anglo-American movement for woman's rights, see Margaret McFadden's *Golden Cables of Sympathy.*

[20] HBS, letter to Mary Ann Evans [George Eliot], 2 May [1869], Berg Collection, NY Public Lib., NY.

[21] HBS, letter to Mary Ann Evans [George Eliot], 2 May [1869], Berg Collection, NY Public Lib., NY.

[22] In *Sensational Designs*, Jane Tompkins bases her entire argument on how to read mid-century American novels by women on this very idea. "Stowe's very conservatism—her reliance on established patterns of living and traditional beliefs—is precisely what gives [*Uncle Tom's Cabin*] its revolutionary potential. By pushing those beliefs to an extreme and by insisting that they be applied universally . . . , Stowe means to effect a radical transformation of her society. . . . [And] the new society will not be controlled by men, but by women" (145).

[23] ESP, letter to Henry W. Longfellow, 22 August 1878 (bMS Am 1340.2 [5815]), Houghton Lib., Harvard U., Cambridge. Phelps terms this same quality of feminine strength in *Doctor Zay* "dangerous and sacred feminine nerve" (111).

[24] HBS, letter to Mary Ann Evans [George Eliot], 2 May [1869], Berg Collection, NY Public Lib., NY.

[25] HBS, letter to Mary Ann Evans [George Eliot], 23 September 1872, Berg Collection, NY Public Lib., NY.

[26] "The ordinary lot of the ordinary young woman," wrote Phelps, "is one of the most miserable and unnatural things in comfortably civilized life" ("Unhappy" 250).

[27] In her *Chimney Corner* pieces, Stowe employed a masculine narrator by the name of Christopher Crowfield. For more about Stowe's anonymous publications, see Hedrick, pages 370–379.

[28] For instance, Stowe clearly admired Eliot's Dinah Morris and linked Dinah's power as a preacher to the kind of succor Phelps herself had tried to provide with *Gates*. "We have had a war that has put almost every family into mourning," Stowe explained in a letter to Eliot. "Like the old land of Egypt there is scarce a house where there is not one dead—& hence this sudden increase of spiritualism[.] It is the throbbing of the severed soul to the part of itself that is gone within the veil— . . . For me my faith is that of *Dinah* your loveliest & most living creation—[.]" But while Stowe recognized the "throbbing of the severed soul" as a pain in need of the relief of strong weakness (simultaneously "lovely" and "living" or vital), she never spoke against the Church's decision to keep women from the pulpit. On the other hand, Phelps openly asserted in her newspaper columns that if, indeed, women were supposed to be religiously superior and of higher moral quality than men, then it was high time the church allowed women to preach. "The Christian church will be a long while in regaining the treasure which it has lost," Phelps warned, "through stifling the voice of the Spirit of God which burns upon women's lips" ("United Head" 306). HBS, letter to Mary Ann Evans [George Eliot], 2 May [1869], Berg Collection, NY Public Lib., NY.

[29] HBS, letter to Mary Ann Evans [George Eliot], 2 May [1869], Berg Collection, NY Public Lib., NY.

[30] Extending the definition of appropriate occupations for women is a favorite Phelpsian theme. In particular, see her articles "Too Much Conscience," "The Song of the Shirt," "A Talk to the Girls," "Unhappy Girls," and "What They Are Doing."

[31] Phelps is quick, however, to defend marriage as an institution and to disclaim the belief that advocates for woman's rights are antimarriage: "The great mass of advocates of womanhood suffrage are God-fearing people, who believe in the holiness of marriage, as they believe in the holiness of Heaven" ("New Earth" 1). See, too, Phelps's retendering of a marriage service in "A Dream Within A Dream" from the 19 February 1874 issue of the *Independent*.

[32] At one juncture, Phelps declares, "[a]s a general thing, it is next to impossible for a woman with the care of a family on her hands to be a successful writer. The majority of the exceptions made their literary reputation before marriage"' ("What Shall" 519). Phelps herself remained single until very late in her career.

[33] Although not a complete list of Phelps's magazine and newspaper articles from the early 1870s, a beginning scholar should examine "Unhappy Girls," "The Song of the Shirt," "Rights and Relatives," "'The United Head,'" "What They Are Doing," "Women and Money," "Men and Muscle," "'The True Woman,'" "The 'Female Education' of Women," "A Dream Within a Dream," and "A Word for the Silent" which, respectively, contend for equitable marriage relations, female self-reliance (including monetary autonomy), equal education for women, and argue that women's right to gainful occupation and intellectual stimulus are ordained by God. For articles that directly treat the issue of suffrage, see Phelps's "The Gist of the Matter," "The Higher Claim," and "The New Earth."

[34] At the conclusion of *Uncle Tom's Cabin*, Stowe recommends, "There is one thing that every individual can do,—they can see to it that *they feel right*. An atmosphere of sympathetic influence encircles every human being; and the man or woman who *feels* strongly, healthily and justly, on the great interests of humanity, is a constant benefactor to the human race" (624).

[35] Stowe visited England on two separate occasions, first in 1853 at the invitation of two Glasgow anti-slavery ladies' societies in order to receive a petition from half a million women abolitionists in Scotland, England, and Ireland. The petition, entitled an "Affectionate and Christian Address of Many Thousands of Women of Great Britain and Ireland to their Sisters the Women of the United States of America," was presented to Stowe by the Duchess of Sutherland. Along with the twenty-six volumes of the "Address," the Duchess of Sutherland gave Stowe a gold bracelet in the form of a shackle—on one link was stamped the date of the abolition of slavery in England; another link remained blank, to be inscribed with the date on which Americans would abolish slavery. Stowe returned to England in 1856 in hopes of establishing a British copyright for her novel *Dred*, and it was on this second trip that she had her interview with Lady Byron. Stowe printed her reminiscences about England in a travelogue entitled *Sunny Memories of Foreign Lands*, and her brother Charles Beecher kept a record of their tour in his journal, published in 1986 by the Stowe-Day Foundation as *Harriet Beecher Stowe in Europe*.

[36] Yet this assumption does not actually contradict her belief that England originated fiction. The persisting paradox of fiction, of course, is precisely that fabricated narratives pretend to be true or are accepted as a truer version of truth.

[37] "Your mind," Stowe once marveled to Eliot, "has in the most airy play of its imagination that English definiteness that refuses to exhale in a mist & turn to a mere cloud." HBS, letter to Mary Ann Evans [George Eliot], 15 April 1869, Berg Collection, NY Public Lib., NY.

[38] As her biographers Mary Angela Bennett and Carol Farley Kessler note, after her mother's death when Phelps was eight years old, she grew up in an environment in which "intelligent, even instructed men" met "the phenomenon of a superior woman" with perplexity—"as it was then for such men to understand such a woman at all" (*Chapters* 134). Phelps referred to this dynamic as Andover men's "feudal view" of women.

[39] Indeed, with the momentous success of her first novel, Phelps entered a literary realm she had already long associated with a writer like Stowe. For example, Phelps made many, ongoing demurrals that *The Gates Ajar* was destitute of literary ambition. Stowe herself had insisted from the beginning that God had dictated *Uncle Tom's Cabin* and that she had acted as a mere medium for His word, and almost thirty years after the publication of *Gates*, Phelps reconstructs her writing process in almost exactly the same language Stowe had used to depict writing *Uncle Tom*. "The angel said unto me 'Write!,'" Phelps declares, "and I wrote" (*Chapters* 95).

[40] For instance, in Charles Beecher's journal of his mother's first British tour, he watched Stowe sit on a bench in Shakespeare's house and ruminate "[if] Willy's mother used to say . . . 'Bill, come in & eat your supper.' And in he came out of the street, then crept in here to the

chimney corner, took his porringer, ate his bread and milk, and looked in the fire to see the figures" (63). See Hedrick, pages 266–269.

[41] HBS, letter to Theodore Wolfe, 7 October [1885], Katharine S. Day Collection, Harriet Beecher Stowe Center, Hartford.

[42] In 1854, the Nebraska Bill proposed to let the settlers themselves decide whether these states would be slave or free. Stowe organized a petition drive to thwart the bill, using money she had received during her first visit to England. See Hedrick's twenty-first chapter, "Andover, Kansas, and Europe: 1854–1857."

[43] For a carefully documented overview of English criticisms of *Uncle Tom's Cabin* as well as a synopsis of British support for the Southern cause before and during the Civil War, see Wendy F. Hamand's "'No Voice from England': Mrs. Stowe, Mr. Lincoln, and the British in the Civil War."

[44] Lady Byron, letter to HBS, 18 October 1856, folder 245, Beecher-Stowe Collection, Schlesinger Lib., Radcliffe Institute for Advanced Study, Cambridge. This letter includes the reference to sending sixty-three pounds.

[45] For excellent studies of how Phelps and Stowe attempted to negotiate the emerging model of professional authorship in the latter half of the nineteenth century, see Susan Coultrap-McQuin's *Doing Literary Business* and Sarah Robbins's "Gendering Gilded Age Periodical Professionalism."

[46] Elsewhere in *Chapters* Phelps explicitly named the amount of her first payment for *The Gates Ajar*: "'Your book is moving grandly,' [wrote James T. Fields]. 'It has already reached a sale of four thousand copies. We take pleasure in sending you'—He enclosed a check for six hundred dollars, the largest sum on which I had ever set my startled eyes" (109). She defended her choice to name figures by espousing a "cold-blooded view"—one deliberately meant to dim "the rosy dreams of those young ladies and gentlemen" (85); apparently, Phelps believed such a mere sum would serve to dissuade those who would "write for a living."

[47] To give but one example, in an 1887 edition of *The Critic*, a journalist writes, "Now that the ocean steamers are beginning to take abroad their summer freight of globe-trotting Americans . . . , it is interesting to learn the summer plans of the literary class, to know where the men and women who live by the pen will pass the dog-days, and what work they will be engaged upon, if they do not abandon themselves wholly to physical ease and intellectual lotus-eating. The plans of many well-known authors are revealed in the following paragraphs, and some further secrets of the same sort may be betrayed in the next number" ("Summer Plans" 263).

[48] Although Phelps was hyperbolic in her characterization of the press as "the Most Holy Inquisition" which put her "to the question"—finally forcing her to decide she was "not adapted to reading the views of the press about my own writing"—her lengthy explanations of why she left off reading reviews coupled with two full chapters dedicated to *Gates* in a twelve-chapter autobiography leads one to believe Phelps actually enjoyed detailing *Gates*'s extensive and on-going reception (*Chapters* 118–119).

[49] Of the "inconveniences" Phelps experienced attempting to draft *Gates* while still living under Austin Phelps's roof, she writes, "Doubtless something would have been done to relieve them had I asked for it; or if the idea that my work could ever be of any consequence had occurred to any of us" (*Chapters* 103). It is telling that her father scorned authorship as a viable vocation for women; in particular, he thought authorship a detriment to a woman's accomplishment as a mother or, for that matter, as a dutiful daughter. In an antisuffrage essay on the political status of women, Austin Phelps insists, "Once fill a young woman's mind with the notion that it is a grander thing to be a speaker on the platform than to be a wife in a Christian home, that it is a nobler distinction to be a successful author than to be the happy mother of children, that it is more honorable to head a half-score of 'committees' for public service than it is to be a loving daughter in a father's house, the model of refinement to younger brothers and sisters, and you can no longer find a place of honor in her thoughts for the mission of either daughter, wife, or mother" (*My Portfolio* 111).

[50] Elizabeth Stuart Phelps the former, Phelps's mother, was the author of didactic "Kitty Brown" Sunday-school works and pious domestic novels, including *The Sunny Side; or, a Country Minister's Wife*, that, according to Phelps, sold 100,000 copies its first year (*Chapters* 12). Phelps herself was christened Mary Gray and only took her mother's name sometime after her death in 1852. In *Chapters*, Phelps confides, "My mother, whose name I am proud to wear . . . , [was at] the time of her death . . . at the first blossom of her very positive and widely-promising success as a writer of the simple home stories which took such a hold on the popular heart. . . . Her last book and her last baby came together, and killed her. She lived one of those rich and piteous lives such as only gifted women know; torn by the civil war of the dual nature which can be given to women only" (11–12). For more information on the first Elizabeth Stuart Phelps, see Phelps's *Chapters*, especially "An Andover Home"; Austin Phelps's "Memorial" in *The Last Leaf from Sunny Side*; Sarah Stuart Robbins's *Old Andover Days*; Nina Baym's *Woman's Fiction*; and Carol Farley Kessler, both her *Elizabeth Stuart Phelps* (especially chapters one and four) and "A Literary Legacy: Elizabeth Stuart Phelps, Mother and Daughter."

[51] This quotation comes from an unidentified clipping in the University of Virginia's Phelps Collection entitled "Elizabeth S. Phelps. Her Work as an Author—Her Girlhood and Her Married Life." See box "Barrett-Ward," accession no. 6997–E. The clipping is dated 6 November 1892.

[52] Presumably, the author meant a chromo of the Annunciation.

[53] See, too, *Women Authors of Our Day in Their Homes*.

[54] See "Elizabeth S. Phelps. Her Work as an Author—Her Girlhood and Her Married Life," 6 November 1892, box "Barrett-Ward," Elizabeth Stuart Phelps Collection (#6997–E), Clifton Waller Barrett Lib., Special Collections, U. of Virginia Lib., Charlottesville.

[55] "There never was & never will be another woman like Lady Byron," Stowe tells Fanny Fern, "it was as good as seeing an angel right from the other side." HBS, letter to Sara Willis Parton [Fanny Fern], July 25, [1869], Sophia Smith Collection, Smith College, Northampton.

[56] It is interesting to note how closely, in terms of imagery and metaphor, Stowe's depiction of Lady Byron is related to Phelps's construction of her Sphinx. For example, in a letter to her daughters, Stowe assures them that, through *Vindicated*, "Lady Byrons voice will rise clear as the sun fair as the moon, & terrible as an army with banners." In turn, in a magazine article on true womanhood as symbolized through the Sphinx, Phelps writes, "Fair as the moon, clear as the sun, and terrible as any army with banners will be the face which, out of the desert of her long watch and patience, [the Sphinx] will turn upon the world" ("The True Woman" 1). HBS, letter to Hatty and Eliza Stowe, n.d. [November-December, 1869], folder 150, Beecher-Stowe Collection, Schlesinger Library, Radcliffe College, Cambridge.

[57] Stowe wrote her first letter to Eliot on April 15, 1869. Thirteen of her lengthy and sometimes illegible letters to Eliot survive, held in the Berg Collection at the New York Public Library. Partial and often inaccurate transcriptions are published in Charles Stowe's and Annie Fields's respective biographies; Marlene Springer's "Stowe and Eliot: An Epistolary Friendship"; and Margaret Wolfit's "The Toast to the Immortal Memory." However, Wolfit's lack of accuracy is lamentable, and Fields appropriates, in toto, her text from Charles Stowe. Thus, for those who wish to read part of this correspondence, I recommend Charles Stowe's *Life*, although he made significant changes to Stowe's original punctuation and often omitted or added entire phrases, and Springer's excerpts, which are excellent. That said, neither source is complete. (Springer claims, in her footnotes, that an E. Bruce Kirkman was "currently editing the letters," although that was in 1986 and no publication exists from Kirkman.) A fourteenth letter must exist. Gordon Haight, the editor of the *George Eliot Letters*, notes that Stowe presented Eliot with an illustrated edition of *Uncle Tom's Cabin* in 1879 that included an autographed letter. This book and manuscript were sold at Sotheby's in 1923—see volume 7, footnote, page 132. Of course, Eliot's side of the correspondence is complete and scrupulously correct, as edited by Haight.

[58] HBS, letter to Mary Ann Evans [George Eliot], 15 April 1869, Berg Collection, NY Public Lib., NY.

[59] HBS, letter to Mary Ann Evans [George Eliot], 15 April 1869, Berg Collection, NY Public Lib., NY.

[60] Although this angle is beyond the scope of my immediate focus, I think a compelling study might be made of gender and desire in Stowe's personal correspondence. In particular, I have found fascinating material in letters between Stowe and her brother Henry and in other places where their mutually producing and often amalgamated identities are discussed. For instance, in an unpublished manuscript held in the Parton Papers at Smith College, "Fanny Fern: An Informal Biography," Ethel Parton tells the story of how, when Stowe was a teacher at the Hartford Female Seminary and Fern was her pupil, one day Stowe and Henry secretly changed clothes. "Henry had become Harriet and Harriet had become Henry." Donning Henry's trousers, waistcoat, and hat, Stowe looked like a "more than passable Beecher youth," and Henry, in Stowe's hoop-skirt, mantilla, and bonnet seemed the very "spit and image" of his sister. Relatedly, in "The Flower in the Cleft" Janet Emig reads the entire Stowe-Byron controversy as a screen for exonerating Henry, who was rumored to have had an affair with a

parishioner. The parishioner was none other than the spouse of Theodore Tilton, the editor of *The Independent*—a rival to Henry's own editorship of the *Christian Union*, and the man who blasted Stowe's article on Lady Byron. While the charge of this affair wasn't made public until 1872 when Victoria Woodhull announced it at a lecture, Emig links Stowe's sense that Henry was under attack to the incest themes of "True Story" and *Vindicated*. By accusing Byron of incest, who had been an adolescent heartthrob for Stowe, Emig's argument is that Stowe invested Byron with her own unacknowledged desire for her brother and was able to restore Henry, as well as herself, to a kind of virtuous innocence. Of Henry and the accusation against him, Stowe wrote to Eliot in 1876: "This [situation] has drawn on my life—my hearts blood—He is *myself*—yes—I know you are the kind of woman to understand me when I say that I felt a blow at him more than at myself. I who *know* his purity, honor[,] delicacy—know that he has been from childhood, of an *ideal* purity." The *Wuthering Heights* overtones in this passage are obvious, and, interestingly, in nineteenth-century reviews of "True Story" and *Vindicated*, Stowe's depiction of Byron is often linked to the character of Heathcliff. See Hedrick, pages 374–379; HBS, letter to Mary Ann Evans [George Eliot], 18 March 1876, Berg Collection, NY Public Lib., NY.

[61] HBS, letter to Mary Ann Evans [George Eliot], 2 May [1869], Berg Collection, NY Public Lib., NY.

[62] HBS, letter to Mary Ann Evans [George Eliot], 18 March 1876, Berg Collection, NY Public Lib., NY.

[63] HBS, letter to Mary Ann Evans [George Eliot], 2 May [1869], Berg Collection, NY Public Lib., NY.

[64] HBS, letter to Mary Ann Evans [George Eliot], 23 September 1872, Berg Collection, NY Public Lib., NY.

[65] HBS, letter to Annie Fields, 9 May [1869] (FI 3985), Fields Papers, Huntington Lib., San Marino. Stowe mistakenly calls Mrs. Henry Wood "Mrs. Henry Ward," presumably because her own brother's name was Henry Ward Beecher.

[66] ESP, letter to Mary Ann Evans [George Eliot], 26 February 1873, Beinecke Rare Book and Manuscript Lib., Yale U., New Haven. While, in this study, the transcripts of Phelps's letters to Eliot all come from first-hand transcriptions of the originals held at the Beinecke Library at Yale, recently George Griffith has published the whole of Phelps's correspondence with Eliot in *Legacy*. See "An Epistolary Friendship: The Letters of Elizabeth Stuart Phelps to George Eliot."

[67] ESP, letter to Mary Ann Evans [George Eliot], 26 February 1873, Beinecke Rare Book and Manuscript Lib., Yale U., New Haven.

[68] Annie Fields knew both Stowe and Eliot well, and when Eliot expressed a desire to Fields to correspond with Stowe, Fields immediately passed along the information.

[69] ESP, letter to Mary Ann Evans [George Eliot], 26 February 1873, Beinecke Rare Book and Manuscript Lib., Yale U., New Haven.

[70] HBS, letter to Mary Ann Evans [George Eliot], 15 April 1869, Berg Collection, NY Public Lib., NY.

[71] HBS, letter to Mary Ann Evans [George Eliot], 15 April 1869, Berg Collection, NY Public Lib., NY.

[72] HBS, letter to Mary Ann Evans [George Eliot], 3 August 1869, Berg Collection, NY Public Lib., NY.

[73] HBS, letter to Mary Ann Evans [George Eliot], 3 August 1869, Berg Collection, NY Public Lib., NY.

[74] In a subsequent letter, Stowe explains, "Now because I have *felt you* your impersonal soul in so many hours I send this book to you as one should write a letter—it is so much an expression of *my own* inner thinkings. . . . I have felt always since I read you, such a *kinship*—as if you were as something part of myself and I have talked to you of this & that in many a lonesome hour." HBS, letter to Mary Ann Evans [George Eliot], 2 May [1869], Berg Collection, NY Public Lib., NY.

[75] This emotion bespeaks desire as well as identification, a theme that deserves more exploration. In a comparable manner, Stowe writes to Lady Byron, "I left you with a strange sort of yearning throbbing feeling—you make me feel quite as I did years ago a sort of girlishness quite odd for me—I have felt a strange longing to send you something dont smile when you see what it turns out to be I have a weakness for your pretty parian things—. . . . So I send you a cup made of primroses—a funny little pitcher quite large enough for cream & a little vase for violets & primroses—which will be lovely together & when you use it think of me That I love you more than I can say as I often think how strange that it is that I should *know* you—you who were a sort of legend of my early days—that I should love you is only a natural result—You seem to me to stand on the confines of that land where the poor formalities which separate hearts here pass like mist before the sun & therefore it is that I feel this language of love must not startle you as strange or unfamiliar." HBS, letter to Lady Byron, 2 June 1857, folder 245, Beecher-Stowe Collection, Schlesinger Lib., Radcliffe Institute for Advanced Study, Cambridge. Although her article analyzes only the American context and is now almost twenty-five years old, the best source on the history of Victorian female relationships continues to be Carroll Smith-Rosenberg's "The Female World of Love and Ritual: Relations between Women in Nineteenth-Century America."

[76] Phelps calls Eliot a "Queen" in her poetic eulogy "George Eliot"; an "Apostle" in her first letter to Eliot in February of 1873; and one of "two great Georges" (in addition to George Sand) in an accompanying letter to the Booklovers Reading Club's *Hand-book to The World's Great Woman Novelists.*

[77] ESP, letter to Mary Ann Evans [George Eliot], 27 May 1877, Beinecke Rare Book and Manuscript Lib., Yale U., New Haven.

[78] ESP, letter to Mary Ann Evans [George Eliot], 1 December 1876, Beinecke Rare Book and Manuscript Lib., Yale U., New Haven.

[79] Phelps provides this anecdote on "Dan" from her autobiography: "I had a little dog in those days. . . . The name of that dog, by the way, was Daniel Deronda; and one day it fell to me, with my own ears, to overhear these authenticated words:—'Mamma?' It was a little fellow who spoke, tugging at his mother's fingers as he scrambled over the boulders. 'Mamma,

I want to know;—is this where the Derondas live?' Such was human fame; and such will it ever be . . . ! Worse might befall me than to be known as one of the Derondas" (*Chapters* 196–197).

[80] One enthusiast exclaimed in a letter to the editors of the *Woman's Journal*, "[O]ur Queen Elizabeth of literature is of to-morrow and all the rest of time" (322).

[81] ESP, letter to Mary Ann Evans [George Eliot], 26 February 1873, Beinecke Rare Book and Manuscript Lib., Yale U., New Haven.

[82] ESP, letter to Mary Ann Evans [George Eliot], 26 February 1873, Beinecke Rare Book and Manuscript Lib., Yale U., New Haven.

[83] ESP, letter to Mary Ann Evans [George Eliot], 26 February 1873, Beinecke Rare Book and Manuscript Lib., Yale U., New Haven.

[84] Edith Simcox was a friend of Eliot and Lewes and deeply in love with Eliot, although Eliot never returned her sexual advances. For more on Simcox, see Gordon Haight's *George Eliot: A Biography*.

[85] HBS, letter to Mary Ann Evans [George Eliot], 26 September 1872, Berg Collection, NY Public Lib., NY.

[86] HBS, letter to Mary Ann Evans [George Eliot], 23 September 1872, Berg Collection, NY Public Lib., NY.

[87] ESP, letter to Mary Ann Evans [George Eliot], 1 December 1876, Beinecke Rare Book and Manuscript Lib., Yale U., New Haven.

[88] Stowe said of Dinah, "For me my faith is that of Dinah[,] your loveliest & most living creation." Calvin, her husband, concurred: "of all your portraitures the female preacher in Adam Bede is the one I have most loved." Calvin went so far as to say, "I have prayed earnestly & wished intensely that you might be just such a preacher yourself." HBS, letter to Mary Ann Evans [George Eliot], 2 May [1869] and Calvin Stowe, letter to Mary Ann Evans [George Eliot], 30 May 1869, both in the Berg Collection, NY Public Lib., NY.

[89] HBS, letter to Mary Ann Evans [George Eliot], 20 April [1873?], Berg Collection, NY Public Lib., NY.

[90] HBS, letter to Mary Ann Evans [George Eliot], 15 April 1869, Berg Collection, NY Public Lib., NY.

[91] In her first letter, Stowe asks, "following you through all the lanes and winding high ways & by ways of religious thought one often asks *where* does this pilgrim find *home*? — What is the *rest* of this explorer? I see your footsteps sometimes in places where one is both glad & sorry to see that another has been—glad because the heart always throbs at sympathetic tokens[,] sorry because; there was there no water and no rest." HBS, letter to Mary Ann Evans [George Eliot], 15 April 1869, Berg Collection, NY Pubic Lib., NY. To this query, Eliot replied, "[W]hat you say as to your wonder or conjecture concerning my religious point of view[,] I believe that religion . . . has to be modified—'developed,' according to the dominant phrase—and that a religion more perfect than any yet prevalent, must express less care for personal consolation, and a more deeply-awing sense of responsibility to man, springing from sympathy with that which of all things is most certainly known to us, the difficulty of the

human lot. . . . As healthy, sane human beings we must love and hate—love what is good for mankind, hate what is evil for mankind" (*Letters* V: 31). Although secular, Eliot's articulation of a universal moral consciousness was directly in keeping with Stowe's own Christianized version.

[92] HBS, letter to Mary Ann Evans [George Eliot], 3 August 1869, Berg Collection, NY Public Lib., NY.

[93] ESP, letter to Mary Ann Evans [George Eliot], 1 December 1876, Beinecke Rare Book and Manuscript Lib., Yale U., New Haven.

[94] ESP, letter to Mary Ann Evans [George Eliot], 1 December 1876, Beinecke Rare Book and Manuscript Lib., Yale U., New Haven.

[95] There is no extant manuscript copy of these lectures, and the most we know of their specific content comes from Phelps's own letter to Eliot in December of 1876. "The lectures were four in number. The first gave just enough of a résumé of the history of fiction to make them partly understand what conditions the artist of to-day must meet, and what a public he enters; with the slight biographical material . . . which you yourself had so kindly favored me, to introduce your name.

The second; treated somewhat of the mechanism of novels; and of your Plots.

The third; of your Characterization, and Style.

The fourth; of your Purpose.

The invitations to repeat the lectures, which come in, all indicate that people are thirsty for anything about George Eliot." ESP, letter to Mary Ann Evans [George Eliot], 1 December 1876, Beinecke Rare Book and Manuscript Lib., Yale U., New Haven.

[96] See, for instance, "Concerning Women" and "Miss Phelps's Lectures." Two years later, in March of 1878, Phelps and a group of women making up The Massachusetts Society for the University Education of Women attempted to endow a woman's professorship at Boston University. The proposed endowment was in accord with Phelps's ideals of professional femininity, both assertive and soft at once: "Those who care to have women as nobly placed as men now are, having positions which receive the same salaries and privileges, if the same duties, and all those who feel that over a girl's education womanly tenderness and presence should preside equally with masculine instruction, are asked to aid in this object" ("A Woman's Professorship" 101).

[97] See "Miss Phelps's Lectures."

[98] In a letter to George Bancroft, Eliot iterates this belief, commenting, "I take my objection to furnishing particulars about myself for any compendium. . . . It seems to me that just my works and the order in which they have appeared is what the part of the public which cares about me may most usefully know" (*Letters* VI: 68).

[99] Including this pamphlet, there were a number of other British publications that reproached Phelps's work, including *"The Gates Ajar," Critically Examined*; *Faith of Fancy? An Examination of "The Gates Ajar"*; *The Door Was Shut. An Answer to "Gates Ajar"*; and *Antidote to "The Gates Ajar."* There were, in addition, circulars that applauded Phelps's novel, although they were fewer in number. See, for instance, *"Watching at the Gates." A Reply to "The Gates*

Ajar" and *What Shall We Say About "The Gates Ajar"? Some thoughts suggested by the proposed "Antidote."* Copies of these pamphlets are housed in the British Library's Manuscripts Collections.

[100] HBS, letter to Mary Ann Evans [George Eliot], 15 April 1869, Berg Collection, NY Pubic Lib., NY.

"THE WILD AND DISTRACTED CALL FOR PROOF"

[1] Cartoon, *Merryman's Monthly*, October 1869.

[2] A year after completing *Uncle Tom's Cabin*, Stowe explained to an English admirer: "I wrote what I did because as a woman, as a mother I was oppressed & broken-hearted, with the sorrows & injustice I saw, because as a Christian I felt the dishonor to Christianity—because as a lover of my country I trembled at the coming day of wrath." HBS, letter to Lord Denman, 20 January 1853 (HM 24162), Huntington Lib., San Marino.

[3] James Osgood, assistant editor to James T. Fields for the *Atlantic Monthly*, published "The True Story of Lady Byron's Life." One of Stowe's biographers, Forrest Wilson, maintains that Fields knew nothing of the article as he was in Europe at the time it was published. "When James T. Fields got home and saw the havoc," Wilson writes, "he was so angry that Harriet dared not write to him for several months, transacting her professional business with Mr. Osgood" (541–542). Another Stowe biographer, Fields's spouse Annie, seconds this interpretation, quoting Oliver Wendell Holmes as having said, "Mr. Fields was absent in Europe . . . and his sub-editor, fearing to lose Mrs. Stowe as a contributor altogether, assented to her request to print the Byron paper" (320–321). Simultaneously, a copy of the article headed an edition of England's *Macmillan's Magazine*. The British version included an introductory statement from the editor, which states in part: "The following paper, from the pen of Mrs. Beecher Stowe, on Lady Byron's life and relations to Lord Byron, is the first complete and authentic statement of the whole circumstances of that disastrous affair which has been given to the world. Painful and appalling as are the details, the time is come when they can no longer be concealed . . . [, and] all former judgments, being based on insufficient data, must of necessity be henceforward invalidated or superseded" (377).

[4] "We have had three storms this autumn," Holmes wrote to his friend John Lothrop Motley, "1. The great gale of September 8th, which I recognized while it was blowing as the greatest for fifty-four years. . . . 2d. The Byron whirlwind, which began here and travelled swiftly across the Atlantic; and 3d, the goldstorm, as I christened the terrible financial conflict of the last week. About the Byron article I confess that, great as I expected the excitement to be, it far exceeded anything I had anticipated" (Morse II: 183). And, indeed, the "whirlwind" was as ubiquitous as it was strong. From American big-city periodicals like the ***New York Times, New York Albion, New York Daily Tribune, New York Herald, New York Ledger, Frank Leslie's Illustrated Newspaper, Harper's Weekly, Boston Commonwealth, Boston Morning Journal, Independent, Nation,*** and ***Chicago Tribune*** to the smaller rags including the ***American Bibliopolist, American Scotsman, Buffalo Express, Citizen and Round Table, Republican,*** the Charleston ***Daily Courier,*** Columbus ***Evening Bulletin*** and Hartford ***Courant*** to a slew of

British newspapers and magazines such as the celebrated *Blackwood's* and the widely distributed London *Times* as well as the *Athenaeum, Daily News, Daily Telegraph, Examiner and London Review, Illustrated Times, Nonconformist, Orchestra, Pall Mall Budget* and *Gazette, Period, Public Opinion, St. James Magazine, Saturday Review, Spectator, Temple Bar, Tomahawk,* and *Vanity Fair*—Stowe was castigated for daring to cast "dirt upon [Byron's] coffin" and pelt "with pitiless mud the escutcheon of one of England's Greatest Men" ("Let the Dead Rest" 1).

[5] Apart from Southern criticisms, Stowe received censure from English pundits as well; see "'No Voice from England': Mrs. Stowe, Mr. Lincoln, and the British in the Civil War" by Wendy F. Hamand.

[6] In her dissertation, Nancy Henry argues that with the *Key*, Stowe signals her acceptance of the position of self-proclaimed author in relation to her public. "[S]he would never again claim," notes Henry, "that God had written something for which she was responsible" (31). Henry points out Stowe's rhetorical repositioning at this time to incorporate fact-driven modes of value into the *Key*; however, Henry does not go one step further to theorize why Stowe's audience refused to believe "The True Story of Lady Byron's Life" where they had, at least in the Northern states, accepted the *Key* as reliable even though it constituted a similar admixture of fact and fiction.

In addition to differences in cultural predispositions toward "fact" between 1851 to 1870, it should also be noted that the *Key* and *Vindicated* sustain other crucial distinctions. The *Key*, for instance, provided real-life stories to support *Uncle Tom's Cabin*, a novel that dealt with atrocities affecting millions of blacks in the United States. *Vindicated*, on the other hand, focused on a single bad marriage and, as I mention in chapter one, failed to extrapolate the one instance to larger marital iniquities affecting millions of women. Importantly, too, the *Key* was able to furnish "actual" stories and documents that "proved" Stowe's novel, whereas, as I argue throughout this chapter, *Vindicated* did not have a single corroborating piece of "evidence" apart from Stowe's private conversation with Lady Byron. Finally, the *Key* dealt with a volatile and contentious political and social institution; *Uncle Tom's Cabin* wasn't the only statement against slavery. Yet *Vindicated* took up a topic for which there was no set group of sympathizers and, in point of fact, no real social contest. Guiccioli wasn't a tenth as famous as Stowe herself, and had Stowe let the matter go, very few people would have purchased and read Guiccioli's book. Ironically, Stowe's expose actually fueled Guiccioli's sales as well as the sales of Lord Byron's poetry.

[7] For the sake of clarity, all page numbers for "The True Story of Lady Byron's Life" come from the *Atlantic Monthly* edition.

[8] This point has been debated by one of her modern biographers, Forrest Wilson, who writes, "It is remarkable that none discovered the astonishing fact that much of [Stowe's] argument . . . was based on a misrepresentation of fact, and a deliberate one. Not one critic or enemy ever found it, and Harriet died with her guilty secret intact. . . . Critics picked at such flaws as her misspelling of Miss Milbanke's name and her inaccurate statement that the Byrons' married life had lasted two years, but never once saw that in her *Atlantic* paper, which,

she cried so passionately in her book, she had written in answer to the review in *Blackwood's*, she did not mention that review at all. The explanation is, of course, that when she wrote her dreadful gossip for the *Atlantic*, she did not know of the *Blackwood* review. It had not yet been published" (549–550).

[9] Unquestionably, Stowe had understood the potential media miscarry before "True Story" even appeared. To Osgood, she had written, "[T]his article is very important and will probably make a good deal of sensation," and she had confided to Fanny Fern, "I am just as scared as I can be . . . —and its all in print in the September Atlantic & now I feel fairly frightened at what I have done; & ready to run behind a door." In the same letter, however, Stowe also insisted that her decision to expose Byron was "right and just." In fact, Stowe never wavered from the conviction that defending Lady Byron was legitimate. When negative reviews of her article appeared, she asked one of her colleagues, William Patton, "What is the duty of a woman in my situation who sees a distinct effort once more to bring into circulation the Byron poetry by whitewashing his character & blackening that of his wife?" And as to the question of her "christian duty in the premises," Stowe informed Patton, "I am easy about that." Sixteen years later, in 1885, Stowe's position remained unchanged: "[W]hat I wrote on the Byron question was at the time I wrote it perfectly authenticated & . . . I have never regretted the writing of it." See HBS, letter to James Osgood, 23 June 1869 (HM 24368), Fields Papers, Huntington Lib., San Marino; HBS, letter to Sara Willis Parton [Fanny Fern], 25 July [1869], Parton Papers, Sophia Smith Collection, Smith College, Northampton; HBS, letter to William Patton, 2 September 1869, Acquisitions, Harriet Beecher Stowe Center, Hartford; and HBS, letter to Theodore Wolfe, 7 October [1885], Katharine S. Day Collection, Harriet Beecher Stowe Center, Hartford.

[10] Actually, the fact that novels continued to favor such wide-spread appeal might have everything to do with the telegraphic revolution. As people had greater access to global information and became less and less tied to a local idea of "community," novels may have provided an illusory sense of connectedness. See *A Fictive People* by Ronald Zboray.

[11] The editor's preface to the *Macmillan's* issue did, in fact, name the author as "Mrs. Beecher Stowe," although in the article itself, as in the American version, the narrator calls herself "the writer."

[12] John Hooker, a representative to the Connecticut state legislature, drafted amendments to revise laws excluding married women from holding property. Stowe wrote to Eliot of Hooker's efforts: "Massachusetts has *half* done this work—New York *half*—but if the amendments just drafted by my brother in law John Hooker & now before the house pass, Connecticut will have the proud superiority of being the first state since Louisiana to recognize ***the absolute equality of woman in the marriage relation***[.] The men are all right enough when they see what we want and are more than ready to right us." HBS, letter to Mary Ann Evans [George Eliot], 2 May [1869], Berg Collection, NY Public Library, NY.

[13] See Calvin Stowe, letter to James T. Fields, 1 January 1870, Fields Papers, Huntington Lib., San Marino.

[14] John Hooker, letter to Isabella Hooker, 18 November 1869, correspondence 1869 September-December (folder two), Isabella Hooker Collection, Harriet Beecher Stowe Center, Hartford.

[15] John Hooker, letter to Isabella Hooker, 20 November 1869, correspondence 1869 September-December (folder two), Isabella Hooker Collection, Harriet Beecher Stowe Center, Hartford.

[16] John Hooker, letter to Isabella Hooker, 1 December 1869, correspondence 1869 September-December (folder two), Isabella Hooker Collection, Harriet Beecher Stowe Center, Hartford.

[17] John Hooker, letter to Isabella Hooker, 4 December 1869, correspondence 1869 September-December (folder two), Isabella Hooker Collection, Harriet Beecher Stowe Center, Hartford.

[18] Upon the publication of Tilton's review, Stowe exhorted her friend William Patton to print a rebuttal of Tilton's views in the name of the Christian press. "It was in accordance with [your] delicate appreciation of noble & wise things that, instead of plunging at once, as Tilton has done, into the Byron question, *you* as I understand called on me for more knowledge of facts. To you therefore I look to [keep] the religious press from the shame & disgrace that has fallen on it thro Tiltons incapacity to understand the simplest elements of practical Christianity as presented in the life of a saintly woman." Stowe continued, asking a series of rhetorical questions meant to exculpate her own, as well as Lady Byron's, motives and spark the sympathy of a believing Christian: "What was the duty of a christian wife who discovers her husband & the father of her unborn child in deadly sin, has never once been thought of— What is the *duty* of a woman who is in some sort personally responsible for the circulation of a poisonous & demoralizing literature by her husband—when she & he are both leaving the world forever & these works are to decend [sic] to future generations?—What is the *duty* of a woman in my situation who sees a distinct effort once more to bring into circulation the Byron poetry by whitewashing his character & blackening that of his wife?" It is important to note that around the same time Tilton made his critique, he was simultaneously accusing Stowe's brother Henry of having had an affair with his wife. HBS, letter to William Patton, 2 September 1869, Acquisitions, Harriet Beecher Stowe Center, Hartford.

[19] Henry Ward Beecher, letter to HBS, 24 August 1869, Katharine S. Day Collection, Harriet Beecher Stowe Center, Hartford.

[20] HBS, letter to James Osgood, n.d. [August or September 1869] (HM 24349), Fields Papers, Huntington Lib., San Marino.

[21] Burton Bledstein explains that with the rise of professional culture in America, "A man was his 'word' or the words others used about him. . . . Universally and freely shared, available to all, words could provide a measure for categorizing people in a democratic society. . . . A Mid-Victorian used the written word as if he were defending it in a public courtroom. To place an opinion in writing was to make it final, commit the writer to its veracity, document a position and submit that position to the impartial reading of a third party" (73, 75).

[22] However, Stowe does contend that Byron himself reacted to the public criticism of his poetry as if his art were the substance of fact. In particular, Stowe cites *Blackwood's* initial condemnation of Byron's representation of Lady Byron as Donna Inez: "March 15, 1820.—Writes, and dedicates to I. Disraeli, Esq., a vindication of himself in reply to the 'Blackwood' on 'Don Juan,' containing an indignant defense of his own conduct in relation to his wife, and maintaining that he never yet has had an opportunity of knowing whereof he has been accused" (*Vindicated* 80).

[23] After *Lady Byron Vindicated* came out, the *Nation*—a periodical that had roundly abused Stowe's "True Story" and had a history of publishing negative reviews of Stowe's novels—recognized that the "only additional proof" Stowe had added were "more extended and explicit reports of the conversation in which Lady Byron revealed the secret" (2). See the Rev. of *Lady Byron Vindicated.*

[24] For instance, the second paragraph of the book begins, "I have not thought it necessary to disturb my spirit and confuse my sense of right by even an attempt at reading the many abusive articles that both here and in England have followed [my] disclosure" (1). I should note that this assertion is false, insofar as it is clear Stowe read many of her critics because *Vindicated* is a minute, point-by-point refutation of claims made against her argument in the "True Story" that goes so far as to quote many of her detractors.

[25] Stowe iterates this line in "True Story": "The interview had almost the solemnity of a death-bed avowal" (311).

[26] HBS, letter to James Osgood, n.d. [August or September 1869] (HM 24349), Fields Papers, Huntington Lib., San Marino.

[27] HBS, letter to James Osgood, 16 October [1869] (HM 24358), Fields Papers, Huntington Lib., San Marino.

[28] HBS, letter to Gamaliel Bailey, 9 March 1851 [typescript, original lost] (Ms. A.1.2.20.9), Department of Rare Books and Manuscripts, Boston Public Lib., Boston.

[29] As Susan Wolstenholme points out, most everyone who has written about the "The Byron Scandal" has added his or her two cents to this question of motive, whether Stowe's intentions were "pure" or "profane" in revealing Lady Byron's secret. Other twentieth-century studies on this subject include: Jean Willoughby Ashton's "Harriet Stowe's Filthy Story"; Alice Crozier's "Harriet Beecher Stowe and Byron"; Frank Lentricchia's "Harriet Beecher Stowe and the Byron Whirlwind"; Susan McPherson's "Opening the Open Secret"; and, relatedly, Paul Baender's "Mark Twain and the Byron Scandal." In addition, almost all Stowe's notable biographers have discussed her potential motive(s) as well, including Annie Fields's *Life and Letters of Harriet Beecher Stowe*; Joan Hedrick's *Harriet Beecher Stowe: A Life*; Charles Edward Stowe's *The Life of Harriet Beecher Stowe Compiled from her Letters and Journals*; Edward Wagenknecht's *Harriet Beecher Stowe: The Known and the Unknown*; and Forrest Wilson's *Crusader in Crinoline.*

[30] Cartoon, *Will-O'-the-Wisp*, 25 September 1869.

[31] Cartoon, *The Comic Monthly*, October 1869.

[32] Cartoon, *Fun*, 18 September 1869.

[33] A commentator for *The Tomahawk* unwittingly yet aptly assessed the paradox of a press claiming to abhor libel at the same time it compulsively writes and rewrites it: "We fearlessly challenge that reckless malignancy which, biting its lips over such a congenial morsel of scandal as this, imputes to all who will not join in its rabid assumption of virtuous indignation, the crimes that it gloats over while it deplores. We are content to be classed by such creatures with the irreclaimable votaries of vice, because we have protested against the beastly curiosity which lays bare the repulsive secrets of the lives of those who were great in spite of their moral blemishes" ("Byron Scandal" 125).

"A MORE *LIVING* INTEREST"

[1] According to Frank Mott's rubric for nineteenth-century bestsellers in the United States, *Adam Bede* was quickly a bestseller while *Silas Marner* became one as schools adopted it as part of their standard curriculum. Mott concludes that both novels "doubtless owe much of their great American popularity to their settings of humble family life" (136).

[2] Though not considered a strict American bestseller according to Mott's designation (although Lewes wrote to Blackwood that the novel "seem[ed] to have surpassed *Middlemarch*" in America), *Daniel Deronda* earned wide critical attention in both the United States and England and certainly garnered handsome royalties (*Letters* VI: 312). For 1876 alone, Eliot records an income of £1700 from *Harper's* and £5840 from *Blackwood*'s (VII: 364). And in addition to the *Harper's* and *Blackwood*'s serial circulations, from 1876–1879, Eliot notes that a total of 22,494 bound copies were sold. This level of distribution and profit is thrown into relief by one of Eliot's modern biographers, Gordon Haight: "Lewes' total earnings after 1855 barely equalled what [Eliot] earned from *Daniel Deronda* alone" (*George Eliot* 491).

[3] For a solid, informational reading of *Daniel Deronda*'s reception in England, see Russel Perkin's *A Reception-History of George Eliot's Fiction*, and for a thorough bibliography of Eliot criticism in England throughout the nineteenth century, see Constance Fulmer's *George Eliot: A Reference Guide*. There are a number of collections of Eliot criticism, often spanning fifty to a hundred years, that provide certain nineteenth-century reviews or summaries of criticism of *Daniel Deronda*. Some of the best include: David Carroll's *George Eliot: The Critical Heritage*; Gordon Haight's *A Century of George Eliot Criticism*; and Karen Pangallo's *The Critical Response to George Eliot*. However, there is no thorough book chapter or article that deals directly with the American reception of *Deronda*—with the exception of various parts of Jack Wilson's dissertation, "George Eliot in America," which is not the most accurate source. To locate most American reviews and notices, see the following two bibliographies: perhaps the best source for American criticism of any nineteenth-century British novel is the *Literary Index to American Magazines, 1850–1900* edited by Daniel A. Wells. In addition, George V. Griffith has cataloged notices, reviews, and articles on George Eliot in America between 1858 and 1881; see "George Eliot's American Reception, 1858–1881: A Bibliography."

[4] HBS, letter to Mary Ann Evans [George Eliot], September 25, 1876, Berg Collection, NY Public Lib., NY.

[5] See "The Jewish Reception of *Daniel Deronda*" by Shmuel Werses for a detailed account of this debate in German and English newspapers, including the Hebrew press. According to Werses, Eliot knew little if nothing of this controversy. Werses's article is also an excellent resource on the various Hebrew translations of *Daniel Deronda*.

[6] For instance, as A. V. Dicey explained in the *Nation*, "The very name of the book points to a misunderstanding between the readers and the author. They cared for Gwendolen Harleth" ("I" 230).

[7] HBS, letter to Mary Ann Evans [George Eliot], September 25, 1876, Berg Collection, NY Public Lib., NY. As a rule, Stowe is a terrible speller: "Gwendolin" is not a typo. Indeed, she often spelled Eliot's name "Elliot."

[8] In 1877, northern and southern states made a compromise over Jim Crow practices that, in effect, sabotaged Reconstruction and made both the history of African-American people as well as the topic of slavery unfashionable among white populations, and beginning in the early 1880s, the United States Congress began to pass legislation that would limit and exclude the immigration of certain populations primarily based on literacy requirements.

[9] In her diary, Eliot foresaw that her readership on both sides of the ocean would be biased against Jewish themes. "What will be the feeling of the public as the story advances I am entirely doubtful. The Jewish element seems to me likely to satisfy nobody" (*Letters* VI: 238).

[10] For more information on the rise of American realism and various high-art periodicals, see Nina Baym's *Novels, Readers, and Reviewers* as well as Nancy Glazener's *Reading for Realism*.

[11] Both Stowe and Phelps, for instance, repeatedly invoked *Adam Bede* as the touchstone against which they measured all of Eliot's subsequent work. Writing of the godlessness in *Deronda*, Stowe lamented, "If this is the last result of modern culture . . . —do your best & dont hope for comfort or help[,] then what a mockery is our existence! But I *know* in whom I believe — & you when you wrote Dinahs prayer with poor Hetty . . . — knew fullwell what a power there is in the living Christ to say to the impotent 'Rise up & walk.'" Phelps echoed this assessment, claiming that if both *Deronda* and *Middlemarch* had "held the Christian trust of Adam Bede," they would have been artistically greater books, "inasmuch as faith is philosophically broader than doubt and art to be perfect, must worship." See HBS, letter to Mary Ann Evans [George Eliot], September 25, 1876, Berg Collection, NY Public Lib., NY and ESP, letter to Mary Ann Evans [George Eliot], December 1, 1876, Beinecke Lib., Yale U., New Haven. Note, too, that the description of Amos Barton in chapter five of *Scenes of Clerical Life* actually predates the realist manifesto in *Adam Bede* and is just as forceful in its articulation of a Wordsworthian appraisal of the common man.

[12] At least one contemporary reviewer named *Daniel Deronda* a "romance." Robert E. Francillon, writing for London's *Gentleman's Magazine*, argued that if "George Eliot can be said to have shown any serious fault as an artist, it is that she has hitherto almost timidly kept to the safe ground of probability. . . . [But] Romance is the form of fiction which grapples with fact upon its whole ground, and deals with the higher and wider truths—the more occult wisdom—that is not picked up by the side of the highway" (384). Francillon found

Deronda so distinct from all of Eliot's previous, "realistic" work that he claimed "it is practically a first book by a new author, and must be judged accordingly" (396).

[13] HBS, letter to Mary Ann Evans [George Eliot], September 25, 1876, Berg Collection, NY Public Lib., NY.

[14] While Eliot doesn't mention specific requests to break off the engagement, she tells Blackwood that "People in their eagerness about my characters are quite angry, it appears, when their own expectations are not fulfilled—angry, for example, that Gwendolen accepts Grandcourt" (*Letters* VI: 241). Note, too, that this is the first half of a two-part, unsigned review by Dicey in *The Nation*. The second part appeared on the 19th of October, 1876, pages 245–246.

[15] I realize that Daniel's identity may not be "stable." As Cynthia Chase has famously argued, the novel works to undermine its very insistence on Daniel's Jewishness by relying on a metaleptic narrative structure that negates both "the proof that the text requires and the referent that it excludes"—i.e., Daniel's circumcision (224). But for the purposes of my argument, what is important is Gwendolen's perception of Daniel as coherent and secure, and the novel's relentless juxtaposition of the two in binaried terms: Gwendolen as a psyche "not yet formed," Daniel as a "formed" individual but not yet aware that he is such; Gwendolen as an amateur singer, Daniel as a consummate one; Gwendolen as self-absorbed, Daniel as altruistic; Gwendolen as the epitome of whiteness, Daniel as a representative of dusky "foreignness"; Gwendolen's lost paternity, Daniel's lost maternity; etc.

[16] For a rather simplistic reading of Gwendolen's relationship to the mirror, see Jenijoy LaBelle's *Herself Beheld*. Primarily LaBelle summarizes the various mirror scenes in the novel, equating Gwendolen's connection to the glass with her increasing entrapment and loss of autonomy throughout the story.

[17] As Jennifer Wicke notes in *Advertising Fictions*, "Advertising begins its nineteenth-century genesis in England, but it achieves its full momentum as an industry and inseparable partner of capitalism in America" (54).

[18] While St. Cecilia was not a favorite female subject among the Pre-Raphaelites like Ophelia or The Lady of Shalott, Edward Burne-Jones designed both a stained glass and later, with William Morris, a tapestry depicting St. Cecilia holding a small hand organ. As is typical of Burne-Jones, St. Cecilia is dressed in a loose garment and sandals, and her hair is undone, flowing down her back. Edward Burne-Jones and his wife Georgiana (or "Georgie") were close friends of Lewes and Eliot.

[19] George Eliot read *The Scarlet Letter* at least twice before writing *Daniel Deronda*, and she would have been familiar with the sexually charged scene between Hester Prynne and Arthur Dimmesdale in the woods: "[Hester] took off the formal cap that confined her hair; and down it fell upon her shoulders, dark and rich, with at once a shadow and a light in its abundance, and imparting the charm of softness to her features. There played around her mouth, and beamed out of her eyes, a radiant and tender smile, that seemed gushing from the very heart of womanhood. A crimson flush was glowing on her cheek, that had been long so pale. Her sex, her youth, and the whole richness of her beauty, came back from what men

call the irrevocable past . . ." (220).

[20] The scene where Queen Hermione masquerades in the guise of a statue is from Shakespeare's *The Winter's Tale*, Act V, Scene III.

[21] Prior to the *tableaux*, Klesmer already evaluated and censured Gwendolen's singing—another venue Gwendolen exploits since she is said to have the "rare advantage of looking almost prettier when . . . singing than at other times" (48). In a neat turn-about, Gwendolen's singing disturbs Klesmer enough to turn him to stone: "Herr Klesmer stood like a statue—if a statue can be imagined in spectacles; at least, he was a mute as a statue." Yet Klesmer is not—and, indeed, cannot be—the kind of statue Gwendolen becomes. Unlike Gwendolen, Klesmer is a poor figure for a sculpture, and his spectacles demonstrate that he is too real—i.e., too modern and quotidian—to be a work of art. The narrator quickly corrects its mistake, amending that Klesmer isn't a statue but simply as quiet as one.

[22] This subject was another favorite among the Pre-Raphaelites. Two years following the publication of *Deronda*, Edward Burne-Jones painted a *Pygmalion and the Image* series.

[23] See Eliot's comments from her *Daniel Deronda Notebooks*, edited by Jane Irwin. Obviously, white has many connotations, Gwendolen's dresses are often white, and she is pictured repeatedly as having a white countenance. Importantly, however, these descriptions always hearken back to the idea of Gwendolen as both a beautiful or "fair" piece of art and a woman whose sensibilities have been, in the words of Gilbert and Gubar, frozen or killed into art. An interesting study would be one that juxtaposed Gwendolen's whiteness against the times she deliberately wears black (in both love-making scenes at Offendene, for instance) and against the times she blushes—which, the narrator tells us, only happens when Gwendolen is surprised.

[24] *Deronda's* narrator explains, "[T]he most powerful of all beauty is that which reveals itself after sympathy and not before it. There is a charm of eye and lip which comes with every little phrase that certifies delicate perception or fine judgment, with every unostentatious word or smile that shows a heart awake to others; and no sweep of garment or turn of figure is more satisfying than that which enters as a restoration of confidence that one person is present on whom no intention will be lost. . . . The more obvious beauty . . . , begins by being an apology for folly, and ends like other apologies in becoming tiresome by iteration . . . a manifold sympathy over a monotonous attraction" (239).

[25] One cannot help but draw another analogy—Mrs. Glasher living at Gadsmere in the middle of a coal mining district. In a sense, the diamonds embody her as well, hardened after so many years "underground" and, ultimately, acquiring monetary value (i.e., when her son becomes heir to Grandcourt's estates).

[26] Before her marriage to Grandcourt, the novel spends a good deal of time detailing how Gwendolen believes her marriage—unlike her mother's—will "not be of a middling kind, such as most girls [are] contented with" (38–39).

[27] The feminist literary histories of the nineteenth-century that consider the public/private and surface/depth contradictions of Victorian femininity are too numerous to mention, and so I choose to list ones that have been of the greatest interest and assistance to me. For British

studies, see Nancy Armstrong's *Desire and Domestic Fiction*, Nina Auerbach's *Woman and the Demon*, Sandra Gilbert and Susan Gubar's *The Madwoman in the Attic*, and Mary Poovey's *The Proper Lady and the Woman Writer*. For American, see Nina Baym's *Woman's Fiction*, Nancy Cott's *Bonds of Womanhood*, and Jane Tompkins's *Sensational Designs*.

[28] I am indebted here to Kathy Psomiades's *Beauty's Body*. Although Psomiades does not link professionalism with British aestheticism, her study explores how bourgeois femininity enabled, defined, and was produced by the aesthetic impulse.

[29] Perusing the rest of the description, one could argue that Gwendolen herself is a parody of such heroines, sans religion.

[30] Catherine Gallagher discusses this economy as specifically prostitutional, wherein sex, like sensational novel writing, is unproductive yet simultaneously lucrative. While Gallagher also describes what she terms the "moral economy" Eliot constructs in opposition to such literary exchange, she contends that Eliot simultaneously "establishes a . . . metaphoric core of anxiety for her own work [where] [t]he guilt of illegitimate genealogical appropriation may be occluded, but the guilt of usurious and whorish commercial appropriation then immediately opens up" ("George Eliot" 47). Incidentally, these are themes Gallagher traces through an entire eighteenth-century oeuvre by women writers; see *Nobody's Story*.

[31] Like Stowe, Eliot singles out Mary Elizabeth Braddon's novels as representative of popular trash. Lewes, incidentally, does the same, and with Stowe sets Eliot's work above "Miss Braddon & the sensation mongers of the day" (see HBS, letter to Mary Ann Evans [George Eliot], September 23, 1872, Berg Collection, NY Public Lib., NY). In a letter to Blackwood on offering cheap editions of *Deronda*, Lewes gibes, "While Mrs. Henry Wood, Miss Braddon, Wilkie Collins etc. sell their novels at 6/- surely G.E. may expect a public?" (*Letters* VI: 345).

[32] See "Silly Novels by Lady Novelists," Eliot's note on "Authorship" from *Leaves from a Notebook*, and her essay "Debasing the Moral Currency" from *Impressions of Theophrastus Such*.

[33] In my judgment, Nancy Henry—the one analyst who has treated the Stowe-Eliot correspondence with a critical eye—misreads Eliot's intentions regarding audience as well as Stowe's assessment of Eliot's relationship to her public. In Henry's dissertation, she quotes a letter from Eliot to Clementia Doughty (Mrs. Peter Alfred) Taylor, a feminist who pressured Eliot to take a more active public role in the Woman's Rights Movement. To Taylor, Eliot claims, "My function is that of the *aesthetic*, not the doctrinal teacher—the rousing of the nobler emotions, which make mankind desire the social right, not the prescribing of special measures, concerning which the artistic mind, however strongly moved by social sympathy, is often not the best judge. It is one thing to feel keenly for one's fellow-beings; another to say, 'This step, and this alone, will be the best to take for the removal of particular calamities'" (*Letters* VII: 44). Henry cites this quotation as emblematic of Eliot's growing disregard for her public, arguing, "[Eliot] continued to write, not only enigmatically, but defensively, resenting the judgments of critics even when sales were high" (29). In turn, Henry contends that Stowe never proscribed to such a model. "Stowe found 'mystification' and intellectualization threat-

ening to democratic principles because for her the ideal society depended upon a well-educated public, and she accused Eliot of violating these principles through the increasingly elevated style of writing she adopted" (12). To prove her point, Henry quotes from Stowe's letter about *Middlemarch*, focusing, however, on Stowe's commentary about Eliot's elevated style and language rather than Stowe's main idea, which is that Eliot needs to revitalize her writing with a Christian animus. Thus Henry juxtaposes Eliot's aesthetic against Stowe's "concern with the dissemination of information to the people and her own involvement in the construction of narratives appropriate for the consumption of the many" (29). Here Henry ignores two complex aspects of both Stowe's and Eliot's respective aesthetics. First, as previously mentioned, Stowe was equally concerned with her art's "fineness" as with its far-reaching message. Stowe fusses over Eliot's exalted style not so much for its impenetrability but because it perpetuates the form of beautiful art without the soul of a Christian moral; in other words, Stowe felt that Eliot's beautiful writing was wasted if not in the service of Christ. Second, Eliot was indeed seeking a way to influence the popular social mind. Writing to Stowe about *Daniel Deronda*, Eliot explains, " There is nothing I should care more to do, . . . than to rouse the imagination of men and women to a vision of human claims in those races of their fellow-men who most differ from them in customs and beliefs" (*Letters* VI: 301). Hence Eliot was not trying to turn away from her audience; rather, as noted to Taylor, Eliot hoped her work would rouse universal sympathies. In this manner, Eliot actually parallels aesthetic declarations from both Stowe and Phelps; all three desire to influence society at a universal level; all three glorify the immortality of literature over the immediacy of political advocacy and social movements.

[34] HBS, letter to Mary Ann Evans [George Eliot], 25 September 1876, Berg Collection, NY Public Lib., NY.

[35] For further discussion of how Eliot was received in book reviews by American critics—especially as the epitome of a realist writer—see George Griffith's "George Eliot, Realism, and the American Press, 1858–1881."

[36] In this manner, American critics placed Eliot and her work quite close to their appreciation of Stowe as a sympathetic writer, especially on questions of race. Whipple found the Jewish pathos in *Deronda* quite akin to that of blacks in the United States. Citing the moment when Mordecai admits that he has been chided by his own people, Whipple claims that the scene bears a resemblance to "the chill of heart which a thoroughgoing New-England Abolitionist of the old type might have experienced when he found numbers of free negroes in the Northern States despising their enslaved brethren in the States of the South" (51).

[37] Richard Brodhead explains that in the years between 1860 and 1900, "the *Atlantic Monthly*, *The Century Magazine*, and *Harper's Monthly Magazine* achieved an identification as the three American 'quality journals.' This means that these three journals produced the same high or distinguished zone in the literary realm that the classical museum or symphony orchestra produced in art or music, a strongly demarcated high-status arena for high-artistic practice" (124).

[38] These adjectives come from "'Deronda' and 'Middlemarch'" in the *Galaxy*; "George

Eliot's 'Daniel Deronda'" in *Scribner's Monthly*; and "Daniel Deronda: A Conversation" in the *Atlantic Monthly*.

[39] HBS, letter to Mary Ann Evans [George Eliot], September 25, 1876, Berg Collection, NY Public Lib., NY.

[40] These numbers are from two historical studies of Jews in America: Lee M. Friedman's *Pilgrims in a New Land* and David Rausch's *Friends, Colleagues, and Neighbors*.

[41] For all of these aspects of Jewish history as well as others, see *Pilgrims in a New Land*.

[42] Since the image of the black slave woman was America's cultural metonym for the intersecting threats of race and sex, these anxieties over the figure of the Alcharisi might also have something to do with yet another contemporary movement: the organization, on the part of black women, for suffrage, fair pay, and greater social autonomy. Although African-American women gained national prominence in the 1890s with the publication of the first widely read novels by black women writers, the establishment of the National Association of Colored Women, and their participation in the World's Congress of Representative Women in 1893, African-American women were already part of the political scene as early as 1869 with the highly publicized speeches of Frances Ellen Watkins Harper across much of the East Coast. In league with Frederick Douglass, Harper was a firm supporter of black suffrage, taking a stand against Susan B. Anthony and Elizabeth Cady Stanton who wished to place sex over race in securing the vote. For instance, at the American Equal Rights Association meeting held in 1869 in New York City, Harper and Douglass took Anthony and Stanton head-on in terms of this issue. Douglass quipped that "this Equal Rights meeting [has] been pre-eminently a Woman's Rights meeting," and Harper concurred, "When it [is] a question of race, [I] let the lesser question of sex go. But the white women all go for sex, letting race occupy a minor position" (Buhle 267). Moreover, 1876—the same year *Deronda* appeared—was a particularly tense period for the suffrage movement as a whole. Apart from numerous local celebrations, Philadelphia sponsored a Centennial Exhibition, and on July 4th, members of the National Woman Suffrage Association held a rally to protest the reading of the Declaration of Independence by having Stanton read their own Declaration of Rights for Women—a document that did not include a specific clause on black women's rights. Harper remonstrated Anthony and Stanton for this omission and gave popular lecturers—often to black women's groups—against the adoption of white female suffrage over universal franchise. Concurrently, Harper encouraged black women to work outside the home, even against seemingly insuperable odds. In 1869, she commented that when she was living in Boston, "there were sixty women who left work because one colored woman went to gain a livelihood in their midst" (Buhle 268). But notwithstanding this kind of hardship, in her 1878 article "Colored Women of America," Harper argued that black women need not be tied to the domestic sphere, and she gave various examples of black women as property owners, plantation managers, entrepreneurs, and sole supporters of their families. "When I was in Mississippi," recalls Harper, "I stopped with Mr. Montgomery, a former slave of Jefferson Davis's brother. His wife was a woman capable of taking on her hands 130 acres of land, and raising one hundred and seven bales of cotton by the force which she could organise. Since then I have received a very inter-

esting letter from her daughter, who for years has held the position of Assistant Post-mistress. In her letter she says: 'There are many women around me who would serve as models of executiveness anywhere. They do double duty, a man's share in the field, and a woman's part at home'" ("Colored Women" 11). For more about Harper, see Hazel Carby's *Reconstructing Womanhood* as well as Elizabeth Ammons's *Legacy* profile. In 1892, Harper published *Iola Leroy; or, Shadows Uplifted*, a novel dealing with the lives of Southern freedmen after Reconstruction and including the fraught topics of racial passing and miscegenation. Also, for the complete text of Stanton and Anthony's Declaration of Rights, see *The Concise History of Woman Suffrage*.

"PROCLAIMING THE ROYAL LINEAGE TO THE AVERAGE MIND"

[1] This information comes from Phelps's autobiography, and all of her biographers—Bennett, Coultrap-McQuin, Kelly, and Kessler—have assumed her figures are accurate. See *Chapters from a Life*, page 111. Mott lists *Gates* as a "better seller" in America, although he does not provide precise figures.

[2] Before *Gates*, Phelps had, in fact, received kind letters from John Greenleaf Whittier and Thomas Higginson complimenting her first well-known short-story "The Tenth of January"—a story about a devastating factory fire that marked, at least for her, "the first recognition which [she] received from literary people" (*Chapters* 92).

[3] ESP, letter to Henry W. Longfellow, 21 March 1879 (bMS Am 1340.2 [5815]), Houghton Lib., Harvard U., Cambridge.

[4] For instance, just as *The Gates Ajar* was written to succor women who had lost relations and lovers to the Civil War, *The Silent Partner* was intended to expose the sordid working conditions of New England factories, while *Doctor Zay* was calculated to confront prejudice against female doctors.

[5] ESP, letter to Madam, 14 February 1880, Elizabeth Stuart Phelps Collection (#6997), Clifton Waller Barrett Lib., Special Collections, U. of Virginia Lib., Charlottesville.

[6] Recorded in her autobiography, *Chapters from a Life*, other such aspects of Phelps's ideal self include Christian faith, a commitment to the abolition of animal vivisection and bootleg liquor, a conviction that women should have the right to vote, and a belief in homeopathy as a practical system of therapeutics. The last chapter of her memoir outlines Phelps's life creed along these points.

[7] ESP, letter to Mary Ann Evans [George Eliot], 1 December 1876, Beinecke Rare Book and Manuscript Lib., Yale U., New Haven.

[8] As in *The Story of Avis*, Eliot's Armgart is an exceptional, talented artist, one who spurns an offer of marriage from Count Graf Dornburg, a man who, like Romney Leigh, assumes that "A woman's rank / Lies in the fullness of her womanhood: / Therein alone she is royal" (*Collected Poems* 128). And Armgart responds to Graf's proposal in terms that prefigure Avis Dobell's reaction to Philip Ostrander. "Yes, I know / The oft-taught Gospel: 'Woman, thy desire / Shall be that all superlatives on earth / Belong to men, save the one highest kind– / To be a mother. . . . Let [Nature] be / arbitress; she gave me voice / Such as she only gives a

woman child, / Best of its kind, gave me ambition too, / That sense transcendent which can taste the joy / of swaying multitudes" (128). See Jack Wilson's article "Competing Narratives in Elizabeth Stuart Phelps's *The Story of Avis*" wherein he reads *Avis* as a *künstlerroman* displaced by a *bildungsroman*: a novel necessitating the death of the female artist in favor of the female reformer. Examining two parallel narratives, or what he terms "architexts," Wilson supports his trajectory by triangulating *Aurora Leigh* and *Armgart* with *Avis*. Wilson argues these two narratives inhabit *Avis* "as a result of frequent allusion," and make "the object of interpretation in *The Story of Avis* . . . not a text but the interaction of textual fields" (61). In sum, Wilson sees these three narratives engaged in related and, at some level, superimposed struggles between issues of aesthetics versus ethics, where, for all three, ethics prevails. Avis Dobell's quest for identity, notes Wilson, follows the same paths pioneered by Aurora and Armgart—paths that "lead to ethical and spiritual enlightenment only [while] the aesthetic vocation . . . slip[s] away" (66). Yet Wilson's reading of *Avis* is incomplete, neglecting the larger context of Phelps's personal correspondence and copious articles on female aesthetics and ethics—works that move to amalgamate, rather than choose between, such antipodes.

[9] In the 1840s and 1850s, academies established especially for women artists were started in Philadelphia with the School of Design for Women in 1844 and in New York with the Cooper Union-Free Art School for Women in 1859.

[10] R. S., letter to James Claghorn, 11 April 1882, Collection of the Archives, The Pennsylvania Academy of the Fine Arts, Philadelphia.

[11] As a sort of culmination to these contentious events surrounding the professional education of female artists, the 1876 Centennial International Exhibition in Philadelphia served to crystallize art as one of a number of new professions in the United States. Bringing together artists and their work from across the nation and housing them in a central museum, the Exhibition served to display the ideological processes of capitalism through art and technology via a more recherché outlet than, say, London's Crystal Palace of 1851 that focused entirely on manufactured commodities or P. T. Barnum's Museum on Broadway that housed oddities and pedestrian entertainments. Yet the Exhibition's overall purpose was identical to these other ostentatious displays of industry, wealth, and eclecticism: to theatricalize commodities as symbols of American cultural value and its production. Integral to this project's success was the display of art not just as "art" but as spectacle, as an advertisement for America's erudition. Thus the Exhibition's planning committee members erected Memorial Hall, a building meant to democratize all kinds of commodities, including art, by placing them all together in a central locale where people from every walk of life could access "culture" in a common space: a kind of republican ideal.

Originally, works by women artists were to be shown side-by-side with men's, yet shortly before the Exhibition opened the Director-General of the Exhibition's Commission, a Mr. Goshorn, informed the women's art organizer Elizabeth Duane Gillespie that there was no more room in the main building to display the women's work. Gillespie was the great-granddaughter of Benjamin Franklin, originally approached by the chair of the Centennial Board of Finance to help the Board raise funds for the Exhibition. Gillespie agreed to help on the condition that women's art, inventions, and products be given space in Memorial Hall, viewing this concession as a means to represent the spirit of "true nationhood." She told her own female committee members that the promised space would "make the occasion more attractive and impressive and productive of the kind and social feeling among the inhabitants of the whole country" (Paine 6). Undaunted by Goshorn's exclusion and under Gillespie's supervision, the Women's Centennial Executive Committee raised enough money to construct a building apart from the central exhibit, the Woman's Pavilion. The Pavilion was subsequently billed as a celebration of women's achievements in all the professions, including the fine arts. Indeed, as Judith Paine notes, the Pavilion was "provocative because it was unprecedented. Although world's fairs were common during the nineteenth century, never before had there been a separate building exclusively devoted to women's work" (5–6). Yet radical feminist groups were not quite so enthusiastic. Being segregated from the main building—as if women could not participate in the commemoration of American art and were relegated to the likes of a summer house—the Pavilion was also "no true exhibit of woman's art," at least according to Elizabeth Cady Stanton (314). Stanton argued that "true" woman's art could not exist as long as women were beholden to men in both law and culture. "[U]pon its walls," she insists, "should have been hung . . . framed copies of all the laws bearing unjustly upon women—those which rob her of her name, her earnings, her property, her children, her person" (316–317). For Stanton, an accurate portrayal of woman's art would have consisted of objects made by females in factories: cloth, shoes, paper. Thus the Pavilion served to catalyze basic concerns to all women pursuing art in the 1870s: the commodification of their art as capitalist spectacle (a threat to all artists after the Civil War); an emphasis upon the exceptionalism of female artists (set apart from the "norm"); the question of whether exceptionalism could stand-in for female universalism (a basic tension within the culture of professionalism); and an increasingly elitist and structured system of the arts that necessitated a perilous negotiation of gender, work, and artistry for women painters, sculptors, actors, and, of course, writers.

[12] For a related historical study of the treatment of aestheticized female sexuality in Victorian painting, see Anne Anderson's "Life into Art and Art Into Life."

[13] For Avis, instantaneous sympathy with strangers is "very natural": "The artist's world is peopled with the vanishing of such mute and unknown friends; and the artist's eye is privileged to take their passports as they come and go" (39). In terms of a native sense of effect, Avis is said to be "too much of an artist ever to choose an awkward pose: she would have writhed under one . . . had she been dead" (168). And nature, for Avis, is one great canvas: "Upon the palette of the sky relaxing Nature spread her colors, as the human artist does, deepening from the pallor to the flesh" (216). These brief examples demonstrate how the narrator develops Avis's innate, aesthetic sympathy with the elements around her into the affected role of a perpetual artiste.

[14] With this assertion, Avis had much in common with actual American women artists of this period. For instance, Harriet Hosmer, the most famous female sculptor after the Civil War, admitted in a personal correspondence, "I am the only faithful worshipper of Celibacy,

and her service becomes more fascinating the longer I remain in it. Even if so inclined, an artist has no business to marry. For a man, it may be well enough, but for a woman on whom matrimonial duties and cares weigh more heavily, it is a moral wrong, I think, for she must neglect her profession or her family, becoming neither a good wife and mother nor a good artist. My ambition is to become the latter, so I wage an eternal feud with the consolidating knot" (35).

[15] It is interesting to note that Stowe herself was quite anxious about "French influences" on young women readers, especially the "physicalness" of French fiction. At the same time Stowe was declaiming against the invasion of the Guiccioli book, itself characterized as French corruption (having first been published in French), Stowe confessed a parallel nervousness over the invasion of George Sand's "French" notions into the Woman's Rights movement. While Stowe readily admitted Sand's artistic acumen—"George Sand writes exquisite french—her style is something wonderful"—it was the carnal exoticism of her narratives that troubled Stowe, indicating their capacity to beguile a mass group of women readers. Hedrick explains, "Stowe feared that the 'simple American women' were likely to follow down this dangerous path [of free love] out of sexual ignorance—or to put it in Stowe's terms, ignorance of things '*French*'" (372). In a letter to one of Elizabeth Cady Stanton's political rivals, Mary Livermore, Stowe confessed, "George Sand's writings are more physical and animal in their descriptions of animal love than those of *any* man—even any Frenchman & it is this *physicalness* that is disgusting." See HBS, letter to Henry Ward Beecher, n.d. [summer 1870], Beecher Family Papers, Sterling Memorial Lib., Yale U, New Haven; HBS, letter to Mrs. [Mary] Livermore, n.d. [August? 1870] (Ms. P.91.37.124), Department of Rare Books and Manuscripts, Boston Public Lib., Boston.

[16] Couture, 1815–1879, is also known for his lavish use of color, sometimes described as "strident." For an overview of his work and position in nineteenth-century art circles, see Albert Boime's *Thomas Couture and the Eclectic Vision*. A study that examines Couture's American influence (including his affect on American pupils) is Jane Van Nimmen's *Thomas Couture: Paintings and Drawings in American Collections*.

[17] The same censures stemming from the belief that live nude subjects jeopardized female artists' virtue were made against viewing anatomizations. Although women were permitted to watch actual dissections as early as 1860 in a single-sex course, certain aspects of the anatomy class continued to frustrate women's desire for equal education. In 1882, Elizabeth Macdowell wrote to Thomas Eakins of the Pennsylvania Academy about material and attitudinal inequities between the separate anatomy classes: "There are several good girls who are seeing the [dead body] for the first time, and they can get a very poor conception from such a dried up dismantled mass. The boys monopolize the alternate mornings . . . , leaving us no opportunity to see the new subject." Macdowell adds, "When we have come in contact with [the boys,] there are some four who are both noisy and rude making it very unpleasant." Elizabeth Macdowell, letter to Thomas Eakins, 31 January 1882, Collection of the Archives, The Pennsylvania Academy of the Fine Arts, Philadelphia.

[18] Whereas Waldo's invalidism teaches him the value of "feminine strength," Philip's dependency upon Avis (physically, spiritually, emotionally, and, in the end, economically) makes him doubt his manhood and engage in a flirtation with Barbara Allen. For an outstanding reading of the courtship between Waldo Yorke and Dr. Zaidee Atalanta Lloyd, see Timothy Morris's "Professional Ethics and Professional Erotics in Elizabeth Stuart Phelps's *Doctor Zay*."

[19] Writing at the turn of the century, the painter Wassily Kandinsky describes his relationship to painting with heterosexist, imperialist, and sexually violent symbolism: "Thus I learned to battle the canvas, to come to know it as a being resisting my wish (dream) and to bend it forcibly to this wish. At first it stands there like a chaste virgin . . . and then comes the wilful brush which first here, then there, gradually conquers it with all the energy particular to it, like a European colonist" (Doy 55). Although this example is much more excessive in how it genders (and racializes) the act of painting, Avis's imagery also conceives of the painter/painted relation in such masculine/feminine terms.

[20] It is not entirely implausible to suppose that when Avis is equated with statuary, such moments are taken from the example of Gwendolen Harleth. Phelps was clearly taken with Eliot's novel, naming her spaniel "Daniel Deronda" and writing a short story with Gwendolen as its main character. See Phelps's "An Hour With Gwendolyn [sic]."

[21] "I do not mean to paint portraits," Avis admits to Coy, "though Courture said I probably must, in America" (*Avis* 59).

[22] Until just after the Civil War, almost all female painters worked in miniature, still life, and landscape genres; if they painted portraits, most often they copied already existing paintings of famous visages (e.g., republican leaders), assisted their distinguished father- or husband-painters by copying portraits for them, or painted likenesses of female friends and family members. There are notable exceptions; in the 40s, Sarah Miriam Peale was the leading portrait artist in Baltimore and then St. Louis for thirty more years. For a more thorough discussion of notable women artists through the 1870s, see Charlotte Streifer Rubinstein's *American Women Artists*.

[23] See Laura Mulvey's classic article on the dynamics of scopophilia in Hollywood cinema, "Visual Pleasure and Narrative Cinema."

[24] Amy Schrager Lang discusses a similar phenomenon in terms of Phelps's *The Silent Partner* where Perley Kelso and Sip Garth's respective gender differences are "offered as the product of class position" (273). Lang reads this displacement through the historical lens of the debate surrounding labor practices in the 1870s.

[25] Where Gwendolen's whiteness signals her fear and frigidity (e.g., the glass reflecting "so many women petrified white"), Avis's signals her racial power. Both women, however, avoid blushing in the conventional way of nineteenth-century heroines—when either is aroused or angered, they both turn white.

[26] Conversely, when Avis blushes, the blush is coded as a physical marker of feminine modesty, even to the point of contrasting such a mark with her position as a professional: "But when, standing with her gloved hand upon a column . . . her eyes gone rebel to all but the

instinct of the moment, starting, she stirred and turned away [from Philip's gaze], she felt a great tidal wave of color surge across her face. If the eye of that amber god across the Madeleine had caught an artist, it had held a woman. Avis became aware of this with a scorching, maidenly self-scorn" (39). When aroused, her blush imprisons rather than empowers Avis: "The scorching color slowly rose, lighted, sped, fired her face, brow, and neck: when [Philip] saw it, he knew that he had never seen her blush before. She seemed to stand imprisoned by that blush, as if it had been a physical paralysis or pain" (102). Thus, the blush imperils Avis, relegating her to a position of stereotypic femininity—it is a metonym for Avis's bodily, erotic passions, a literal stain upon her cheek that calls into question Avis's purity. Her fascination with the color red provides a parallel to her blushes, since she is aware of its sexual danger, and it is often used in combination with the bodily blush. Once she marries Philip, however, she refigures both her blushes and the color red in terms of appropriate, marital romance. Wrapping herself in a carmine shawl after their honeymoon, she tells Philip that carmine "is one of the colors made from the cochineal. . . . I have always fancied that they throb with the life that has been yielded to make them" (133). Thus, the color is transformed into a metaphor, here, of her relinquished maidenhood. "She blushed gently: she was glad [Philip] thought the carmine suited her; she loved it too well to wear it at hap-hazard. . . . She would not wear this color except for him."

[27] It is not an exaggeration to figure Waitstill in such terms: the novel begins and ends with quotations from Thomas Bulfinch's "Age of Chivalry" where King Arthur entrusts Sir Galahad in the quest for the Sangreal or Holy Grail. Clearly we are to associate Avis with the good-hearted King, the Grail with the attainment of "Womanhood" or feminine strength, and Waitstill with the forthright Galahad, this "purest of knights," an overt Christ figure in Bulfinch's rendition of the Camelot mythology (Bulfinch 419).

[28] Other "New Woman" novels by Phelps engage in similar modes of gender comparison and substitution, yet keep such comparison to middle-class men or working-class women. For instance, Aunt Winifred's class and race are secured in juxtaposition to boorish men: "I looked [the Deacon] over again,—hat, hoe, shirt, and all; scanned his obstinate old face with its stupid, good eyes and animal mouth. Then I glanced at Aunt Winifred as she leaned forward in the afternoon light; the white, finely cut woman, with her serene smile and rapt, saintly eyes. . . ." (*Gates* 104). *The Silent Partner*'s Perley Kelso is naturalized as a white, middle-class philanthropist in relation to Sip Garth, a "little brown" factory worker: "Whereas Perley has become 'healthy' and 'happy,' her 'womanly, wonderful face . . . beg[ging] for nothing' but 'opulent and warm . . . ,' Sip remains, for all her faith, poor and dark: 'a little rough, brown girl,' with 'nothing saintly' about her" (Lang 283–284). And *Doctor Zay*'s brand of femininity establishes itself as privileged *vis-à-vis* Waldo Yorke, the prototypic bourgeois male: "She had her dangerous and sacred feminine nerve under magnificent training. It was her servant, not her tyrant; her wealth, not her poverty; the source of her power, not the exponent of her weakness. . . . The young man acknowledged from the bottom of his heart that she was a balanced and beautiful creature. He had read of such women. He had never seen one" (*Doctor Zay* 111).

[29] Rosemarie Thomson analyzes how disabled women are necessary to the rhetorics of reform in *The Silent Partner*, *Uncle Tom's Cabin*, and *Life in the Iron Mills*.

[30] A fine example of this caricature can be found in Mary Wilkins Freeman's short story "A New England Nun." The prudish and finical old maid found a good deal of play in the writings of so-called local colorists, including Freeman, Sarah Orne Jewett, and Kate Chopin. Even though the old maid was a farcical standby, however, I should point out that writers like Freeman and Chopin employed this very element of her character against their readers, inviting them to laugh at her while implicating that laugh in the very structures of stereotyping that circumscribed her social position in the first place.

[31] Without making too much of the red-toed stockings, I believe it is no accident that the toes are red rather than green or purple or orange. Throughout *The Story of Avis*, the color red—"carmine" to Avis—is a symbol of erogenous and artistic passion in women.

[32] In March of 1877, *The Literary World* asserts in its "Literary News" section that "Elizabeth Stuart Phelps is at work on a story, which is to take up the woman question; and is said, by those who have seen parts of it, to be her best book" (163). Come June, however, they print the following retraction: "We are authorized to say that the story which Miss Elizabeth Stuart Phelps is writing is not, as has been whispered through the papers, on the 'woman question,' if this term means woman suffrage, or what is generally understood by the vague and comprehensive expression 'woman's rights.' It does, indeed, relate to women, as all interesting stories do, or, rather, as an interesting story does when told by a person of the marked individuality and sympathetic genius of Miss Phelps" (17). Phelps herself never called *Avis* a suffrage novel; rather, in addition to what she saw as its aesthetic merits, she truly believed her novel was a vehicle for universal kinship between herself (as author) and her women readers. In a letter to an admirer of *Avis* dated April 1878, Phelps writes, "I try to help women; I love women; and when they make me aware that they are conscious of help, or recognize my purpose, I am stronger for the next step. Such letters as yours do both." ESP, letter to Sarah Knowles Bolton, 5 April 1878, Bolton-Stanwood Family Papers, American Antiquarian Society, Worcester.

[33] Indeed, Avis is also said to be Artemis—the Greek, virgin huntress who is perfectly happy without men, taking care of women and animals in childbirth.

[34] Phelps may have first come to embrace the Sphinx from a passage in Barrett Browning's *Aurora Leigh*. Aurora describes her Muse as "the Muse-Sphinx," with "purple-braided head" and eyes that "start between the boughs / As often as a stag's" (32–33). That Phelps was mesmerized and perplexed by this figure, and that this figure was able to contain paradoxical elements of womanhood (e.g., "veiled or free" below), is clear in the following poem she wrote for the 1879 graduating class at Andover's Abbott Academy. The poem is aptly titled "The Sphinx":

> O glad girls' faces, hushed and fair! how
>   shall I sing for ye?
> For the grave picture of a sphinx is all that
>   I can see.

Vain is the driving of the sand, and vain the
desert's art;
The years strive with her, but she holds the
lion in her heart.

Baffled or fostered, patient still, the perfect
purpose clings;
Flying or folded, strong as stone, she wears
the eagle's wings.

Eastward she looks; against the sky the
eternal morning lies;
Silent or pleading, veiled or free, she lifts
the woman's eyes.

O grave girls' faces, listening kind! glad will
I sing for ye,
While the proud figure of the sphinx is all
that I can see. (366)

[35] For instance, when Philip first admits his love to Avis, we are told that she resists like "a great, dumb, protesting goddess, whom some light hand had just dragged from the bosom of the earth to the glare of day" (64).

[36] As Phelps writes in one of her magazine articles on the dangers implicit in any notion of conventional Victorian womanhood, "'The true woman,' . . . earth has never seen. . . .

[W]hen through family, church, and state woman the equal of man herself disowns and exiles women the subject, and when generations have brought the laws of inheritance to bear upon such a race of women; when children and children's children have perpetuated their struggling strength, and dropped their lingering weakness—only then can we draw the veil from the brows of the TRUE WOMAN. Only then shall this sad Sphinx—who lost her crown and received her curse for the love of knowledge, yet who has woven out of her love to man the web of earth's purest dreams and holiest deeds—unclose her marble lips and lift her weary head to take her well-earned blessing.

Fair as the moon, clear as the sun, and terrible as any army with banners will be the face which, out of the desert of her long watch and patience, she will turn upon the world" ("The True Woman" 1).

[37] There is, however, one more substitution beyond the Sphinx that actually links *The Story of Avis* to the discourses of "natural" or patently feminine modes of production. Although the novel and the ideal of the Sphinx did not sit well with reviewers in America and England, the representation of Avis's life and work are catalysts, ones that point toward the "salvation" of all women, but finally with the creation of Waitstill, not the Sphinx. Waitstill is a creation that potentially thwarts the complications and contradictions so rife in an aes-

thetic marketplace: she is live, not static like a two-dimensional painting; she is changeable, liquid, permeable, "priceless." She is generations, not an individual or individuating thing.

[38] For instance, Avis cannot claim the title of professional painter until she has passed through a series of special rituals, including various levels of training abroad, trying to make her career in two years after returning home, and, ultimately, taking a place as a painting instructor, i.e., as an expert who must continue to display her esoteric knowledge in service of her society in order to maintain her professional status. For a comparison of Phelps's construction of female artistry in *Avis* to Nathaniel Hawthorne's in his contemporaneous novel *The Marble Faun*, see Deborah Barker's "The Riddle of the Sphinx."

[39] For example, see Thomas Richards's *The Commodity Culture of Victorian England*, Lori Merish's *Sentimental Materialism*, and Jennifer Wicke's *Advertising Fictions*. Richards treats advertising in England from 1851–1914; Merish locates her discussion of gender and/as commodity in nineteenth-century American literature; and Wicke treats the same period and subject as revealed in literature and popular images in the United States (although she does have a chapter on Dickens).

[40] ESP, letter to Mary Ann Evans [George Eliot], 26 February 1873, Beinecke Rare Book and Manuscript Lib., Yale U., New Haven.

Bibliography

Alcott [Nieriker], May. *Studying Art Abroad, and How to Do It Cheaply.* Boston: Roberts Brothers, 1879.

"American and Foreign Art." *Frank Leslie's Illustrated Newspaper* 10 November 1883: 178.

Ammons, Elizabeth. "Legacy Profile: Frances Ellen Watkins Harper (1825–1911)." *Legacy* 2.2 (Fall 1985): 61–66.

"An Appeal from American Authors." *The Critic* 5 (6 February 1886): 65.

Anderson, Anne. "Life into Art and Art into Life: Visualizing the Aesthetic Woman or 'High Art Maiden' of the Victorian 'Renaissance.'" *Women's History Review* 10.3 (2001): 441–462.

Anonymous. Letter. *Pall Mall Gazette* 7 September 1869: 3.

Armstrong, Nancy. *Desire and Domestic Fiction: A Political History of the Novel.* New York and Oxford: Oxford UP, 1987.

Ashton, Jean Willoughby. "Harriet Stowe's Filthy Story: Lord Byron Set Afloat." *Prospects: Annual of American Cultural Studies* 2 (1976): 373–384.

Auerbach, Nina. Rev. of *Work* by Louisa May Alcott, *The Story of Avis* by Elizabeth Stuart Phelps Ward, *Anne* by Constance Fenimore Woolson, *The Anglomaniacs* by Constance Cary Harrison, and *The Descendant* by Ellen Glasgow. *Nineteenth-Century Fiction* 33.4 (March 1979): 475–483.

———. *Romantic Imprisonment: Women and Other Glorified Outcasts.* New York: Columbia UP, 1986.

———. *Woman and the Demon: The Life of a Victorian Myth.* Cambridge: Harvard UP, 1982.

Austin, Alfred. *A Vindication of Lord Byron: The True Story of Lady Byron's Life.* London: Chapman and Hall, 1869.

Baender, Paul. "Mark Twain and the Byron Scandal." *American Literature* 30 (January 1959): 467–485.

Barker, Deborah. "The Riddle of the Sphinx: Elizabeth Stuart Phelps's *The Story of Avis.*" *Literature Interpretation Theory* 9.1 (September 1998): 31–64.

Barrett Browning, Elizabeth. *Aurora Leigh.* 1856. Ed. Gardner B. Taplin. Chicago: Academy Chicago Publishers, 1992.

Baym, Nina. *Novels, Readers, and Reviewers: Responses to Fiction in Antebellum America.* Ithaca: Cornell UP, 1984.

———. *Woman's Fiction: A Guide to Novels by and about Women in America, 1820–1870.* Ithaca: Cornell UP, 1978.

Beecher, Charles. *Harriet Beecher Stowe in Europe: The Journal of Charles Beecher.* Ed. Joseph S. Van Why and Earl French. Hartford: The Stowe-Day Foundation, 1986.

Bennett, Mary Angela. *Elizabeth Stuart Phelps.* Philadelphia: U of Pennsylvania P, 1939.

Benson, Eugene. "George Sand and the Marriage Question." *Revolution* 7 July 1870: 1–2.

Bledstein, Burton J. *The Culture of Professionalism: The Middle Class and the Development of Higher Education in America.* New York: W. W. Norton and Co., 1976.

Blumin, Stuart M. *The Emergence of the Middle Class: Social Experience in the American City, 1760–1900.* Cambridge: Cambridge UP, 1989.

Boime, Albert. *Thomas Couture and the Eclectic Vision.* New Haven: Yale UP, 1980.

"The Bookman." *The Critic* 20 (January 16, 1892): 45–46.

Bowker, R. R. "Daniel Deronda." *International Review* 4 (January 1877): 68–76.

Bradbury, Malcolm. *Dangerous Pilgrimages: Trans-atlantic Mythologies and the Novel.* New York: Viking Penguin, 1996.

Brodhead, Richard. *Cultures of Letters: Scenes of Reading and Writing in Nineteenth-Century America.* Chicago: U of Chicago P, 1993.

Browne, W. H. Rev. of *Middlemarch. The Southern Magazine* 12 (March 1873): 373–380.

Buhle, Mari Jo and Paul, ed. *The Concise History of Woman Suffrage.* Urbana: U of Illinois P, 1978.

Bulfinch, Thomas. *Bulfinch's Mythology: The Age of Fable, the Age of Chivalry, Legends of Charlemagne.* 1855. Ed. Bennett Cerf and Donald Klopfer. New York: The Modern Library, 1934.

"The Byron Case." *The Saturday Review* 11 September 1869: 343–344.

"The Byron Controversy." Scrapbook. Hartford: Stowe-Day Library, 1869.

"The Byron Scandal." *The Examiner and London Review* 25 September 1869: 618.

"The Byron Scandal." *The Nonconformist* 20 October 1869: 1011.

"The Byron Scandal." *Public Opinion* 25 September 1869: 380–381.

"The Byron Scandal." *The Tomahawk* 18 September 1869: 125–126.

"The Byron Scandal." *Vanity Fair* 11 September 1869: 146.

"The Byronizers." *The Spectator* 25 September 1869: 1121–1122.

Carby, Hazel. *Reconstructing Womanhood: The Emergence of the Afro-American Woman Novelist.* New York: Oxford UP, 1987.

Carr, Cornelia Crow. *Harriet Hosmer: Letters and Memories.* New York: Moffat Yard and Co., 1912.

Carroll, David, ed. *George Eliot: The Critical Heritage.* New York: Barnes and Noble, 1971.

Charvat, William. *The Profession of Authorship in America, 1800–1870.* 1968. Ed. Matthew J. Bruccoli. New York: Columbia UP, 1992.

Chase, Cynthia. "The Decomposition of the Elephants: Double-Reading *Daniel Deronda.*" *PMLA* 93 (1978): 215–227.

Child, Lydia Maria. "The Byron Controversy." *Independent* 14 October 1869: 1.

Clarke, Arthur C. *How the World Was One: Beyond the Global Village.* New York: Bantam Books, 1992.

Cohen, Monica. *Professional Domesticity in the Victorian Novel: Women, Work and Home.* Cambridge: Cambridge UP, 1998.

"Concerning Women." *Woman's Journal* 11 November 1876: 1.

Conrad, Peter. *Imagining America.* New York and London: Routledge, 1980.

"The Contributor's Club." *Atlantic Monthly* 40 (November 1877): 615–625.

Cooke, George Willis. *George Eliot: A Critical Study of Her Life, Writings, and Philosophy.* Boston: James R. Osgood and Co., 1883.

Cott, Nancy. *The Bonds of Womanhood: 'Woman's Sphere' in New England, 1780–1835.* New Haven: Yale UP, 1977.

Coultrap-McQuin, Susan. *Doing Literary Business: American Women Writers in the Nineteenth Century.* Chapel Hill: U of North Carolina P, 1990.

———. "Elizabeth Stuart Phelps: The Cultural Context of a Nineteenth-Century Professional Writer." Diss. U of Iowa, 1979.

Crozier, Alice. "Harriet Beecher Stowe and Lady Byron." *Critical Essays on Harriet Beecher Stowe.* Ed. Elizabeth Ammons. Boston: G. K. Hall, 1980. 191–199.

Cunliffe, Marcus. *In Search of America: Transatlantic Essays, 1951–1990.* London: Greenwood P, 1991.

Curti, Merle. *The Growth of American Thought.* New York: Harper and Row, 1951.

Curtis, George William. "Editor's Easy Chair." *Harper's New Monthly Magazine* 39 (1869): 764–767. Rpt. in *Critical Essays on Harriet Beecher Stowe.* Ed. Elizabeth Ammons. Boston: G. K. Hall, 1980. 184–189.

Dean, A. *"The Gates Ajar," Critically Examined.* London: Hatchards, Piccadilly, 1871.

"'Deronda' and 'Middlemarch.'" *Galaxy* 5.22 (November 1876): 698–701.

Dicey, A. V. "Daniel Deronda-I." *The Nation* 23 (12 October 1876): 230–231.

———. "Daniel Deronda-II." *The Nation* 23 (19 October 1876): 245–246.

Dickens, Charles. *Martin Chuzzlewit.* 1844. New York and Oxford: Oxford UP, 1997.

Dickinson, Gideon. *The Wanderer; or, Life's Pilgrimmage. A trip to England and Scotland described in verse, with introduction and notes dealing largely with Mrs. Stowe's Lady Byron Vindicated, and the Beecher scandal.* Boston: H. H. Clark and Co., 1888.

Douglas, Ann. *The Feminization of American Culture.* New York: Anchor Books, Doubleday, 1977.

Doy, Gen. *Seeing and Consciousness: Women, Class, and Representation.* Washington, DC: Berg Publishers, 1995.

DuBois, Ellen Carol, ed. *The Elizabeth Cady Stanton-Susan B. Anthony Reader: Correspondence, Writings, Speeches.* Boston: Northeastern UP, 1992.

"Editor's Easy Chair." *Harper's New Monthly Magazine* 68 (May 1884): 965–970.

Eisler, Benita, ed. *The Lowell Offering: Writings by New England Mill Women (1840–1845).* New York: Harper and Row, Pub., 1977.

Eliot, George. *Adam Bede.* 1859. New York: Thomas Y. Crowell and Co., 1893.

———. "Authorship." *Leaves from a Notebook: The Complete Works of George Eliot.* Vol. 6 Boston: D. Lothrop and Co., 1885. 275–278.

———. *Collected Poems.* Ed. Lucien Jenkins. London: Skoob Books Publishing, 1989.

———. *Daniel Deronda.* 1876. Ed. Terence Cave. New York and London: Penguin Books, 1995.

———. *Impressions of Theophrastus Such.* 1879. Ed. Nancy Henry. Iowa City: U of Iowa P, 1994.

———. *Daniel Deronda Notebooks*. Ed. Jane Irwin. Cambridge: Cambridge UP, 1996.

———. "Silly Novels by Lady Novelists." 1856. *Selected Essays, Poems, and Other Writings*. Ed. A. S. Byatt and Nicholas Warren. New York and London: Penguin Books, 1990. 140–163.

Emig, Janet. "The Flower in the Cleft." *Bulletin of the Historical and Philosophical Society of Ohio* 21.4 (October 1963): 223–238.

"European Peasants and Immigrants." *Atlantic Monthly* (May 1893): 233–234.

Fields, Annie. *Life and Letters of Harriet Beecher Stowe*. Boston and New York: Houghton, Mifflin and Co., 1898.

"Five American Magazines." *The Literary World* 11 (6 November 1880): 392–393.

Fox, John. "The Character of Lady Byron." *Temple Bar* October 1869: 334–354.

———. "Lord Byron's Married Life." *Temple Bar* June 1869: 364–393.

———. *Vindication of Lady Byron*. London: R. Bentley, 1871.

Francillon, R. E. Rev. of *Daniel Deronda*. *Gentleman's Magazine* 17 (October 1876): 411–427. Rpt. in *George Eliot: The Critical Heritage*. Ed. David Carroll. New York: Barnes and Noble, 1971. 382–398.

Freedberg, S. J. *Painting of the High Renaissance*. Cambridge: Harvard UP, 1961.

Freedman, Jonathan. *Professions of Taste: Henry James, British Aestheticism, and Commodity Culture*. Stanford: Stanford UP, 1990.

Friedman, Lee M. *Pilgrims in a New Land*. Westport: Greenwood P, 1979.

Fulmer, Constance. *George Eliot: A Reference Guide*. Boston: G. K. Hall, 1977.

Gagnier, Regenia. "A Critique of Practical Aesthetics." *Aesthetics and Ideology*. Ed. George Levine. New Brunswick: Rutgers UP, 1994. 264–282.

———. *Idylls of the Marketplace: Oscar Wilde and the Victorian Public*. Stanford: Stanford UP, 1986.

Gallagher, Catherine. "George Eliot and *Daniel Deronda*: The Prostitute and the Jewish Question." *Sex, Politics, and Science in the Nineteenth-Century Novel*. Ed. Ruth Bernard Yeazell. Baltimore: Johns Hopkins UP, 1986. 39–62.

———. *The Industrial Reformation of English Fiction: Social Discourse and Narrative Form, 1832–1867*. Chicago: U of Chicago P, 1985.

———. *Nobody's Story: The Vanishing Acts of Women Writers in the Marketplace, 1670–1820*. Berkeley: U of California P, 1994.

"The Gates Ajar" Criticised and Corrected by an Englishwoman. London: Geo. John Stevenson, 1872.

Geison, Gerald L., ed. *Professions and Professional Ideologies in America*. Chapel Hill: U of North Carolina P, 1983.

"George Eliot's 'Daniel Deronda.'" *Scribner's Monthly* 13.1 (November 1876): 133–135.

Gilbert, Sandra and Susan Gubar. *The Madwoman in the Attic*. New Haven: Yale UP, 1979.

Gilman, Arthur et al. *Poets' Homes. Pen and Pencil Sketches of American Poets and Their Homes*. Boston: D. Lothrop and Co., 1879.

Glazener, Nancy. *Reading for Realism: The History of a U.S. Literary Institution, 1850–1910*. Durham: Duke UP, 1997.

Griffith, Elisabeth. *In Her Own Right: The Life of Elizabeth Cady Stanton*. New York: Oxford UP, 1984.

Griffith, George V. "An Epistolary Friendship: The Letters of Elizabeth Stuart Phelps to

George Eliot." *Legacy* 18.1 (2001): 94–100.

———. "George Eliot, Realism, and the American Press, 1858–1881." *American Periodicals* 9 (1999): 36–54.

———. "George Eliot's American Reception, 1858–1881: A Bibliography." *Bulletin of Bibliography* 44.3 (1987): 193–196.

Gwendolen, a sequel to George Eliot's Daniel Deronda. Boston: Ira Bradley and Co., 1878.

Haight, Gordon, ed. *A Century of George Eliot Criticism.* Boston: Houghton Mifflin Co., 1965.

———. *George Eliot: A Biography.* New York and Oxford: Oxford UP, 1968.

———, ed. *The George Eliot Letters.* 9 vols. New Haven: Yale UP, 1955.

Halsey, Francis Whiting, ed. *Women Authors of Our Day in Their Homes: Personal Descriptions and Interviews.* New York: James Pott and Co., 1903.

Halttunen, Karen. *Confidence Men and Painted Women: A Study of Middle-Class Culture in America, 1830–1870.* New Haven: Yale UP, 1982.

Hamilton, Gail. "Gail Hamilton Once More: *The Story of Avis*—A Review in IV Parts." *The New York Daily Tribune* 12 Feb. 1878: 2. Pt. 4 of a series.

Harper, Frances E. W. "Colored Women of America." *Englishwoman's Review* 15 January 1878: 10–15.

———. *Iola Leroy; or Shadows Uplifted.* 1892. Oxford: Oxford UP, 1988.

Harper, J. Henry. *The House of Harper: A Century of Publishing in Franklin Square.* New York: Harper and Brothers, 1912.

Hawthorne, Nathaniel. *The Scarlet Letter.* 1850. New York: Penguin Books, 1986.

Hedrick, Joan. *Harriet Beecher Stowe: A Life.* New York and Oxford: Oxford UP, 1994.

Henry, Nancy Elizabeth. "Originating Fictions: Harriet Beecher Stowe and George Eliot." Diss. U of Chicago, 1994.

Hinds, Barbara. "The Lyceum Movement in Maine." Thesis. U of Maine, 1949.

Honour, Hugh. *The New Golden Land: European Images of America from the Discoveries to the Present Time.* New York: Pantheon, 1976.

Hollander, Anne. *Seeing through Clothes.* Berkeley: U of California P, 1993.

Howe, Julia Ward. "Mrs. Stowe's Vindication." *Woman's Journal* 22 January 1870: 17.

Howitt, William. Letter. *Daily News* 13 September 1869: N. pag.

Huber, Christine Jones. "The Pennsylvania Academy and Its Women." Philadelphia: Pennsylvania Academy of the Fine Arts, 1974.

Jackson, Stanway. *Faith or Fancy? An Examination of "The Gates Ajar."* London: Elliot Stock, 1871.

James, Henry. "Daniel Deronda: A Conversation." 1876. *George Eliot: The Critical Heritage.* Ed. David Carroll. New York: Barnes and Noble, 1971. 417–433.

———. Notice of *Daniel Deronda. The Nation* 22 (24 February 1876): 131.

Johannes, George the Count. "A letter from George the Count Johannes to the *New York Herald.*—September 4: The Libel upon Lord Byron and His Sister Augusta Nailed to the Pillory of Falsehood . . ." [New York?]: n.p., 1869.

Kelley, Mary. *Private Woman, Public Stage: Literary Domesticity in Nineteenth-Century America.* New York and Oxford: Oxford UP, 1984.

Kelly, Lori Duin. *The Life and Works of Elizabeth Stuart Phelps, Victorian Feminist Writer.* Troy, New York: The Whitston Publishing Co., 1983.

Kessler, Carol Farley. *Elizabeth Stuart Phelps*. Boston: Twayne Publishers, 1982.

———. "A Literary Legacy: Elizabeth Stuart Phelps, Mother and Daughter." *Frontiers* 5.3 (Fall 1980): 28–33.

LaBelle, Jenijoy. *Herself Beheld: The Literature of the Looking Glass*. Ithaca: Cornell UP, 1988.

Lambert, Royston. *Beloved and God: The Story of Hadrian and Antinous*. London: Weidenfeld and Nicolson, 1984.

Lang, Amy Schrager. "The Syntax of Class in Elizabeth Stuart Phelps's *The Silent Partner*." *Rethinking Class: Literary Studies and Social Formations*. Ed. Wai Chee Dimock and Michael Gilmore. New York: Columbia UP, 1994. 267–285.

Larson, Magali Sarfatti. *The Rise of Professionalism: A Sociological Analysis*. Berkeley: U of California P, 1977.

Leavis, F. R. *The Great Tradition: George Eliot, Henry James, Joseph Conrad*. London: Chatto and Windus, 1948.

"Let the Dead Rest." *The Tomahawk: A Saturday Journal of Satire* 123 (11 September 1869): 1.

Letter. *Woman's Journal* 8 October 1887: 322.

Levine, Lawrence W. *Highbrow/Lowbrow: The Emergence of Cultural Hierarchy in America*. Cambridge: Harvard UP, 1988.

Leymarie, Jean. *French Painting: The Nineteenth Century*. Trans. James Emmons. Cleveland: The World Publishing Co., 1962.

"Literary News." *The Literary World* 7 (March 1877): 163.

"Literary News." *The Literary World* 8 (June 1877): 17.

"The Lounger." *Illustrated Times* 9 October 1869: 230–231.

Lurie, Alison. *The Language of Clothes*. New York: Random House, 1981.

Macaulay, Thomas Babington, Thomas Moore, Leigh Hunt, et al. *The True Story of Lord and Lady Byron*. London: J. C. Hotten, 1869.

Mackay, Charles, ed. *Medora Leigh: A History and An Autobiography, with an Introduction and Commentary on Charges against Lord Byron by Harriet Beecher Stowe*. New York: Harper and Brothers, 1870.

Maguire, Francis. "George Eliot." *International Review* 7 (1879): 17–32.

Marcus, Sharon. "The Profession of the Author: Abstraction, Advertising and *Jane Eyre*." *PMLA* 110.2 (March 1995): 206–219.

McFadden, Margaret. *Golden Cables of Sympathy: The Transatlantic Sources of Nineteenth-Century Feminism*. Lexington: UP of Kentucky, 1999.

McLuhan, Marshall and Quentin Fiore. *The Medium is the Massage*. New York: Simon and Schuster, 1967.

McPherson, Susan. "Opening the Open Secret: The Stowe-Byron Controversy." *Victorian Review* 27.1 (2001): 86–101.

Merish, Lori. *Sentimental Materialism: Gender, Commodity Culture, and Nineteenth-Century American Literature*. Durham: Duke UP, 2000.

"Miss Phelps's Lectures." *Boston University Beacon*. 15 November 1876: 28.

"Miss Phelps's New Novel." Rev. of *The Story of Avis*. *The Literary World* 8 (November 1877): 97–98.

Morris, Timothy. "Professional Ethics and Professional Erotics in Elizabeth Stuart Phelps's *Doctor Zay*." *Studies in American Fiction* 21.2 (Autumn 1993): 141–152.

Morse, John T., Jr. *Life and Letters of Oliver Wendell Holmes*. 1896. Introduction. Earl N. Harbert. 2 vols. New York and London: Chelsea House, 1980.

Mott, Frank Luther. *Golden Multitudes: The Story of Best Sellers in the United States.* New York: MacMillan, 1947.

"Mrs. Beecher Stowe and Lady Byron." *The Spectator* 4 September 1869: 1038–1039.

Mulvey, Christopher. *Anglo-American Landscapes: A Study of 19th-Century Anglo-American Travel Literature.* Cambridge: Cambridge UP, 1983.

Mulvey, Laura. "Visual Pleasure and Narrative Cinema." *Screen* 16.3 (Autumn 1975): N. pag. Rpt. in *Feminisms: An Anthology of Literary Theory and Criticism.* Ed. Robyn R. Warhol and Diane Price Herndl. New Brunswick: Rutgers UP, 1993. 432–442.

"New Books." Rev. of *The Story of Avis. Philadelphia Inquirer* 31 Oct. 1877: N. pag. Rpt. in "Four Contemporary Reviews." *The Story of Avis.* Ed. Carol Farley Kessler. New Brunswick: Rutgers UP, 1985: 273–274.

Oliphant, Margaret. "American Books." *Blackwood's Magazine* 110 (October 1871): 422–442.

Paine, Judith. "The Women's Pavilion of 1876." *Feminist Art Journal* 4.4 (Winter 1975–1976): 5–12.

Pangallo, Karen L., ed. *The Critical Response to George Eliot.* Westport, CT: Greenwood P, 1994.

Perkin, Harold. *The Rise of Professional Society.* New York and London: Routledge, 1990.

Perkin, J. Russell. *A Reception-History of George Eliot's Fiction.* Ann Arbor: UMI Research P, 1990.

Phelps, Austin. "Memorial." *The Last Leaf of Sunny Side.* By H. Trusta. Boston: Phillips, Sampson and Co., 1853.

———. *My Portfolio: A Collection of Essays.* New York: Charles Scribner's Sons, 1882.

Phelps [Ward], Elizabeth Stuart. *Chapters from a Life.* Boston and New York: Houghton, Mifflin, and Company, 1897.

———. "The Christmas of Sir Galahad." *Independent* 23 (7 December 1871): 1.

———. *Doctor Zay.* 1882. Afterword. Michael Sartisky. New York: The Feminist P, 1987.

———. "A Dream within a Dream." *Independent* 26 (19 February 1874): 1.

———. "The 'Female Education' of Women." *Independent* 25 (13 November 1873): 1409–1410.

———. *The Gates Ajar.* 1868. Ed. Helen Sootin Smith. Cambridge: Harvard UP, 1964.

———. "George Eliot." Rev. of *George Eliot's Life. Harper's Weekly* 14 February 1885: 102–103.

———. "George Eliot." *Independent* 33 (3 February 1881): 1.

———. "George Eliot. Her Jury." *Harper's New Monthly Magazine* 62 (May 1881): 927.

———. "George Eliot's Short Stories." *Independent* 37 (30 April 1885): 1–2.

———. "The Gist of the Matter." *Woman's Journal* 22 July 1871: 226.

———. "The Higher Claim." *Woman's Journal* 28 October 1871: 343.

———. "An Hour with Gwendolyn." *Sunday Afternoon* 3 (March 1879): 230–234.

———. "Last Words from George Eliot." *Harper's New Monthly Magazine* 64 (March 1882): 568–571.

———. "Letter to the Educational Director of the Booklovers Library." *The Booklovers Reading Club Hand-Book to Accompany the Reading Course Entitled, The World's Great Woman Novelists.* Educational Dir. Frederic W. Speirs. Philadelphia: The Booklovers Library, 1901: 121–123.

———. "Men and Muscle." *Independent* 23 (31 August 1871): 1.

———. "Miss Elizabeth Stuart Phelps's Poem for The Birthday Garden Party to Harriet Beecher Stowe." *The Atlantic Monthly Supplement* 50 (August 1882): 1–16.

———. "The New Earth." *Independent* 23 (28 September 1871): 1.

———. "Rights and Relatives." *Woman's Journal* 23 September 1871: 298.

———. *The Silent Partner*. 1871. Afterword. Mari Jo Buhle and Florence Howe. New York: The Feminist P, 1983.

———. "The Song of the Shirt." *Woman's Journal* 2 September 1871: 274.

———. "The Sphinx." *Scribner's Magazine* 18 (July 1879): 366. Rpt. in *Songs of the Silent World, and Other Poems*. Boston: Houghton, Mifflin and Company, 1885. 97–98.

———. "Stories that Stay." *Century* 58 (November 1910): 118–123.

———. *The Story of Avis*. 1877. Ed. Carol Farley Kessler. New Brunswick: Rutgers UP, 1985.

———. "Too Much Conscience." *Independent* 23 (3 August 1871): 3.

———. "'The True Woman.'" *Independent* 23 (12 October 1871): 1.

———. "Unhappy Girls." *Woman's Journal* 12 August 1871: 250.

———. "'The United Head.'" *Woman's Journal* 30 September 1871: 306.

———. "What Shall They Do?" *Harper's New Monthly Magazine* 35 (September 1867): 519–523.

———. "What They Are Doing." *Independent* 23 (17 August 1871): 1.

———. "Women and Money." *Independent* 23 (24 August 1871): 1.

———. "A Word for the Silent." *Independent* 26 (1 January 1874): 1633–1634.

"Polychromatic Portraits.—No. 1." *The Period* 30 October 1869: 2.

Poovey, Mary. *The Proper Lady and the Woman Writer: Ideology as Style in the Works of Mary Wollstonecraft, Mary Shelley, and Jane Austen*. Chicago: U of Chicago P, 1984.

———. *Uneven Developments: The Ideological Work of Gender in Mid-Victorian England.* Chicago: U of Chicago P, 1988.

Postman, Neil. *Amusing Ourselves to Death: Public Discourse in the Age of Show Business*. New York: Penguin Books, 1985.

———. *Technopoly: The Surrender of Culture to Technology*. New York: Vintage Books, 1993.

Powderly, T. V. "A Menacing Eruption." *North American Review* 147 (January 1888): 165–166.

Preston, Harriet Waters. "The Story of Avis, and Other Novels." *Atlantic Monthly* 41 (April 1878): 486–494.

Psomiades, Kathy. *Beauty's Body: Femininity and Representation in British Aestheticism.* Stanford: Stanford UP, 1997.

"Public Prepossession for Byron." *The Spectator* 11 September 1869: 1066–1067.

Rausch, David A. *Friends, Colleagues, and Neighbors: Jewish Contributions to American History.* Grand Rapids, MI: Baker Books, 1996.

Rev. of *Daniel Deronda. The Edinburgh Review* 144 (October 1876): 442–470.

Rev. of *Lady Byron Vindicated. Nation* 6 January 1870: 2.

Rev. of *The Story of Avis. The Chicago Tribune* 10 November 1877: 9.

Rev. of *The Story of Avis. The Galaxy* 24.6 (December 1877): 855–857.

Rev. of *The Story of Avis. The Nation* 26 (21 March 1878): 202.

Rev. of *The Story of Avis. NY Times* 15 October 1877: 2.

Richards, Thomas. *The Commodity Culture of Victorian England: Advertising and Spectacle, 1851–1914.* Stanford: Stanford UP, 1990.

Robbins, Sarah. "Gendering Gilded Age Periodical Professionalism: Reading Harriet Beecher Stowe's *Hearth and Home* Prescriptions for Women's Writing." *"The Only Efficient Instrument": American Women Writers and the Periodical, 1837–1916.* Ed. Aleta Feinsod Cane and Susan Alves. Iowa City: U of Iowa P, 2001. 45–65.

Robbins, Sarah Stuart. *Old Andover Days: Memories of a Puritan Childhood.* Boston and New York: Pilgrim P, 1908.

Robertson, John. Letter. *Pall Mall Gazette* 14 September 1869: 3.

Robinson, Harriet H. *Loom and Spindle: Or Life Among the Early Mill Girls.* New York: Thomas Y. Crowell, 1898.

Rothblatt, Sheldon. *The Revolution of the Dons: Cambridge and Society in Victorian England.* New York: Basic Books, 1968.

Rubinstein, Charlotte Streifer. *American Women Artists from Early Indian Times to the Present.* Boston: G. K. Hall and Co., 1982.

Said, Edward. *Beginnings: Intention and Method.* New York: Basic Books, 1975.

Sánchez-Eppler, Karen. "Bodily Bonds: The Intersecting Rhetorics of Feminism and Abolition." *Representations* 24 (Fall 1988): 28–59.

Schaffer, Talia and Kathy Alexis Psomiades. Ed. *Women and British Aestheticism.* Charlottesville: UP of Virginia, 1999.

Scott, Donald M. "The Popular Lecture and the Creation of a Public in Mid-Nineteenth Century America." *Journal of American History* 66 (March 1980): 802–805.

———. "The Profession that Vanished: Public Lecturing in Mid-Nineteenth-Century America." *Professions and Professional Ideologies in America.* Ed. Gerald L. Geison. Chapel Hill: U of North Carolina P, 1983. 12–28.

Smith-Rosenberg, Carroll. "The Female World of Love and Ritual: Relations Between Women in Nineteenth-Century America." *Disorderly Conduct: Visions of Gender in Victorian America.* New York: Oxford UP, 1985. 53–76.

Spring, Elizabeth T. "Elizabeth Stuart Phelps." *Our Famous Women. An Authorized Record of Their Lives and Deeds.* Hartford: A. D. Worthington and Co., Publishers, 1884. 560–580.

Springer, Marlene. "Stowe and Eliot: An Epistolary Friendship." *Biography* 9.1 (Winter 1986): 59–81.

Standage, Tom. *The Victorian Internet: The Remarkable Story of the Telegraph and the Nineteenth Century's On-line Pioneers.* New York: Walker and Co., 1998.

Stansell, Christine. "Elizabeth Stuart Phelps: A Study in Female Rebellion." *Massachusetts Review* 13. 3–4 (1972): 239–256.

Stanton, Elizabeth Cady. *Eighty Years and More (1815–1897).* 1898. New York: Source Book P, 1970.

———. "The Moral of the Byron Case." *Independent* 9 September 1869: 1. Rpt. in *Critical Essays on Harriet Beecher Stowe.* Ed. Elizabeth Ammons. Boston: G. K. Hall and Co., 1980. 174–176.

Storer, Richard. "Leavis and 'Gwendolen Harleth.'" *F. R. Leavis: Essays and Documents.* Ed. Ian MacKillop and Richard Storer. Sheffield: Sheffield Academic P, 1995. 40–49.

"The Stowe-Byron Controversy." Scrapbook. Boston Public Library. 3 vols. [1869].

"The Stowe-Byron Controversy: A Complete Résumé of Public Opinion; with an Impartial Review of the Merits of the Case, by the Editor of 'Once a Week.'" London: Thomas Cooper and Co., [1869].

Stowe, Charles Edward. *The Life of Harriet Beecher Stowe Compiled from her Letters and Journals.* 1889. Detroit: Gale Research Co., 1967.

Stowe, Harriet Beecher. "The Chimney-Corner. The Woman Question: Or, What Will You Do With Her?" *Atlantic Monthly* 16 (December 1865): 672–683.

———. *Lady Byron Vindicated: A History of the Byron Controversy, from Its Beginnings in 1816 to the Present Time.* Boston: Fields, Osgood, and Co., 1870.

———. *Sunny Memories of Foreign Lands.* 2 vols. Boston: Phillips, Sampson, and Company, 1854.

———. "The True Story of Lady Byron's Life." *Atlantic Monthly* 24 (September 1869): 295–313.

———. "The True Story of Lady Byron's Life." *MacMillan's Magazine* 119.20 (September 1869): 377–396.

———. *Uncle Tom's Cabin; or, Life among the Lowly.* 1852. Ed. Ann Douglas. New York: Penguin Books, 1986.

"Summer Plans of Literary Workers." *The Critic* 10 (28 May 1887): 263–266.

Taylor, Bayard. *Critical Essays and Literary Notes.* New York: G. P. Putnam's Sons, 1880.

Thomson, Rosemarie. "Aberrant Bodies: Making the Corporeal Other in Nineteenth-Century American Cultural Representations." Diss. Brandeis U, 1993.

Thoreau, Henry David. *Walden.* 1854. *The Portable Thoreau.* Ed. Carl Bode. New York and London: Penguin Books, 1975. 258–572.

Tidy, Charlotte Elizabeth. *The Door Was Shut. An Answer to "Gates Ajar."* London: William MacIntosh, 1873.

Tilton, Theodore. "The Byron Revelations." *Independent* 26 August 1869: 1.

Tompkins, Jane. *Sensational Designs: The Cultural Work of American Fiction, 1790–1860.* New York: Oxford UP, 1985.

Trachtenberg, Alan. *The Incorporation of America: Culture and Society in the Gilded Age.* New York: Hill and Wang, 1982.

The True Story of Mrs. Shakespeare's Life. Boston: Loring, Publisher, [1869].

Twain, Mark. *The Autobiography of Mark Twain.* 1917. New York: Harper and Bros., 1959.

Van Nimmen, Jane. *Thomas Couture: Paintings and Drawings in American Collections.* New York: Clarke and Way, 1970.

W., J. S. *Antidote to "The Gates Ajar."* London: Hodder and Stoughton, 1870.

"Watching at the Gates." A Reply to "The Gates Ajar." London: S. W. Partridge and Co., 1871.

Weisbuch, Robert. *Atlantic Double-Cross: American Literature and British Influence in the Age of Emerson.* Chicago: U of Chicago P, 1986.

Wells, Daniel A., ed. *Literary Index to American Magazines, 1850–1900.* Westport, CT: Greenwood P, 1996.

Werses, Shmuel. "The Jewish Reception of *Daniel Deronda.*" *Daniel Deronda: A Centenary Symposium.* Ed. Alice Shalvi. Jerusalem: Jerusalem Academic P, 1976. 11–43.

What Shall We Say About "The Gates Ajar"? Some thoughts suggested by the proposed "Antidote." London: Watson and Hazell, Printers, 1871.

Wheildon, William Willder. "Lord Byron and the Stowe-Byron Controversy, 1869–1886." Scrapbook. Boston Public Library. 1887.

Whipple, Edwin P. "Daniel Deronda." *North American Review* 124 (January 1877): 31–52.

Wicke, Jennifer. *Advertising Fictions: Literature, Advertisement, and Social Reading*. New York: Columbia UP, 1988.

Wilbour, Charlotte. "Harriet Beecher Stowe." Rev. of "The True Story of Lady Byron's Life." *Revolution* 9 September 1869: 149.

Willis, Nathanial Parker. *Memoranda of the Life of Jenny Lind*. Philadelphia: Robert E. Peterson, 1851.

Wilson, Forrest. *Crusader in Crinoline: The Life of Harriet Beecher Stowe*. Philadelphia: J. B. Lippincott, 1941.

Wilson, Jack H. "Competing Narratives in Elizabeth Stuart Phelps' *The Story of Avis*." *American Literary Realism* 26.1 (Fall 1993): 60–75.

———. "George Eliot in America, Her Vogue and Influence, 1858–1900." Diss. U of North Carolina at Chapel Hill, 1965.

"A Woman's Professorship in Boston University." *Woman's Journal* 30 March 1878: 101.

Wolfit, Margaret. "The Toast to the Immortal Memory." *George Eliot Fellowship Review* 20 (1989): 60–62.

Wolstenholme, Susan. "Voice of the Voiceless: Harriet Beecher Stowe and the Byron Controversy." *American Literary Realism* 19.2 (Winter 1987): 48–65.

Woodmansee, Martha and Peter Jaszi, ed. *The Construction of Authorship: Textual Appropriation in Law and Literature*. Durham: Duke UP, 1994.

Zboray, Ronald J. *A Fictive People: Antebellum Economic Development and the American Reading Public*. New York and Oxford: Oxford UP, 1993.

Index

F

G

H

Z